THE
MAGISTRATE'S
TALE

ALSO BY TREVOR GROVE

The Juryman's Tale

THE
MAGISTRATE'S
TALE

Trevor Grove

BLOOMSBURY

First published 2002
This paperback edition published 2003

Copyright © 2002 by Trevor Grove

The moral right of the author has been asserted

Bloomsbury Publishing Plc, 38 Soho Square, London W1D 3HB

All papers used by Bloomsbury Publishing are natural, recyclable products made
from wood grown in sustainable, well-managed forests. The manufacturing
processes conform to the environmental regulations of the country of origin.

A CIP catalogue record for this book
is available from the British Library

ISBN 0 7475 6183 4

10 9 8 7 6 5 4 3 2 1

Typeset by Hewer Text Ltd, Edinburgh

Printed and bound in Great Britain by
CPI Antony Rowe, Chippenham and Eastbourne

CONTENTS

ACKNOWLEDGEMENTS

My thanks to all those mentioned in the text who agreed to talk to me, including law lords, politicians, bench chairmen, justices' clerks, legal advisers, lawyers, court officials and, in particular, fellow magistrates on my own and other benches. Prison, probation and YOT officers were also enormously helpful, wittingly or unwittingly. I hope I have reported them accurately.

My special gratitude to Harry Mawdsley, then Chairman of the Magistrates' Association, for encouraging this project from the start and, along with Ann Moody, former chair of the Haringey Bench, and John Hajdu, JP, for reading the typescript and offering invaluable advice.

My thanks to Ronald Blythe and Penguin for letting me quote a sizeable chunk from *Akenfield*, and to Peter Milford of St Vincent College, Gosport, for letting me use his excellent mock trial.

Sir Robin Auld refused me an interview, on the grounds that he had turned down all other approaches from the media regarding his review of the criminal justice system – but volunteered to write a foreword to this book instead. I could not have been more surprised and pleased.

FOREWORD
by the Rt. Hon. Lord Justice Auld

The Magistrate's Tale should not be regarded as a sequel to Trevor Grove's *The Juryman's Tale*, though it is as compelling a story and as penetrating an analysis of our criminal justice process. This tale is of his odyssey in becoming, and two years 'novitiate' as, a magistrate. It is an odyssey in which he chronicles, sometimes wryly, his growing affection for magistrates and respect for the justice they administer. For those who are magistrates, or who are otherwise involved in the system of summary justice, the story is as informative as it is engaging. For those who may be thinking of following him, and for the many who are unfamiliar with what magistrates do, his account is a highly readable and practical guide.

The magistracy of which Trevor Grove has become a member is a truly remarkable body of people. No other country in the world relies, as we do, on lay magistrates – unpaid volunteers – to administer the bulk of criminal justice. Magistrates' Courts deal with about 95 per cent of all prosecuted cases. Magistrates, over 30,000 of them, sitting usually in panels of three, handle 91 per cent of that work, the balance being undertaken by professional magistrates, now called District Judges (Magistrates' Courts). As he observes, the magistracy owes its longevity and vitality to its willingness to change and evolve with the times.

Trevor Grove's experience of lay justice as exercised by a jury in partnership with a judge in the Crown Court led him to follow what he discovered was a well-worn path from juror to magistrate. It is plain from his account of his magisterial colleagues and the nature of his work that he considers the journey to have been worthwhile. Instead of the old stereotype of an authoritarian, largely middle-class and late-middle-aged male bench, he found it to be composed, in general, of a wide variety of men and women from all walks of life and ethnic backgrounds. All or most of them in his tale come over as persons with a refreshing humility and anxiety, not only to perform well forensically, but also, in the process, to do good for society and individuals in the cases before them. As his graphic accounts of many individual cases in his 'home court' in Highgate and in other courts all over the country well illustrate, this is often a nigh impossible task given the social and family conditions that generate and nourish crime. Yet, despite local geographical and demographic differences and traditions, the picture is generally the same – benches reasonably representative of the wide mix of the local communities from which they are drawn, taking their job seriously and trying to combine greater 'professionalism' with practicality and common sense.

One of the most striking impressions of *The Magistrate's Tale* is how much we now expect from magistrates, as unpaid volunteers, in the discharge of their civic duty. Criminal law, both substantively and in its rules of procedure and evidence, has become one of the most technical and difficult areas of the law to administer. Trevor Grove's account reveals the extent of their task – most of them without any legal qualifications. There are increasingly frequent training sessions – some of them in the evenings and over weekends. There are many extra-curricular activities including attendance at periodic meetings of the local bench, speaking at schools and visiting probation centres, young offender institutions and prisons. Many magistrates also represent their bench on various inter-agency bodies, ever multiplying with the increasing governmental momentum towards 'joined-up' working in the criminal justice system.

However, there is a danger if all this is pushed too far. Magistrates should not become so legally trained and give such time to their role as to adopt the mantle of 'quasi-professional' judges. If they were to do so, it would be at the expense of their standing as ordinary members of the public bringing fairness and good sense to the job. In the legal and procedural technicalities of their work, they have the invaluable support and guidance of their justices' chief clerks and legal advisers, another body of persons whose critical contribution to the success of the system runs like a thread through Trevor Grove's account. Long may it remain that way.

Chapter 8 records the comment of Lord Bingham, the Senior Law Lord, that if we were inventing the system from scratch we probably would not have come up with the lay magistracy, but that is not an argument against it. My work on the Criminal Courts Review led me firmly to the same view. I believe that Trevor Grove's engaging and perceptive work should go a long way to securing a wider understanding of the immense value of magistrates to our system of criminal justice. The end of his tale is, I hope, a pointer to a happy ending to the imminent public debate and legislation on the matter, namely, preservation and strengthening of lay justice at all levels of trial. Certainly, both the story and the way he tells it encourage optimism.

Robin Auld

CHAPTER I

The Unprofessionals

'You could say it is a remarkable act of faith in the good sense
of ordinary people'

For four o'clock on a Monday afternoon, the Middlesex Guildhall Crown Court was unusually busy. Across Parliament Square
in the House of Commons, MPs were in a state of excitement,
having just concluded a ballot to elect a new Speaker. The tourists
drifted like autumn leaves between the Houses of Parliament and
Westminster Abbey, entangling themselves in the ribbons that
marked the perpetual construction sites. Rush hour had begun,
though it was impossible to tell: all day long the traffic around the
square had been moving no faster than a glacier.

But normally at this time, peace would be descending on the
Middlesex Guildhall. British justice generally adjourns for the
day at 4 p.m. Remand prisoners would be loaded into their vans
and locked into cramped little cubicles like battery hens for the
journey to Pentonville or Wormwood Scrubs. Barristers would
be de-wigging themselves, ushers lighting up and making tea.
The place would be emptying.

Instead, on this particular October afternoon, the lobby of
the Guildhall was in polite turmoil. People were coming into the
building in a stream, queueing to pass through the metal
detector, emptying their pockets of keys and change. They
arrived in pairs, chattering animatedly. They appeared to be
respectable, middle-aged, middle-class Londoners. The men
wore suits and ties. The women were dressed as for shopping
in the West End. They were met by a flow of people also trying
to get through the metal detector but in the opposite direction.
There were dozens of them and they were plainly busting to
leave the building. This lot were a good deal scruffier than those
coming in. Many were much younger. Almost none of the men

had ties; several wore jeans and trainers. They looked tired and crotchety, as though they had just got off a long-distance coach from Scotland.

At first glance, you would have assumed there was nothing much in common between those going out and those coming in. So would they, probably. In fact the two groups had something very much in common, and their confluence amidst the gloomy stonework of the Edwardian courthouse was full of social and historical significance. The significance was this: the people entering the building were ordinary Londoners, except that half of them were about to be sworn in as lay magistrates. Those who were leaving were also ordinary folk, except that all of them had just finished a day's unpaid work as jurymen and women.

Here then, passing each other in the entrance to one of the capital's oldest courts, were representatives of the two most defining human elements of this country's criminal justice system: not judges, barristers or solicitors, never mind Lord Chancellors or Lord Chief Justices, but the lay magistracy and the lay jury.

'Lay *adj* . . . non-professional, amateur [. . . from Late Latin *laicus*, ultimately from Greek *laos* people],' says the dictionary. An American or Australian tourist, peering in under the Guildhall's mock medieval porch, would know all about juries: their post-colonial homelands are strong upholders of trial by one's peers. But they would know little or nothing about the lay magistracy since, in the first place, it is an institution nowadays unique to this country and, in the second, most people here don't know much about it either.

Briefly, the facts are these. There are around 30,000 lay magistrates, more grandly known as Justices of the Peace, in England and Wales. (Scotland has its own system.) They generally sit in threes, usually for half a day a week. They hear charges, they decide whether defendants are to be remanded on bail or in custody, they hold trials and sentence the convicted. They preside in those most delicate of tribunals, the youth and family courts.

These people are all volunteers, drawn from local communities. They have no legal qualification, and they are not paid a penny for what they do other than modest allowances. (There are also some ninety-five full-time professionals, previously known as stipendiary magistrates but now as district judges, who help in the busiest courts; but let's leave them aside for the moment.) Magistrates deal with the overwhelming majority of all criminal cases in this country – more than 95 per cent of them. They consign the remainder – the most serious matters, such as murder, rape and robbery with violence – to the crown courts for trial by jury.

Foreigners find it incredible that we place the day-to-day application of the criminal justice system almost entirely in the hands of these justices and jurymen, these mere amateurs. But that is what it boils down to. And indeed, the more you think about it, the more extraordinary it is. Here we are at the beginning of the twenty-first century, when nearly every human undertaking is so specialised that even office cleaners need a written qualification to land a job, relying on unqualified Tom, Dick and Harriet, plus another nine odds and sods in the case of a jury, to take some of the most important decisions facing any civilised society – decisions which deeply affect the lives of victims as well as offenders, and can have a profound impact on the whole community.

You could say this is obviously crazy. Or you could say it is a quite remarkable act of national faith in the good sense of ordinary people. What I say is that the roots of democracy in this country may be a lot healthier and more tenacious in our criminal courts, where we don't usually think to look for them, than in many other institutions, notably a Parliament increasingly treated with disdain by the Government and consequently, as we have seen, with worrying indifference by the electorate.

I was at the Guildhall that afternoon in a bid to relive the past. A little over a year earlier I had come to this same place to be sworn in as a magistrate myself. It wasn't as nerve-racking as taking the juror's oath, with all the worry of a trial to follow, which I had done more than once. But it was certainly what's called 'a memorable occasion', like a first communion or a bar mitzvah – which meant that in fact one's mind was too scrambled to remember all that much about it.

There were some twenty of us being sworn in. We were each allowed one relative or friend to witness the event. I brought my mother, which increased the sense of undergoing some sort of rite of passage. An usher sat the would-be Justices of the Peace along green-upholstered pews in the well of Court 2, in strict order. It was a great high room with a beamed ceiling, carved oak stalls along the sides facing inwards like a college chapel, and a splendid raised dock at the rear of the court which could have doubled as the bridge of a small steamship. The onlookers sat in the stalls, beneath an array of portraits rich in dress swords and buckled shoes. One depicted the eighteenth-century magistrate Sir John Fielding. Only later did I discover him to be a splendid role model for those of us in court that afternoon.

Sir John was famous for being not only judicious but also blind, like Justice herself. He was also the half-brother of an even more famous JP, Henry Fielding, the author of *Tom Jones*. Henry was appointed to the Middlesex bench in 1749 and presided over his own courthouse at his home in Bow Street. The two Fieldings became celebrated for their fairness and incorruptibility. Henry campaigned against capital punishment, but at the same time was vigorous in trying to reduce London crime. He and John set up a body of professional thief-takers, known as the Bow Street Runners, who were the forebears of the Metropolitan Police. Henry took what we should now call a proactive view of his judicial role. He started a local paper, the *Covent Garden Journal*, in which he regularly ran the following notice: 'All persons who shall for the future suffer by robbers, burglars, etc., are desired immediately to bring or send the best description they can of such robbers, etc., with the time, and place, and circumstances of the fact, to Henry Fielding, Esq., at his house in Bow Street.'

Oddly, the portrait of half-brother John, who succeeded Henry at Bow Street, shows him in an open-necked shirt, looking more like a poet than a JP. Even today, a tie is considered *de rigueur* in court. But no doubt this was Sir John in his weekend togs. The judge who was presiding over our ceremony, by contrast, was in full fig. Colourfully sashed, belted and bewigged, he beamed down on us from an immense throne.

One by one we trooped into the witness box, swore our oaths, were congratulated by the judge and went back to a new set of places, still in very strict order so that we didn't bump into each other entering and leaving the pews. His Honour then delivered a homily, of which I remember little except that he advised us to avoid putting the letters 'JP' after our names even though we were entitled to, and never to use them to curry favour, wield influence or avoid a parking ticket. Afterwards, we had tea and digestive biscuits and my mother said loudly that my delivery of the oath was the best of the afternoon. This made me feel about fifteen years old instead of fifty-four. At least she wasn't wearing a hat. I put her in a taxi and raced off to the sybaritic refuge of the Savoy's American Bar, where I had planned to meet my wife.

The new JP ordered a large G and T. I experienced my first pang about drinking, even though I wasn't driving that evening. This would soon become a regular nagging worry, complete with vividly imagined newspaper headlines along the lines of 'Drink-drive magistrate disgraced'. Then I caught sight of a dark-haired woman who looked familiar. She too was knocking back a stiff one with a slightly guilty air. I realised she had been at the Guildhall that afternoon. Hurrah. It was another newly-sworn member of the judiciary of England and Wales. We exchanged magisterial glances, grinned, and raised our glasses to each other. Only an hour on the bench, and two of us, at any rate, were already hitting the grog, which I found reassuring.

ANYTHING TO DECLARE?
I decide to apply, and fill in the forms

Why would any normal person want to become a magistrate and sit in judgment on his or her fellow men? Maybe a minority of those who apply are small-time Savonarolas, burning with zeal to punish society for its sins: they would almost certainly be discarded by the appointments system at a very early stage. But as for the majority, my impression is they are far from being instinctive authoritarians. Many are encouraged by their employers or trade unions to put themselves forward in the public interest. Some respond to an advertisement in the press or an item on local radio for the same reason. They say things like 'I felt it was time for me to put something back into society', or 'I think it is a job people *ought* to want to do'.

Others are simply cajoled into it by a well-meaning JP friend, as I was. Rhoda was a neighbour. We played family tennis together. What I hadn't taken fully on board was that she was also a magistrate. Then she discovered I was writing a book about the jury system, the consequence of my having been a juryman on a long and engrossing kidnap trial at the Old Bailey. I have since learnt that experience of jury service is what inspires a good many of those who volunteer to become magistrates. In any event, Rhoda must have detected the symptoms of incipient judicial junkiedom. She began an unpushy courtship. The appeal was to civic conscience rather than worldly vanity: someone had to perform this important task. The days when being a JP was considered a valuable social distinction and had what H. G. Wells called 'the aura of a minor knighthood' had long since gone.

The consequence was that about a year later, having examined at least a dozen reasons why I did not want to be a magistrate and found them all pretty feeble, I sent a letter off to an official called the Secretary of Commissions, asking for an application form. I did not accompany it with a case of whisky, as one former holder of that office remembered happening in the old days. I was not burning with ambition to be elevated benchwards, merely putting myself in the way of the judicial press gang, should it wish to pick me up.

Volunteering is a mug's game, as everyone knows. 'You, you and you,' the sergeant-instructor in my school's army cadet corps barked during an exercise one wet winter's day. 'You've just volunteered to lay your bodies over that stretch of barbed wire so that the rest of the platoon can march over you. Carry on!' Happily, the wire wasn't barbed, but the platoon marched over us with glee. I thought it was a lesson I would never forget. So what was I letting myself in for this time?

The application form arrived and I put it aside for several months. It was an inquisitive document – eight pages poking into one's personality, politics and pastimes. 'Please indicate ethnic origin' was just the start of it. 'Do you have the ability to sit and concentrate for long periods of time?' it went on. 'Which political party do you generally support?' 'What is the occupation of your spouse or partner?' 'Are you a Freemason?'

You are asked to list recreational interests and activities, membership of clubs and societies. 'Please give details of any criminal convictions which you have, including motoring offences.' Then, with clumsy menace: 'Is there anything in your private or working life, or in your past, or to your knowledge in that of any member of your family or close friends, which, if it became generally known, might bring you or the Magistracy into disrepute, or call into question your integrity, authority or standing as a magistrate?'

Your pen hovers over the box marked 'No' while you conduct a quick mental check of your friends and relations, among whom drink, drugs, adultery and parking on double yellow lines are not unknown. What sort of outrage does it take to bring the magistracy into disrepute these days, you wonder.

Robert Shallow JP would not have had an easy time filling in this application form. Remember that feeble old lecher in *Henry IV, Part 2* boasting about the time he and Falstaff 'lay all night in the windmill in Saint George's field' dallying with Jane Nightwork

– though 'she never could away with me'. (Falstaff: 'Never, never; she would always say she could not abide Master Shallow.')

Shakespeare evidently had a low opinion of the magistracy. Even the fat knight is full of scorn. Though he admits they had 'heard the chimes at midnight' together, Sir John speaks witheringly of his former boon companion: 'I do see the bottom of Justice Shallow . . . Lord, Lord, how subject we old men are to this vice of lying! This same starved justice hath done nothing but prate to me of the wildness of his youth, and the feats he hath done about Turnbull Street; and every third word a lie . . .'

'I do remember him at Clement's Inn, like a man made after supper of a cheese-paring. When a' was naked he was for all the world like a forked radish, with a head fantastically carved upon it with a knife: a' was so forlorn, that his dimensions, to any thick sight, were invisible: a' was the very genius of famine; yet lecherous as a monkey, and the whores called him mandrake: a' came ever in the rearward of the fashion . . .'

So Shallow was a whoremonger and a liar, but a justice nonetheless. Well then, OK. Emboldened, you put a tick in the 'No' box. Were you to tick 'Yes', it seems that would be the end of it, since there is no space provided to detail or explain the disreputable matter. It would simply mean disqualification, I imagine, no questions asked.

The trickiest bit of the form requires applicants to describe briefly why they wish to become a JP, having regard to the 'six key qualities' that a magistrate must possess, namely 'good character, understanding and communication, social awareness, maturity and sound temperament, sound judgment, and commitment and reliability'. I make this nine rather than six key qualities, but never mind: numeracy is not one of them.

Modesty makes one hesitate at this juncture. There must be a trap here. If you are so replete with understanding, maturity, sound judgment and reliability – in short, wisdom, Mr Solomon – how come you aren't too busy ruling the kingdom or at least chairing a New Labour quango to have the time to be a magistrate?

The young have no difficulty with this kind of self-assessment, since they are endlessly writing reams on why they would make such top-notch candidates for this course or that job vacancy. Guileless university admissions tutors and human resources officers have created a whole generation of master embellishers who, in addition to the key magisterial qualities listed above, are also caring, keen on cinema, concerned about the environment and don't smoke. My daughters' CVs make my eyes water.

In any event, feeling embarrassingly goody-goody, I filled the space with a lot of words like 'worthwhile' and 'community' and hoped that the three referees I had listed at the back of the form would make good the gaps in a down-to-earth fashion.

I sent off the completed application. Time passed. A primary head teacher friend warned me not to hold my breath. She would have made an outstanding magistrate but had been turned down flat, without any explanation. She must have come across as too fair-minded, she said bitterly. In fact, I have since learned, she applied at a time when there was a glut of teacher JPs on our bench, and it was thought undesirable to have such a high proportion of magistrates from any one profession. There is a 15 per cent ceiling currently in force.

In my own case I knew there were several factors against my candidature. I was over fifty. I was white. And I was middle class. The effort to make the magistracy more representative of the population at large has been going on for decades, but it was given fresh impetus after 1997 by Labour's Lord Chancellor, Derry Irvine. He was especially keen to raise the proportion of applicants from ethnic minorities and blue-collar occupations. It was also thought a good idea to get younger people on the bench, to the extent of positively discouraging the over-fifties. I didn't object to any of this, so long as they were not talking quotas. But it meant that the only thing I had going for me apart from the fact that I fulfilled the statutory qualification of living within the area and being under sixty-five was, unusually, that I was a man. Although the sex ratio of JPs around the country is roughly fifty-fifty, there is concern in some areas that there are now more female than male applicants. Could this be a rare case of anti-discrimination favouring my own gender, for once?

Eventually word came in the form of a letter from my local magistrates' court, telling me to stand by for an interview. A month or so later (it was now May 1998) came another letter, this time with a date for me to present myself at the Tottenham Court Road offices of the Secretary of the Middlesex Area Advisory Committee on Justices of the Peace – one of the ninety-four such bodies around the country which 'advise' the Lord Chancellor on the appointment of new magistrates. (It is unusual for the advice to be rejected.) There was an instruction to visit a court to observe it in session. I was to fill in an 'observation form' and take it with me to the interview.

So I went along to our local courthouse in Highgate, North London, spent a morning on the public seating at the back of Court 1 and filled in my form as events slowly, confusingly and sometimes inaudibly unfolded. I had to note the time court commenced business, explain why there were seats provided for the press, identify the justices, the crown prosecutor, the defendant and the clerk of the court. It was not a demanding task, especially as I had spent many long hours in crown courts as a juror. The only case to grab my attention was that of a man found to be drunk in charge of his car. In fact he had been in the back seat very sensibly fast asleep, with the keys in his pocket. Even so he was disqualified, which struck me as unfair. This was my first encounter with mandatory sentences, a topic which makes many magistrates uneasy.

So it had been a dull morning, enlivened only by what looked to my ignorant eye like an obvious injustice. Oh dear. Foreboding deepened when a letter came from the Middlesex Area Advisory Committee seeking yet more information about my ethnicity, together with a questionnaire 'approved by the Commission of Racial Equality'.

ORIGINS OF THE SPECIES
A very potted history

What was I letting myself in for? Perhaps I should look a little more closely at the institution of which I was seeking to become a part. It had an immensely ancient and rather dizzying past, I discovered.

It is usual to trace the history of the magistracy to as far back as 1195. That was the year when King Richard I commissioned a number of knights throughout the kingdom to keep the peace in their localities, while he was away crusading and earning his soubriquet 'Coeur de Lion'. Their job was to pursue and catch evil-doers and they were known as *Custodes Pacis*.

Gradually these Keepers of the Peace took on a judicial as well as a policing role. But it was not until the passing of an Act in 1361 that the Keepers formally became Justices for the first time. The Act required three or four upright men in every county to be appointed Justices of the Peace, the first of our public institutions to have a statutory origin. Among a mass of other duties, they were required to 'pursue, arrest, take and chastise' offenders. Four times a year, at what came to be known as Quarter Sessions, they had 'to hear and determine all manner of felonies and trespasses done in the same county'.

These were not their only functions, however. Being not only the worthiest but also, I imagine, the bossiest of the local gentry, these early JPs soon amassed a swathe of other responsibilities, among them the maintenance of roads and bridges, the administration of the poor laws, dealing with beggars, running the prisons, fixing wages, controlling prices and recruiting men for the militia. Their appetite for public service seems to have been insatiable. During the sixteenth century they began sitting in twos and threes without a jury rather than waiting for Quarter Sessions to come round. In due course these summary proceedings were officially recognised and came to be known as Petty Sessions, which increased and formalised the justices' influence still further. Under the Tudors it was the task of JPs to prosecute recusants and for a time during the Commonwealth they even performed marriage ceremonies in place of priests. For centuries, in other words, the Justices of the Peace ran almost everything to do with local administration in England and Wales, while also acting as instruments of central government. On top of all this, many of them were Members of Parliament. They were the Mr Bigs, or more often the Sir Bigs, of their time, among the most powerful men in the land.

This did not necessarily make them model citizens. Sir Francis Drake and Sir John Hawkins were both JPs, despite the former's early history as a privateer and the latter's murky past as a slave trader. In 1693 there was a complaint to the Privy Council about justices 'who come and take the King's wages and, before half the business is done, betake them to the tavern'. The opportunities for abuse were manifold. In London, corruption among lay magistrates grew so rife during the late eighteenth century that the Government was obliged to appoint stipendiaries to stop the rot.

It was not until the nineteenth century that justices were shorn of their non-judicial powers. First they lost their policing duties, when modern police forces were established; then most of their administrative functions under the Local Government Act of 1888, although vestiges such as liquor licensing and tax enforcement remain. There were moans at the time that without the governmental work, public-spirited men – such as the author of *On the Origin of Species*, the late Charles Darwin JP, had been and the novelist Thomas Hardy JP still was – would stop volunteering to be justices.

The historian F.W. Maitland thought the JP's days were numbered: 'He is cheap, he is pure, he is capable, but he is doomed.' (The same sorts of anxieties about loss of status were voiced in 2001, when it was feared Lord Justice Auld's review of the criminal courts would recommend that benches be chaired by professional judges, thus reducing magistrates to token laymen.) However, Maitland was proved wrong. The freeing-up of JPs to concentrate on judicial work led to a rapid expansion of summary matters for them to deal with, and in 1925 large numbers of cases which had previously been triable only by judge and jury were added to their jurisdiction. It was a resounding vote of confidence in the lay magistracy and set the pattern which still applies today, whereby JPs dispose of the great bulk of all the criminal cases in the land.

Other changes have led to the progressive democratisation and de-gentrification of the magistracy. Attempts to widen the class base from which JPs were chosen were tentative at first, but gathered momentum during the second half of the twentieth century. Today people from almost every kind of background, occupation and ethnic minority are to be found on the bench, though the public is only dimly aware of it. This was one of the frustrations facing Harry Mawdsley when he became the new chairman of the Magistrates' Association in April 2000. 'The image of the magistracy is a big challenge,' he told Frances Gibb of *The Times*. 'We're seen not only as middle class but upmarket middle class. The reality is different. On my bench in South Cheshire we have train drivers and postal and hospital workers – not just doctors and nurses. One newly-appointed JP in Liverpool bought a suit especially to sit on the bench.'

In 2001 one of the youngest JPs in the country was 28-year-old Jim Murphy, a postman and union official who sits on the Mid-Sussex bench at Haywards Heath. The first black magistrate, a Jamaican called Eric Irons, was appointed to the Nottingham bench in 1962, since when there has been a steady increase in the number of non-white JPs.

As for gender, roughly half the country's justices are now women, but it was not until the zippily-entitled Sex Disqualification (Removal) Act 1919 that they were allowed to sit as magistrates. The first woman JP was Mrs Ada Summers, Mayor of Stalybridge. The widow of a local ironmaster, she was an active Liberal and keen suffragist, evidently a formidable figure. She was sworn in on 31 December 1919 and thus became the first woman ever to adjudicate in an English court.

So much for history. What it taught was that, as with all Britain's great institutions, the longevity of the lay magistracy was due not to its rock-like immutability but to its willingness to change and evolve with the times. To the would-be Justice of the Peace in the closing years of the twentieth century, therefore, the past was not much more useful as a guide than a London tube-map would have been to Richard the Lion-heart.

QUESTION TIME
I am interviewed – and accepted

These days candidates for the magistracy must undergo two interviews. In my own case there was just one, but it was quite a grilling. I had no idea what to expect. I was put in a small room and instructed to study two hypothetical cases. One of them concerned a youth who had resisted arrest and hit a policeman. As I was reading up the case, a woebegone figure exited from a door behind me, looking like an actor at an audition who'd just been given the don't-call-us-we'll-call-you treatment.

I entered through the same door to find myself facing a panel of people arranged in an L-shape. There were some five or six of them. They inspected me silently, then the chairman began putting questions. Every so often one of the others would join in. It was like an oral version of the application form. We got stuck for a while on the matter of political affiliation. There is less emphasis on this matter now, in recognition of the fact that since the 1997 and 2001 elections, party labels are no longer much of a guide to either a person's class or politics. But then it was still regarded as important. I said I usually voted Tory but had defected to Labour at the last election and might or might not do so again.

This threw them. They tried to make me plump for one party or the other. They had to satisfy the Lord Chancellor that they were delivering a balanced intake. The task was made no easier if candidates didn't or wouldn't fit into political pigeonholes.

Just for the present, I persisted, I was a New Labour Conservative. A former Lord Chancellor, the late Lord Hailsham, was once faced with a similar problem when asked to approve a candidate for a notoriously Tory bench. The applicant, it was argued, was a '*Liberal* Conservative'. Lord Hailsham responded pithily: 'A Liberal Conservative is a Conservative and not a Liberal, just as a fly-button is a button and not a fly.' Button or fly, at least I was able to satisfy my inquisitors (again) that I wasn't a Freemason, something which evidently bothers the powers that be a good deal. Masons must go round feeling like Ku-Klux Klansmen these days.

We got onto the case of the imaginary youth who had hit the policeman trying to arrest him. I said it was pretty hard to reach a sensible decision about sentencing without knowing all the circumstances, such as what the lad was being arrested for, how hard the blow was, whether he had a previous record and so on. However, on the face of it, I thought probation might be appropriate. This was one of those Bateman cartoon moments: the man who . . . thought probation was the proper punishment for biffing a policeman. The panel sucked their teeth, looked aghast at each other and sternly at me. Didn't I realise that assaulting a policeman was a very serious offence, possibly deserving imprisonment, and wasn't that as it should be? I stumbled about a bit, just stopping myself from saying that, surely, giving and receiving the odd whack was all in a week's work for the men and women in blue. That would certainly have been unwise.

An Asian woman asked sweetly if I was prejudiced in any way and I said yes, everyone was. She looked a bit taken aback – I had obviously committed another Bateman. (In retrospect, I think she was just putting it on. Apparently this is a standard question, and anyone who claims to be prejudice-free is regarded as unsound.) So what were my prejudices? I found cars full of young men menacing, I said, especially if they had their sound systems turned up; and I felt hostile towards yobs with cropped hair waving lager cans. 'You'd be dealing with a lot of those types of people as a magistrate,' said my interrogator pointedly. 'I know. We've got one of them at home,' I said, thinking of my shaven-headed teenage son. 'But as a magistrate I hope I'll be able to put aside my prejudices. They're usually ill-founded anyway.' Gulp, I thought. Is that really what I believe?

The inquisition lasted perhaps forty minutes. I couldn't tell how well or badly I was doing since it was like taking part in a game without knowing the rules. Was I coming across as too liberal or not liberal enough? Did my three or four parking tickets a year really show I had 'a cavalier attitude to the law', as someone suggested? My questioners were polite, thorough and non-committal. I left the room feeling like the man who had been in before me had looked. Hovering in the air was an unspoken 'We'll let you know'.

It wasn't until mid-November, five months later, that they did so. The Advisory Committee wrote to say it was 'minded' to forward my name to the Lord Chancellor 'with a recommendation that you be appointed a magistrate'. Well, well. Either it was a case of beggars can't be choosers or the interview panel had not found me too old, white, middle class and soft hearted after all.

But hang on. Not so fast. 'Before proceeding further the Advisory Committee wishes to receive from you the assurances set out in the enclosed Declaration and Undertaking.' Note the admonitory capitals. I had a premonition I was about to be asked once again whether I was a Freemason.

The glossy form required me to acknowledge and undertake: 'that it will be my duty to administer justice according to the law; that my actions as a magistrate will be free from any political, racial, sexual or other bias; that I will be circumspect in my conduct and maintain the dignity, standing and good reputation of the magistracy at all times in my private, working and public life; that I will respect confidences; that I will complete all training which may, from time to time, be pre-scribed . . .' and so on through a number of other solemn promises which reminded me gloomily of my brief, inglorious spell as a Boy Scout.

I also had to undertake to inform the Chairman and Clerk to

the Justices of my Petty Sessional Division 'of any impending criminal or civil proceedings, including divorce, against me, or in which I become involved in my capacity [eh?], and of the outcome; if I become bankrupt or involved in any other financial difficulties or if a Company, of which I am a Director, goes into liquidation . . .' and, ah yes indeed, I must also inform them 'if I become a Freemason'. My late Uncle Gordon, a saintly man who would have made a model magistrate, was a mason. I was beginning to feel like joining the Brotherhood just to see what happened.

Months went by, interrupted by a teasing sort of letter from the Advisory Committee which said that *if* the Lord Chancellor decided to appoint me, then I would need to be on stand-by for the swearing-in ceremony sometime in April. The Clerk to the Justices at Haringey Magistrates' Court, which would be my bench *if* I was accepted, also wrote in the conditional tense, outlining the training schedule I would have to undertake *in the event* of the Lord Chancellor approving my appointment.

All this is pretty testing of the would-be magistrate's patience and resolve. The whole procedure had already taken over a year. In the meantime one had been quizzed, scrutinised and repeatedly asked to testify to one's own fair-mindedness and incorruptibility, with an insistence that began to make one feel distinctly unworthy: I was not putting in for canonisation, after all. Yet still nothing was finalised. It was getting to the point where I might be tempted to commit some minor crime just to reassert my membership of the human race.

Then the long-awaited letter arrived, signed by Anthony Moore, secretary to the Middlesex Advisory Committee. 'I have heard today,' he wrote, with an unusual show of urgency, 'that the Lord Chancellor has appointed you a Justice of the Peace. The Committee sends you its sincere congratulations.' I was to take the Oaths (two of them), or if I preferred Solemn Affirmations, before His Honour Judge J. Inman ten days hence at 4 p.m. Meanwhile, 'in black ink or type', there was another questionnaire to fill in.

CHAPTER 2

Without Fear or Favour

*'The sentencing guidelines are only guidelines. You must
exercise your judgment'*

Returning to the Middlesex Guildhall that October afternoon
as a fully-fledged JP to see the next lot of Haringey magistrates
being sworn in was rather gratifying. After just a year and a bit
on the bench I was scarcely a veteran, but at least I was no
longer a new boy. I could watch the woman smoking secretively
at the end of the corridor and the man rehearsing the wording of
the oaths with a slight sense of superiority. Been there, sworn
that.

But still, the occasion was not without solemnity. The Justices
of Middlesex have had their headquarters on this site since the
early nineteenth century. The present building was completed
shortly before the outbreak of the First World War. During the
Second, occupied Europe's governments-in-exile snuggled up to
the Mother of Parliaments on the other side of the square and
held all sorts of legal hearings here, including courts martial. So
there was a good deal of history in the air as the score or so of
postulant JPs from the London boroughs of Haringey and
Ealing waited to take their vows.

In charge of the ceremony was the secretary of the Middlesex
Advisory Committee, the same Tony Moore who had written
that they were 'minded' to recommend me as a magistrate.
Today he was minded to be very chatty. As he watched his new
charges assemble, he told me proudly that the Middlesex
magistracy had now got a 21 per cent ethnic minority representation, which compared pretty well with the 24 per cent
proportion in the working population of the area as a whole.
(Subsequently these figures turned out to be over-optimistic, as
they were based on the old 1991 Census. The true proportion

was nearer 18 per cent ethnic minority justices as compared with a 33 per cent ethnic minority population – but it was encouraging that the 2000 intake of new JPs in Middlesex included 22 per cent non-whites.)

At that moment a self-assured figure thrust his way into the scrum of departing jurors and bustled purposefully through the metal detector. His eyebrows preceded him by a good half-inch, giving him a strong resemblance to a horned owl. This could only be the judge. He was wearing a waxed country coat and carrying a squashy holdall which presumably contained his robes. Mr Moore greeted him affably and everyone shuffled into Court 3.

Once upon a time, this was the Middlesex County Council Chamber. It is a fine lozenge-shaped room, with a splendid fan of benches for the councillors. The armrests are carved with the heads of hares and dragons. In front of each place where the councillors once sat there is a small device with two buttons, one labelled 'FOR', the other 'AGAINST', relic of an ingenious mechanical voting system which even then must have put the House of Commons to shame. I wondered what the magistrates-to-be would make of these fateful buttons. Perhaps they'd recognise with a slight flinch that soon they too, modest Caesars of the modern day, would be required to give the thumbs up or down to some hapless defendant in the dock.

The judge had shed his waxed coat and was resplendent in mauve, black and cerise. He was flanked by the chairs of the Haringey and Ealing benches, looking less decorative in their mufti but also a good deal less daunting. The first to take the oath was an Asian man. He was followed by a black woman. Shortly afterwards came a Mr Cohen and then a woman in a headscarf who swore on the Koran. Tony Moore must have been purring at this demonstration of ethno-religious diversity.

The oath is in two parts, both of which would come as a bit of a jolt to a fervent republican since they place the monarchy very decidedly at the pinnacle of British justice. Middlesex magistrates have time to mull over this before committing themselves,

since they are sent the script some days before the ceremony –
on a pink sheet of paper for those who plan to swear and a
yellow one for the affirmers. This is what the pink version says:

> 'When your name is called, advance to the Clerk's desk and
> take the appropriate Book. Holding the Book in your uplifted
> hand, face towards the Judge and say aloud the words of the
> Oath, viz:-
>
> "I, (full name), do swear by Almighty God that I will be
> faithful and bear true allegiance to Her Majesty Queen
> Elizabeth The Second, her heirs and successors, according
> to the law."
>
> *Pause for breath, then on to the second part:*
>
> "'I, (full name), do swear by Almighty God that I will well
> and truly serve our Sovereign Lady, Queen Elizabeth The
> Second, in the office of Justice of the Peace and I will do right
> to all manner of people after the laws and usages of this
> Realm without fear or favour, affection or ill-will."'

I think the last bit of this is rather fine: plain words with neither
a trace of swagger nor any equivocation about the need to be
unbiased and fair-minded. At least a couple of the oath-takers
that afternoon seemed to find them moving, gulping a little as
they promised to do right to all manner of people – not just
without ill-will, which was to be expected, but without affection
either, a curiously striking notion.

One by one they took the pledge. The judge leant down to
congratulate them and shake each of them by the hand when
they had finished. It was like a school prizegiving without the
prizes. The new JPs went back to their places with a mixture of
piety and pleasure on their faces. Inappropriately, they reminded me of communicants returning from the altar rail.

The judge's homily was encouraging: 'Welcome to one of the
oldest judicial offices in the land,' he began, then quickly got to
the heart of the matter. 'You must accept the law for what it is,
whatever its imperfections . . . But you are not a rubber stamp.

The sentencing guidelines are only guidelines. You must exercise your judgment.'

Ah, judgment. Not such an easy matter in today's non-judgmental world. The little buttons in front of us saying 'FOR' and 'AGAINST' recalled a less ambiguous age. But the good guys don't wear white hats nor the bad guys black hats any more. These days saints have tarnished haloes, sinners have deprived upbringings and absolutely everyone is a victim. Yet when it comes to exercising judgment in the courtroom, there's not much room to fudge the matter. You can't abstain. It is bail or custody, guilty or not guilty, prison or probation.

Tea or coffee? The ceremony was over. Some of the new JPs looked as though they would have preferred the question to be: red or white? The whisky-loving novelist Kingsley Amis thought those the three most depressing words in the English language; but you could tell all that swearing to do right to all manner of people had given some of the chaps a bit of a thirst. Never mind. The biscuits were quite nice and the gaggle of my new colleagues on the Haringey bench were animated. Our chairman, Ann, with her Napoleonic haircut, strode among them like a genial general meeting a fresh batch of recruits. It is customary for the chairs of benches not to sit on interviewing panels, in case they should be thought guilty of influencing decisions for or against a candidate. So this was her first encounter with the reinforcements. One of them, I was pleased to see, was a man who looked even older than myself. Another was a young woman positively blushing with pleasure. 'I have always wanted to do this,' she told me. 'It was something I thought people *should* want to do. But it took me ages to work up the courage to apply.'

They were a bunch of ordinary North Londoners, keen to get involved in public service for one reason or another, yet with only the haziest notion of what being a magistrate would entail. The public image is no guide. The media never seem able to make up their minds about JPs. One day they are tweedy little Hitlers, unbendingly dishing out the law. The next they are bleeding-heart liberals incapable of responding adequately to the people's righteous anger. I warm to that amiable *Daily Mail* columnist Keith Waterhouse's view of magistrates. 'Those easy-going coves,' he called us. But I suppose the gathering at the Guildhall would have been rather scandalised by that definition.

IN WHICH WE SERVE
The training begins

We began our training in the spring of 1999. The novice magistrate's induction to the mysteries of the criminal justice system is more taxing than it once was. Twenty or thirty years ago, newcomers were simply dumped on the bench and expected to learn from experience, in much the same way that callow ex-public schoolboys used to be sent out to run the British Empire. It was assumed that the right sort of people from the right sort of background had an innate ability to do the right sort of thing. This assumption was often hideously misplaced. One hears stories of crass, patronising or simply ignorant behaviour on the benches of not so long ago that make one's toes curl. One still encounters such mastodons here and there, but now that JPs have to undergo regular appraisal, they ought not to survive much longer.

These days the training consists of several half-days observing the courts in action and a series of quite demanding evening seminars. My first observation turned out to be an eye-opener. I had been warned that a good deal of what magistrates had to do was inhumanly boring: long hours spent dealing with unpaid parking fines, neglected TV licences, noise abatement orders and the like. I was braced for a tedious morning.

Magistrates' courts differ strikingly around the country. Some are cosily Dickensian, like the Shire Hall in Bury St Edmunds; some vastly imposing, such as the turreted Victoria

Law Courts in Birmingham. The finest modern courthouse I have seen is in Leeds, which combines the convenience of a hotel conference complex with glitzy 1990s design and state-of-the-art security. Alas, the Haringey bench's main place of business does not compare with any of these. It is a boxy, concrete, 1950s building off the Archway Road, on the way into town along the A1, situated between a defunct police station and a Jaguar showroom. I have since grown quite fond of it, but on that spring morning, as I nudged into the staff car park alongside a Securicor prison van disgorging its human cargo, it seemed tawdry and dispiriting.

Courts 1 and 2 are in keeping with the exterior: high-ceilinged, characterless oblongs with a raised platform and closed-fronted desk across one end for the bench. The clerk sits on a sort of half-landing beneath the bench with computer, phones and boxed set of Stone's Justices' Manuals to hand, giving a strong impression that this is, as it were, the courtroom flight deck – which in effect it is. There are varnished plywood pews for the lawyers in the well of the court and a narrow, glassed-in dock to one side, with a door leading down to the basement cells. The spindly lectern supporting a small heap of holy books in tattered cloth covers turns out to be the witness box. A royal coat of arms, a thermometer, a clock, and a sign with a crossed-out human ear indicating facilities for the hard-of-hearing fail to enliven the walls.

Nor was the cinema-style public seating at the rear of the court an uplifting venue from which to observe justice at work. The half-dozen or so people around me looked variously sad, shifty or downright menacing. On some of the chair-backs were hardened blobs of chewing gum and attempts at finger-nailed graffiti. Someone better equipped had etched 'Up White Hart Lane' on the cheap veneer, this being Tottenham territory.

The court got to its feet and bowed to the bench. The bench bowed back. The chairwoman said 'Good morning' in a head-mistressy manner. The usher called the first case on her list. The action began. This was a charges court, with many of the defendants in custody and most of them up before the bench for the first time. So there were no trials, and matters moved forward at amazing speed – sometimes too briskly for me to follow what was happening.

The first up was a man accused of indecently assaulting 'a female person'. He gave his address through a Kurdish interpreter as the Whittington Hospital, a mile or so down the Archway Road. The bench appeared to know exactly what they were dealing with and speedily ordered him to be re-detained there under Section 3 of the Mental Health Act.

The door to the cells was opened again and in place of the mentally disturbed Kurd came a 40-year-old man charged with possessing an imitation firearm, threatening to kill a married couple with it and assaulting the wife, 'occasioning actual bodily harm'. He was from Haringey's notorious Broadwater Farm Estate, scene of the lynching of PC Blakelock in the Tottenham race riots of 1985. No bail for him. He would be remanded in custody and committed for jury trial to Wood Green Crown Court.

Next on the usher's list were two angry-looking black girls accused of crack cocaine dealing. According to the police, drugs had been found in their underwear and in 'the vaginal area'. A search of their premises had discovered 'rock-like substances' and a pair of electronic scales. 'We will not accept jurisdiction,' declared the bench, meaning that the matter was too serious to be dealt with by magistrates and would have to go up to the crown court.

There followed a procession of alleged lesser offenders including shoplifters, several drink-drivers, three likely lads with gelled hair and shiny ties accused of stealing a guitar, a young man charged with being in possession of 'an article which had a blade or was sharply pointed, namely a knife'. The majority pleaded guilty, as is generally the case.

However, an alleged rapist would have to go before a jury. And so would a thin little fellow with darting eyes who needed a Turkish interpreter. I would come across other men charged with rape in the coming months. But the Turk was my first and so far only alleged murderer. I stared at him with extreme interest, but there was nothing at all about his manner to suggest whether he might or might not have killed the woman with whose death he was charged. Of course he would have to be committed to the higher court, but for now he was remanded in custody. 'Take him down,' came the order and he padded meekly below, handcuffed to his guard.

It had been a busy, slightly alarming and wholly riveting morning, but apart from the rape and murder charges, not at all untypical. My subsequent court visits as an observer confirmed the pattern. Most of the defendants were young and male. Those in work were a rarity. A high proportion spoke poor English or none at all.

I referred to a slim, grim document produced by Haringey council in 1999 called the *Crime and Disorder Audit* and there was the backdrop to these seedy courtroom dramas, spelt out in black and white with coloured pie charts. In terms of income, housing, educational attainment, health – in fact almost any indicator one cares to name – this much-blighted borough is one of the twenty most deprived districts in the country. By one definition, it has the highest unemployment rate of any local authority in England and Wales. Compared with London as a whole, it has an exceptionally high ratio of young inhabitants to old. In two wards more than a quarter of the population are under sixteen. Since in general, as the audit states bluntly, 'offenders in all categories of crime tend to be male and in the fifteen to nineteen age group', what I saw happening in the courts was scarcely surprising.

The missing bit of the picture, not specifically mentioned in the audit, was that around 45 per cent of the borough's 221,000 inhabitants belonged to ethnic minorities, if one included Greeks, Turks and an estimated 20,000 refugees and asylum seekers, who represented about 9 per cent of the total population. Haringey already offered to provide translations of the *Crime and Disorder Audit* in Bengali, Chinese, Greek, Gujarati,

Kurdish, Somali, Turkish and Urdu. It seemed an odd omission not to be including the languages of Eastern Europe, too, as Bosnians, Kosovans, Albanians, Poles, Romanians and Chechens found their way from the south coast ports to join the polyglot throng. At the last count it was reckoned that the people of Haringey spoke over 190 different languages including Bini, Loa and Tumbuka.

Perhaps the bench, too, should be worrying about how to reflect the increasingly multicultural locality it was supposed to represent. 'Race', in the loose sense in which it is used these days, is not just a black and white issue. The Lord Chancellor was able to boast that 8.8 per cent of the 1999 intake of new magistrates nationwide were from the ethnic minorities. But we sometimes behave as though the terms 'Afro-Caribbean' and 'Asian' covered all racial definitions and cultural distinctions. Settlers from Vietnam, China, Russia, Iran or Ecuador wouldn't go along with that.

THE CLASS OF '99
We discover each other – and the cells

Meanwhile, as spring turned to summer, our training sessions in the evenings began to make sense of what we were seeing and hearing during our daytime court visits. These were quite formal, two-hour affairs, complete with agendas, slides, work sheets and coffee breaks. They took place in the Highgate courthouse retiring room. This is the magistrates' mess as well as the place to which they remove themselves to discuss verdicts and sentences out of the court's hearing. Again, retiring rooms differ markedly. Birmingham JPs have spacious premises, including a library-cum-reading room whose opulence makes you think you are in a Pall Mall gentlemen's club rather than a Midlands courthouse. We, by contrast, have a dullish, low-ceilinged room largely filled with tables and chairs, with a coffee-maker and scullery at one end and our library at the other.

The scullery is the source of Safeways orange squash, custard creams and ginger nuts, presided over by the amiable Len. He is known as the court keeper and has a special pair of tongs for squeezing tea-bags. By 'our library', in contrast to Birmingham's, I mean a single set of shelves containing some undisturbed rows of law reports, a few dozen volumes of wider interest with titles like *The Changing Image of the Magistracy, Second Edition*, and a wrinkled school exercise book for recording withdrawals and returns. The nicest thing about the room is that it overlooks a pretty paved garden with a raised gravel flower bed where magistrates and court staff go to stroll or smoke among the laurels on sunny days.

Search warrants, community sentences and prisons not really being suitable subjects for outdoor discussion, however, our training took place inside, with the curtains drawn. Our trainers were the court clerks, those key figures around whom the magistrates' courts pivot and without whom the whole system would quickly disintegrate into legal chaos. Their job is to manage the court hearings and to advise the justices on points of law. We are now supposed to call them 'legal advisers' rather than clerks. When I asked one of them why, he said that the word 'clerk' had been thought to have lowly Victorian connotations. What stuff and nonsense, say older magistrates – like the suggestion that teachers should be called 'learning professionals' in order to increase their public esteem. Well, what's in a name? Even if journalists such as myself were officially redesignated 'recording angels', the public would still regard us as hacks.

Esteem arises from merit, and the legal advisers have plenty of that, call them what you will. Those who have any dealings with them have a high regard for these men and women, all of whom are qualified solicitors or barristers and know their stuff meticulously. One fellow magistrate with long experience of the public sector tells me they are its most dedicated and effective members. Anyway, Haringey's 150 JPs are looked after, thank goodness, by eleven of these supremely patient and able figures.

Their chief is Mr Fillingham, who is almost never referred to by his first name, Graham, and runs the whole caboodle with impressive calm and competence. He began in the magistrates' court service as a teenage teaboy, and now has the sonorous joint title of Justice's Chief Executive and Clerk to the Justices. It was under his and his team's auspices that we began to learn the difference between a conditional discharge and a suspended sentence.

But who were we, exactly, the ten new members of the Haringey bench who had been sworn in together a few weeks earlier and were now being dished out with folders, schedules, yearbooks, diaries, documents from the Ethnic Minorities Advisory Committee, questionnaires, entry codes and stiff plastic cards to raise the barrier into the court car park? We knew no more about each other than a group of singles starting on a course of evening salsa classes.

We sat in a polite semicircle and said our names: Chloe, Kate, Anthea, Gabrielle, Menen, Jennifer, Kristina, Clive, Joyce, Trevor. Eight women, two men. I guessed I was the oldest at fifty-four and that the youngest of us was in her early thirties. There was no urgent need to get to know each other, as there is in the panicky atmosphere of a newly-sworn jury. In fact it was months before I knew all our occupations. For the record they were, in the same order as above: Citizens' Advice Bureau adviser, university maths lecturer, jewellery importer, health lecturer, retired human resources manager, senior manager in the Post Office, special needs teacher, educational consultant, pharmacist, freelance journalist. A fair old mix, though it was interesting to note the preponderance of the public sector. This is true of the magistracy as a whole. Perhaps it is axiomatic that people who have already chosen to go into public service professionally are drawn to do more of it on a voluntary basis. But it is also the case that many public sector employers are contractually compelled to give staff members a certain amount of paid 'public service leave' each year. Private employers, regrettably, are under no such obligation.

The class of '99 got on well together, as the legal advisers took us painstakingly through the rudiments of bail, verdicts and sentencing. But there was no group dynamic about these training sessions. We didn't bond as a team, as I like to think most juries tend to, because we knew full well we never would be a team. Quite the reverse, in fact. Those in charge of the court rota would do their best to see that for the next year or so none of us sat together, since no chairman would want to be flanked by two wet-behind-the-ears wingers. One was more than enough.

The nearest we got to a bit of bonding was our visit to the cells, a new experience for all. We descended the stairs leading from the dock in Court 1, feeling like visitors to the underworld. At the bottom was a bare, windowless lobby with a board listing the day's custody cases in felt-tip, and the prisons from which they had been brought. Most were marked 'PV' for Pentonville, a few miles south of us and quite close to the notorious women's jail in Holloway.

Securicor now handled all the transporting and guarding of prisoners for the Haringey courts, it was explained. Not so long ago there was a busy police station next door, but in the deplorable drive for cost-cutting and efficiency, the place was abandoned. This not only pleased the Treasury but also, wickedly, made it look as though local crimes were down, because there was no one to report them to. Mugging victims and the finders of stray dogs heading gratefully for Highgate's sole blue lamp were now doomed to disappointment. These days the nearest station was miles away in Hornsey and the only police in the court building were liable to be there as witnesses. Having seen some of the court's clientele, not just in the dock but also in the public seating, I didn't find this news altogether reassuring. Through a door we could see the Securicor staff's cheerless little cubbyhole. It contained a kettle, some coffee mugs and a poster of a big girl in a small bikini. Presumably the women jailers were inured to this kind of thing.

A corridor studded with red alarm buttons led off the lobby.

This was where the cells were. We went into one of them. It was chillingly oppressive: a stark, empty box containing nothing but a coffin-like bench, or maybe bed, with a hard wooden lid. A doorless cubicle en suite contained a steel toilet, no paper. The inner wall of the cell adjoining the corridor was pierced by a tiny round window like a porthole in a bathysphere. Other than that the cell was utterly featureless, without a knob or bump or projection of any kind which might be used by a prisoner to hang himself or beat his brains out.

Close to the ceiling was a pattern of opaque glass bricks. The small amount of daylight they let in somehow increased the sense of hopelessness the cell conveyed. We resurfaced in the courtroom from which, in just a few weeks' time, we would be sending people down to the dispiriting dungeons from which we had just emerged. It was a melancholy thought.

By now we had been given a schedule of our sittings, known as the rota. One new JP was horrified at the number of her expected appearances. 'That's once a week until the millennium,' she wailed. We were allowed to exchange dates among ourselves or with any other willing magistrate. There was a flurry of telephone calls to arrange swaps. 'I'm abroad for three weeks in August.' 'I just can't do Hanukkah.' 'I'm away for the Christmas holidays.' 'Help!' Well, as I said, volunteering is a mug's game.

CHAPTER 3

Absolute Beginners

*'It's a job no one on earth thanks you for doing, while there
are lots who question your motives'*

Outside in the courthouse garden a blackbird was singing.
Inside, we were TICing and TWOCing and TDAing – in other
words, picking up jargon. To TIC is to take into consideration,
as in 'other offences'. To TWOC is to take a vehicle without the
owner's consent, as distinct from a TDA which stands for
taking and driving away, though I shouldn't have thought
the irate victim would notice the difference. A youth under
eighteen on trial for one of these offences might well find
himself being looked after in court by someone from YOT,
the Young Offenders Team, then remanded on bail for a PSR,
or pre-sentence report. He could be given an ASBO (antisocial
behaviour order) or he might be banged up in a YOI, a young
offenders' institution. ABH, actual bodily harm, is less serious
than GBH, grievous bodily harm. What makes the assault G
rather than A is the intent to cause serious injury. A reasonable
sentence for ABH might be a community service order, or CSO,
except that its name has now been changed to a community
punishment order, so it would be a CPO.

Such was the unfamiliar ABC we new JPs of the Haringey
PSA (Petty Sessions Area) were trying to learn PDQ before we
found ourselves in court actually having to do the business.
Fortunately there was no barrister's Latin to learn, though I've
since noticed that bench chairmen and women dearly love a
chance to roll '*sine die*' (no fixed day) around their tongues. My
Latin master would have insisted on pronouncing it 'sinnay
deeay'. The way they say it sounds ominously like 'sign, die'.

It was not intended that we should have a detailed knowledge
of the law in the way, say, a grammarian has a detailed

knowledge of a language. We merely had to be able to understand it and follow its basic rules with reasonable competence,
guided when necessary by the legal adviser. For example,
magistrates need to know about court procedure, about the
burden of proof, the rules of evidence, the requirement for the
key elements of the prosecution case to be disclosed to the
defence, and so on. We should be aware of PACE, the Police
and Criminal Evidence Act 1984, which lays down the proper
manner in which suspects should be arrested and interviewed.

We learnt that the reward for an early guilty plea, which
saves both time and expense, was one-third off the appropriate
sentence, and that the maximum sentences we could impose
were a £5,000 fine and six months' imprisonment. The exception to this was where a defendant was found guilty of more
than one 'either-way' offence, in which case the punitive-
minded could give two consecutive maximum jail sentences,
adding up to a whole year behind bars – although the prisoner
would usually be released on licence after half that time.

The phrase 'either-way' offence referred to a set of crimes
which were neither so serious that they were indictable only,
which meant they could be tried only in the crown court, nor so
relatively petty that they were summary only, and had therefore
to be heard by magistrates. They included, for example, fraud,
dangerous driving, theft, burglary and indecent assault. As
things stood then, before Lord Justice Auld published his
criminal courts review in 2001, it was left to the defendant
to choose which mode of trial he preferred, the choice being
between a relatively knowing bench of three magistrates and a
dozen complete novices sitting in the jury box. The point was
that while juries were more likely to give a defendant the benefit
of the doubt, sentences in the crown court tended to be heavier
than those the magistrates imposed. Naturally we hoped those
charged with 'either-way' misdeeds would choose trial by
magistrates rather than trial by jury, since such cases tended
to be a good deal more interesting than a routine driving
without insurance or a drunk and disorderly.

Highgate Magistrates' Court. It is a Monday morning and the district judge, or stipe as everyone still calls him, Mr Wiles, is dealing with people charged over the weekend. He is quick and decisive. Whereas a bench of three lay magistrates must hold whispered consultations or go out to the retiring room to make up their minds, he merely reflects briefly and then pronounces. His manner is cool but not chilling. He is kindly towards a frightened Romanian girl who pleads guilty to stealing a couple of T-shirts from a BHS store. 'We went in there: we had the opportunity; we took the opportunity,' she confesses in a low voice through the interpreter. 'I am very repentant about it.' He gives her a conditional discharge for six months, which means she must stay out of trouble for that period of time or she'll be brought back to court and re-sentenced. My guess is she'll never be in trouble again.

A traumatised-looking boy is brought up from the cells wearing a white paper suit splattered with blood. He was arrested on Friday, says the prosecutor, for stealing a cream cake worth 79p from a supermarket. 'Oi, that's not true,' interjects the lad in the dock indignantly. 'It was a doughnut.' He was pounced on by the supermarket security staff and slightly injured. When the police were called and searched him, they found a small amount of cannabis. At the police station he'd gone a bit wild, been locked in a cell where he went wilder still, injured himself, damaged his clothes and had to be put into the police-issue paper pyjamas. What a nightmare weekend. The defendant looks as if he can scarcely believe the sequence of events that followed from his helping himself to a 79p doughnut. Mr Wiles deems him to have been punished enough by his three nights in the cells. Quite enough, I'd say.

Our next training session was on trial procedure and verdicts. The prosecution had to prove each element of its case, said the trainers. Section 9 evidence was a written statement accepted by both sides. The order of play was explained: the prosecutor's opening speech, examination-in-chief of the first prosecution witness, cross-examination of the witness by the defence, re-examination by the prosecutor and so on until the prosecution had concluded its case and it was the turn of the defence to bring on its witnesses, who would endure the same three-part examination. If the defending advocate had made an opening speech before calling evidence, then the prosecution had a right of reply. Otherwise, the defence had the last word. Most of us had a fair grasp of all this anyway, but it became clearer when the clerks gamely played out the trial of a shoplifter called Mr Pincher. The police witnesses, inevitably, were Officers Nickem and Catchem.

The following week the subject was sentencing, the purposes of a sentence being: punishment, protection of the public, deterrence, reparation/compensation, and rehabilitation. It is an interesting list, when you think about it, for it is not always easy to give the same weight to each of those aims. A short custodial sentence provides little scope for rehabilitation, for example. Nor is a man sent to prison as a reparation to society in general in the best position to compensate the victim in particular.

These were deep waters, we realised, scanning the longish list of sentences available, from a conditional discharge via fines, compensation orders, probation (now community rehabilitation) orders, community service (now punishment) orders, electronic tagging and so on all the way up the scale to custody. Until the middle of the nineteenth century, it didn't stop there. Justices had the power to sentence felons to transportation and death – and used it with great frequency.

Fortunately, JPs are not left to flounder. On every bench and in every retiring room there is an invaluable lifebelt in the shape of a stiff folder containing the sentencing guidelines. These guidelines are drawn up by the Magistrates' Association (a voluntary body to which most JPs belong) with the approval of the Lord Chancellor and the Lord Chief Justice, and do exactly what they say: they suggest a range of appropriate punishments and levels of fine for all the criminal offences we commonly have to deal with. In a few motoring matters, such as drink-driving, there are mandatory endorsements and periods of disqualification. But otherwise the bench is encouraged to use its own judgment, while staying within these reasonably wide parameters. 'They are of course only guidelines,' says the Lord Chancellor. 'They do not curtail your independent discretion to impose the sentences you think are right, case by case. But they exist to help you in that process. And, importantly, they help to assist the magistracy to maintain an overall consistency of approach.'

That last point is indeed important. A perennial beef against JPs used to be, and to a lesser extent still is, their inconsistency. One of the chief justifications of the lay magistracy is that it provides local justice. But too often local justice has simply been a euphemism for startling local discrepancies. For example, where a bench in a university town would be lenient towards cannabis smokers, a quiet country court might treat them as if they were Colombian drug barons. Attitudes towards prostitution in a city with a big red-light district could differ sharply from those in a rural market town. This was punishment by postcode, said the critics.

The guidelines have supposedly done much to even out these differences, though they have not got rid of them completely. When a new scale of recommended fines for driving without insurance was published in September 2000, carefully graded to take earnings levels into account, I was startled to hear a JP in another London borough say that her bench simply ignored them. The new guideline fine for someone on a middling income was £220. Her bench had always preferred a sum of £350 so they were jolly well sticking to it, she trumpeted, making it plain she thought guidelines were for cissies.

THE TOTTENHAM TRAIL
I encounter our other courthouse

One of our observation sessions had to be in a court other than Highgate. I chose the neighbouring London Borough of Enfield, which was not very adventurous of me, since I would soon become a regular visitor there anyway. The reason for this was that Haringey magistrates have not one but two places of business: besides the premises in Highgate, they also share part of Enfield's rather splendid 1930s courthouse in Tottenham, some three or four miles away to the east. For Haringey to have court facilities there makes sense. There is more crime in Tottenham than any other part of the borough, so for many defendants this is the closest courthouse to get to – and the easiest to pay their fines at if convicted.

To make the short journey from genteel Highgate to rough-and-tumble Tottenham is to cross one of those cultural-socio-economic frontiers that are forever reshaping and redefining London. One minute you are driving through Hornsey in the shadow of Alexandra Palace, past a handsome Victorian pumping station, the next you go under a railway bridge and quite suddenly find yourself in . . . I was about to write 'a foreign land' until I remembered William Hague's problems during the 2001 election campaign. So let me re-phrase that: quite suddenly you find yourself in what *looks like* a bustling foreign city, though which city it would be quite impossible to say. Turnpike Lane is not a ghetto. It is more like a permanent exhibition of immigrant entrepreneurialism. There are women in veils and African robes, men in turbans and Rasta tams, all moving about busily, carrying briefcases, hauling trolleys, parking vans. The greengrocers display okra and plantains, yams and sweet potatoes. You pass the Al Halal Fried Chicken shop, the Bangla Bazaar, the Chinese Herbal Centre, the Al Amin Butchers, Tawakal Trading, Parnassus Travel and a Lebanese minimarket. There is Turkish coffee, Malaysian satay,

Thai takeaway and the Jashan Indian Restaurant, a favourite of the *Spectator* magazine's restaurant correspondent. Amidst this jumble of cultures and nationalities placidly rubbing commercial shoulders sits the aptly-sited office of the Haringey Racial Equality Council.

On my first journey I got lost among the streets of terraced housing east of the Lane. I stopped and lowered the window to ask a passer-by the way. He looked at me narrowly for half a second and before I'd even opened my mouth said: 'You're looking for the courts, right?' I stared at him wide-eyed. 'How did you know that?' I blurted out. The man laughed. 'Dressed like that? Couldn't be anywhere else, mate. That's the only place you'd be going round here wearing a jacket and tie.' This was unnerving. Just a few minutes earlier I had been merrily spotting Greek Cypriots by their worry beads and Ethiopians by their handsome cheekbones. Now here was I being categorised just as superficially and probably more accurately in a single glance which had immediately identified me as a lawyer, magistrate or possibly a plainclothes policeman. To this white citizen of London N15 I belonged to a tribe just as distinct as – and possibly even more alien than – anyone on the pavements of Turnpike Lane. What was disturbing, I thought, as I set off to follow his directions, was that he had so instantly marked me down as someone connected with Them rather than Us. Was that the impression JPs generally made? Unfortunately, this was probably so.

On our part, magistrates soon learn that first impressions are often unreliable. That very morning, as I drove up to the Tottenham courthouse, I noticed a tall black guy lounging beside the entrance smoking, and at once assumed I'd be seeing him in the dock an hour or so later. This was not because he was black but on account of his menacing shades and round leather hat, like an Afghan guerrilla's. Half an hour later, as I was familiarising myself with the retiring room, in strode this same cool dude bearing a tray of coffee and biscuits: he was a popular member of the courthouse staff, one of the keepers, and his name was Charles. Later he showed me a good place to park my Piaggio motor scooter. 'That's where the police leave their bikes,' he said. 'It'll be safe there.' I should jolly well think so. This was a courthouse car park, after all.

The atmosphere in the Tottenham retiring room was a good deal more formal than at Highgate. Down the middle of the room, taking up most of the space, was a long, heavy, board-room-style table which was the preserve of the Enfield magistrates and their legal advisers. At the head sat a chairman figure who, once all had taken their places, rapped the table and proceeded to assign the day's work in the manner of a CO issuing battle orders to his officers. We Haringey-ites had a very much smaller table near the door and kept our voices down during the Enfield briefing. It was hard not to feel we were intruding. Since then I have got used to this rather unsatisfactory sharing arrangement, which must be even more annoying for Enfield, whose courthouse this principally is. But I still sense a detectable sniffiness between the two benches. A question to which the Lord Chancellor might be keen to know the magistrates' answer would be: which bench would you rather be tried by, Haringey or Enfield? I bet we'd each vote in favour of our own lot. If so, that would not only demonstrate local loyalty, but would also, if you think about it, be quite reassuring to the public.

Tottenham Magistrates' Court. A much more handsome courtroom than Highgate: carved oak furniture in 1930s style, solid and reassuring. A man whose upper garment consists of no more than a vest stretched over his enormous biceps explains sullenly why he can't pay off his fine at £10 a week. He has five children, he says, and begins stumbling through their ages. A baffled look creeps over his face and he counts his fingers. He realises he has forgotten one. Six children, he corrects himself sheepishly.

It is astounding how so many defendants turn up to court without a penny in their pockets, or so they say.

Obviously those faced with a fine know that if they admit to having cash on them they'll be encouraged to hand over a down-payment. But they must think the magistrates are cretins, or so old as to believe that Londoners still go everywhere on foot, like the young Charles Dickens. What, not even the bus fare home? Come off it. One man threatened with a body search leaves the courtroom to consider the matter, and reappears moments later to say that after all he can pay the whole fine by cheque – cheque! – right away.

A man enters the dock, listens to the charges and says firmly: 'I'm pleading guilty because the police told me this would cut things short. But I'm not guilty, though I'll stick with pleading guilty.' The bench is in a fix. They try to persuade him that if he isn't really guilty it would be unjust for them to accept his plea. He really must plead not guilty and let them set a date for a trial. But, no, he won't budge and that's that. Guilty, then.

A heavy-set 36-year-old pleads guilty to stealing a pair of trousers. In mitigation, he says he's a grandfather with a lot of dependants. His record shows he has been in prison four times – for theft, drug trafficking and rape. Now he's a shoplifting grandpa. How are the mighty fallen.

FIRST SITTING
My debut on the bench

The big day arrived. What should I wear? No one had said a word to us about correct court garb. Women magistrates seemed surprisingly free and easy about their wardrobes. Some turned up in trousers and jumpers; most favoured a modest sprinkling of jewellery. The men, with fewer variations open to them, generally stuck to dark suits, plain shirts and subdued ties. But I couldn't help thinking of my encounter with the man in Tottenham and wondering whether it was such a good idea for male members of the bench to look so uniformly like bank managers. I ran an eye over my three usable suits, which ranged from the funereal to the frivolous, and hummed and hawed a bit.

Eighteen months later one would have taken the matter more seriously. Early in 2001 the *Daily Mail*, ever on the lookout for new manifestations of political correctness, ran a story under a great big four-decker headline: 'Why magistrates won't be asked to look "sober and respectable",' it fumed. Allegedly the Lord Chancellor was about to act on an 'equality report' from his advisers which recommended that 'any dress code should be rigorously checked for cultural bias, as terms like "sober" and "respectable" are likely to mean very different things to different people and are a minefield for prejudice and assumption'. Horrid visions of magistrates in sweatshirts and leather jackets rose momentarily to mind.

What these patronising busybodies chose to ignore was that sobriety and respectability mean pretty well the same all over the world. Indeed in many societies these qualities are more highly prized than they are here. This is the notice outside a magistrates' court in Barbados, for example, where it is not just the bench who have to attire themselves smartly: 'All persons attending court must dress appropriately,' it warns. 'No jeans, no tights, no miniskirts, no earrings worn by males. Hairstyles must be worn tidily.' In London courts that would rule out three-quarters of the public.

In any event, since in this country there is no such dress code that I am aware of, there is no need for it to be rigorously checked for cultural bias. So the Lord Chancellor has very sensibly kept mum on the subject. My own view is that magistrates should dress in the way they personally feel appropriate for what is, after all, a pretty serious occasion. In the case of men that might conceivably include an open neck and no tie in the manner of Israeli politicians, but certainly not jeans and flip-flops. Come to think of it, a gown such as the ushers wear would overcome most of these difficulties in a trice. Uniquely,

City of London justices do still wear blue and black robes, having held on to a tradition long since abandoned everywhere else.

Anyway, when the day of my first sitting dawned I rather daringly chose a Jon Snow-ish tie with an abstract fruit-salad design and a blue tweed jacket instead of a suit. As a gesture of solidarity with the common man this minute adjustment to the usual uniform was pathetic, but at least it showed I had given some thought to the role in which I was about to make my debut.

This took place in the Tottenham courthouse. Over coffee in the retiring room the court clerk took us through the morning's list of cases. I was just a touch nervous. It wasn't as though one was going to have to perform in any way. The chairman or woman does all the talking. The two wingers merely have to look alert and put on a dumb show of understanding what's afoot. Still, filing into a courtroom which has been ordered to its feet at your entrance, exchanging bows with the assembly and being addressed as 'Your Worships' is all bound to make one a trifle self-conscious, anxious not to trip over a chair-leg or knock the water carafe onto the legal adviser's head.

It was mostly minor stuff that morning. There were several applications for extended pub licences and a man accused of assaulting a woman – one of those frequent instances of domestic violence which would probably collapse when the victim decided not to give evidence, preferring a brute of a partner to no partner at all. It looked as though my inaugural sitting was to be something of an anticlimax. But then came a sad young Somali who had been found guilty of drawing unemployment benefit fraudulently, and whom our bench was now to punish. The Probation Service had drawn up a pre-sentence report which, in its compressed and unemotional form, told a bleak tale.

Back in the early 1990s, with Somalia in a state of violent anarchy, the man and his family had had their lives threatened. They were forced to flee. His wife and children sought refuge in

Kenya while he came to the UK in the hope of being able to earn enough money to send some back to them. As a political refugee, he had been granted indefinite residence. Desperate to maintain his family, he had cheated the Department of Social Security out of between £2,000 and £3,000, nearly all of which was dutifully sent to Kenya. He seemed genuinely repentant, eager to make amends, and offered to compensate the DSS at the rate of £100 a month. We sentenced him to 200 hours' community service. He thanked the bench gravely.

I found all this quite cheering. It seemed to me that the matter had been dealt with fairly, not just in the court's eyes but also in the offender's. Nevertheless, one was left with the dismal reflection that the anxieties which had led to his misbehaviour remained painfully unresolved. For the next eighteen months or so, as he toiled to pay off his debt to this benevolent yet alien northern society, the plight of his wife and children thousands of miles away would be even more miserable than it had been before.

My first actual trial took place some days later, also at Tottenham but in a tiny courtroom without a proper dock and with no direct access to the cells. A small brass plate screwed to the magistrates' desk said: 'This court is 17 feet long and 16 feet wide wall to wall.' Why there is a need to have these measurements permanently before the bench's eyes I cannot imagine. Since motoring offences are often heard in this court, perhaps the idea is to provide a sort of ready-reckoner when dealing with such cases. 'How far from the other car were you, Mrs So-and-so, when you noticed you were about to ram it? About twice the width of this room, would you say? It is 16 feet wide wall to wall.' At any rate, it was an intimate scenario and one rather hoped the defendant would not be of a violent disposition.

The young woman who appeared before us was not violent but she was certainly aggressive. She had pleaded not guilty to ignoring a noise abatement order by playing music loudly in the small hours and annoying the neighbours. A long-haired tech-

nical officer from the council gave evidence. He had the unenviable job of checking out such incidents with his decibel
measuring equipment, usually at unsocial times and often
threatened by inebriated party-goers. He had been called to
this woman's address at 3.30 a.m. to test the noise level. He said
firmly: 'In my opinion it constituted a nuisance.'

It was a relatively trivial matter, unless one happened to live
next door to the defendant. But still, there was a toughish
discussion in the retiring room before we decided she was
guilty. Persuading myself she had been avoiding the truth
was not a snap decision. What shook me was that after the
verdict, when the prosecutor came to present her record to the
bench prior to sentencing, it turned out that she had a long,
turbulent history of noise offences and of not paying her fines
for them. She had been lying unflinchingly all through her
evidence. So here was the first of many lessons in human
duplicity which one couldn't help learning and yet which
one would have to school oneself to discount, for fear of
becoming cynical and case-hardened. Whatever else we had
picked up from our training, the presumption of innocence
must remain paramount.

*Highgate. A 20-year-old Chinese man is accused of raping
his underage sister. His family have been in London as
refugees for some years. His father and mother are both in
court, looking sorrowful. According to the prosecution,
the defendant has been committing 'chronic, repetitive
penile penetration' on his sibling since before she even
became a teenager. The sallow young man listens impassively as all this is relayed to him by a Cantonese interpreter. Obviously the case is so serious it will have to be
heard in the crown court, but we must decide what is to be
done with him in the meantime.*

*Incredibly, the mother pleads for her son to be given bail
while awaiting trial, even though this would mean his
living at home for several weeks, under the same roof as*

his sister-victim. I ask myself: is this a situation where political correctness demands we should give due weight to the mores of another culture, the kind where in a parent's eyes male offspring are invariably in the right and must always take precedence over mere daughters? Absolutely not. One of the key reasons for refusing bail is a reasonable fear that the defendant will interfere with prosecution witnesses. We remand the man in custody.

COURT REPORTS
In which the newcomers compare notes

Kate threw a Sunday drinks party for the class of '99. It was a lovely summer's day. We sat around a table on the terrace eating olives and drinking abstemiously while a gaggle of spouses toped rather more heartily at the bottom of the garden. Most of us hadn't seen each other since we began sitting. We were eager to exchange notes. There was general agreement: court was nearly always interesting, occasionally bewildering, sometimes deeply dispiriting. Our chairmen and women had mostly been helpful and considerate. Any worries we'd harboured about the lay magistracy being a po-faced, authoritarian-minded institution had been largely dispelled. Perhaps we would come to be more critical in the light of experience, but for the time being everyone seemed impressed – and secretly relieved, maybe, that their motives for becoming a JP were unlikely to be betrayed. What we were doing seemed on the whole to be a good thing.

A year later, when I had decided to write this book, I asked some of my colleagues to recall those early reactions. They were still enthusiastic. The role of the magistrate was not just socially valuable but also personally worthwhile, said Jennifer, a senior manager in the Post Office. 'I felt I'd discovered real life. It has helped me focus on what's really important. It has shown me a way I can make an input to society. That's been a surprise. I hadn't expected that.' I was reminded of what the nineteenth-century French political writer Alexis de Tocqueville said about juries, that they are 'a peerless teacher of citizenship'.

Gabrielle is herself a Frenchwoman, a health lecturer who has lived in this country for thirty-five years and thought she might be barred from becoming a JP because of her nationality. Somewhat to her surprise she wasn't. 'Nobody said a word,' she confided in a richly-accented undertone, even though there was no one to overhear us. There were certainly grounds for doubt on the matter. Even that eminent authority on the history of the lay magistracy Sir Thomas Skyrme KCVO CB TD JP DL has only gone so far as to say, 'There is reason to believe that even a foreign subject may legally be appointed a magistrate', before going on to relate how Princess Chula of Thailand was turned down for the Cornwall bench in 1962. However, when I rang the Lord Chancellor's office I was told there was no problem with foreign residents on the bench, so long as they were prepared to take the oath of allegiance. Two years later, this advice would have to be revised, but at the time there was no bar to my Continental colleague's appointment.

'After all this time living here I wanted to put something back,' said Gabrielle, and plainly she felt she was doing so. 'I admire the fact that ordinary people get involved. My French friends are surprised that we do it – and for no pay! So they assume it must be some kind of an honour, and when I say no, they're very impressed. I think maybe they are a bit envious of what we have: real popular justice. It is a very *révolutionnaire* idea.'

The only male in our intake other than myself was Clive, a colourful figure approaching fifty with a grey beard, long ponytail to match and a clamorous taste in shirts. He had turned up for our first training session at the Highgate court-house wearing an electric blue yarmulke and sandals, which showed a certain independence of spirit. To my eyes he looked strikingly unmagisterial, though I dare say he wouldn't have fooled my Tottenham friend. Before he became an educational consultant he was the head of a Liverpool comprehensive. Labour Party member and sandal-wearer, Clive did not fit the public's traditional image of the male magistrate as a crusty conformist with his golf clubs in the boot of the car.

It was an image he himself had been taken in by. 'Initially, one of the reasons I wanted to become a magistrate was to re-balance the bench against all those retired colonels. In fact what I discovered was an infinitely more careful and coherent system than I'd expected.' Right from the start, he was agreeably surprised. 'The structure of decision-making allows room to apply your own judgment. But it also challenges thoughtless prejudices, liberal and reactionary alike. It makes you justify your reasoning within the boundaries of the law.'

Did left-wing friends think it odd that he had wanted to become an authority figure and join the establishment? Some of them did, but Clive had a sharp response. 'There's a way in which you can be a liberal and just stand aside, without getting your hands dirty. You complain about everything but you do nothing. You don't make a difference.'

That sort of fastidiousness made him impatient. 'There's this Third World charity I'm chairman of – a sort of Jewish equivalent of Christian Aid. People ask, what's the point of it? You can only help a few families or maybe at most a small village – what about all the millions of other desperate people? To which I say, surely it's better to do something, however little, than just stand there picking holes and wringing your hands.

'I'd thought for a long time about becoming a magistrate. There was a tradition of public service in my family. Running a school in Liverpool and then working for the local education authority, I was very aware of social needs and the lack of equal opportunities. My landlady in Liverpool was a long-serving JP and she was very persuasive about the social value of the lay magistracy.'

But what if one didn't like a particular law, the Poll Tax for example? 'Well, you can argue about how to apply it – or you can walk away by resigning. It's like collective responsibility and the Cabinet. Magistrates are under the fairly solemn constraints of the oaths they have taken. I think most of them must feel pretty committed to the law of the land. The point is to try to make it work humanely.

'Something I wasn't prepared for was my change in attitude to locking people up,' Clive reflected. 'Even though I was a committed liberal, I'd always been a bit careless about prison. There were some people who had to be put away and that was that. Now I realise that locking someone up even briefly is a severe responsibility. What about his children? His job, if he has one? Will it turn him into a hardened criminal? Too short a sentence and there's no chance of rehabilitation; too long and he's institutionalised. These are very difficult judgments.'

Like myself, Clive was intensely bothered by the problem of sentencing asylum seekers. They usually had no money for a fine, since they weren't allowed to work in their first six months here and their benefit came in the form of vouchers. They were often unsuitable for community service because of the language barrier. Yet it was plainly wrong to send someone to prison simply because there was no other suitable sentence. 'I'm horrified by what's going on here,' says Clive. 'In this money-driven society, keeping a man so impoverished that he can't afford even a small fine is just provoking petty crime.'

Kate, mathematician and university teacher, had also puzzled some of her friends by becoming a magistrate. She had been drawn to it partly as a result of a lifelong curiosity about the law which had not been wholly satisfied by marrying a lawyer. 'But also, I felt that being a JP was something people should be willing to do, even though as a child of the Sixties – Essex University, lefty politics and all that – I didn't exactly warm to the idea of magistrates.' Even now, she said, people who discovered she was on the bench were often suspicious. 'It's a job no one on earth thanks you for doing, while there are lots who question your motives. They want to know what right you have to be judging others, and at first that was a question I often asked myself.'

Until one has sat quite a number of times, it is hard to know what being a magistrate is like. Kate searched libraries and bookshops for helpful material, as most of us did, but there was almost nothing of a non-academic nature. At her interview she was perturbed that the panel seemed so keen to pin down her political allegiance. She insisted she was uncommitted, but could see it didn't go down well. Like me, she was asked about prejudice. She answered that as a teacher one was quick to make judgments about a class, to recognise types, but one also learned to put those first impressions aside.

None of this had given her much of a clue as to what to expect, but the reality had, on the whole, been reassuring. There were no politics in the retiring room at all. Indeed, it would be impossible to be sure how any of our colleagues voted. As for prejudice, she had encountered none whatever. Beyond a mild animus against defendants who chewed gum in the dock, neither had I.

Everyone had a first sitting story – well, not always a first sitting, since in most cases these had been as uneventful as my own, but an early experience that had shaken or surprised them. One woman recalled her bench having to deal with a youth facing several robbery charges. These were so serious he would have to be sent up to the crown court for trial, but meantime they had to decide what to do with him while he was on remand. After much soul-searching the bench decided to keep him out of prison and grant him bail. Four days later this woman's 15-year-old son and a few friends were effectively kidnapped by a violently threatening young man wielding a knife. He forced them all to empty their cashpoints, then hung on to two of them until midnight, when he could have a second go at withdrawing the maximum cash allowance on their cards. The boys escaped and found their way home, but it had been a dangerous and frightening experience. What made her son's account so chilling, said his mother, was his description of their assailant. Horrified, she realised that it was almost certainly the same youth she had bailed the previous week. 'One knows the issues intellectually,' she said. 'This brought them home emotionally in a shocking way.'

The worry of having made a wrong decision can be haunting. As Lord Devlin wrote of the even heavier responsibilities which sometimes burden juries, 'the sleep of the final verdict is disturbed by the nightmare of miscarriage'. One woman in our intake could not erase a particular scene which had occurred soon after she started sitting. She was sharing the bench that day with two male justices. The case concerned a man accused of raping a very young girl, a relative of his. There had been many delays. The case had been in court several times already and now the man was due to be committed to the crown court for trial. However, once again the prosecution wanted more time to prepare, and asked for a further adjournment. This is always a delicate matter. Magistrates are under constant pressure to avoid unnecessary hold-ups and to be especially wary of granting adjournments unless there are persuasive reasons.

Despite the gravity of what the defendant was charged with (and nothing can be much graver than the rape of a minor), the bench eventually decided not to grant the adjournment. The usual arguments in such a situation are that the prosecution has had more than enough time to get its act together and that it would be unfair to keep the man on remand any longer. They knew the consequence of their refusal would be that the prosecutor would offer no evidence and so the case would be dismissed. On the basis that although the bench would in effect be freeing the man, the police could always re-charge him, the novice magistrate reluctantly agreed.

The chairman announced their decision. At that moment the female probation officer who was sitting in the court shot a look of horrified reproval at the woman magistrate. 'I shall never forget it,' she said. 'That look said that as a woman and a mother I should have known better and tried harder. I knew she was right. It was a tough lesson.'

But there were rewarding experiences, too. 'The best thing

about being a magistrate,' said Clive, 'is when you feel you've caught someone at the right moment to do something positive about his life, to stop some young guy who's in court for the first time sliding down the slippery slope. That is a wonderful feeling.'

STORM SIGNALS
A legal revolution in the offing

Virtuously, I went along to an introductory evening about the forthcoming Human Rights Act, a prospect which was throwing all manner of magistrates, both novices and veterans, into a tizzy. The incorporation of the European Convention on Human Rights into English law would represent the most important change to our legal system this century – and magistrates would be in the front line.

The event was held in one of those soulless Bloomsbury hotels which make you want to apologise personally to any tourists unfortunate enough to be lodged there. The place looked and felt like a coach terminal. There was a large turnout of magistrates from all over the Middlesex area, demographically varied in appearance and apparel. A non-participant couldn't possibly have guessed what it was we all had in common.

The proceedings opened on a dramatic note. Someone from the Magistrates' Association, of which I was a brand new member and which styles itself, justly, as the Voice of the Magistracy, drew our attention to two articles which had lately appeared in *The Times* and the *Financial Times*. They speculated that the Government was thinking of winding down the lay magistracy. 'This government had no hesitation in getting rid of hereditary peers,' boomed the man at the microphone defiantly. 'It is hostile to lay magistrates. We are fighting for our survival.'

Wow! This was stirring stuff. I had read the articles myself with some alarm, and formed the impression that because they appeared within days of each other, they looked suspiciously like a kite-flying exercise. Perhaps the Lord Chancellor and/or Home Secretary Jack Straw wanted to test public opinion on the matter. If so, then this was the proper way to react. Wouldn't it be something if this control-freakish New Labour administration actually managed to turn law-abiding magistrates into rampant militants?

After this the rest of the evening fell somewhat flat, as we were led painstakingly through the eighteen Articles of the European Convention on Human Rights. But it raised some interesting conundrums. For example, did not the prohibition of slavery and forced labour, Article 4, conflict with the sentencing of offenders to do unpaid work under community service orders? (The answer was no, it did not: there was a special provision to allow this.) And what about the possibility of a clash between Article 8, which is about the right to privacy, and Article 10, which concerns the freedom of expression – a stark problem for the press? (What about it, indeed? One could already hear the silky sound of lawyers rubbing their hands.)

Naturally the adoption of the new Act had given legalistic phrase-makers a chance to shine. The Convention, we were told, was a 'living instrument'. It embraced the 'doctrine of proportionality' and in applying it we should adopt the 'purposive approach'. This means one need not always take a strictly legal view of the law, but should consider what purpose the drafters had in mind – a notion which could spawn all sorts of mischief, I should imagine. But I did rather like the phrase used to describe the concept of fair representation for both sides in court: 'equality of arms'. It seemed to hark back to the medieval days of trial by ordeal, one popular test of a man's guilt or innocence having been ordeal by single combat, the assumption being that God would favour the injured party.

Before we left we were invited to fill in a form assessing our reactions to the evening's events. One question asked whether we thought the 'learning outcomes' of the event were 'met'.

Fortunately, one was able to apply the purposive approach to interpret this crass piece of illogicality. In any event, the real outcome of the evening so far as I was concerned was that it raised two themes which were to provide a continuo accompaniment throughout my first two years as a JP: human rights and the future of the lay magistracy.

CHAPTER 4

Now and Then

'Thirty years ago the old "It's a fair cop, guv" spirit still prevailed'

By the time autumn arrived, I was beginning to get the hang of things. Certain patterns of misbehaviour were becoming familiar, particularly where they concerned motoring offences. But as for other kinds of crime, no two cases were ever quite the same, although drugs and drink were a regular part of the background. Typical was the case of the 20-year-old Buddy Holly lookalike who appeared before us one morning. He was charged with stealing several pairs of sunglasses, a toaster and a shirt. (The randomness of what people like this take when they are thieving is pathetically telling.) He pleaded guilty. It was a routine minor shoplifting for which he would have received a routine minor sentence – until his previous record was disclosed.

It emerged that the thefts had taken place when he was not only on a conditional discharge for one offence, but also in breach of a probation order for another. He was a heroin addict with a dismayingly long history of stealing to pay for his habit. He was living with his girlfriend and, inevitably, there was a child. Clearly, the appropriate sentence was a problem because of his failure to respond to community penalties in the past. Equally clearly, unless his addiction was checked, Haringey magistrates would be seeing a lot more of him over the coming years. We adjourned the case for the probation service to prepare a pre-sentence report, hoping it would find him suitable for drug treatment. In other words, we passed the buck. It was the correct thing to do. But it left me feeling both frustrated that we were not able to see the thing through ourselves and relieved that it was not our bench that had to decide the sentence in what was pretty obviously a hopeless case.

This sense of despair became familiar. Not long after Buddy Holly, the bench I was on had to deal with a 35-year-old Turk likewise accused of serial theft. He had spent a day on a snitching spree in Wood Green, one of the main local shopping areas: £60 worth of Tottenham Hotspur's bobble hats, £120 worth of South Park dolls, £101 worth of Manchester United football kit and a couple of sandwiches. It was the sandwiches that were his undoing: he was spotted taking them by a security guard. He was an £80-a-day heroin addict who had breached probation for such offences on previous occasions. He had no fixed abode, no job, no family, no anchor of any kind in his awesomely chaotic life.

The sentence would obviously have to be postponed for a report, but what about bail? The chances of his reoffending while on remand were high. But would he fail to surrender to bail when the date of his sentencing came round? On the whole we thought this unlikely, given his guilty plea, his record of previous appearances and his apparent willingness to co-operate with the probation service in preparing his PSR. What we hoped was that the report would consider him suitable for one of the local authority's intensive drug rehabilitation courses. That would obviously be a more positive sentence than sending him to jail. In which case, what was the point of locking him up in the interim for several weeks, knowing that drugs are as readily available in prison as they are outside, probably more so? After much discussion, we decided to grant bail with stiff conditions, uneasily aware that this was possibly an instance of hope triumphing over experience.

A young man pleaded guilty to assaulting a woman in a pub. When the incident was explained by the prosecution it sounded less like a beating than a bit of rough manhandling. We could have dealt with that straightforwardly. However, it turned out that the defendant was already in prison for another matter and undergoing treatment for alcohol abuse. What to do? The tempting solution was to give him a short custodial sentence to be served concurrently with the existing one. That would be convenient and cost-free. On the other hand it would add another prison sentence to his record and make his offence seem graver than we reckoned it was. So we gave him a twelve-month conditional discharge, which meant no further punishment if he did not reoffend within a year, plus £50 costs. It was a good decision, I thought.

Drink reared its head again with a man called, let's say, O'Malley, a squat, red-faced Irishman in a leather jacket with no shirt underneath and his pale belly showing above his belt buckle like a harvest moon. His eyes were screwed up as though he was facing into a Saharan sandstorm. He was obviously suffering the hangover from hell. He had allegedly attacked his wife with a chair-leg at three in the morning. But he pleaded not guilty on the grounds that she was the instigator, having overdosed on antidepressants. He did not resist arrest. If granted bail, he said he would go to stay with his son two miles away. However, when we checked on the map, his son's place was actually only a couple of blocks from his own home. Mr O'Malley couldn't confirm this as he was unable to understand the map and had, according to his solicitor, 'certain problems with reading'. As an alternative abode he proposed his mother's in East Acton. This sounded promising. But she was not on the phone. Then, when the police tried to establish her whereabouts, it turned out no such address even existed. The man had plainly not seen his mother for years. Nevertheless, bearing in mind that every defendant has a right to be remanded on bail unless there are persuasive reasons against, we reluctantly bailed him to stay with his son, crossing our fingers that he wouldn't go round the corner and rough up the main witness for the prosecution, namely Mrs O'Malley.

(It is not only defendants who can suffer from confusion. One obliging fellow pleaded guilty to a charge even though the prosecution had brought him to court under the wrong name,

₃ age and the wrong address. Had he been legally ˰˰ᴖ˰ᴖᴖnted I imagine he would have been got off in a trice and the Crown Prosecution Service would have had to go back to square one. As it was the poor chap made himself a martyr to candour and the CPS was let off the hook.)

Deciding whether or not to grant bail requires judgment and experience. Concerns for the public's safety and the defendant's rights are often in conflict. The difficulty of the undertaking was brought home to me one day when the bench spent a long time discussing the case of a youth who was to be tried for malicious wounding. With extreme reluctance but also a sense of having come to the proper conclusion in the particular circumstances, we gave him bail. As soon as he had left the courtroom the clerk turned to us and said he thought we would like to know the defendant was likely to be out on bail for no longer than one or two minutes. The police were outside the door. He was about to be charged with rape and would be remanded in custody. I felt both foolish and relieved that, no thanks to us, the public was to be safeguarded after all.

Not all bail decisions are complicated. It required an effort not to take a dim view of the defendant who was brought up from the Tottenham court cells in handcuffs one autumn afternoon. He was a furious-faced black youth with a haircut like a brick balanced on an egg. He was accused of breaking into fruit machines with two accomplices at an amusement arcade. When the manager tried to stop them, the defendant allegedly threatened to stab him in the face with a screwdriver and the trio calmly carried on their work. Traced and arrested, the defendant turned out to have a long record of committing crimes while on bail and failing to show up for court hearings. We hardly paused before refusing bail, giving our reasons as the risk of his failing to surrender to bail for his next court hearing and the likelihood of his committing further offences. Back to custody he slouched.

OLD ROGUES
Things ain't what they used to be

This lad had brought an atmosphere of hostility into the courtroom. With younger defendants that is not unusual. They often give the impression of being completely alienated from their surroundings. They act as if they are in a room full of beings from another world who have no right to keep them there – people older than themselves, wearing strange clothes and speaking an unfamiliar language. With my old fart hat on, I wonder whether we have paid a high price for becoming less class-ridden and more egalitarian. Society used to be less fair, but at least everyone had an idea of what it was, how it worked and where they fitted in to it. In that admittedly dispiriting phrase, people 'knew their place'.

Now we are disorientated. Some of these young people barely seem to know what society is, never mind that they have a right to a place in it. They postpone adulthood, then turn up in court like orphans, without a single relative to support them. They feel rejected, so they respond with rejection. They demand 'respect' for themselves, but have no notion of showing it to others. Hence the mingled indifference and indignation they bring with them into the dock. It is a way of saying in body language: 'I refuse to recognise the authority of this court – or any authority at all.'

Sometimes this angry attitude persists in older offenders, and no doubt there is nothing new in that. On the other hand, reading through newspaper cuttings of thirty years ago, it is hard to avoid the impression that in those days there was a closer affinity between the dock and the bench. The old 'It's a fair cop, guv' spirit still prevailed. There was an acknowledgement by defendants that the magistrates had a job to do, and by the magistrates that it should be done with humanity and understanding. They might be on different sides, but they were part of the same community.

My former colleague Yvonne Thomas wrote a regular court report for the London *Evening Standard* in the early 1970s called 'Slice of Life'. Today her stories have a cosily Rumpolian ring. This was her account of how Sir Frank Milton, the Chief Metropolitan Magistrate, dealt with a vagrant called Robert who had been found sleeping by the warm air vent behind the Strand Palace Hotel:

He was enjoying a kip at 12.35 a.m. with free central heating when the police came and told him and his mates to push off. When a policeman came back a short while later, Robert was still there – which is why this small, stocky man, with an Edinburgh accent you could cut, stood in Bow Street court next morning.

Robert came tidy to court: a dark-blue suit which did him no discredit, a sweater underneath and suede shoes. He stood in the dock with his bristly chin up, shoulders back, defiant – like a man who was not going to give up a good air vent for nothing. And why, one might wonder, should he leave a warm bit of pavement for a colder patch when most people were at home and asleep anyway?

This was just what Sir Frank wanted to know. 'Is there really any harm in sleeping there?' he asked.

The police constable said there had been complaints. 'A large number of people living rough converge at the hot air vents at night and people have to step off the pavement,' he said.

'Are there any pedestrians at that time of night?'

'There are a few, sir.'

Robert listened with his chin raised high, long hair swept back off his forehead, the picture of an independent man being greatly irritated by trivialities. 'Are there any questions you want to ask?' Sir Frank inquired.

'Nope!' roared Robert.

'Are there any witnesses you want to call?'

'I don't believe in witnesses, sir.'

'No? Well, there are quite a lot of witnesses I don't believe in either,' Sir Frank said agreeably. To the constable: 'You say it is necessary to bring these wretched people in?'

'We do get a lot of complaints, sir.'

People like Robert have to lose in the end, but he dropped not a jot of his defiance. He told the probation officer that he earned £2.20 a day working in a kitchen. 'He says he doesn't want to spend the money on a bed for the night and his attitude is it's his own business,' said the probation officer.

'It's a point I'm inclined to agree with,' Sir Frank said, 'so long as he is not a nuisance to other people.' And he fined Robert a fiver.

There is a beguiling innocence about all this, despite the paternalistic overtones. Another Chief Metropolitan Magistrate liked to quote a comment from one of the regular drunks at Bow Street. On being given a lenient sentence, the man beamed and said: 'Thank you, guv. You're a gent. There aren't many of us left.'

Here follows a case which would almost certainly have been dealt with differently a generation later, hypersensitive as we have now become to the slightest hint of child abuse:

Standing in the dock was itself an agonising punishment for Horatio, who came over from Trinidad to make good. He gripped the rail and twisted his fingers and when the charge was read out to him he sighed deeply and looked skyward. 'Guilty,' he said with a groan.

Horatio, aged thirty-two, came to London to find a good job (he found one as a clerk, earning £30 a week) and to take examinations, to be qualified. He expected to be sent to prison for what he had done: indecently assaulting a little girl aged ten. His life lay in ruins. He looked bitterly ashamed.

Horatio's problem was that he worked so hard there was no time for the lighter side in his curriculum. As soon as he got back from the office to his one-room bedsitter in Islington he opened his law books and worked for his exams. He hadn't had time to make friends. But he was very fond of the Nigerian landlady's three little daughters. They often called in to say hello, knocking politely at the door first. Horatio gave them sweets and sometimes a few pennies and they were friends.

One day Rosie, aged ten, knocked at his door. 'Come in,' he called, and in she sauntered, looking sweet, and sat down as usual for a chat.

'She told me her Daddy and Mummy were out,' Horatio confessed later. He assaulted Rosie by touching her but did not, a doctor decided later, interfere with the girl. 'I would not do her any harm,' Horatio said, looking desperately respectable in his dark, well-pressed suit and pinstriped shirt. Rosie did not think much of the incident, but mentioned it to her father quite a long time after. He called the police and a doctor.

'Is there anything you want to say?' the Old Street magistrate asked Horatio.

'Yes, sir. If you are sentencing me to imprisonment . . .'

'I think that is most unlikely. I am putting the case back till later in the morning for a probation report.'

When he came back, the probation officer confirmed that Horatio was working with such single-mindedness he had neglected the social side of his life. The magistrate spoke very sternly to Horatio; told him that young girls had to be protected and any other such incident would lead to imprisonment. There would be a conditional discharge for two years.

'You will be punished severely for this offence as well should you come before the court again on a similar charge.'

'I do assure you, sir . . .' started Horatio.

'Stand down,' yelled the jailer, cutting through Horatio's assurances and ushering him out of court.

There is one significant little word that crops up in these exchanges. Younger Brits have long since discarded it, overcompensating for the deference of a previous age. Oddly enough, Americans of every class still use 'sir' to convey guarded respect and to deflect aggression. In this last of Yvonne Thomas's columns, 'sir' is still current, just. But the boy's sulky manner is a foretaste of what lay ahead:

Jo isn't the sort of chap who gets into trouble. He is a tall, 17-year-old West Indian who came to England with his parents, two brothers and sister a couple of years ago, settled down well in his Holloway school and left with a handful of exam passes.

So why was he standing in the dock staring stonily ahead while his father wept in the witness box, wiping away the tears with one hand, nervously hitching up his trousers with the other? 'This is my best son,' cried Jo's father, the only comprehensible words as the tears rolled down his cheeks.

Jo looked without expression at the magistrate, head up and shoulders back in his orange shirt and brown suit. He was charged with carrying an offensive weapon: a banister rail.

What happened with Jo was this: He walked a friend home one evening, then set off for his own house and on the way picked up the white-painted banister rail. As it happened, some policemen were coming off duty and noticed Jo walking along with his big stick. There had been trouble between white and coloured youths in the neighbourhood, but Jo did not look as if he was out for trouble.

When Jo saw the police he dropped his stick and when asked about it made the stock reply that he had it in case he was attacked. In court Jo denied saying that. 'I was never picked on before so I wasn't expecting to be picked on,' he protested.

Why had he got the stick, the magistrate asked.

'It looked like the sort of stick I could use for tying up flowers in the garden.'

'Why did you drop the stick when the police appeared?'

'I didn't. It fell from my hand.'

'When it fell, why didn't you pick it up, if you wanted it to tie flowers in the garden?'

'I hadn't got time; the police came. I didn't mean any harm with it.'

'I am satisfied,' the magistrate said, 'that you were carrying the stick and that it was not intended as a stake for your garden. I find the case proven.' He asked the defendant: 'Will you give me an undertaking that you will not carry a weapon again?'

'I wasn't carrying a weapon, sir,' Jo said.

'This is a weapon.'

'I've never carried a weapon before,' Jo insisted.

'Will you ever do it again?' the magistrate asked sharply. Jo was silent. 'Well, will you give me an undertaking?' No reply from Jo.

The magistrate sent Jo from the courtroom and spoke to the boy's father. 'Will you go and get a bit of sense into him?' Some minutes later Jo's father went to the witness box and Jo returned to the dock. Jo's father started crying.

'I don't say that he had any intention of hitting anyone, but if the occasion had arisen, he could have,' the magistrate explained. He conditionally discharged Jo for twelve months. Father and son left the courtroom together.

What dates that case is the presence of the boy's father. He came to court not only to support his son but also to try to repair the family's shame. The magistrate deliberately involved him and no doubt took his paternal concern into account in giving Jo a light sentence. Today, sadly, the chance of an Afro-Caribbean youth coming to court with a mother or a sister is not high. For his father to be there would be a rarity.

THE WAY WE WERE
A country magistrate remembers

Of course there was masses wrong with the benches of yester-year. As recently as 1947 a quarter of all sitting magistrates were over seventy and only one in a hundred was under forty. JPs were scarcely at the cutting edge of social progress. In her witty autobiography, *Hons and Rebels*, Jessica Mitford recalled the monstrous Uncle Tommy, her father's brother, a retired naval captain who enjoyed making his nieces' flesh creep with traveller's tales of eating stewed black babies among the cannibals. In the 1920s Uncle Tommy was a magistrate. He belonged to the old fire and brimstone school, and gloried in the fact that he had the right to attend county hangings. He was particularly proud of having given a three-month jail sentence to a woman driver who accidentally ran her car into a cow on a dark night. 'Clap 'em in the brig,' he roared. 'That's the only way of getting these damn women off the road.'

Just as male magistrates still suffer from a public image which is wildly outdated, so their female colleagues tend to be caricatured as beefy battleaxes in brogues with strangulated accents. However, even in the days when there was a good deal of truth in the accusation that most women JPs were either county ladies or the wives of well-heeled businessmen with time on their hands, this did not necessarily mean they were a bunch of insensitive reactionaries.

One of the most engaging voices in *Akenfield*, Ronald Blythe's enduring portrayal of a Suffolk village written in the 1960s, is that of Mrs Christian Annersley, a magistrate for twenty-five years and chairman of the tiny, seven-strong local bench. She is candid about being a toff. 'I suppose we would be called upper-class – in fact, we could hardly be called anything else,' she tells Blythe breezily. Nevertheless, everything she says conveys humour and understanding. 'There is no doubt that today's magistrate is a far better person than his predecessor.

He goes to conferences, he goes to prisons, reads the law and does try to find out. Whereas before it was simply Colonel Bloggs who prided himself on being just an ordinary decent chap, and all that this implies. Rigidity. Ignorance.'

Mrs Annersley has an abundance of that key quality in a successful magistrate, curiosity. 'I think what I actually enjoy about the bench is that it is simply endlessly interesting. How people live, how people behave, how they think – and all at this vulnerable, naked moment in their existence . . . Good people in a muddle, bad people and just poor low people who never have an earthly.'

She remembers the way rural life was just after the Second World War when 'this part of Suffolk was very basic. There was incest and bestiality on the one side, an American soldier getting drunk and driving into a brick wall on the other, and people riding bicycles without lamps in the middle.

'In the village there was always the Bad Family. Every village had one and we knew them all. They came up over and over again, and we watched them going slowly, inevitably downhill . . . It is a dreadful thing to say, but nothing can make any difference for some people. Since then I have visited schools and borstals, prisons and hospitals, and there they are. One can pick them out. They are cursed in some way.

'Our village Bad Family – father and three grown-up sons – doesn't feel any shame, I am sure,' she says shrewdly. 'Their lives are a little war, winning and losing, mostly losing . . . Our Bad Family isn't bad at all – just stupid. But they'd sooner be called bad than stupid.'

The scale of crime in that pre-motorway era was reassuringly local and predictable. Stealing women's underwear off clothes-lines was a popular offence, probably provoked by erotic bra and knicker ads. Panty-stealers were on a par with 'indecent exposure people' – lonely, nervous fantasists. 'Of course, they are always put on probation,' says Mrs Annersley. 'We never treat them unkindly.' And there were Peeping Toms: 'This was a real old village thing. You never really hear of it now. It was all part of the old frustrated, cooped-up feeling, I suppose.' Those were the days when culprits were still inclined to blush at being fined a pound and having their names in the papers for getting a bit rowdy on a Saturday night or shouting 'Fuck off' at a policeman. She had never had a murder case in twenty-five years. There were no poachers any longer, nor the stealing of lead from the church roof, which had been a popular local crime just after the war.

The Akenfield bench sat fortnightly and were usually through by lunchtime, which would be a laughably light case load these days even for a country courthouse. They don't seem to have been a particularly pompous lot. 'We know everybody and it can be a bit embarrassing when a personal friend comes up,' says their chairwoman. 'Then you can either pretend it's all a great joke or you can sit back. Any magistrate can push his chair back if he doesn't want to sit on a case.'

Furthermore, they showed a degree of sensitivity which isn't always apparent in my own experience, refusing to be what Mrs Annersley calls 'those awful whispering magistrates who go into a huddle before the defendant and the court. We *always* retire for our considerations. This means that not only do you take greater trouble over your decision but that you look as though you do.'

Mrs Annersley's thoughts on punishment touch a chord. 'There are so many ways in which you know you are doing the wrong thing – because there is no right thing to do. You know at heart where prison is no answer, yet the man will be sent to prison.' All the same, having been liberal and 'psychological' all her life, Mrs Annersley tells Ronald Blythe, she has now reached the conclusion that 'punishment is a good thing. That punishment really gets it off the chest of a great many people. They think, "Well, I've paid!" If people can accept the fact that they have paid they can either go on being a happy criminal or they can stop being a criminal.'

So much for the snobbishness and bigotry which supposedly characterised the old-style woman magistrate of the shires. But perhaps Mrs A. can be relied on to say something fatuous about the importance of ladies wearing hats in court. Not so. 'None of us women magistrates wear hats,' she says firmly. 'I won't wear one. I get confused in a hat. My head gets hot and I get hopeless.'

When I asked Ronald Blythe for permission to quote from his book, he sent a postcard to say yes. He described Mrs Annersley and those of her kind who still sit on benches up and down the country in a striking sentence. 'They are what used to be called "racy women",' he wrote admiringly: 'sensible, good-hearted, loving and amused by life.'

LADY OF MANY HATS
Poachers, probation and penal reform

After many months of relentless research, I had yet to meet a single woman who had ever worn a hat in court. Was the hat-wearing lady magistrate of yore no more than a myth dreamed up by the beak-bashing tabloids? I was beginning to think so. Then I met Sue Baring.

The reason for our encounter had nothing to do with head-gear. I had asked to talk to her because she was not only an ex-magistrate and former chair of the Inner London Probation Committee, but also the current chair of the British Institute of Human Rights – and this was the very week in which the Human Rights Act was to come into force. JPs all over the country were biting their nails about it, despite the hours of training we had all put in. The prospect of having to give the reasons for verdicts in open court, as required under the Act, was causing particular trepidation. Hitherto benches had always behaved like juries rather than judges, and simply pronounced their decisions with no explanation whatsoever. Sue, however, was cock-a-hoop that the European Convention was at last to be incorporated into British law. She came to the door of her Notting Hill house looking triumphant, brisk and pretty, in a pale grey trouser suit. The Act, she said immediately, was an entirely good thing. Magistrates would soon realise there was very little to worry about. End of subject.

(She turned out to be right, and giving reasons proved to be an aid to decision-making which was welcomed by even the most die-hard magistrates.)

Sue Baring's twenty-one years on the bench, from 1965 to 1986, straddled the period between the Akenfield era and the present. Given her subsequent, awesome career in voluntary public service – which, besides those offices already mentioned, has embraced the Parole Board, the National Council for the Resettlement of Offenders, the Howard League for Penal Reform and the board of the Almeida Theatre in Islington – there is no doubt whatever that she would have been grabbed as a magistrate however rigorous the selection procedure. But in her day and for someone of her comfortable background, she confessed, the matter was a *fait accompli*. After she had her fourth child, her father-in-law decided that hanging about at home and belonging to the Women's Institute would not be enough to keep the energetic Mrs Baring properly occupied. He would find her something to do. He happened to be the Lord Lieutenant of Hampshire. The next thing she knew she was being sworn in as a JP on the Winchester bench. 'There was an interview, but it was a pure formality,' she told me, a touch shamefacedly.

'We were a very middle-class bunch. There wasn't a single person of any other colour, though there were quite a lot of local teachers and business people. We mainly had to deal with poachers, unruly soldiery and naughty Winchester schoolboys, though there was quite a bit of burglary too.' She made it sound like Akenfield Magistrates' Court, only writ a little larger. I noted that poaching seemed to have survived in Hampshire for longer than it had in Suffolk.

Later Sue moved to London and sat in the south-east of the capital, dealing with offenders from Greenwich and Woolwich – 'a very different crowd'. One of her first sittings involved the committal of five South London villains charged with counter-feiting enormous sums of money. 'They all had broken noses and cauliflower ears. Quite an awakening after dealing with slow-speaking poachers and drunken squaddies.'

It was the Labour mayor of Winchester who persuaded her to become involved with the Probation Service. It became a life-long interest. Probation officers have a wide range of respon-sibilities, from preparing pre-sentence reports to supervising the whole gamut of community punishments and dealing with those who breach them. 'In general I'm in favour of community sentences,' said Sue, who knows the subject from both sides of the bench. 'In the long run they are far less damaging to society than locking people up for short periods of time and doing nothing with them while they're in prison.

'The Probation Service has strengthened and wised up a good deal over the years. Well, it had to. In the days when it saw its task as being chiefly to "assist, advise and befriend" everyone thought it was a soft touch. Under New Labour, Jack Straw wanted to go to the other extreme and change its name to the Correctional Service, which had a more punitive ring to it. But it would have been a silly thing to do. The then Lord Chief Justice, Tom Bingham, refused to attend a Probation Service conference if Straw persisted in changing its name.' The proposal was dropped. Sue laughed. 'Lord Bingham did very well on our behalf.'

New magistrates like myself worry a good deal about the limited variety of sentences available to us. But twenty or thirty years ago things were much worse, and prison was far more often the chosen option – as Mrs Annersley had remorsefully told Ronald Blythe. Sue has seen the alternatives greatly ex-panded in her time. She was enthusiastic about modern means of making people, particularly young people, confront their offending behaviour – anger management, drug and alcohol rehabilitation, and so on. 'With everyone you unravel some-thing that is very badly awry in their personal lives which leads them to offend.' But she didn't underrate the difficulties. 'Those who make the laws don't understand the chaotic lifestyle of these young people. They can't be *anywhere* on time. They are incapable of getting up in the morning. There's no one to get them out of bed, no discipline,' she exclaimed, though more in sorrow than in anger.

Still, these were not reasons for falling back on custody. 'I would very strongly say that community sentences are less damaging for society and the person. At least they are doing something a little bit reparative. I'm on the side of society, of the communities in which people grow up, both good and bad, and to which the criminal has eventually to return. I am very much in favour of making more harmonious communities. You can help to achieve this by community sentences firmly and rigorously applied, or an extremely good meld of prison and rehabilitation such as in a prison like Grendon.'

Plainly, despite the *noblesse oblige* manner in which Sue Baring became a JP some forty years ago, with the aid of her Lord Lieutenant papa-in-law, her experiences in the judicial and penal world have moved her in a liberal direction. As I said goodbye I asked what she thought of Ann Widdecombe's Conservative Party Conference gaffe in Bournemouth the previous day, when the shadow Home Secretary had demanded zero tolerance for people found in possession of cannabis. Sue raised her eyebrows. 'Surely,' she said, 'they can't really want to criminalise a whole generation.' Nor they did. By the next morning, Miss Widdecombe's Tory colleagues were queueing up to confess to youthful experiments with spliffs.

So what was I saying earlier about hats? Sue said she was seventy, which I found hard to believe. She looked at the very least ten years younger, certainly too young to have belonged to the elusive hat-wearing generation of lady magistrates. But no. Eureka! When I played back the tape of our discussion, this is what I heard: 'Women had to wear hats on the Winchester bench in those days. It was *de rigueur*. I only had old, battered wedding hats. One day I said to the chairman, would it matter terribly if I didn't wear a hat this afternoon. I wanted to go to the hairdresser in the lunch hour. He said: "My dear Mrs Baring, the frivolity of your hats makes absolutely no difference to the dignity of this court. I think, in fact, it would be better if in future you didn't wear them at all".' So there it was: Sue Baring, of NACRO, the Howard League and the ever-so chic Almeida, had worn a hat in court. At long last, my quest was over.

Highgate. An example of the sob story as mitigation. The defendant, a small, foxy Irishman, has pleaded guilty to drink-driving, as well he might: he was three times over the limit. Worse, this is not the first time. He's been done twice before for the same offence and on the last occasion was disqualified for four years. 'But the wife's pregnant, you see,' he explains. 'And we were planning to emigrate to New Zealand.' (The relevance of this unlikely bit of information is unclear, but I think it's intended to show a general willingness to turn over a new leaf: an intention to emigrate to the Antipodes comes up quite often.)

'Then me brother turned up unexpectedly from abroad. I hadn't seen him for a long time. He said our mother was seriously ill. I was very upset. Gutted. So me brother and me went to have a few drinks. And when I got into the car, I clean forgot I was drunk, Your Honour.'

Another small man, an Italian, who has pleaded guilty to smashing up his girlfriend's answerphone and beating her. They have been sitting at the back of court happily holding hands. But under a general edict to take domestic violence seriously, we have to proceed. The whole exercise seems slightly surreal. On top of the court costs, there is the interpreter's fee. The case has to be adjourned for a PSR. Back they'll have to come again, plus interpreter, no doubt still holding hands.

A string of charges of 'loitering for the purposes of prostitution' in Seven Sisters Road. Since most of the girls don't show up, we listen to the police witnesses in the absence of the defendants. One cheery WPC says that when she challenged a well-known prostitute and asked her what she was doing the girl replied: 'I'm just going out to buy a bagel.'

Once we have found the cases proved, we examine the print-outs of previous convictions and sentence by rote: £75 fine plus costs. One gets the impression that getting fined is all in the week's work for these women and they probably couldn't care less. The routine is broken when a strikingly good looking black woman puts in an appear- ance. She displays a challenging cleavage, wears a saucy hat and pleads not guilty. Curiously, the police officer in the witness box fails to describe her as a known common prostitute, with supporting evidence, as the charge re- quires. This is the only type of case in English law apart from driving while disqualified where a person's previous record may – in fact must – be presented as part of the prosecution evidence. In this case there is none, so we find the case not proved, and the lady sashays out of court with a disdainful smile.

LEFT WINGER
The London JP who put the idea into my head

The first Justice of the Peace I ever met was Illtyd Harrington. I was in my early twenties and all I knew about magistrates was culled from the pages of P.G. Wodehouse. Lord Emsworth and Sir Gregory Parsloe-Parsloe were both JPs, as was Wodehouse's own father. Illtyd did not fit the picture. He was the deputy leader of the now defunct Greater London Council. He was distinctly Old Labour: Welsh, garrulous, jolly and outspoken. He was also what used to be called a confirmed bachelor. In short, he was about as far removed from Mrs Annersley's Colonel Bloggs as it was possible to be, and although the same vintage as Sue Baring, he certainly never had a father-in-law who was the Lord Lieutenant of Hampshire. He is, however, a member of a posh gentlemen's club, the Savile, and that was where we met.

It must have been thirty years since I had last seen him but he looked much the same: florid-faced, grey-bearded and rumpled-suited. With a red Aids ribbon in his buttonhole, the old leftie seemed mischievously out of place among the pinstripes and Spy cartoons. He was obviously a favourite with other members. They bought him drinks and joshed him about his former County Hall colleague Ken Livingstone, now Mayor of London. He greeted Winston Graham, author of the *Poldark* books, as 'Your Eminence', and informed me that Robert Louis Stevenson and Ralph Richardson had both been Savile men.

According to the club rules we weren't supposed to have even a notebook in front of us in the public rooms, let alone a tape recorder. We had one of each, which suited my host's subversive instincts. The club's dapper Chilean manager wafted by. 'One of General Pinochet's victims,' whispered Illtyd darkly. He continued in the same conspiratorial vein as we talked, muttering into my ear and running his words together in spates of anecdotage. When I played the tape back later it sounded like Dylan Thomas reciting *sotto voce* in the next room.

Illtyd had been a JP in the London borough of Brent for thirty years. He joined the bench in 1967, rising from winger to become a youth magistrate and a chairman. 'I became a magistrate as a career move,' he said candidly. A self-confessed slave to local government, he did it to please his political masters. 'The Labour Party was always keen to have its own people on the bench. They wanted me to do it, so I did.' Political allegiances aside, however, the requirement for balanced benches was less of a priority then than it is now, even in the metropolis. 'The bench mainly consisted of a kind of lower middle-class squirearchy, often ruled over by strong-minded clerks,' he said. 'There were a few working-class magistrates, such as railway workers and postmen, but not all that many. The local Guinness headquarters was a very good source of JPs.'

In some ways, oddly enough, it was less important to have a socially representative bench in those days. Although class consciousness was still acute, society as a whole was more united and had a sense of shared values. 'There was a fierce moral core among working people,' Illtyd reflected. 'I'm not sure it's there any more in a big city like London. The local courts, the local newspapers and the local community all played their part: they had a common sense of moral law. The press would comment on cases in a way that reflected this, and people took notice.

'But still, it was often rough justice. I remember writing a piece in the *New Statesman* about how we were constantly having to punish West Indians who couldn't understand why it was illegal to sell alcohol to their guests when they were throwing a party in their own homes. It was just their way of financing the booze. But they were breaking the law.

'The courts spot social change much faster than the politicians. There used to be lots of Irish pubs in the area and there was a tremendous amount of drunkenness. But then alcohol started to give way to soft drugs and we noticed there was less violence – for a time, anyway.'

Some JPs were slower or less willing than others to sense the climate of the time. 'There was one woman magistrate I remember . . . we were dealing with an awful case: a black youth had attacked a boy and a girl in Carnaby Street, *screwed* them *both*, then stolen their wallets. And do you know what this woman magistrate's reaction was? She said: "What were they doing out after 10 pm?"

'Once I was sitting with two women JPs on the case of a single mother with several small children. She was in a hopeless state, and had broken into a phone-box and stolen a few pence. They wanted to send her to Holloway – to jail for heaven's sake!'

Not that Illtyd was a softie. On one occasion which still rankles an alleged drug pusher not only turned up late but, when he did eventually arrive, casually wheeled his bicycle into the courtroom. Unimpressed by the gravity of the proceedings, he then proceeded to start eating his packed lunch in the dock. Illtyd and his colleagues were not amused. First they convicted him of possession. Then they sentenced him to twenty-eight days in jail for contempt of court.

A world away from Akenfield and Winchester, the Brent magistrates often found themselves dealing with very serious matters. 'Some terrible things were going on. There was a big housing estate where the police discovered a gang of Balkan refugees had kidnapped a whole lot of their own young girls and were forcing them to work as prostitutes. Now you've got the Russian Mafia and the Triads.

'I had some of the first Jamaican Yardies in my court. They'd been operating from a council estate. They each had several passports and were obviously very organised and very danger-ous, though for some reason the police insisted they weren't. So there were no cops around when I left the court. Instead there was this large, menacing mob outside. They looked very belli-gerent. Luckily I had a driver and he quickly bundled me into the car and we got away.'

But in 1996 he wasn't so lucky. He was attacked by a gang of black muggers. The incident left a very strong impression on him. 'A while later I was having lunch at *The Times* and said something light-hearted about the incident maybe having made me too prejudiced to stay on the bench any longer. Afterwards I thought, oh dear, journalists are a leaky lot. So I decided I'd better tell the Lord Chancellor I wanted to step down before he asked me to.'

Perhaps it was just as well. Although Illtyd Harrington hasn't a racist cell in his body, a Labour JP candidly prepared to describe the Macpherson report's attack on institutional racism in the police force as 'a disaster' might have had an awkward time remaining on the bench.

Tottenham. A Polish man is in the dock on three motoring charges, a familiar treble: no insurance, no MOT, no driving licence. The defendant didn't know British drivers had to have insurance and an MOT, he claims, but he does have a driving licence. He produces a tatty bit of paper that looks as though it has been through the D cycle in a washing machine more than once. It is a Polish licence. But that's no use if he's been in the country for longer than a year – which he has, much longer. He appears to be astonished at this piece of news, then angry as we dish out the fines. This scene is played out week after week in the Haringey courts.

A man with dreadlocks is charged with crashing his car into a bus. 'No,' he says, pleading not guilty. 'It wasn't a car; it was a moped.' The prosecutor looks exceedingly foolish. Case dismissed.

Mr Antonio, who is accused of having failed to give his address after bumping into another vehicle, says indignantly, 'But I just gave a kiss to the car'.

The morning concludes with an application from a social worker for a warrant to pick up a raving manic-depressive who pours lighter fuel over her neighbour's car and threatens to torch it. According to my friend Marjorie Wallace (who founded the mental health charity SANE), 90 per cent of mental health patients in hospital wards were voluntary when she started in 1986. Fifteen years on, she says, 70 per cent are sectioned, coming into acute wards through the courts. Most of them are on drugs. So much for 'care in the community'.

CHAPTER 5

First Impressions

*'She wore a leopard-skin hat and a great cloak of what
looked like zebra hide'*

During my novitiate I often found it quite hard not to be
influenced by my first impressions of a defendant. Although
we had all been schooled to allow for class and cultural
differences in the way people behaved, it took an effort not
to be pleased by good manners and turned off by rude ones.
Humans react as instinctively to a smile or a scowl as do dogs to
a wagging tail or bared teeth. On the whole defendants and
witnesses behave pretty straightforwardly in court, given that
they are invariably very tense. But you also have to be able to
deal unemotionally with the tough guys who 'diss' you by
snarling their replies or turning their backs on the bench, just
as you musn't feel over-sympathetic to those who show respect.

I remember an anxious little man who pleaded not guilty to
owning a car in an unroadworthy condition and kept addressing both the clerk and the chair as 'My Lord' despite the fact
that the chair was actually a woman. As the police witness
recited a catalogue of faults on the car, from bald tyres and a
corroded chassis to a radio that might at any moment burst into
flames, the defendant's face fell. 'Can you forgive me, My
Lord?' he burst out, turning to the bench almost in tears.
The chairwoman spoke to him kindly. 'Do you mean you'd
like to change your plea to guilty?' 'Oh no. I am not guilty,
please, My Lord.' All the same, he earnestly wanted to be
forgiven just for having caused so much trouble. One's heart
bled.

The way people dress for a court appearance should be of
even less concern to us than how they behave. Yet it still strikes
me as odd that in this acutely fashion-conscious age so many

defendants don't seem to give any thought at all to the possible effect of their appearance. Surely they have the wit to see that looking reasonably clean and tidy can only play in their favour. Or maybe they haven't. My colleague Clive, who is very aware of how his own ponytailed appearance on the bench can favourably impress a defendant, has interesting thoughts on this subject. 'I'm struck by how so many defendants fail to dress up,' he says. 'It makes you think: they can't even be bothered to *try* to influence us. No wonder they don't get jobs. The trouble is so many of them don't even have a Sunday best. They're so disconnected from any formality, any real *occasions* in their lives, that they've no idea how to invest events with significance.'

The days have long gone when unrespectably dressed defendants were sent home and told to put on a collar and tie. During the 1940s and 1950s it slowly came to be accepted that it was OK for people to come to court in their ordinary working clothes. Perhaps the trouble now is that many of those we see in court not only don't have a Sunday best, they don't have 'working' clothes either, because in the conventional sense of the word they don't have any work. So they show up looking as if they've just come from a football match or the gym, like the young woman accused of having a cannabis farm in her attic. The police said they'd found 4,000 marijuana plants thriving away under the roof – a little Medellín in a North London semi. This was big business, with a production capacity worth £500,000 a year. For her court appearance the alleged plantation owner, who would certainly face a prison sentence if found guilty, chose dingy leggings and a Holmes Place sweatshirt.

You learn not to read anything into tattoos and body-piercing (one of our male clerks sports a discreet earring). But the defendant who turned up in full rocker gear, complete with studded leather gauntlets and 'Harley Davidson' emblazoned across his chest, clearly didn't want to be mistaken for a respectable member of the bourgeoisie. More ambiguous was the outfit selected by a young man who pleaded not guilty to a motoring offence. I'd have thought it was asking for trouble to go on trial with the one word 'PROBABLY' inscribed in giant letters on one's T-shirt.

An example of how looking the part might assist one's case broke the tedium of an afternoon's motoring hearings at Tottenham one day. A young African with an immensely posh accent and a natty suit denied that he was guilty of failing to tax his car. He was a law student and arrived in court loaded with legal books. These were to help him argue that his car was such a wreck it could not properly be described as 'a mechanically propelled vehicle'. It was more of an ex-vehicle, he said Python-esquely. His witness was a garage mechanic called Ringo who confirmed that the car was beyond repair and that he had agreed to take it to a crusher yard. It must surely have added to the believability of Ringo's evidence that he came to court straight from his garage, wearing a boiler suit and holding up the Bible to take his oath with a very oily hand.

Likewise, when the young defendant explained that he was not disputing the facts but basing his defence on a matter of law, it may well have lent weight to his argument that he looked and sounded like an Old Bailey barrister minus the wig. He was obviously aware of the danger of overplaying the role. 'I don't want to come across as being brazen or conceited,' he said plummily as he began quoting from Halsbury. Nevertheless, he cited a case called Smart v. Allen which had the clerk scurrying to his own law books. We concluded that he was right. We let him off. Of course I would deny we were influenced in any way by the mere appearance of the defendant and his witness. All the same, to anyone who thinks it doesn't matter a bean how you present yourself in court I would commend this tale of two suits, the lounge and the boiler, for consideration.

Sometimes people who do dress up for the occasion achieve odd results, like the girl who came along to interpret for her friend, Miss Mputu. Miss Mputu herself was pretty striking, with hair dyed scarlet. But her friend would have stood out in a mardi gras parade. Already quite tall, she was wearing tennis shoes with five-inch platform soles, a bikini top, a bare midriff and an enormous plastic hat painted all over with twinkling goldfish, from beneath whose rim she chattered and giggled with infectious merriment. I can't remember what we decided about Miss Mputu, but I suspect it was nothing too bad.

Another African lady who evidently thought a court appearance demanded some display arrived looking like a tribal queen. She wore a leopard-skin hat and a great cloak of what looked like zebra hide. She took her place in the witness box with difficulty, as she was a very large woman. Once she was settled, she gave her evidence, in French, as though she were granting an audience to some pipsqueak colonial governor. In fact she was explaining why she had not paid her £400 of motoring fines. The reason, she said, was that her husband was only a student and they had five children. Life was '*très difficile*' – though not as *difficile* as the lives of some other fine defaulters we heard from that afternoon, like the girl with a ring through her nose who shrugged 'I'm on probation and my partner's in custody', or the chap who had not been paying his fines because he had mental health problems *and* flu *and* when he sent a friend to collect his benefit this friend, who was an alcoholic, never came back.

We gave the African queen another chance to pay off what she owed in instalments. She waved a hand regally and gave the bench her blessing. '*Dieu vous bénisse*,' she announced as she heaved herself out of the witness box. We were indeed blessed to have seen her splendid performance.

While on the subject of defendants' appearance, it is worth noting that in June 2001, soon after David Blunkett became the first blind Home Secretary, the Lord Chancellor lifted the ban on blind people serving as magistrates, which had been in place since the 1940s. Despite the example of the famous blind JP Sir John Fielding in the eighteenth century, the view two hundred years later was that a magistrate who could not observe the demeanour of the man in the dock or read the paperwork in a case was unsuited to be on the bench. However, after a three-year pilot scheme involving nine blind justices, there was persuasive evidence not only that the ban was unnecessarily discriminatory, but that a visually impaired member of the bench could be a positive bonus. The blind could detect nuances in a witness's voice that might be ignored by sighted colleagues, for example. The need for documents such as pre-sentence reports to be read aloud, instead of skimmed in silence as is the usual practice, turned out to be of benefit to the whole bench. Perhaps even more to the point, as one of the blind magistrates in the pilot scheme observed: 'The fact that I'm unlikely to be influenced by someone's appearance may mean I'm more impartial.'

Highgate. Chairing the bench today is my recently appointed mentor, Barbara. This is a new national initiative whereby every novice magistrate is given an experienced JP to act as a personal adviser. We must do a set number of sittings together over my first two years. Haringey is one of the first benches to institute mentoring and everyone is curious to see how it works. Barbara and I are getting on fine, though I don't like being known as a 'mentee', the vile word that's been dreamt up to describe the mentored ones. It makes one sound like a cross between a fibber and a sea-cow.

Every defendant this morning is in custody. Two young brothers have been charged with threatening behaviour but only one of them is in court. The unusual aspect of the affair is that they are accused of threatening each other. We bind over the one who's present to keep the peace in the sum of £50. (That's the amount he will forfeit if he misbehaves.) But we have to warn him that should he be attacked by his absent brother, who has not been bound over, he will be at a disadvantage. He says he doesn't mind.

An Artful Dodger-ish lad has been brought in on a warrant. There are two other outstanding warrants for his arrest and he recently failed to show up for a court hearing. Barbara asks him why. He says it's because of the 'stress' he's under, as many do. More originally, he also blames the fact that his mother has got eczema on her feet.

A tough 22-year-old white girl stands accused of entering a friendly old couple's house by pretending to have been beaten up by her boyfriend and needing help, then stealing a few pounds and some family photos. She is amazingly self-possessed: 'Can I just check the charge?' she inquires in a practised tone. 'Is it for burglary?' Satisfied on this score, she indicates a not guilty plea. She's as thin as a splinter. All at once she begins chatting loudly with a girlfriend on the public seating at the back of the court, talking over the heads of the lawyers. Her friend stands up to show off a new tattoo on her waist before being ejected by the usher.

The clerk studies precedents of burglaries involving deception, for example where the thief gained access by pretending to be a meter reader. All of them got jail sentences of at least a year, he advises. The maximum sentence the magistrates' courts can impose is only six months. All the same, in the interests of speed and because of the small value of what was stolen, we decide to accept jurisdiction rather than pass it up to the crown court. The case is adjourned for trial. The girl is happy about that, but makes no application for bail because, we deduce, she's already in prison for another matter.

We have a longish discussion about whether to bail a man charged with entering a house at night while the owners were asleep, and stealing cash and documents. Burglary of a private dwelling is always a serious offence. It is aggravated when it takes place at night with people on the premises, so we have already refused jurisdiction. If found guilty he may well go inside for a longish time. The question is whether he should be kept in custody until his crown court hearing. On the one hand he has a record, including two serious spells in jail. On the other he was going straight for a long time before this alleged lapse, and he is forty-two, an age when men tend to shed some of the foolhardiness of youth. (Though I go along with not being racist or sexist, I am adamantly ageist.) So we are minded to grant him bail. Another factor in his favour is that he's in work. What kind of work? He is employed by a security firm, Your Worships.

HYPOTHETICAL CASES
A training weekend in Hertfordshire

I set off for the Ashridge Business School with mixed feelings. The heart did not lift at the prospect of a Saturday and Sunday of back-to-back lectures punctuated by coffee breaks and meals *en masse*, rounded off with a bout of late-night drinking – the usual pattern of away fixtures of this kind. On the other hand the promise of nearly two days of uninterrupted instruction held a sort of swottish appeal. Our training so far had been presented in gobbets. Here might be a chance for us to string them together and become joined-up justices.

Ashridge was a sprawling Victorian pile with late 1960s add-ons. It looked like a cross between a thriving public school and a rather dull holiday camp. One needed a map to find the way around. There was a gym, a pool and attractive gardens – a wonderfully ironic setting in which to learn about dealing with thieves and crack-dealers. There seemed to be lots of different groups attending courses and functions, but the general impression was of a bonding weekend for Conservative parliamentary candidates. Almost everyone was dressed in Marks & Spencer sweaters and not very distressed jeans. Behind a tall yew hedge I came across the moving spectacle of a dozen blind people groping their way through the grounds in crocodile formation, each holding on to the person in front so as not to bump into a wall or tumble down a ha-ha. They looked like

John Singer Sargent's famous painting of gassed soldiers in the First World War. In fact, it turned out they weren't blind at all, merely MBA students taking part in an exercise designed to inculcate team spirit and interpersonal trust.

'Aim,' said the slide that went up on the screen to launch our first session: 'To complete basic training.' The heart sank. We were back in the land of 'learning outcomes'. Would the whole weekend be spent looking at skew-whiff projections of bullet points echoing what the lecturer had just said? Thank goodness, no. Almost immediately we were divided up into groups, each under the tutelage of two legal advisers, and sent off to different rooms. Our group was subdivided into three-person 'benches'. We were now to embark on a series of practical exercises.

For the rest of the day we were plunged into a sort of virtual reality crime-fest. Should we grant this pushy policeman's application for a search warrant, given that his reasons were based on no more than an anonymous tip-off? Ought we to adjourn the case of a schoolmaster accused of indecent assault so as to give him time to find a character witness, bearing in mind the alleged victim was a 12-year-old child and would be kept in nervous suspense for at least another fortnight? Would we grant bail to a youth pleading not guilty to theft, considering his patchy previous record? We tried a man for burgling £268 worth of trousers. We had to sentence a driver who admitted to speeding but pleaded in mitigation that he was rushing a doctor to the scene of an emergency, then a man of previously pious character found guilty of defrauding the church organ fund of which he was the treasurer.

What made these hypothetical cases so absorbing was that each 'bench' had to muddle its way through to a decision by itself, unaided by chairman or legal adviser. We were guided only by the small amount of training and experience we remembered, plus that famous common sense which I strongly believed in as far as jurors were concerned and on which I likewise based my faith in the lay magistracy. If it wasn't quite a judicial version of *Survivor*, there was certainly an element of being up a creek without a paddle.

Only once we had reached a conclusion and given our reasons for it did the tutors step in with comments and criticisms. Most telling of all was comparing the decisions of one's own 'bench' with those of the others in the room. Sometimes they were strikingly different. This would have been alarming, were it not for the fact that the differences so pointedly illustrated the difficulties involved. They showed that misjudgments arose less from our undoubted legal ignorance than thoughtlessness and faulty reasoning. They demonstrated the degree to which a magistrate's liberal or illiberal instincts might unconsciously bias his or her understanding. A defendant's freedom – or a victim's faith in justice – could hang on such nuances.

The day was voted a great success. My colleague Kate said what she liked was the chance to talk as well as train. Between sessions there was much discussion of a kind we normally never had, about what one might call the philosophy, or perhaps the morality, of what we were doing. How should we rank, say, shoplifting compared with fare-dodging? Was driving without insurance as bad as driving while drunk? Why was it considered that a community service order was a graver penalty than a fine? The former is purposeful and may be instructive whereas fines probably do more harm than good and might even be the cause of further crimes. Could a short custodial sentence ever be rehabilitative? Was it really sensible for the magistracy to spend so much of its time acting as a tax enforcer? Such matters had seldom been raised during our earlier training. Perhaps they should have.

In the evening there was a quiz. Even to our own eyes there was something pretty bizarre about twenty-five Justices of the Peace perching on sofa-arms and squatting on the floor, pens poised over paper, like a demure version of a Sunday night pub quiz at the Pig and Whistle. To an intruder or, heaven help us, a fly-on-the-wall documentary director, the proceedings would have seemed grotesque.

'What is the prescribed limit of alcohol for driving, expressed in a) breath, b) blood, c) urine?' was one of the jollier questions. [Answer: a) 35mgs, b) 80mgs, c) 107mgs.] Others were along the lines of: 'What is the minimum term for a sentence of imprisonment?' [Answer: five days] and 'What is the age of criminal responsibility?' [Answer: ten]. The grimmer the topic, the greater the merriment. When the correct answers were read out there were unseemly hoots of triumph and groans of disappointment. A quartet of sari-clad Indian ladies from another North London bench got an astounding 100 per cent correct.

Later that night, over after-dinner drinks, a magistrate from a neighbouring borough told me about a perfectly legal way of buying tobacco on the Internet and diddling the excise man. Apparently you order several cartons of fags from a supplier in Greece, where the tax is minimal, and they are then sent here by courier, purporting to be a gift from Petros or Andrea. Since I was trying to stop smoking, the information was tantalising but useless. What was pleasing was to be told about the scam by a Justice of the Peace. You see how ordinary and human magistrates really are? Perhaps it would be in the interests of democratic justice for me to remain a smoker after all, like so many of our clients in the dock.

On my way to our first session on Sunday morning I skidded on some mossy paving stones and fell on my back. I wasn't hurt, but within an hour I was pressed to fill in a claim form. Horrors. Was this yet another instance of the compensation culture or were the Ashridge people simply nervous at the idea of being sued by a magistrate? Either way it was deeply irritating. Rolling stones may gather no moss but in the middle of a moist English January paving stones do. Grown-ups should be expected to know this. *Caveat ambulator*. Case dismissed.

Tottenham. A Kurdish kebab shop owner is charged with malicious wounding with a knife. He will be committed to the crown court in due course, but in the meantime he wants his bail amended so he can come back to London.

One of the conditions of his bail has been that he should live with friends in Lowestoft, not just for the safety of the prosecution witnesses (who presumably include the stab victim) but also for his own. What is going on here? The defence lawyer explains. According to the police there is a high level of hostility between blacks and Kurds in the area of the kebab shop. But the shop owner thinks it will be safe for him to return because his cousins have been running the place in his absence and there have been no violent incidents.

Here is an unpleasant glimpse of the racial antagonism which faces many minority groups, not from the native population but from each other. Every now and then ripples rise to the surface of similar tensions between, for example, Turks and Kurds, Turkish Cypriots and Greek Cypriots, or black Londoners of Caribbean as against African backgrounds. The magistrates' courts know they are there; so do the police. But despite the official requirement for the courts to stamp on racially aggravated crime with extra-heavy penalties, this minority-on-minority version of it is seldom acknowledged, which may suit the politically correct but must seem unfair to those who are victims of it.

The case of the Kurdish man poses a tricky decision. We must not inflame a racist feud, nor put either him and his family or the prosecution witnesses in danger. On balance we decide the defendant is probably in a good position to judge the risks, so we allow him to return to London and his livelihood while he awaits his trial by jury.

POSITIVE PUNISHMENT
Seeing community sentences at work

On a Saturday morning in March 2000, I went to visit the senior probation officer in charge of community service for

Haringey and Enfield. This was part of our training, but I was also curious to see what happened to the men and women whom we sentenced to perform unpaid weekly work in lieu of sending them to jail. It sounded all very sensible in the abstract, but what was it like in reality? Although all the main political parties subscribe to the idea, there are plenty of members of the public who think it is a soft option.

Hilary was a cheery, efficient woman, plainly a strong believer in the value of community service orders (as they were then known). 'People do learn something,' she said. 'They discover quite a bit about problem-solving, even if it's no more than how to get from A to B in time for work. For many of them, work itself is a new experience.' As she drove two other Haringey magistrates and myself to see current community service projects in action, she gave us some background. At any one time her small team of seven community service officers and ten project officers were dealing with 250 offenders, she explained. Nearly all of them performed their service on Saturdays.

The maximum CSO of 240 hours translates into almost a year of working every Saturday for seven hours. The most anyone is allowed to do in a single week is twenty-one hours. Offenders must report for work at 9 a.m. If they are more than fifteen minutes late or don't show up at all they are breaking the conditions of their order. It used to be the case that the probation service was less stringent about how many failures to attend they would overlook before sending the offender back to court, but now things have toughened up. In the past on average three or four offenders in every ten failed to complete their orders. Some had valid medical reasons for not complying, but many just couldn't be bothered. Now, after two failures, back to court they must go where there will be, in pure Straw-speak, a 'presumption of imprisonment'. We have yet to see how effective this crackdown turns out to be, but it plainly has the potential to increase the already swollen prison population.

'The most difficult are the 16 and 17-year-olds,' Hilary said with feeling. 'Teenagers don't *do* waking up in the morning, or walking anywhere. The boys are the worst. Sometimes we try to help by going to collect them from a pick-up point. Girls tend to be a little more disciplined.' When offenders failed to turn up at all, a formal warning letter would be sent inquiring about the absence. If there was no reply, the probation office applied for a warrant. The trouble was the police were often too short of resources to execute them promptly.

One big problem surrounding community punishment orders, as they are now called, is the health and safety regulations. Offenders are treated as employees for legal purposes, which means the authorities can be held responsible for real or imagined injuries. The consequence is yet another example of the risk-averse compensation culture at its most frustrating. Litter-picking or graffiti-cleaning are suitable projects on a canal bank or a housing estate, for example, but not on main roads, because of the danger from passing cars. I have encountered this problem outside London too. Never mind that these worthwhile tasks, when undertaken at all, are willingly done by law-abiding council employees and others. Criminals must apparently be treated with greater consideration, because of the local authorities' understandable fear of being sued. This is ridiculous, in my view. The quickest and most effective way to end the plague of graffiti in our cities would be to give offenders the unpleasant task of scrubbing them off. The public would be readier to accept this as a tough, worthwhile punishment if the work being done was more obviously visible and useful.

As it is, much community service tends to consist of low-risk work such as painting and gardening. But even here, the regulations can cause difficulties, because every offender must have read to him and clearly understand the precautions he needs to observe for his own safety, such as not drinking the turps or sloshing paint in his eye. The snag is that so many of the offenders in our borough are on the wrong side of the language barrier. So a non-English-speaking Romanian or Kosovan cannot be put to work unless there is someone else in the group who can interpret for him, which is not always simple to arrange. I have been in court when a pre-sentence report pretty well ruled out community service because of the offender's language difficulties. Others usually considered unsuitable for community service (apart from obvious cases such as the disabled or single mothers of small children) include those with records of serious violence, sexual offences or disabling drugs and drink problems, but that is readily understandable.

We visited three sites that Saturday morning. The first was a childcare centre which was being redecorated in agreeably acid colours. There were several young men and an older one, working hard and cheerfully. We chatted and they all agreed this was a better punishment than a fine, though it is supposedly a worse sentence. 'It's more positive, man,' said one. 'You feel you're achieving something.' The loss of their Saturdays was a real hardship, especially for those who had jobs during the week, said his mate. 'But hey, I'm learning a bit about decorating, and I reckon that may be useful.' In charge was a smiling young black man called Russell. He regularly runs community service projects like this one to earn extra funds while studying sociology and criminology at London University. A former painter and decorator himself, he must not only supervise the job and instruct his charges in how to use their tools, but also maintain discipline and report breaches.

I was impressed by Russell, and by the other supervisors we met that morning. Without people like this, who must have tact and leadership qualities as well as professional skills, the whole system would be unworkable. At a Victorian church in Tottenham we watched a gang of youngsters tidying up the churchyard in the rain. There had been two failures to appear that morning, which apparently wasn't too bad going.

Our last visit was to a large community centre where the CSO brigade of about ten men was toiling away at cleaning and repainting the hotel-size kitchen which served the whole complex. This was truly hard and disagreeable work. The place was grimy, greasy and full of awkward corners. Layers of congealed fat had to be cleaned off the stoves and walls. A tattooed Michelangelo was on top of some scaffolding working at the ceiling. As I was watching him, wondering how they'd got around the safety regulations, a huge fellow with a shaved head came and loomed over me in what I hoped was a friendly fashion. 'Hey,' he said, looking at me closely. 'You're one of the geezers who sentenced me.' I gulped. Had there been the smallest menace in his manner I'd have fled, but he was grinning. I said I remembered him, which seemed only polite, but not what we'd sentenced him for. 'Breach of community service order,' he laughed. Rather than imprisoning him, as Mr Straw would presumably have preferred, we had fined him and told him he could continue with his CSO from where he'd left off, rather than start his hours all over again. He said he thought that was very fair of us and since then he had not once failed to appear for work. Then we shook hands and he went back to his scrubbing brush.

I had found the whole morning heartening. As a method of punishing people quite severely while at the same time producing a tangible benefit for both the offender and society, community service seemed far preferable to both fines and custody. Fines, even if they are paid, further impoverish those who are already poor. Prison damages families, diminishes job prospects and makes the antisocial more so. Of course CSOs would not do for the most serious and dangerous criminals. But for those who are not, which is the majority, this seems to me a good kind of sentence, one whose scope ought to be continually explored and expanded.

I was impressed to read in the Magistrates' Association magazine an account of community service projects in Humberside. They included not only environmental work and construction jobs but litter-picking on council estates and helping in charity shops. The manager of one cancer shop said that a number of offenders who were placed with her by the probation service even came back afterwards as volunteers.

I have a feeling that the reforming Middlesex magistrate

Henry Fielding would have approved of all this. In 1751 he wrote *An Enquiry into the Causes of the Late Increase in Robbers*, which not only inveighed against hanging as the routine means of punishment but also considered the criminal not as a doomed outcast of society but as a potential citizen. Centuries before Mr Blair, he was one of the first to think in terms of the causes of crime as well as crime itself. 'Nay, as the matter now stands, not only care for the public safety, but common humanity, exacts our concern,' he argued, 'for that many cart loads of our fellow-creatures are once in six weeks carried to the slaughter, is a dreadful consideration; and that this is heightened by reflecting, that, with proper care and proper regulations, much the greater part of these wretches might have been made not only happy in themselves, but very useful members of society, which they now so greatly dishonour in the sight of all Christendom.'

Since that Saturday morning tour, as I have already mentioned, a community service order has become a community *punishment* order. 'I have no problem with the idea of punishment,' Hilary said firmly. 'One of the aims of the service is the "proper punishment of offenders", after all.' Probation itself has also changed its name. We must now learn to talk about a community *rehabilitation* order. In fact, I think the new terms are an improvement. They describe in plainer English what these sentences are about. However, there was a slight hitch over the reborn version of the old combination order. The CO, as its name implied, was a combination of probation and community service. There was no good reason to alter it. However, the jargon jugglers at the Home Office came up with community rehabilitation and punishment order. It was only after all the bumf had been printed, the story goes, that someone realised a sentence whose acronym was CRAPO might not get taken very seriously. The shredders went into action. Goodbye CRAPO: hello CPARO. Come back combination order. In fact, I bet it doesn't go away.

Highgate. A man pleads guilty to possession of a Class B drug – a small bag of cannabis which he handed over to the police. Like so many such cases, the prosecution arose pretty much by accident. The bloke was stopped for driving his motorcycle dangerously and shooting traffic lights. The stuff came to light as the result of a routine search. The police then had little alternative but to prosecute for possession as well as the offences which had originally drawn their attention. This happens all the time. I get the impression a charge of possessing – as opposed to cultivating or supplying – a Class B drug is nearly always a by-product, rather than the main purpose, of a police initiative.

If that's so, then I think it is a sensible approach. Not many people I know take Ann Widdecombe's hard line on soft drugs. Although I have yet to hear any magistrate speak out openly in favour of legalisation, plenty of us have teenage children. We live in the real world. Convictions tend to be punished with a conditional discharge or the minimum fine suggested by the sentencing guidelines: £100 plus costs was the going rate in 2001. In other words, there is no strong sense that we are dealing with a grave social ill here, even though the law implies otherwise. What is worth thinking about is that being drunk and disorderly is not only considered a lesser offence but much less often leads to a charge. Yet we know from our own statistics here in Haringey that excessive drinking is involved in more than half of street crimes, 65 per cent of murders and 75 per cent of stabbings. Only the drunken motorist, be he only a milligram over the limit, gets really heavily sat on. Everyone knows this is a rather cockeyed state of affairs.

Stop Press: Home Secretary David Blunkett has announced his intention to reclassify cannabis as a Class C drug. Possession will no longer be an arrestable offence. The Government has at last surrendered to the common sense views put forward in Lady Runciman's excellent report for the Police Federation. Even true-blue Tories like Peter Lilley and the editor of my old paper, the Telegraph, *are pleased, and so am I.*

CHAPTER 6

Crime and Punishment

'The defendant spat in his captor's face and shouted "Fuck
you! Fuck you!"'

The three Romanian asylum seekers who emerged from the cells
in Tottenham one day were not prepossessing. Two of them
were under eighteen and so had to be treated as youths. They
were brought out of the dock, sat in the well of the court and
addressed by their first names. The press, though there were no
journalists present, was instructed not to identify them. They
seemed quite indifferent to this special treatment. All three were
wearing smart jeans and designer trainers and gave off a strong
smell of tobacco which wafted up to the bench. They were
pasty-faced, blank-gazed and even the 16-year-old had a five
o'clock shadow.

I had never seen the courtroom so full. Apart from the
defendants there were three lawyers, the prosecutor, an interpreter, a social worker, a probation officer, a policeman, several
members of the public and no fewer than four security guards.
This was evidently a serious matter.

There were twenty-five charges against each defendant,
which the clerk read out in a passionless monotone. Each
charge related to the theft of a cash or credit card and its
subsequent use to steal sums of between £200 and £600 from
the issuing bank or building society. The total amounted to
nearly £40,000, all stolen during the ten-month period the
defendants had been in London.

The CPS had to decide whether to prosecute on the sub-
stantive charges or on a charge of conspiracy, which would be
an automatically indictable offence and go to a higher court.
This was to be for another hearing, but in the meantime we had
to decide whether to bail them. Objections to bail were that they

might fail to surrender, having no very fixed abodes or ties to the local community, and that they might commit further offences. Despite the shortness of their stay in the UK, they had already been in trouble. Their records included a caution for theft, an eighteen-month conditional discharge for theft and a drink-driving offence.

The three listened impassively. Two of the defendants said they were claiming asylum because they were Gypsies who had been persecuted in their homeland. They did not look like Gypsies to me, but then how should I know? The third youth, who did look like a Gypsy, wasn't one. He was a Catholic, also a downtrodden minority back in Orthodox Romania, apparently.

The prosecutor outlined what it was alleged these three had been up to. There had been a spate of card thefts in the spring of 2000 in Wood Green. Victims describing what happened recalled that they had been involved in 'conversations with foreign-sounding males' just before they discovered that their pockets or bags had been picked. The police installed CCTV near High Street cash machines in the area and that was how they targeted the suspects. The cameras apparently spotted the trio, plus two others who were not in court, going through a regular routine. One of them would lounge near the cash point pretending to be talking on his mobile phone. In fact he would either see or overhear a pin number being entered and dial the number into his mobile. The gang would then follow the victim, distract his or her attention and steal the card. Later they would use the stored pin number to withdraw the maximum amount of cash.

Subsequently, a new method of stealing the cards was perfected. While the person was still standing at the cash machine one of the youths would tap him or her on the shoulder pretending to have picked up a dropped £10 note. Meantime another member of the gang would snatch the card just as it was being ejected and race off. So skilfully was this done that the victim would often be unaware of what had happened, either forgetting that the card had not been returned or assuming the machine had swallowed it for some reason. The technique now has a name: shoulder-surfing. Very quickly the thieves amassed thousands of pounds.

The 16-year-old was remanded into the care of the local authority. The other two were more problematic. Their lawyers argued that the police evidence was suspect and that the TV camera footage would not prove their clients were the culprits. Besides, as asylum seekers without papers, dependent on social security, where would they run to? Almost anywhere in Europe, perhaps, given that they faced possible jail sentences. We refused bail.

Some weeks later I was sitting in Highgate when the trio and their interpreter returned to reapply for bail. The 16-year-old was to remain in local authority care, but this time the other two made a better fist of it. The oldest of the defendants had somehow gathered together enough money to offer a security of £500, which he was prepared to pay into court. We asked him to increase the sum to £1,000, just to impress on him the seriousness of the business, though the court would probably accept less if his friends could not scrape together the entire sum.

As for the young Catholic, his lawyer had worked hard on his behalf. He was a clever lad, she assured us, with good English. Haringey had found him a bed in a bail hostel and he was being offered a place at the College of North-East London. We were satisfied.

This was not the end of my Romanian saga, however. Only a few days later I was in the Tottenham courthouse, having an interesting morning. It had begun with an application for a warrant under Section 135 of the Mental Health Act 1983. A 35-year-old man needed to be taken into care for his own safety. He had a history of mental illness. He firmly believed he was the King of England, sharing the throne with Queen Elizabeth II. He also claimed to be a senior officer in the IRA. He was prone to go into pubs and denounce everyone there as devils. His latest problem was that he had begun scratching himself crazily and was liable to injure himself.

The warrant would allow him to be seized, by force if necessary, and taken to St Ann's Hospital for seventy-two hours. The bench must weigh such applications very carefully. The evidence of a single social worker, even on oath, is not a lot to go on. By means of such denunciations supposed witches were burnt in the Middle Ages and the Soviet Union locked up dissidents, claiming they were mentally deranged.

We granted the warrant. Then into the dock ambled a familiar figure. I recognised him as one of the Romanians awaiting trial for the card thefts. I had seen him twice before and knew his previous record because of his bail applications. So I told the clerk that I would probably have to withdraw from the bench. He returned after a discussion with the young man's lawyer and said not to worry. I could stay on the bench. I guessed the defendant was going to plead guilty to whatever he was charged with, which would mean my knowledge of his past misdemeanours was immaterial.

He was accused of common assault and, sure enough, pleaded guilty. The prosecutor described what had happened. It was early evening. An off-duty police sergeant in plain clothes had seen the defendant acting suspiciously in a bus queue and arrested him for attempted theft. The sergeant alerted the bus driver, who called the police for assistance.

The arrested man apologised, then without any warning tried to punch the sergeant, who managed to deflect the blow. He pushed the policeman and the two men fell out of the bus door locked together. There was a struggle. When they rose to their feet, the defendant ran off. The sergeant gave chase and caught him. The defendant spat in his captor's face and shouted, 'Fuck you! Fuck you!' At Hornsey police station he denied common assault. Now, however, he had changed his mind and pleaded in mitigation that he didn't know the man was a policeman: he thought he was a bus conductor. This of course made no difference whatsoever. Assaulting someone in a position of authority is a serious matter whether it concerns the Metropolitan Police Commissioner himself or the humblest traffic warden. Nor had he pleaded guilty at the earliest opportunity.

Once again I heard the man's story: how he had fled Romania after being racially threatened and had been in England a year. He was living on benefits of £35 a week. He had four previous offences to his name: drink-driving, driving while banned, driving without insurance and attempted theft. The other matters for which he was awaiting trial were not mentioned, of course, nor did I discuss them with my colleagues. What we did learn, however, was that this young asylum seeker had already been sentenced to a community service order of 200 hours – which so far he was performing acceptably. We decided to adjourn for a pre-sentence report. It would be for another bench to decide whether to send him to jail for his assault on the police sergeant or to extend the CSO. Knowing what I knew about the charges still hanging over his head, the chances of his staying out of prison very long did not look promising. I wondered, as I had so often in the case of asylum seekers/ economic refugees coming before us, whether he might come to regret the great gamble he had taken in leaving his own country to seek his fortune here.

Highgate. An afternoon of dealing with people convicted or pleading guilty at previous hearings who have now returned, accompanied by pre-sentence reports, to learn their fate. We spend half an hour before going into court reading the PSRs in the retiring room. They are prepared by the Probation Service, usually on the basis of one in-depth interview. On the whole, they are conscientious pieces of work, though older magistrates tend to think they err on the side of leniency. At its conclusion the report will recommend an appropriate sentence. It has to be said this very rarely runs to custody. All the same, most of the PSRs I have dealt with were thoughtful, persuasive and not at all badly written, though invariably depressing.

Today we have a man guilty of stealing a few small things from a tourist's rucksack. Were he a first-time offender we'd probably have been thinking of a conditional discharge. But the PSR discloses he is very far from having a clean record. It includes four fines, three probation orders, two community service orders and no fewer than six prison sentences. If Labour's plans to crack down on repeat offenders were in force, we'd have had to send him back inside. But he is not violent. He is not in any sense a major criminal. So instead, given the relatively minor crime he has committed and his apparent remorse, we put him on probation, and I am sure we are right.

Far more disturbing is the case of a woman convicted of biting a female police officer. According to the PSR she has no criminal record, but a terrible history of violent abuse by her ex-partner. There are sickening photographs attached to the report. They show a tiny, naked woman pitifully covered in black and crimson bruises. She weighs just over six stone. In the women's refuge where she fled for safety she was further assaulted by a bigger, bullying woman. When we go into court having read the PSR, there she is, looking as if she had just been released from Belsen. We order her to pay £25 compensation to the WPC and give her six months' probation – though what we intend that to mean is half a year's supervision and protection.

VIOLENCE IN COURT
The ones that got away

One sultry Monday afternoon in Tottenham we were nibbling digestives and drinking tea, waiting for a trial to get under way, when the clerk asked whether we had heard about the fracas on Saturday. Saturday courts deal with Friday night drunks and thugs considered too much of a menace to be released on police bail. Often they include real bad-hats. They are all in custody and so must be dealt with promptly. On this particular Saturday an especially rough customer had broken his way out of the dock, smashing the toughened glass and leaping into the well of the court in an attempt to get away. It had taken three security men to restrain him.

This made me sit up a bit. I confess that the matter of magistrates' safety had frequently flitted through my mind. These days there is no regular police presence in courthouses. If there are any officers on the premises they tend to be there as witnesses, i.e. truncheonless, handcuffless and for all one can tell without even a whistle about their persons. In the smaller courtrooms the defendant is only a few feet from the bench. I had been told there was a panic button, but no one seemed certain where it was or who would come to the rescue if one pressed it. The nearest police station was miles away in Hornsey. Our water jugs are made of glass, not plastic, which seems short-sighted in view of the number of times these homely items have apparently been hurled across courtrooms at the heads of justices and judges.

Sensing that he had our close attention, the clerk went on gleefully, recalling an occasion when a man leapt out of the dock, caught hold of a chandelier and swung himself towards the bench like Douglas Fairbanks Sr. Another prisoner had come into the dock armed with a razor blade mounted in a toothbrush handle and slashed three people before he could be disarmed.

A short while after this conversation, an unnerving incident occurred in Berkshire. The papers were full of it the next day. Two prisoners charged with burglary had escaped from Slough Magistrates' Court after masked gunmen burst into the courtroom. The gang were disguised as security staff – perhaps being clever enough to realise that if they had pretended to be policemen they would have looked out of place in a courthouse these days. They were armed with a pistol and a sawn-off shotgun. They fired a shot into the courtroom ceiling, then raced off with the two men (a third refused to leave the dock) and jumped into a waiting getaway car. No one was shot but a plainclothes police officer was hit on the head with the butt of a gun.

That must have livened up the Slough bench's afternoon. How would I have reacted in such a situation? Dived for the floor? Sat there paralysed? Our training has not even touched on such eventualities. A colleague told me about a recent murder hearing where she had been puzzled to see five huge figures with very short haircuts and bulges under their suits squashed in among the lawyers. Then she noticed the public seating was filling up with grim-faced black men of similar dimensions. It was a Yardie matter, she realised nervously, and the bulky characters in the well of the court were armed policemen, on guard for an escape attempt. The most recently constructed secure docks have floor-to-ceiling bulletproof glass and must be pretty well impregnable. But that wouldn't stop a determined desperado holding a bench hostage until the door was opened to release his chum. What is it the Convention of Human Rights says about equality of arms? Perhaps the bench should have a Smith & Wesson handy.

Highgate. Liam is facing a strangely old-fashioned-sounding charge. The Crown alleges that he 'without lawful authority or reasonable excuse, had with you in a public place, namely Stamford Hill N16, an offensive weapon, namely one truncheon'. Everyone is assembled for Liam's trial: magistrates, clerk, prosecutor, defence lawyers, police witnesses. Everyone, that is, except the defence's sole witness, Liam's mother. We are mildly agog. Will she say it wasn't a truncheon but some harmless domestic utensil, namely a rolling pin?

The trial has already been adjourned twice. So where is Mum, for heaven's sake? Inquiries reveal that she has stayed at home 'because the gasman was calling that day'. Ye gods. Her son is in court and rather than come to his aid she waits in for the gasman. Matters could proceed without her, but we are so full of the Human Rights Act and the need to give Liam a fair trial that we reluctantly agree to adjourn again.

In the same court some days later we do proceed with a trial even though the defendant himself has not put in an appearance. It is a dangerous driving case, a more serious matter than carrying an offensive weapon, namely one truncheon. The driver allegedly knocked down a man on a zebra crossing, fracturing several of his limbs. According to the police witness, the accident occurred at 4 a.m. and the defendant was in fancy dress. Sadly the officer gives no further details. There is more prosecution evidence, from an effusive Greek who looks like Zorba, as played by the late Anthony Quinn. He says he was there and saw what happened. He tells the court that the victim's friends begged him to be a witness as 'we are the same people'. 'But I said I am not the same,' bellows the witness, wagging a finger emphatically. 'I am Greek Cypriot. This man was Turkish. The Turks are the enemy of my people. They invaded our homeland. But still I do speak the truth.'

We believe he does speak the truth and find the driver guilty. Unfortunately we cannot disqualify him in his absence since we might then put him in the position of unwittingly committing a crime, were he to carry on driving. So he will have to be brought to court on a warrant and sentenced in person.

Two lads stole a credit card, says the prosecutor, and used it to order a brand new £5,500 Ducati motorbike. The owner of the card reported its theft to the police, so the police cunningly disguised themselves as motorcycle delivery men and brought the Ducati round themselves. The boys came to the door bursting with excitement at the prospect of owning such a magnificent machine. Then the police pounced. It was a classic sting, yet astonishingly the two boys plead not guilty. How will they try to wriggle out of it? Once again we are fated not to know the answer. We

adjourn the case for trial. It is one of the crosses magis-
trates bear that they almost never see a contested case
through from beginning to end.

SLIPPED DISCS
The tedium of the car tax court

High on the list of non-judicial chores magistrates would rather
the bench could shed, up there with council tax defaulters and
TV licence evaders, come road tax dodgers. These people are
summoned in huge batches and a whole morning or afternoon
is devoted to them. The first time I was handed the court list on
one of these occasions I reeled. There were eighty-one names
printed on it: we would be there until midnight or at any rate
Newsnight. Happily, only ten of them turned up, which I learnt
was about the usual score. This is generally a bad move by the
no-shows, since we will fine them in their absence as if they were
of middling income, not knowing anything about their financial
circumstances. That means £95–£110, plus the outstanding
duty and costs.

Dealing with the non-appearances takes on the rhythm of a
litany. The charge is always the same, i.e. that so-and-so 'kept
on a public road a mechanically propelled vehicle which was
unlicensed, contrary to Section 29 (1) and (3) of the Vehicle
Excise and Registration Act 1994'. The clerk adds his or her
own bit of patter: '27 June, no reply, good service' – meaning
that the summons was properly served on that date, usually by
post. The prosecutor briefly and wearily gives the evidence. We
find the matter proved and announce the fine. On and on it goes
with such a sense of relentless inevitability that I once heard a
chair say 'Proved' before the prosecutor had even given his
evidence.

When people do show up, the bench is so grateful for the
interruption it thanks them effusively. Sometimes they have
incontrovertible reasons for not having paid the tax, for ex-

ample having given away the car or been in prison or, in the case of one indignant individual, both. A young woman insisted that she had sold the car in question three years earlier and brought along the purchaser to prove it. A towering black man with a gold safety-pin in his ear went into the witness box. He said he was called Wendy. The court couldn't very well disbelieve him since not only was he on oath but he was wearing a necklace across his massive chest spelling out the name in shiny silver letters. (I have also encountered a miserable-looking defendant called Romeo and another who told us, without a trace of irony, that his first name was Lucky.)

Some of those who turn up for these sessions come to complain about the fines imposed on them *in absentia* and argue for the sum to be reduced. Such was the case of a beautifully-dressed young man who showed us his housing benefit documents to prove he was on low income. Otherwise, in his charcoal suit and mauve tie, he would have been taken for a banker or an African diplomat. In fact, he told us, he was an ex-salesman of crystals, fossils and other New Age mineral goods. And what did he do now? 'I'm a children's nanny,' he said with a shy smile. Although some London nannies do pretty well these days, we reduced his fine considerably and he offered a down payment of £20 there and then.

'Best to get it over and done with,' he said, with nanny-knows-best briskness.

'That is music to our ears,' replied the incredulous chairman. And it was.

Tottenham. Here are the names in full of those summoned to appear before our bench accused of motoring offences this Monday afternoon: George Amo, Adam Clarke, Costas Constantinou, Hasan Demir, Oner Duman, Toyfun Geltav, Colin Howard, Paulinus Ihenakaram, Guylan Kalanda, Vallipuram Kathirkamanathan, Ismail Krasniqi, Klodian Luzi, David Margolis, Atay Mehmet, Filo Mputu, Mercy Nabirye, Mohammed Reza Nazari, Daniel Osifu-

wa, Russell Robinson, Maharanie Sukhu, Huseyin Uras, Dwayne Williams, Brian Bive Wonga, Everton Young.

It doesn't take much experience to know that a number of these people will be asylum seekers or recent refugees. Indeed, of the four who bother to show up, one says in very broken French that he speaks nothing but Lingala, a Congolese language, so we have to adjourn his case to find a Lingala interpreter.

There is a serious public hazard here which is not widely recognised. A great many foreigners settling in this part of London are plainly driving around in a way which could pose a real danger to other road users. Some of them may never have taken a driving test in their lives. Typically those summoned to court will have neither insurance, nor a legal driving licence, nor an MOT. One cannot really be too surprised. Many asylum seekers and refugees are living in wretched circumstances. They survive on vouchers or minimal benefits and are not officially allowed to work until they have been here for a while. Of course there is a black economy out there. But even if these poor people can earn enough to buy an old A or B registration Fiesta, it is not very likely they could also afford to insure, test and tax it properly, never mind go through the costly palaver of getting a full British driving licence (a foreign licence, if they have one, is only good for a year). When caught, their usual excuse is either that they were driving someone else's car or that they were ignorant of the law or more probably both. The fact that many of them may be touting for custom as illegal late-night minicab drivers in the West End one doesn't care to think about.

Of course it is hard to know someone is driving illegally until he is stopped by the police for some other reason. But at least we could ensure that the immigration authorities tell newcomers about our motoring regulations in explicit terms. As it is, magistrates are often in the ludicrous position of having to fine an impoverished offender, like the Polish man who was trying to keep his wife and two children on total benefits of £77.80 a week, less than it would have cost him to insure his car. A short period of disqualification might be a more sensible sentence.

A few weeks later in the same courthouse the afternoon's motoring list runs to ninety-six alleged offenders. This is how the list begins: Acikgul, Adjl, Ali, Amissah, Arbon, Atamturk, Ayadoun, Bashkim, Baliche, Berou, Bulger . . . I say to my wife when I get home: 'There's going to be trouble about asylum seekers before long.' That was in the winter of 2000.

FINE TUNING
A bailiff's lot is not a happy one

Four times a year there is a meeting of the Haringey Petty Sessions Area justices in the Highgate courthouse. At the first one I attended, Court 1 was so full that several magistrates had to sit in the dock, looking like a gang of middle-aged Mafiosi. It was the legal advisers who were lording it in the seats where we usually sat, ranged along the bench on either side of the chairman, looking loftily down on us – an apt symbol of our relationship, possibly.

The centrepiece of this particular meeting was an address by the managing director of the firm of bailiffs used by the court to collect outstanding fines. For some reason it had never occurred to me that bailiffs were commercial operators. They make their money by charging collection costs to the offender. It sounds a pretty thankless occupation. For one thing it is not always easy for them to track their targets down. For another, even when they have been found, about a third of them routinely deny they are the persons in question. Nor are the other two-thirds usually eager to co-operate. Very few pay up. Many try to play the system. Others simply can't pay, especially when costs are added –

say, £30 on top of a £100 fine. So the bailiffs have to resort to seizing their belongings.

But that is not straightforward either. Bailiffs can't force an entry, so they tend to go for the cars. The snag here is that an astonishing 20 per cent of the information held by the Driver and Vehicle Licensing Authority in Swansea is incorrect, which can make it hard to be sure of ownership. (The mind reels. I remember the days when a car's logbook told you the whole history of its previous and present owners.) All the same, this is not a statistic offenders should rely on. One man with fifty-four outstanding warrants was enraged when the bailiffs came and coolly took away his Porsche, never to be seen by him again. Once upon a time magistrates might have sympathised with his plight. Today's benches, though, are not so inclined to side with the Porsche-owning classes, and the bailiffs' action was applauded.

Hundreds of thousands of distress warrants are issued every year. The warrant allows property to be seized to the value of the unpaid fine plus the bailiffs' costs. At this stage of the process no part-payments are accepted, so the bailiffs have no alternative but to cart off what belongings they can. If there is no car to seize, they will try to gain entry into the home, though even then they can only take non-essential goods. That leaves TVs, stereos, furniture and so on, which ought to fetch a tidy sum. The trouble is they don't. They get sold at special auctions where everyone knows the sellers are the bailiffs and the bidders have the advantage, so prices are ludicrously low. A £1,000 sofa would typically fetch around £150. The result is that the bailiffs have to seize more property than they would otherwise need so as to raise even a portion of the money.

This was gloomy news. Imposing fines is a disheartening exercise even when you believe offenders can afford them. To learn that lots of them won't bother to pay up anyway simply makes one feel foolish or cynical, or both. At any given moment, apparently, Haringey is owed over £2m in unpaid fines, a situation that is replicated more or less everywhere else in the country. What makes it worse is that this income is deemed by the Government to form part of a court's annual budget. As a device for encouraging the efficient collection of fines this is no doubt very canny, but it is extremely tough on court administrators who have to deal with the shortfall.

After we had absorbed the talk about bailiffs and their unenviable, sometimes dangerous line of business, there arose a discussion about the level of fines imposed when cases were proved in a defendant's absence. The custom is that when an offender fails to show up, he or she is fined as if earning a middling income. If they don't like it, they can come to court and ask for their means to be reconsidered – a timewasting business. Alternatively they just don't pay it, and wait for our new friends the bailiffs to come round. What was being proposed at our meeting was that fines *in absentia* should be based on the assumption of low income. Since that assumption would be correct in 90 per cent of cases, this would avoid people being too heavily fined, save court time and might even lead to more penalties being promptly paid.

However, others were quick to point out that it would be manifestly unjust for a well-off no-show to be fined the same as someone on income support. It would be an invitation to higher income defendants not to turn up in court. In the end it was thought best to leave things as they were. What had been interesting, though, was to witness what one might call the lay judicial mind in action: a group of thirty or forty JPs with a good deal of experience between them debating an aspect of sentencing where the bench has some discretion, and reaching a view based not on the law but on what they eventually agreed was fair and sensible. It seemed to me a good example of the merits of the lay approach. I doubt if a courtroom full of lawyers chewing over the same topic would have felt easy taking such a subjective approach.

As if to prove the point, someone then rose to complain about the fact that magistrates were increasingly being restricted in the use of their discretion, local knowledge, common sense, etc., by orders from on high. There were now mandatory lengths of driving ban for drink-driving, levels of fines and licence endorsements were much more narrowly prescribed, minimum and maximum sentences more strictly laid down, and so forth. The old hands, one gathered, were mildly cheesed off with all this interference. Cecil, a long-serving JP who had impressed me with his chairmanship when I sat with him and was also a trained lawyer, chose this moment to announce his retirement and bid farewell. 'Thirty years ago,' he growled mischievously, 'we had no such thing as consistency. In those days, we were *entirely* capricious.' There was laughter in court, as the newspapers say.

Tottenham. Heading the morning's list is a 28-year-old accused of kidnap, possession of a sawn-off shotgun, a Walter P38 semi-automatic handgun, several rounds of 9mm ammunition, a lock-knife, a weapon 'designed or adapted for the discharge of any noxious liquid, gas or other thing' contrary to Section 5(1) (b) of and Schedule 6 to the Firearms Act 1968, and twenty-three wraps of crack cocaine. This promises to be exciting. We are all busting to get a sight of this alleged Tottenham terminator. But mysteriously and to our great disappointment he fails to show up. Maybe the prison van has been delayed. No one seems to know. I think he must have escaped.

Instead of this one-man assault squad we find ourselves dealing with a sad, shaking, crop-haired girl whose eyes are blank with misery. She huddles in corner of the dock staring at the floor, occasionally weeping. She is wearing a grubby smock and a stud through her eyebrow. She is accused of threatening behaviour in a hospital, where she menaced members of staff with a jagged piece of glass. It's hard to believe it took seven police officers and a can of CS gas to restrain this trembling shadow of a human being.

She won't plead guilty, as she says she threatened no one but herself. She has a point. It was her own throat she had held the shard of glass to. Her lawyer says she suffers from borderline personality disorder, a condition notoriously difficult to diagnose and considered untreatable. It is a borderline case for the magistrates too. The girl is plainly unwell. The case is adjourned for trial, but I am left wondering how a lay bench is supposed to deal with the bad/mad dilemma. Our training has not covered this at all.

BEHIND THE WIRE
Inside Britain's most notorious juvenile jail

As part of our training we were to visit Feltham Young Offenders Institution, a place whose name was loaded with foreboding. It is not only a prison but a remand centre, the only one in the whole of London for 15 to 21-year-olds. From time to time the public becomes aware of Feltham's existence because of some grisly event, such as the murder of Zahid Mubarek, who was battered to death by his racist cellmate, or the suicide of one of its inmates. But to the capital's magistrates the name has a daily familiarity, since that is where all young male defendants remanded in custody must be fetched from or sent to before and after a hearing.

One quickly learns that locking a lad up in Feltham is not something one does with a light heart. In 1996, the then HM Inspector of Prisons, Sir David Ramsbotham, had produced a damning report of conditions there. Two years later he and his team made an unannounced inspection to see how far their recommendations had been implemented. What they found on this visit was even more disturbing. 'I have to disclose to the public,' wrote Sir David, 'not only that the conditions and treatment of the 922 children and young prisoners confined in HM Young Offenders Institution and Remand Centre Feltham are, in many instances, totally unacceptable. They are, in many instances, worse than when I reported on them two years ago and reveal a history of neglect of those committed to their charge and a failure to meet the demands of society to tackle the problem of offending behaviour . . . a picture emerges of an institution and staff overwhelmed.' He called the place 'rotten to the core'.

(On the eve of his retirement in the summer of 2001, Sir David produced yet another withering report, saying that though conditions for the younger inmates had improved, those for the 18 to 21-year-olds were still 'wholly unacceptable'.)

Thus, fearing the worst, we set off at eight o'clock on a Wednesday morning and bombed down the North Circular in the direction of Heathrow airport, against the incoming tide of rush-hour traffic. There were nine of us aboard the minibus, including one of our legal advisers who had come to Haringey from Hull and wanted to get a close-up look at the most notorious of the country's fourteen YOIs. The atmosphere was sombre. We were heading for a place specially designed to incarcerate kids the same age as my own – kids charged with, or already convicted of, some of the worst crimes of which men are capable, including drug-dealing, rape and murder. It was a depressing prospect.

We were not aware we were approaching HM YOI and RC Feltham until we saw the wire. The fence loomed up suddenly, high and forbidding. 'Welcome to Feltham Visitors Centre,' said a sign. 'Serving families and friends.' We had obviously entered territory where irony held no sway, like those unlovely Islington borderlands where the borough shamelessly bids you 'welcome' to littered pavements and mean streets. The visitors' centre was really no more than a caff. What it served families and friends was tea and Cokes and Crunchie bars. It smelled of old fat and Old Holborn and there were notices pinned round the walls. One declared, 'The Prison Service is committed to racial equality', as though to announce it were enough. Another warned that 'A passive drug dog is working in the area and will search visitors'. To newcomers, unused to the jargon, it might occur that an active drug dog would be more satisfactory.

We were greeted by Officer Sharon, bonny, breezy and rattling with keys. She piloted us through a series of slamming and sliding doors until we emerged onto a bleak sort of parade ground. It was flanked by low buildings and workshops which spread across a large acreage within the wire. The place had the forbidding air of a Second World War POW camp without the watchtowers. There were a few flower beds and from some-where, incongruously, the screams of peacocks.

This was the biggest young offenders' unit in western Europe, said Sharon, though it was impossible to tell from her tone whether she considered this a matter for pride or shame. At any one time there were more than 900 lads in residence. They were segregated, the under 18-year-olds being kept away from the older ones. Most of the inmates were on remand, she explained, which meant there was a constant coming and going. Early every weekday morning convoys of prison vans would leave with full loads to do their tour of the London courts, dropping off passengers for their hearings, picking them up afterwards if they had not been released and returning them to Feltham, often to a different cell or even a different block. Old and new inmates would still be arriving late into the evening, so the staff never knew what numbers they would be dealing with from one day to the next. It was unsettling for everyone.

The high turnover made it hard to educate or rehabilitate the boys, Sharon explained. The average length of stay was just over sixty days, though the youths awaiting trial for murder, of whom there were usually several at Feltham, would probably be held on remand for ten months or more. After sentencing, some stayed at Feltham to serve their time, but most were despatched to long-stay young offenders' institutions such as Portland and Huntercombe.

Sharon steered us towards some workshops. We passed a group of youths digging in the flower beds and others pulling laundry carts. They wore red armbands to show they were trusted prisoners and seemed to be performing their tasks with some zeal, grinning as we watched them. Jobs like these or in the kitchens can earn inmates up to £14 a week. 'I'd rather have them out working at something than sitting on their butts all day staring at the lavatory in their cell,' said Sharon, who failed to conceal a streak of motherliness beneath her no-nonsense manner. 'The kids are desperate to work, not just for the money but because they're so bored.' Regrettably, there weren't enough jobs to go round.

In the workshops there were further signs of activity. Young men were plastering and painting a set of rooms inside the mock-up of a flat. They were working towards an NVQ in painting and decorating. Once they had finished doing up the rooms in eye-catching colours, however, they would have only a moment to feel proud of their achievement before painting their handiwork white again so that the next batch of students could start from scratch. It struck me there was a poignant metaphor here, thinking of the hundreds of boys who leave Feltham after serving a successful sentence only to return months later as reoffenders: it's all to be done again. Next door another group were scrubbing and spraying long strips of different kinds of carpeting which had been laid out on the floor. They were doing an NVQ in office and industrial cleaning. 'You need a qualification even for that now,' muttered Sharon, lamenting the fact that as this required an ability to read the warning notices on chemical cleaning agents, illiterate lads were not eligible. It was absurd.

Courses like this are popular for those who are in Feltham long enough to complete them; but again, there is a shortage of places. There is a similar squeeze in the classrooms. The trouble is that because there is a legal obligation to educate the 15 to 16-year-olds, they take up a lot of the teaching resources, leaving less opportunity for the older inmates. The schooling is good, according to Sharon. The classes are small and the sessions short, so as not to overtax attention spans. 'Here we can force them to go to school, unlike at home,' said Sharon. 'For many of them it's the first sustained experience of secondary education they've had. The teachers find it rewarding too. They have more attentive students than they probably would outside, and maybe they're even safer, too. If there's any trouble they call us.' (Not for the first time, it occurred to me that what we really want is not juvenile prisons but secure colleges.)

The rules governing juvenile detainees are now very strict. They must have twelve hours a day of education and exercise, so the young ones tend to hog not only classrooms but also the sports facilities, such as they are. They also have TV in their cells, all of which must seem unfair to the older inmates – especially to those unlucky enough to have an eighteenth birthday at Feltham and find themselves transferred from one regime to the other.

By now we would have been thoroughly lost but for our guide. It was like being below decks on an aircraft carrier. To the accompaniment of clinking keys and ringing gates, we passed through windowless corridors, wings, units, halls and a gym full of alarmingly-muscled young men reeking of sweat. Delicious smells came from the kitchens where chefs assisted by prisoners somehow manage to operate on a budget of just £1.30 per head per day. We looked in at the studio of Radio Feltham, the first prison radio station in the country. It is run by the inmates and puts out a daily programme of music, advice and punchy home-made ads urging listeners to stay off drugs.

On the wall outside the studio was a notice which said: 'Trouble with bullying? Then speak with the anti-bullying officer.' There were certainly some very powerful, frightening-looking individuals around. The merest glance from one of them would count as bullying in my book. There had been more than 5,000 recorded prisoner-on-prisoner assaults over the previous ten years. Bullies are locked up for stints of six weeks or longer in a special unit where the discipline is very strict and where, supposedly, they are taught to understand why their behaviour is wrong.

The Chief Inspector had not been complimentary about Waite Wing two years earlier, but Sharon seemed to think it was now quite effective. In fact I had the impression that things in general had probably improved since Sir David's last visit. There was less of the sullenness I had anticipated; the place seemed clean and, as far as one could tell, the relationship between staff and inmates appeared to be good-humoured. But there is no escaping the fact that this is a densely crowded community of disturbed, volatile, immature young men. The vulnerable are picked on, even at night, when 'window warriors' shout threats at them across the courtyards. Victimisation happens. Boredom happens. There are constant attempts at self-harm and suicide. Boys eat metal bolts and stab themselves.

The 65-bed unit we went into, a prison within a prison, was not a place where anyone would willingly spend much time. The only two visible distractions were an unattended billiard table and the telephone, at which a noisy queue waited to communicate with the outside world. Phonecards are the hard currency of the inside world. There seemed to be a lot of pointless yelling and restless mooching about. No one was reading or writing or even playing cards. The sense of wasted time and blighted lives became even more oppressive when Sharon observed ruefully, 'A lot of these lads have got sons of their own.' It was a dismal thought.

Most cell doors were open. Some of the occupants lay on their beds listlessly, beneath the spread legs of raunchy pin-ups. The most prominent item in each cell, apart from the bed, was the lavatory. Better that than the degrading routine of slopping out, which David Ramsbotham's predecessor as Chief Inspector, Sir Stephen Tumim, fought to put an end to. But still, a room with a loo and not much else must have a lowering effect on the spirits. Hence the hot competition to get a prison job. One of our magistrates asked to be locked into a cell. Sharon obliged. He was let out five minutes later, looking panicky. The solidity of the door with its tiny peephole made one feel horribly confined and powerless, he said.

For many the only relief from the tedium comes from getting stoned. Britain's prisons are dens of drug-taking, despite the constant struggle to stamp it out. About a quarter of the children and youths detained in Feltham are Class A drug users when they are arrested, mainly on crack cocaine and heroin. Every day at Feltham 5 per cent of the inmates are randomly tested for drugs, but cannabis use remains endemic. Visitors are the main source. In the large room where visits take place – more than 50,000 a year – we watched the sniffer dogs go through their paces.

One of our magistrates was given a wrap of cannabis to conceal in his clothes, then we all stood in a line while a friendly-looking spaniel was led up to each of us in turn. When he reached the supposed culprit he sat down resolutely and wagged his tail. This was the passive dog warned about in the visitors' centre. The proactive dog, Dillon, had an entirely different *modus operandi*. Once again one of my colleagues, a laughably undruggy looking chap in a dark suit and tie and heavy spectacles, was asked to pocket the stuff. This time it was a small bag of heroin. As soon as young Dillon was unleashed he appeared to go mad, whizzing round the room at top speed, sniffing in all the corners and under the chairs, nosing the assembled trouser-legs, his tail whirring like a propellor. Finally he got his man. He was rewarded by being given his favourite chewy toy by his handler, and trotted off looking immensely pleased with himself.

Dillon and his passive partner, each worth about £11,000 fully-trained, catch some 170 people a year at Feltham. Nevertheless, a lot of drugs still get through. Inmates and their suppliers become adept at transferring the stuff. They carry it in their mouths or more often up their bottoms. Sharon said a lot of them cut holes in their jeans so they can pass the drugs from bum to bum in a flash. Once the package is *in situ*, the culprit is safe, since intimate body searches are not allowed. This is tremendously frustrating for the prison staff, who are well aware that dozens of their charges are walking around with illegal substances stuck up their behinds twenty-four hours a day. 'Some of them even store their gear up there,' Sharon said, making our eyes pop as we pictured the uncomfortable outlines of needle and syringe.

The prison governor entertained us to coffee in his utilitarian boardroom. Its only prominent decoration was a trophy cupboard in one corner. Among its contents was a shield won by the Quail Unit Murder Charge Group. One didn't like to ask what sport it had been awarded for, but I felt reasonably sure it wasn't badminton. The governor had been appointed only eight weeks earlier and made no bones about the task he had taken on. Five thousand young people came through the gates of Feltham every year, he said, charged with every kind of crime from nicking a sweater to rape and murder. The place was 'a huge transit camp', where the pressures were so overwhelming there was a danger of creating in staff and inmates alike what he called 'an attitude of learned helplessness'. His honesty was impressive, though discouraging. 'Adolescents are impulsive, confused about their own identities and relationships,' he said. 'Bullying is part of the social problem of being a young criminal.' He made it sound as though 'being a young criminal' was a career choice. Maybe that's just what it is for the ill-schooled and socially alienated, without hope for themselves or strong ties with anyone else.

A short while after we met him, the governor resigned – for health reasons. In fact there were to be four governors of Feltham in less than a year. A deputy governor also left, appalled by the case of an inmate who very nearly succeeded in hanging himself and disgusted by what he called the Dickensian conditions of the institution.

I have to say that during our brief visit, gloomy though it was, we had little inkling of things being in quite such a desperate state. Perhaps Sharon's good-heartedness misled us. For example, she seemed to me rightly enthusiastic about the two months of special training given to pre-release prisoners, showing us around the immaculate computer centre where they learn basic keyboard skills, how to manage spreadsheets, use the Internet and so forth. They also get taken to visit a Job Centre, half of them never having even entered such a place before, and are encouraged to enroll for some kind of further education. This all seemed excellent. But even Sharon had misgivings. Gruffly but with feeling she told us about the appalling circumstances most of 'the boys' were going back to after their release. In the essays they wrote about what they'd do first when they got out, the priorities were invariably the same: a McDonalds hamburger, a spliff, a beer and sex, roughly in that order. There was a 76 per cent reoffending rate.

By the time these lads reached the age of twenty-five, she told us, they usually began to stop committing crimes. Until then, lots of older reoffenders would lie about their age in order to get back to Feltham. Bad though it was, the place had become part of their lives. Some of them even thought of it as home. My last view of Feltham was of a hall where shadowy figures appeared to be beating people up and sitting on them. It was a 'control and restraint' class for the staff, said Sharon, and hurried us on towards the prison gates.

Highgate. A young man with an enormous bulge on his left jaw staggers up into the dock from the cells. He's accused of stealing a video recorder and failing to surrender to bail when the case was previously listed. He explains the reason was that his girlfriend had to go into rehab for heroin addiction that day – as if this were as reasonable an excuse as someone going into hospital for a major operation. Ho hum. The boy can barely speak from pain so 'in common humanity', as the chair says, we accept this explanation and adjourn the matter, letting him out on bail to totter off to the dentist. Dear me, we are a soft lot.

A tiny little old lady is in the dock. Sheila is sixty but looks much older. She has a lined, bird-like face and thin grey hair. She too is charged with stealing video equipment, also a packet of prawns and a roll of bin liners from Sainsbury's. The total value of her curiously assorted haul is £135.87. It is hard to believe such a timid, grannyish figure is in jail.

Actually Sheila is not her name, she admits. She has several other aliases. She confesses she had been drinking when arrested and pleads guilty in a deferential manner, calling us 'Your Worships'. She must have been in the courts before. So it turns out. Her file contains an astonishing thirteen pages of previous offences, covering twenty-four years of theft and shoplifting, and several spells in prison. It is not surprising that she has a long history of alcoholism, on top of which she has to care for a mentally-ill niece. Heaven knows what the Probation Service will recommend in the pre-sentence report. Poor Sheila seems beyond both punishment and rehabilitation.

Two young white men are up before us next. They are charged with carrying out several muggings in a manner which put their victims 'in fear of being then and there subject to force'. They had a knife. The Crown needs an adjournment to prepare its case for committal to the crown court. One of the defendants makes no application for bail, but the other does. He argues that he was not picked out at a police identity parade. He says he has a history of mental illness (schizophrenia and manic depression). His girlfriend, with whom he has a 2-year-old child, is at the back of the court. She is persuasive when she promises to ensure he stays out of trouble and takes his medication. On the strength of this, we grant him bail. Not for the first time, the support of a good woman has come to the aid of an otherwise apparently doomed and undeserving male.

A thick-set, mild-looking, middle-aged man is charged with threatening to kill three people in an affray, which he stoutly denies. He is outraged that he is being held in custody. He is a St Vincent businessman in Britain on a working visit, he says. He is forty-nine, a practising Christian with no previous convictions of any kind anywhere. He certainly looks immensely respectable, more like a preacher than a would-be killer. The reason he's in jail is that he has no home address in this country. If he is to be released from prison while awaiting trial, which he pretty obviously deserves to be, we must find a bail hostel in London for him – but there are no vacancies. All we can do is hope the probation officer can come up with something by the end of the day.

This is a shameful situation, but not unusual. The scarcity of supervised local authority accommodation for young people on remand is especially worrying when one considers that in Haringey an unusually high proportion of alleged offenders are NFAs – of no fixed address. A colleague told me of an occasion when the nearest such vacancy for a local North London lad they wanted to bail was in Durham! The provision for girls is worse still: even those as young as fifteen must go to the adult women's prison in Holloway. Britain's capital city offers no alternative secure accommodation.

CHAPTER 7

Leaving London

*'It is a good idea that JPs live, work, move and breathe in the
local community'*

By now I was engaged in writing this book. I hoped there would
be some interest in an account of the lay magistracy that was
aimed at the general public rather than law students' reading
lists and courthouse libraries. I wanted to make the case for JPs
as I had tried to make it for juries in my previous book. The
tradition of lay justice in this country was inspiring and admirable, but could do with promoting.

I also had another motive. There was a worrying feeling in
the air that this unique, and uniquely valuable, institution
might be on the brink of fundamental change. Lord Justice
Auld's appraisal of the criminal courts system had been under
way for some while. The signs were that he would shake up
the status quo. At best he might recommend that lay benches
should be retained, but under the chairmanship of a professional district judge in the more serious cases. At worst JPs
might be done away with altogether. Such were the leaks and
rumours emanating from his inquiry as the new millennium
got into its stride. Time and events were pressing. Whether I
would be celebrating the survival of the lay bench or writing
its requiem was uncertain, but either way I had to get a move
on.

It was clear I had to get out of London and see a bit more of
the world – that is, of England and Wales. It was already
obvious to me that the conditions in which crime and punishment occurred differed sharply all over the country. Haringey
might be fairly typical of cosmopolitan inner citydom, but it
was surely no template for what went on everywhere else. If
much of the justification for the lay judiciary was that it

dispensed local justice, then I should have to visit some of the localities.

I decided to start with somewhere as unmetropolitan as I could imagine: the land of my birth, North Wales. I would head for Wrexham, via a detour to the town where I was born. I had not been there for forty years.

Virgin did not make my trip to Colwyn Bay easy. The 9.03 train which was supposed to get me there changing at Chester did not go to Chester. The Holyhead train, which did, was delayed. Many hours later, we were trundling along beside the slate-coloured Irish Sea, past concentration camps of untenanted caravans and mobile homes, flat-roofed and drab. Hibernating cafés with their shutters nailed down proclaimed 'ICES' and cut-price beer. We pulled into Colwyn Bay, once a respectable holiday town and the wartime base of the Ministry of Food, where my father was posted. Now, I was told, its down-at-heel hotels have become B & Bs for homeless Liverpudlians living on their Giro cheques and fighting in the streets at night.

I queued where it said 'Tacsi'. Although I didn't hear a single word of Welsh spoken during two days in North Wales, monoglot natives were assiduously provided for. Under the sign for 'Toilet' was the helpful translation 'Toiled'. For the disabled there was a 'Toiled anabal'. 'No parking' was 'Dim parcio'. Dim kiddingo.

My tacsi driver was Debbie, who had settled in North Wales from southern Australia, which on this cold, wet morning seemed perverse. Her dream was that one day she would take her children back to her homeland, she sighed. Debbie took me on a dispiriting tour of Colwyn Bay and neighbouring Rhos-on-Sea, where my parents had been billeted. We visited the hideous hotel where my mother went into labour in the middle of singing *Auld Lang Syne*: I was born on New Year's Day. Apparently the hotel was quite a swinging hangout during the war, when the Ministry of Food people virtually took it over. There were cocktails and dinner dances. Now the place smelt of mildew and disinfectant. The whole town had become a dump, grumbled a pensioner in a seafront pub as we gazed out on the dank, empty beaches. He was sorry that a returned native should see it in this state. 'You won't find a magistrates' court here any longer,' he snorted when I told him what I was doing in the area. 'When the crime rate went up, they closed the court down, didn't they? Now they have to take the crooks to Llandudno, don't they?'

This was not the first time I had heard complaints about courts being amalgamated. It is a remorseless trend all over the country, humanity of scale giving way to economies of scale, as is so often the case. The Magistrates' Association's chairman was 'passionately concerned' about the problem. Not so long ago there were twenty-four courts in North Wales. Today there are only nine, and one of them is in Wrexham. It is the biggest population centre in North Wales – about 40 per cent rural, and some 40,000 living in the town itself. The two-storey brick courthouse is a pleasant modern building, though somewhat overwhelmed by the grey tower block next door. This, amazingly, turns out to be the police station – 'a triumph of architecture over utility', in the words of the Wrexham Justices' Clerk, George Tranter. It looks more like the headquarters of North Wales's answer to KGB. During an earth tremor some years ago the whole monstrous building began to sway: the locals had alarming visions of coppers toppling from the tenth floor and prisoners escaping from the holding cells below.

By contrast the courthouse had a reassuring air about it. One entered a comfortable grey-carpeted foyer-cum-waiting room with leather banquettes along the wall and magazines spread out on coffee tables. A striking bronze sculpture of a blind Justice with Apache features stood at one end, its flowing tresses modulating cleverly into a set of scales. My colleagues back in Haringey would have been astonished at such adornments, so very much more alluring than our own Spartan surroundings. This could have been the waiting room of a plush legal practice, except that the clientele were wearing baseball caps and biting their eroded nails. There was the usual huddle of smokers outside the entrance but, unusually, a box for fag-ends had been fastened to the wall and everyone seemed to use it.

George Tranter, who runs the Wrexham court, is a big, bearded, bespectacled man with a genial pedagogic air and a formidable knowledge of his profession, hauling Acts of Parliament into his conversation as readily as if he were talking about the rules of rugby. Over coffee, he described his patch. How very different it all seemed from London. There was petty theft to fund drug habits, he told me, burglary for the same reason, but, being so rural, not a lot of robberies. There was quite a trade in stolen farm implements – drug dealers accepted payment in kind nowadays. I confess I found something rather engaging about the notion of paying for a stash of heroin with a muckspreader and a pair of ploughshares.

According to George, Wrexham didn't have the difficulties of declining tourist areas such as Colwyn Bay and Rhyl, which were forced to take in B & B refugees from Liverpool and Birmingham. Rhyl had a significant drug problem. Why did they choose these places? Because they knew the hotels needed the business and a lot of them had happy childhood memories of seaside holidays there, especially the Butlin's at Pwllheli. The locals used to complain about the English buying second homes in the area: now it was the riffraff from the inner cities who caused resentment.

Ethnic minorities made up less than 1 per cent of the local population. So the magistrates did not get the same opportunities to 'practise their non-racist skills as elsewhere', said George, betraying barely a hint of irony in his tone. 'Maybe as a consequence we have an increased risk of stereotyping.' Not much, I'd have thought, as I listened to the Tannoy system politely summoning defendants into court for their hearings. The names were almost satirically local: Davies, Hughes, Owen, Jones, Thomas, Williams.

The Welsh language, said George, was unique in Europe because it had equal status with English in the Welsh courts. In countries like Switzerland and Belgium there were priority languages for each region. Here in Wrexham a defendant could insist on using either, though it didn't often come to that. 'When we have a Welsh-speaking defendant we generally use an interpreter,' George beamed, though the court reporter for the local newspaper (an ex-Fleet Street man, as he proudly informed me) pointed out that there were enough JPs, clerks and lawyers who spoke Welsh to mount a whole hearing in that language if need be – a noteworthy occasion when it happened, one gathered.

George was robust on the whole question of how local 'local justice' had to be. Certainly it is a good idea that JPs live, work, move and breathe in the local community. They should be aware of local opinion. But they should not be led by it. They were not there to *represent* the local community. Otherwise one would be in danger of accepting that justice in Wrexham could be different from justice in Flintshire. The whole purpose of the sentencing guidelines, after all, was to try to avoid there being a geographical lottery. He observed that although Lord Justice Auld had received representations from magistrates who felt very strongly about their local ties, there had been none from local communities making the same point.

One aspect of North Welsh justice is decidedly unlocal: there are no prisons in the region. The nearest are in Liverpool, Cheshire and Shropshire. This is a major headache with remand prisoners, who might have to be transported to and from court several times before their trials. Wrexham was looking forward to the installation of a direct video link between the court and the jails, an idea that was currently being tried out in Bristol with great success. It meant, for example, that a remand prisoner could make a reapplication for bail on camera instead of spending hours trundling around the countryside in a cramped paddy wagon for the sake of a ten-minute appearance in the flesh. The scheme would save time, money and disruption – and would be a godsend in London, too, I realised, thinking of the Feltham boys.

Most of the Wrexham bench tended to be drawn from the teaching and medical professions and from the farming community, said George. Since 1980 the job market had worked in the employers' favour. Bosses had become more demanding and some magistrates had been forced to resign. The result was that the width of recruitment had been reduced. Once upon a time nationalised industries such as British Gas and the Electricity Board were fruitful sources of JPs. No longer. Now everyone was under more pressure – a complaint I was to hear again and again in other parts of the country.

Fortunately, this did not seem to be affecting the political balance on the Wrexham bench. In fact it closely mirrored the voting patterns in the 1997 election, which showed that the old suspicion that most JPs were Tories was no longer justified. In any case, political partisanship was pretty hard to measure accurately, in George's view. 'The trouble with giving your political affiliation is that once you've put it down on your appointment it stays with you for life, irrespective of whether your vote has stayed the same or not.

'The thought did occur to me,' he went on, 'that for a long time anyone who became a magistrate in the early 1980s would never admit to voting Labour anyway, on the grounds that their sanity might be questioned. Now anybody appointed to the magistracy since the late 1990s might not admit to voting Conservative for precisely the same reason. There are some Plaid Cymru voters on the bench, though in this part of Wales the nationalists are not particularly strong. In two of our constituencies in 1997 they were actually outvoted by Jimmy Goldsmith's Referendum Party.

'On the whole I can say after twenty-five years in the courts that magistrates are very good at putting aside their political differences in the retiring room. The problem is that law and order has become much more of a political football than it used to be. Until the early 1990s there was a more bipartisan approach to criminal justice. Now there is too much reactive legislation. Politicians ignore the old nostrum that hard cases make bad law. There is a danger of magistrates being tagged as fellow travellers with the government lawmakers of the day.'

Despite such concerns, George did not see the lay magistracy withering away. 'I don't think the public in England and Wales would be happy with the removal of lay involvement. Leaving it all to the lawyers would raise people's hackles.' The judges wouldn't like it either. 'Judges tend to be rather against the idea of professional stipendiaries taking over completely. That's partly out of jealousy,' he grinned, 'because whereas a stipe both convicts and sentences, crown court judges can only sentence.'

But he himself was rather in favour of mixed professional and lay benches, as Sir Robin Auld was considering. I suggested this was because a lot of legal advisers rather fancied themselves becoming the professionals in question. The Government would have to turn to them to expand the supply of district judges. He did not disagree. 'If they selected people from our ranks as chairs, at least the JPs would be used to working with them. Two wingers could still outvote the professional chairman, don't forget. Magistrates think they would be too diffident about standing up to him or her. But why do you distrust yourselves so much? Think how much more lay magistrates know about certain subjects than most lawyers – licensing and motoring offences, for example. Totting up the assets magistrates would bring to such a tribunal would be quite an encouraging exercise.' I felt George was humouring me somewhat, but he had a point.

Ten o'clock came. I spent the day doing the rounds of the courtrooms, looking out for differences between Haringey and Wrexham. Some hit you in the eye and ear in a very obvious way: there were no non-white defendants, none for whom English was not their first language and few who even spoke it with a Welsh lilt as opposed to a Lancashire monotone. Every defendant who was not in custody sat in the well of the court, rather than going into the dock, which lent a certain friendliness to the proceedings. There were several older defendants, including a ruddy-faced pensioner with a shoulder bag and stick who stoutly denied being drunk and disorderly and a middle-aged man who was astonished to have been charged with stealing chocolates from a branch of Kwik Save. He had grabbed a small handful of Matchmakers from an open box which was part of a pre-Christmas display. The total value of his haul was £1.49. Surely even in rural Wales this did not amount to a major heist. Nevertheless, as theft is an 'either-way' offence, the clerk was bound to go through the lengthy rigmarole of telling the defendant he could elect trial by jury if he wished. He sensibly settled for a guilty plea and a conditional discharge, leaving everyone wondering why on earth he had been prosecuted in the first place.

Otherwise the day's round-up of alleged malefactors largely consisted of the usual suspects: young people, frequently with drug problems, accused of shoplifting, using stolen credit cards, breaching probation, driving while disqualified, and so forth. It was the same parade of desocialised, disorganised victim-delinquents one can find on any day in any court in the land.

Alice stood out, however: a smartly groomed 49-year-old woman in a tailored overcoat. She was accused of threatening behaviour. She had shouted abuse at another woman in the toilet of a Wrexham nightclub, then in the office of the Prestige taxi firm. At one point she had grabbed hold of her. Alice pleaded guilty. It would have been idiotic of her to do anything else, since incontrovertible evidence was to hand in the form of high-quality CCTV video footage in full colour, which was now played on a big TV set in the courtroom. This was the first time I had seen evidence of this kind and it was immensely convincing. The filmed encounter showed Alice confronting another woman and mutely haranguing her (there was no soundtrack), then chasing her across the road to the minicab office.

'It was merely a verbal confrontation,' said her goateed lawyer by way of mitigation. 'A case of handbags at fifty paces.' The two women knew each other of old. The defendant apparently blamed the victim for the break-up of a friend's marriage. Now she was very embarrassed by the whole episode, and full of remorse. The police had tried to persuade the complainant to settle for a caution, but she refused. The bench gave Alice a twelve-month conditional discharge, which seemed fair to me. Then the court rose for lunch.

The magistrates ate cheese and pickle sandwiches in the small staff canteen. I asked them about the CCTV. They responded with enthusiasm, explaining that there were now cameras covering most of the town centre, under the remote control of excellent operators who were able to focus on incidents as they occurred and even zoom in for a close-up of the participants. Cases of affray had diminished sharply. 'We used to have to sit through endless trials listening to "he hit me" – "no, he hit me first" type of evidence,' said one of the lunchers. 'Now no other evidence is really needed.' They had not yet had a single trial where a defendant had challenged his own identity on film. The police had to watch their behaviour, too. On the whole, the Wrexham JPs felt, it was three cheers for Big Brother.

I was struck by another local initiative, which surely deserved to be copied elsewhere: offenders sentenced to fines were given a paying-in book which they could use at any HSBC branch in the country, knowing that the amount would be immediately credited to their account in the Wrexham fines office. Given the long distances rural folk would otherwise have to travel to make their weekly or fortnightly payments, this was obviously sensible. But clearly it would be just as effective in an urban environment too, making it easier for offenders not only to pay in the money but also to keep track of how they were progressing.

The afternoon was as busy as the morning. In Court 2 a jolly, tattooed, earringed fellow in a fisherman's sweater had been brought in on a warrant for breaching a community service order. He was also wanted by the police in Rhyl. Before he was handcuffed and taken off to Rhyl, he wanted to give a note to his girlfriend, who was sitting in court. The Group 4 security man obligingly suggested he fold the message, but the defendant said he was an old hand at this and that if he folded the paper it would not fit through the slit between the door of the dock and the glass wall surrounding it. The girl took the note, read it, gave the writer a loving look and a wave and off he went to the cells with his chin held high, like a man going away to war.

Later the bench was faced with one of those cases that make magistrates contemplate retiring in despair. A 26-year-old woman who looked fourteen was up on two charges of burgling credit cards and two of using them. She was already on a conditional discharge for a previous offence and admitted the breach. Hers was a sad, familiar story: her two children had been taken into care, she had lost her home, and taken to drugs for consolation. The chances were this was the reverse of the true sequence of events, but what did it matter? The consequences were equally dire either way. She had already been in custody for six weeks and 'had not coped at all well' with prison, according to her lawyer. The magistrates gave her a three-month custodial sentence, knowing full well that as she had already served half that time in jail on remand, she would be released. It was the kindest thing they could do in the circumstances, but everyone knew for sure it would not be long before she was back in court again.

I said goodbye to Gareth, formerly of Reuters, now of the *North Wales Leader*. Gareth said the story of the day, which he had just filed, was undoubtedly that of the well-dressed middle-aged woman whose old animosity led her to behave threateningly in a nightclub toilet. It was not much of a tale by Fleet Street standards. But it was certainly worth running as an everyday story of Wrexham folk.

Tottenham. We hear a local authority application for a woman to be committed to custody for the non-payment of business rates. Imprisoning a person for debt is not something I have yet done and I find the idea disquieting. One thinks of the Fleet and the Marshalsea as belonging to another era altogether.

The defendant is a very large, sad-eyed Nigerian woman with big glasses called, let's say, Sonia. Some years back she had rented premises from the council to run a restaurant. She called it The Refined Bukka and served her own Nigerian cooking. She had not paid her business rates at all between 1994 and 1996, when the council repossessed the place. Three years later she still owed nearly £3,000. The council had tried everything: letters, warnings, even the bailiffs, but Sonia had simply not responded. One could sympathise with their frustration. There was only prison left, they said.

Now Sonia tries to explain what happened. 'I couldn't do business,' she says. 'My restaurant was in a cul-de-sac. No one came.' After six months the failure of the restaurant and the death of her father in Nigeria became too much for her. She'd borrowed money from her family, and even from her church: here were her accounts, on two sheets of paper, written down in laborious longhand, showing outgoings exceeding income in a way that would have drawn a shudder from Mr Micawber. It was no good. She locked up The Refined Bukka and simply forgot about it.

Then came a series of personal problems. She hands a sheet of cheap writing paper up to the bench on which she has written down what happened. 'Dear Judges,' it begins, then goes on to describe how she was violently raped in her own home. The experience has left her suffering from stress and incontinence. 'Life was uneasy for me,' she concludes understatedly. As the clerk and chairman gently question her about these matters, Sonia breaks into sobs and the usher fetches her a box of tissues.

We consider her plight with a good deal of solicitude. The poor woman is plainly decent and pious, but was simply overwhelmed by her cares and incapable of dealing with them. What is more, if the council had acted more decisively in response to her non-payment of the rates instead of allowing her debts to mount, the outstanding demand would not have been half so big. So we remit (i.e. let her off) some of her debt and refuse the application for committal. She is to make arrangements to repay the balance of what she owes. When the chair delivers this decision, she looks as if she will burst into tears again, this time with gratitude. As she leaves the court she turns towards the bench and, with some difficulty, performs a deep, old-fashioned curtsey.

WINDOW ON THE WORLD
The largest law courts west of Moscow

A plump, jolly policeman was coming towards me along the pavement hugging a slim Asian youth who smiled at him cheekily. They were holding hands. This was a bit startling. It appeared the police in Birmingham had taken the Macpherson report rather too much to heart. Then the fierce October sunshine glinted on metal and I saw the handcuffs. Together they strolled into the entrance of the Victoria Law Courts.

Euston station had been in a state of chaos. It was only days after a derailment in which four people had been killed and many injured. Railtrack had imposed a panic regime of speed limits on long stretches of line. This suited the Virgin railway company very well as it could now blame its habitual erratic performance on reasons beyond its own control. The 6.34 had left Euston at 7.32, which was only eleven minutes before the supposed departure time of the 7.43, which hadn't even arrived at its platform by the time we left. The on-board Tannoy announced that despite the extra hour the crew had had to prepare for the journey, the buffet was not open. As we left each station on our route, the guard announced blithely that this was the 6.34 train to Watford Junction, Milton Keynes, Birmingham International, etc. as if its scheduled departure time still meant anything to anyone. The railways' pretentious habit of listing train arrival and departure times in terms of single minutes had never seemed more absurd. Throughout the carriage people muttered into their mobile phones warning that they'd be late. If Sir Richard Branson had a pound for every time a Virgin passenger cursed his name he'd be even richer than he is already.

Birmingham's Victoria Law Courts are magnificent: a palace of red terracotta rampant with ornate towers and balustrades. The foundation stone was laid by the Queen herself in 1887, her jubilee year. There is a stained-glass window showing her bent glumly over a pile of masonry with a trowel in her hand while the mayor stands by, taut with solicitude. When the courts were built, at a total cost of £113,000, they were hailed as the finest modern building in the country. Today it is certainly among the most impressive examples of architectural Victoriana anywhere.

This is the largest court complex in Europe – the biggest west of Moscow. We queued to pass through the security checks. My umbrella was seized and I was given a ticket to retrieve it later. 'Potential dangerous weapon,' glowered the security man. My small folding brolly, bought from an Oxford Street stall in a thunderstorm, was less dangerous than a flyswat, but there you go.

The enormous Great Hall, as big as a railway station, was milling with people: young white and Asian lawyers in sharp suits, shifty-looking lads in £70 trainers with cigarettes in their cupped hands, women in saris, ushers in black gowns. There are some thirty courts here, going at full blast every weekday. The inside of the building is as grand as the exterior, though the high-ceilinged lobbies and echoing corridors are clad in yellow rather than red terracotta. There are admonitory inscriptions on the walls to catch the guilty eye: 'Thou shalt not bear false witness against thy neighbour' . . . 'He that walketh uprightly, walketh surely, but he that perverteth his ways shall be known.'

Any defendant with an ounce of sensitivity towards his surroundings would be daunted by the sheer tremendousness of it all. Here indeed is a temple to judicial authority, plainly designed to imbue a sense of humility and contrition. But a visit to the Gents suggested otherwise. The place had been energetically graffitied. Mostly the results were indecipherable scrawls, shows of inarticulate defiance, though a conscientious citizen had aerosolled 'Kill paedophiles' above the urinals. A tagger, or perhaps a whole gang of taggers, had gone to work on the ceiling with what appeared to be a blowtorch.

Court 1 was a perfect stage set, full of pomp and panelling. The magistrates sat under a great curved canopy, which made them look at once both intimidating and small. The dock was planted right in the middle of the room, surrounded by chest-high oaken rails, with a staircase like the companionway of a man-o'-war leading down to the cells. Unlike the practice at Wrexham, here all the defendants went into the dock, whether they were in custody or not. The first of the day was a man in a suit and tie accused of setting fire to a property and endangering human life – the property in question being his own home and the human life that of his woman partner, who was sitting meekly beside me on the public benches. There was much coming and going – lawyers, defendants, defendants' friends and relations, bowing to the bench as they entered and bowing again as they left. A young man with shoulder-length hair positively genuflected. From the beady way he eyed my notebook I judged he was the court reporter for one of the local papers.

Court 3 was presided over by a brisk-mannered stipe. From the rear one could see three heads in the dock. Two belonged to thick-necked, shaven-skulled white men, the third to a neatly-groomed black man. At a glance you might suspect it was the white men who were the villains, but they were the security men. Two on one suggested that the defendant was potentially dangerous and indeed the charges ran to a whole series of thefts and robberies, some with violence involving lengths of copper tubing and a screwdriver.

The defendant had been in jail before for similar offences but now his solicitor was asking for bail while his client awaited trial. The application was well argued. Although the prosecutor had mentioned DNA, fingerprints and bloodstains, the fact was that the young man had not been picked out at identity parades by a single one of his alleged victims. The defence maintained that because of this man's previous convictions, the police routinely pulled him in whenever there was a spate of muggings and car thefts. But his record also suggested he would not fail to surrender to bail and, by the way, there was his mother, a nurse, sitting at the back of the court to reassure us. I glanced at her. She was a nice-looking woman, but at that moment her face was sorrowful and anxious. The stipe retired to consider the matter, there being some research to be done as to whether the defendant was actually in prison at the time of some of the alleged offences. As the handcuffs were snapped on and he was led down the stairs to the cells, he cast a beseeching look at his mother, as if trying to convince her that this time he really was not the culprit. He was strikingly handsome, an impression enhanced by the thuggish appearance of his guards.

Court 7 had been modernised to make it more escape-proof. It was one of the two most secure courts in the building. Not only was the dock completely enclosed from floor to ceiling in thick, presumably bullet-proof glass but the public gallery was, too. The proceedings were relayed via microphones and speakers, which made it far easier to hear what was going on than the echoing acoustics of the older courts. Sitting behind the glass screen in the public gallery, one was uncomfortably reminded of an American execution suite, with its special viewing room for onlookers.

There were two lads in the fishtank dock with their guards. One was a tiny dreadlocked Rastafarian, the other a spotty, pink-skinned youth. Three squirming girls were sitting in front of me, chewing gum and giggling. They tapped on the glass as the boys were taken down to the cells. 'Melvyn, you've been a naughty boy,' one of them squealed, weirdly unawed by the grimness of the setting.

In Court 6 the chairman of the bench sat on a throne surmounted by a sort of miniature Albert Memorial towering towards the ceiling and topped with a dusty mahogany crown. The effect was rather more satirical than imperious. Two 17-year-olds were brought up. They were as pale as lard and extravagantly pierced. Several similarly unappetising young people had joined me on the public benches. I thought I detected a sudden change of atmosphere in court, a slight mounting of tension. I was right. The two security men in the dock didn't sit down next to their charges as usual, but stayed standing, leaning over the prisoners awkwardly throughout the proceedings. Clearly there was a serious concern that these two, perhaps with the help of their friends sitting next to me in court, might try to leap out of the dock and make a run for it. Such things happen from time to time, which explained the heavy glass screens in the securer courts.

There was a massive bang as the door at the bottom of the stairs was closed behind the two boys. The first time I had heard it I jumped as if a bomb had gone off. But after a whole morning I was beginning to get used to the grisly ritual of prisoners being brought up from and sent down to the cells. On the way up there would be heavy footsteps, the jangling of keys, as guards and prisoners surfaced in single file, linked together by their handcuffs. On the way down the prisoner would lead the way, having to lift the handcuffed arm behind him to the height of his minder's wrist because of the steepness and narrowness of the staircase. Then came the crash of the door, followed by an echoing, thought-provoking silence.

'Mind you, they're really quiet today,' said Helen, the clerk. The court had risen and the prosecutor, an amiable bearded man who looked like a schoolteacher, was showing me the stairs down to the cells. He rightly thought I would find them interesting. This was the stairway to hell: precipitous, worn stone steps, blackened brick walls barely as wide as a man's shoulders, leading to a Dickensian, dungeon-like gloom at the bottom.

'What do you mean, really quiet?' I asked Helen.

'Well, normally,' she began – and at that moment there came a hair-raising woman's scream from somewhere beneath our feet, followed by indistinct shouting.

'Normally, that sort of thing goes on quite a lot,' Helen continued calmly. 'Prisoners yelling and cursing.' Rather a salutary warning to first-time offenders appearing here, I thought. Perhaps we could contrive the same sort of effect back in Haringey, with a tape of howls and groans piped through the courthouse.

I was not invited to visit the Victoria Law Courts cells, which were being refurbished, but I was told there were twenty-two of them, capable of holding more than seventy prisoners at a time. A network of tunnels linked them with nearby Streelhouse Lane Police Station, where another forty people could be held in custody. Plainly Birmingham took its crime seriously.

Up in Court 15, on the second floor, a trial was under way. This was nothing like the courtrooms below: simply a plain, rectangular room with desks at one end for the bench and a slew of other desks and plastic chairs for everyone else. The defendants, two youths, one white, one black, accused of stealing a mobile phone, were slouching on chairs in the middle of the room where we could admire their costly-looking footwear.

Presiding was the man I had a lunch date with, David Bradnock, chairman of the Birmingham bench and a JP for twenty-two years. His sole winger – Birmingham struggles to run to three-person benches, such is the case load – was a kindly looking black woman. It was a small case, but a thorny one, as the CPS was relying chiefly on identification evidence, a notoriously tricky area. Identification is subject to a host of considerations such as the time of day, visibility, distance, whether the witness knew the defendants, and so forth. The closing speech for the defence drew the bench's particular attention to the case of Turnbull v. The Crown regarding identification evidence.

Then we broke for lunch. The chairman took me to his spacious office, via the magistrates' library, a large, ornate room which would be the envy of a St James' club, book-lined and elegantly furnished. After the utilitarian facilities in Haringey, I could only goggle. But then everything at the Victoria Law Courts seemed to be on a grand, not to say an almost industrial, scale.

There were 450 JPs on the bench, David told me – so many that it was necessary to keep a constantly updated 'Who's Who' in the library, complete with photographs and mini-biographies of each justice. They dealt with over 60,000 criminal cases a year, the heaviest serious caseload in the country. Some 2,000 people came through the court entrance every day, and £1.3 million worth of fines were awarded every month – with a 52 per cent collection rate, which was not too bad going. Brummie JPs liked to boast that one year sitting in their courts was equivalent to five years anywhere else. Historically Birmingham had something of a struggle to meet the need for volunteer JPs, which was why it had six stipendiaries. But that year sixty new justices had been sworn in, which was an improvement.

Local companies such as BT, Cadbury's and British Aerospace were courted for support and tended to respond well, said David, himself a property man. He was to have a meeting with Price Waterhouse Coopers at which he hoped to persuade the influential accountancy firm to endorse the lay magistracy with its clients. 'We want them to tell businesses that there is a real value in letting their staff become JPs – it not only shows their commitment to the community but can also improve employees' management and personnel skills.' The Birmingham bench included taxi drivers, factory workers and nursery school teachers, as well as surgeons and college professors. David was very chuffed that the 2000 batch had thrown up a female car mechanic.

Evidently he regarded it as a priority to see that the bench was as representative as possible. Ethnic minorities make up 12 per cent of the population of greater Birmingham, but the bench itself could boast over 20 per cent, including men and women from the Afro-Caribbean, Indian, Pakistani, Bangladeshi and Chinese communities as well as others. There were interpreters for a hundred different languages and Saturday teach-ins for would-be court translators. The chairman said he made a point of having regular meetings with the local press, whose role was important in helping to sustain confidence in local justice. Indeed the very day of our meeting the *Evening Mail* had a story about two law professors from China having lately visited the courts and been much impressed by what they saw. 'It's not just the rest of England and Wales who look to these busy courts for a lead,' said David. Video links with the local prisons (as anticipated in Wrexham) were coming soon. Meanwhile, not only did Birmingham have psychiatric nurses on the court premises, but the city prided itself on having established a system for identifying and diverting those with mental problems at the point of arrest.

As well as the Chinese professors, David Bradnock had also recently played host to Sir Robin Auld, who reassured him in the course of a three-hour meeting that whatever his review's eventual recommendations for reform of the criminal courts, the future role of the lay magistracy was safe. It might even be enhanced if a new intermediate tier of jurisdiction for more serious cases were to involve lay magistrates sitting alongside professional district judges. David had sent a letter passing on the good news to all the members of his bench, he told me. By the way, he added slily, it was worth noting that quite a significant proportion of appeals upheld against Birmingham magistrates' rulings concerned decisions taken by stipes, not lay justices. I only hoped Sir Robin knew that too.

The canteen was packed with lunching magistrates and lawyers. I sat with Sharon, David's winger in Court 15. She had a big, shy smile and a crucifix around her neck. We did not discuss the case, but over chicken curry and fish pasties she told me why she had become a magistrate seven months earlier. Sharon was a 43-year-old social worker dealing mainly with meals-on-wheels and transport for the elderly. It was a colleague who suggested she apply. She sent off for the papers, but did nothing about them for a year, thinking she wasn't cut out to be a JP. Then a friend at her church urged her to do it, arguing that it was important for black people to get involved. 'He said I could help make the bench more representative, and that's what persuaded me.' Once Sharon had taken the plunge and done the training she knew she had done the right thing.

After her group were sworn in there was a gathering at the courts one Saturday hosted by the chairman of the bench for all the new justices and their families. Their employers were also urged to come along, which seemed to me an especially astute piece of public relations. Everyone was shown round the place and told its history, but the main purpose was to help people get to know each other. With such a large number of magistrates, mostly sitting once a fortnight on the same day each week, there was a danger many of them would seldom meet. So this get-together was a measure to tackle the problem, as was the ecumenical service which David Bradnock had inaugurated in the cathedral that year, attended by more than 500 past and present justices.

It was time to return to Court 15. During the lunch break the woman legal adviser had been at her books to see what the Court of Appeal had to say about identification evidence in the case of Turnbull v. The Crown cited by the defence. Now she rose to her feet, looking very business-like in a severely-cut houndstooth jacket, to give an exemplary exposition of the matter to the whole court – which consisted of the two JPs, the prosecutor, the defence lawyers, the pair of indifferent-looking defendants, the mother of one of them, the usher and me. The gist of it, she concluded, just as meticulously as if she had been addressing a packed courtroom in the Old Bailey, was that one must take great care. 'You can be 100 per cent certain you've identified someone and be 100 per cent wrong.'

Armed with this information David and Sharon retired to consider their verdicts. They took a long time about it. The boys lolled across the desks with their heads in their arms while the anxious mother sat in the corridor outside smoking. 'I've got to give it up,' she told me nervously. She had a pinched, worried face. 'I've got emphysema. But life's full of stress, isn't it? I'm even allergic to lettuce,' she added enigmatically. 'I blame the chemical sprays used by the growers. But then I don't like lettuce anyway.' She sighed and lit another fag.

The usher, an agreeable and talkative sort, as most court ushers seem to be, confessed that he too was a smoker but only off-duty. He had taken early retirement from British Aerospace where he had held various senior jobs on the shop floor. He'd decided he wanted to work again, but this time at something different, something to do with people.

'I love doing this,' he said. 'Every day something new. It's what they say about the courts: a window on the world. Do I think better or worse of humanity from what I've seen? Better on the whole. There are some hard nuts. Some kids you know you'll see again and again. But mostly there's some good in them. There's a core of decency, you know.'

As we waited it occurred to me that since the Human Rights Act, which requires magistrates to give full written reasons for their decisions, it was logical to assume that the longer a bench was out on a verdict, the more likely they were to be giving the thumbs-down. An acquittal barely needs explaining: it is simple enough to say you were not convinced by the prosecution evidence beyond reasonable doubt, after all. I asked the lawyers if they thought this was so. They hadn't considered it, they said. Giving written reasons was too new a game. But sure enough when the magistrates returned it was to give a lengthy, thoughtful and detailed explanation of why they had found the lads guilty.

I left them to sort out the tricky matter of sentencing, since I was worried about catching a train back to London. What was tricky about their task was that one of the boys was a youth, being only seventeen. Magistrates in an adult court have a limited range of sentence in such cases: either a conditional discharge or a fine. For any other kind of penalty, the defendant must be referred to the youth court which has much wider powers but where, being a new bench, the case would have to be heard again, assuming a not guilty plea. Everyone looked dismayed by this anomaly, but when I left, whatever they were going to do about the older lad, it looked to me that this was the course they were reluctantly going to have to take regarding the younger – prolonging his uncertainty and adding to the tax-payers' bill.

I caught a train which was only an hour behind schedule. Settling into my seat I opened the *Evening Mail*. A small news item caught my attention. The West Midlands Probation Service had been fined £3,000 on account of two people sentenced to community service orders cutting their fingers on a circular saw in 1998. For heaven's sake! The lawyers who take up such compensation cases should be careful. If their activities frighten local authorities from supporting such projects, the next time their clients are in trouble, community service might be less readily available: custody could be the only option.

CHAPTER 8

A Jewel Beyond Price

'The justices are chosen for their qualities of fairness, judgment and common sense'

I went to see Lord Bingham, the former Lord Chief Justice. He had recently been appointed Senior Law Lord, in part at least to deal with tricky appeals it was anticipated would emerge from the first testing few years of the Human Rights Act. Waves of legal controversy would one day pile up in the House of Lords committee rooms which would have arisen as tiny ripples in magistrates' courts up and down the country.

Lord Bingham was already on record as a supporter of the lay magistracy, having praised it robustly in a recent speech. 'The justices are chosen for their qualities of fairness, judgment and common sense, alert to the needs and concerns of the communities they serve and enabling local issues to be determined locally by local people,' he said.

'And in the eyes of the public they have one great advantage: they are free of the habits of thought, speech and bearing which characterise professional lawyers and which most people find to a greater or lesser extent repellent. The existence of 30,000 citizens distributed around the country, all with a sound, practical understanding of what the law is and how it works, is, I think, a democratic jewel beyond price.'

This was stirring stuff. I wanted to hear more. While waiting in the entrance lobby of the House of Lords I got chatting to Bernardo, the police officer on duty. He was a Galician who had settled in London and joined the Met some years ago. We were just getting onto the interesting subject of illegal immigration and the policing thereof when Lord Bingham came down to lead me up to his office. This was a fine, high-ceilinged room with heavy Puginesque curtains ('standard House of Lords issue

– my wife rather objects') and a view over the rush-hour traffic trundling past Palace Yard.

Lord Bingham is a tallish, thinnish, donnish and very agreeable man whose entry in *Who's Who* would be longer but for the modest abbreviations. 'I'm very much in favour of the lay magistracy,' he said firmly. 'Obviously, efforts must be made to try to make it even better. There are problems in making an institution efficient when it is dependent on people who have got other jobs to do and have to fit it into the rest of their lives.

'If we were inventing the system from scratch, I suspect we probably wouldn't come up with the lay magistracy. But that isn't an argument against it. I have repeatedly claimed that the magistracy is a democratic institution. You have a number of members of the public chosen for their qualities of fairness and good sense, general soundness and practical wisdom, exercising important judicial functions. This has the result that a large number of people in the community actually have hands-on experience of how the law works and what it's all about and are imbued with notions of fairness, of not making your mind up until you've heard both sides. Just as I think the jury is a democratic institution, so I think the lay justices are.'

This had not always been so, he agreed. 'The worst benches of magistrates I've ever encountered were one-class benches. You'd go to a place, a county bench in some smart area of the country, and you would get three people who simply didn't know what a £100 fine meant to somebody on housing benefit and income support. On the other hand I can think of a magistrates' court in East London in the old days when it was regarded as a crime even to own a car, let alone do anything wrong with it.

'Lord Chancellors have genuinely tried extremely hard to get balanced benches. Perversely, it's got more difficult recently to attract manual workers. In the old days the nationalised industries were extremely generous if you were a Justice of the Peace. If you worked for the railway or gas board, it was regarded as a public duty to give you a day off to go and sit.

Whereas now, with everything becoming much more commercial and hard-nosed, the tendency is to say if you have the day off you don't get paid.'

As a young barrister, Tom Bingham often appeared in magistrates' courts in London and the home counties. He remembered it as a useful and generally reassuring experience. Appearing before lay magistrates was different from addressing a jury. 'You'd expect a bench of JPs to be a little less susceptible than a jury might be. On the other hand, if you had a damn good point of law, you'd be better off in front of a stipendiary, because as a trained lawyer he'd be more interested in the matter than a lay bench would.'

Lord Bingham regarded district judges as complementary to the lay magistracy. 'I don't see them as replacing it, though Lord Justice Auld may well be contemplating ways in which JPs and stipes could sit together.' But he seemed to me very determined to guard the lay element against over-professionalisation. For example, he said he had always been 'really insistent on the separation of functions between the justices' clerks and the justices. Years ago I remember that one could go into a magistrates' court and it was obvious to absolutely everybody that there was only one person in the whole court who mattered, and that was the clerk. The magistrates looked extremely foolish. One wondered why they were there at all. One ended up addressing submissions to him. I think it is very important indeed that the clerk should be the professional adviser and that the justices should be the decision-makers.'

It was no doubt Lord Bingham's firm belief in the democratic credentials of the lay magistracy that allowed him to support the Government's plan to restrict a defendant's right to elect trial by jury in 'either-way' cases – a plan which its opponents regarded as profoundly undemocratic. The proposal was that in cases such as theft or sexual harassment, magistrates rather than defendants would decide where they would be best tried. 'I don't favour the defendant having a right to dictate mode of trial. It seems to me a totally appropriate matter for a court to decide,' Lord Bingham insisted, though he was unhappy about the latest version of the Mode of Trial Bill whereby justices would not be able to to take into account a man's previous record in making their decision – which would have helped target the old hands who elect crown court trial simply in order to play the system, often changing their plea to guilty at the last moment.

'Behind this proposed reform is a belief that there are some cases which end up before a judge and jury, at considerable cost to the taxpayer, which simply don't merit it. As Lord Chief Justice I went up to sit in Liverpool for a week and they lined up seventeen cases for me to hear, on the basis that if one of them wasn't effective there'd be another one – and all seventeen defendants changed their pleas to guilty. Is that a good use of court resources and taxpayers' money?

'I imagine quite a lot of lawyers would say you have a right to trial by judge and jury, where you'd have a better chance of an acquittal. But you may very well be punished more heavily if you're convicted in the crown court than you would have been by the justices. The tendency of a lot of criminal defendants is simply to put off the evil day. There is a sort of fecklessness about many of them that means they aren't very rational decision-makers.'

Sentencing such ill-organised and usually impoverished people was always difficult, agreed Lord Bingham when I told him of the problems we often faced in Haringey. 'The dilemma is inescapable. You can't send people to prison simply because they haven't got a bean to pay the fine. I don't think anyone's found an answer to these problems,' he said – though he did rather favour the idea of weekend prisons (as I do), which would give malefactors a taste of custody without affecting their ability to keep a job. Likewise, though he accepted that the Probation Service needed 'a whip it can crack', he was dead against an automatic two-strikes-and-you're-in-jail attitude towards those who breached community punishment or rehabilitation orders more than once. 'These are people who by definition aren't well-disciplined, are sometimes only marginally rational, who don't respond like you or I would to such a threat.'

As for asylum seekers, who seldom had the wherewithal to pay even a small fine and were usually barred from working, Lord Bingham did not see deportation as a practical alternative, although the sentencing guidelines do allow magistrates to make such a recommendation to the Home Secretary. 'I suspect that threatening to send an asylum seeker back to the country he has fled from would be a breach of the Convention on Human Rights,' he said, with the finality of a Law Lord who could envisage the likely appeals procedure and its conclusion all too clearly.

I was looking forward to bringing up this matter with my Galician policeman friend downstairs, wondering what he would make of Lord Bingham's view. It is a well-known phenomenon all over the world that the immigrants of one generation are hostile to those of the next. But PC Bernardo had gone home, no doubt to a slice of *tortilla* and a pot of tea.

Highgate. A busy morning. The matters before us range in seriousness from loitering for the purpose of prostitution to cruelty against children.

A stoat-faced man is up for an indecent assault on an 11-year-old boy. The proceedings may not be reported in detail. The defendant allegedly pushed the boy down to the ground between two cars in a car park, pulled his clothes off and had oral sex with him. He then asked the boy to perform the same service on himself. He was identified, many months later, by DNA evidence from swabs taken from the boy at the time. Today the CPS want another adjournment. Because of the seriousness of the case, we grant it, even though there have already been months of delay, which is good for neither the defendant nor his alleged victim, who is still only a child.

A dreadlocked man is brought up from the cells and

marches into the dock like a cockerel, staring defiantly around the court. He is charged with dishonestly causing to be 'wasted or diverted a quantity of electricity of value unknown'. He pleads guilty to this, but not guilty to common assault and making threats to kill. It was the alleged victim, his landlord, who had assaulted, drugged and kidnapped him, *he maintains.*

What unfolds is deeply depressing. The man started offending when he was quite young. He became addicted to crack cocaine. When other people started using his flat as a drop-in drugs den despite all his efforts to keep them out, he left. He slept on the streets, used his benefits to buy drugs and supplemented his meagre income by begging. He began to suffer from hallucinations and heard 'voices'. He had two small children. He had built up £3,500 of debts and owed a fine to the court which he had not even begun to pay off. Two warrants have been issued for his arrest in that connection, but in any case he is now in prison on remand to the crown court, charged with possessing an offensive weapon. The pre-sentence report is frankly despairing. It could hardly have been anything else.

The man's lawyer says that fiddling the electricity meter was 'a crime of economic necessity'. His client now claims to have given up drugs and is 'trying to start up an Internet café'. The mind boggles. Nevertheless, the electricity company has no idea how much or little power he has wasted or diverted, and compared with the other matters he faces, this one does not seem to weigh heavily in the scales of justice. We decide to fine him a moderate amount for the electricity fraud, but to deem it as payable by a day in the cells, which he has already served. 'So now you're free to go,' says the chairman benignly, before remembering the man's current situation and adding with an embarrassed smile, 'except that I believe you are still in custody'.

P.S. Home Secretary Jack Straw has made a speech in

*the East End of London attacking defence lawyers. 'The
mitigating evidence for conviction is sometimes a load of
old cobblers,' he snorted. 'I was a barrister years ago. If
you were stuck you'd come up with the fact that they had
got a girlfriend who was pregnant, they were getting a job
on the Monday, all sorts of other stuff.' But for sure he
never heard anyone plead for leniency on the grounds that
his client was starting up an Internet café.*

BEAK TALK
As threats to the magistracy mounted, JPs rallied

Rumblings about Lord Justice Auld's review of the criminal
courts system had been piling up throughout the summer and
autumn. JPs received a particular jolt from the evidence sub-
mitted to Auld by the Justices' Clerks' Society, representing the
senior legal advisers and administrative executives in the
magistrates' courts system. It appeared that the sheepdogs
did not, after all, think very highly of the sheep. The JCS
proposed a new, three-tiered court structure. At the top of the
pyramid would be a version of the crown courts, as now. The
medium-level, second-tier bench would consist of a professional chairman flanked by three lay justices to deal with all
imprisonable offences carrying a jail sentence of up to two
years. All other cases, including the whole range of non-
imprisonable offences which presently form the bulk of magistrates' court work, would be heard by a professional judge
sitting alone.

The JCS's submission was tantamount to saying that unac-
companied lay justices were not to be relied upon. It did not go
down at all well with the Magistrates' Association. Chairman
Harry Mawdsley, a former university sports science lecturer,
showed his muscle. 'These proposals would destroy the lay
magistracy as it exists at the present time. There would be no
place for the lay magistracy in the proposed first tier, at best a

subordinate role in the second tier . . . The Magistrates' Association totally rejects these proposals.

'We find it inconceivable that the Justices' Clerks' Society has put forward proposals which completely undermine the lay magistracy. Our relationship with the Justices' Clerks' Society has been a close and important one reflecting the relationship that we have with our justices' clerks at local level. These proposals place that relationship in jeopardy.

'What gives rise to even greater concern and anger is the statement . . . "*we recognise that the current system of lay magistrates and juries has a number of weaknesses in relation to consistency and efficiency*". For the justices' clerks to accuse the lay magistracy of inconsistency when they have the influence and ability to bring about the effective use of the Magistrates' Courts Sentencing Guidelines by every bench in the country is beyond belief. To be accused of inconsistency by those outside the system is bad enough, but this comes from justices' clerks who advise and support magistrates in every aspect of our judicial work . . .'

This was bare-knuckle stuff, one would have thought. But in Haringey the spat caused barely a comment. Relations between justices and clerks remained as friendly as before. In general, however, magistrates shared Mr Mawdsley's belligerence towards possible future threats. In the letters columns of the Association's magazine, *The Magistrate*, lay justices rushed to support their chairman. Les Arnott of South Yorkshire said JPs should not be concerned. 'The Lord Chancellor will have pointed out to Mr Blair that the current magistracy are unpaid volunteers.

'It is inconceivable that a sudden or even gradual changeover to an inferior continental system will be tolerated by a majority of JPs. They will simply resign and such a transition would not and could not take place against the backcloth of fear that justice and the rule of law would descend into anarchy. No such transition could be risked. Fear no more.'

Anne Foot of Bristol and North Avon also called us to the

colours: 'As lay magistrates we must reassert some of the positive aspects of our work:

- Judicial independence, safeguarded because we are unpaid volunteers.
- The knowledge of the local community and their concerns.
- The breadth of experience and background skills that three people draw upon, plus the legal advice from the clerk.
- Magistrates are chosen for their "common sense" and have sworn to act without "fear or favour".
- Of all the areas within the judicial system, we have more members from ethnic minority groups.
- In spite of dealing with over 95 per cent of all criminal cases, only 4 per cent are taken to appeal – which must reflect a confidence in our judicial decisions.'

I dare say Lord Irvine would have agreed with Anne Foot, though C. W. Elton of Merseyside, also in a letter to *The Magistrate*, took leave to doubt it: 'I wonder,' he wrote, 'if I am the only magistrate that finds the pronouncements of the Lord Chancellor concerning the selection of magistrates bizarre.

'Time after time I have read and heard him say that the magistracy should reflect the community we live in and be chosen from a cross section of that community. All very commendable except for the fact that judges are picked from a public school background, followed by Oxford and Cambridge and ending in chambers to become a barrister. How can they preach to us and at the same time not live on the same planet?'

This sentiment was echoed subsequently in a letter to *The Times* from a woman JP, Gill Morrison, challenging the proposition that justice would be better served by replacing lay magistrates with professional district judges. She had never met a judge under forty or one who lived in a council flat, she pointed out, nor were there all that many who were female. By contrast, on her own bench 'my colleagues have come from all backgrounds, every race and religion, and have had some fascinating life experiences, through their work on the buses, council, rag trade, fire service, social work, market trading, to name but a few. They are of all ages.' Everyone, concluded Mrs Morrison stoutly, should do a stint as a JP.

There was another letter in *The Times* that year which demonstrated the magisterial spirit in fiery form. The author was a Mrs Agnes Grunwald-Spier JP. She was provoked by the perplexing appointment of former BBC Director-General John Birt to be the Prime Minister's 'crime adviser'.

'Sir,' she wrote, 'Lord Birt is to be an unpaid adviser to Tony Blair on crime, bringing "a fresh set of eyes to the project instead of years of received wisdom". In other words he really knows nothing about the subject.

'I have been a magistrate since 1984 and now sit on criminal cases and the family panel. I have been continually trained over the years and for this I have never received any payment. I have read hundreds of pre-sentence reports and listened to hundreds of defence solicitors explaining how a particular offence occurred.

'I have three sons aged twenty-one, eighteen and fifteen, and chair a safe house for women in Sheffield. Most of our residents are fleeing domestic violence and/or drug and alcohol related problems . . . I think I, and many others like me, have a better idea of what causes crime and what to do about it. Why does No.10 never ring us?'

Meantime there were honeyed words from the Lord Chancellor. 'Lay magistrates represent civic engagement in the justice system and government has no intention of removing them,' he announced in December 2000. 'The unpaid work of the lay magistracy is greatly valued by the Government and we are committed to ensuring they continue to play a significant part in the criminal justice system.'

The same month came the results of research jointly commissioned by the Home Office and the Lord Chancellor's Department. It was rather encouraging. The report, *The Judiciary in the Magistrates' Courts*, found that 'the lay magistracy is gender balanced and ethnically representative of the population at a national level, whereas stipendiaries are mostly male and white'. It showed that on average a lay magistrate sat in court for 41.4 half-day sessions a year, whereas stipes sat about four days a week – a statistic which lent some weight to the argument that the professionals are liable to be more case-hardened than the amateurs. The research also showed that although district judges were much faster and more efficient than lay magistrates, they were also more likely to refuse bail and make use of 'immediate custody as a sentence', which in turn had significant cost implications, since imprisonment is expensive. All in all, the report seemed to be good news for JPs. It concluded that eliminating or greatly diminishing the role of the lay magistrates would not be 'widely understood or supported' by the general public – a verdict only slightly marred by the finding that 73 per cent of this same general public did not know the difference between lay and stipendiary magistrates anyway.

But still, unease persisted. If Lord Irvine and Sir Robin Auld were not about to consign JPs to the coffin of history, many grumbled, there were other forces at work which might achieve the same result. This was the suspicion that 'they' (unspecified) were deliberately increasing the burden of training sessions and appraisal procedures to the point where existing magistrates would resign in frustration and new applicants would be put off volunteering. Proposed court amalgamations would have the same demoralising effect. Such conspiracy theories were not to be taken seriously. But there was some truth in the accusation that mounting demands on JPs' time were being imposed without careful consideration of the consequences.

I 'met' Anne Walker, Deputy Chair of the South-East Suffolk bench, courtesy of the lively Internet chat room run by the Magistrates' Association. She was a recently-retired member of her area Advisory Committee, which interviews and recommends the appointment of new magistrates. In her nine years on the committee, had she noticed any falling-off of enthusiasm?

She had. The number of applicants had dropped quite sharply from a healthy fifty to sixty a year when she first joined the panel. Anne herself became a JP at the age of thirty-two, but these days very few people as young as that – especially young men – came forward. Now the majority of male applicants were either early-retired or successfully self-employed. The rest simply couldn't afford to take the time off work, never mind commit themselves to the extensive training. The amalgamation of local courts had not helped either. It was not just defendants who were inconvenienced. Some magistrates found themselves having to put up with twenty-mile journeys each way.

All of this might indeed make the idea of becoming a JP seem less attractive than it used to be. Anne said her bench had a good relationship with the Suffolk press, but nonetheless she felt people had far too little positive information about what the magistracy did or the great fund of goodwill which kept local justice alive and well. (Interestingly, she said, among those who did apply to join the bench, quite a number first had their curiosity aroused by the experience of doing jury service – as I did myself.)

What really concerned Anne about the future, however, was the general dwindling of community spirit. People used to be drawn into public service via organisations like the Round Table and Rotary Clubs. These days younger men and women did not want to belong to such bodies. They preferred to live their own lives. In the long run, thought Anne, this tendency to stand aside spelt a threat to the survival of the lay magistracy quite as real as anything Lord Justice Auld or the conspiracy theorists might be dreaming up.

DEFENDER OF JUSTICES
England's top judge praises the amateurs

Having talked to the previous Lord Chief Justice, I thought it would be a good idea to compare his views with those of the present one, Lord Woolf. He readily agreed to see me to talk about the lay magistracy. We had met once before, but it was plainly the subject of the interview rather than the identity of the interviewer that made him so obliging.

I was shown into his offices at the Royal Courts of Justice in the Strand – more vanishingly lofty ceilings and towering bookshelves. These legal lords must suffer from a kind of *de bas en haute* vertigo. It was just three days before the new Lord Chief Justice was going to have to pronounce judgment on the length of time the boy murderers of little Jamie Bulger should spend in detention – a decision which had lately been taken out of the Home Secretary's hands and passed to the judiciary by the European Court of Human Rights. Those who knew Harry Woolf as a humane and liberal judge correctly predicted that he would revert to the original eight-year tariff rather than confirm the fifteen years set by Conservative Home Secretary Michael Howard. For a man about to provoke a great squall of anguished controversy, he seemed completely unruffled, looking at ease in a cosy blue cardigan with leather elbow patches amidst the imprisoning walls of legal tomes all round him.

'Rather different from the last time we met,' Lord Woolf chuckled. It certainly was. On that occasion we had been eating grilled flying fish on a moonlit beach in Barbados. Now he was Lord Chief Justice of England and Wales and we were drinking instant coffee instead of planter's punch.

You would expect him to be a supporter of the lay magistracy. His wife Marguerite is a long-serving JP. From 1986 to 1990 he himself was chairman of the Middlesex Advisory Committee, the body which selects and oversees magistrates for my own area of London. 'One of the particular problems we had to deal with at that time was the relationship between magistrates and the new batch of stipendiaries we were introducing to ease the workload. Not surprisingly, the magistrates were a little bit nervous that they'd be put in a back room to deal with all the rubbish while the stipes got the interesting cases. Fortunately that didn't happen.'

And what about the present day? Lord Woolf drank some coffee and picked his words with care. 'The lay magistracy is a unique and marvellous system,' he said. 'I value it immensely. As far as I'm concerned any reforms would have to be ones which preserved the strengths of the system, which I see as the involvement of the public in the administration of justice in a way which is wholly desirable.

'I think it is unfortunate there is evidence to suggest that some benches are not as ethnically neutral as they should be. I don't know how reliable the research is . . .' He hesitated judiciously. 'I am not sure that the perception is justified. But I believe the better training that magistrates are having now, including racial awareness, will meet that problem.

'Some of my predecessors were not research-friendly. They thought it could be damaging to the independence of the judiciary. I take a different view and think it can only be helpful. Statistical analysis as to punishments – that sort of research can help. In the recent fracas about curtailing the right to trial by jury, the strongest argument that was advanced was a lack of confidence in the magistracy among defendants from the racial minorities. But that's capable of being tackled.

'I see the magistracy as a huge champion of independence in the administration of justice. So it is essential that we tackle such problems as do exist. When I have visitors from abroad, especially from the new East European democracies, one of the aspects of our system which they admire most is the magistracy. They think it's wonderful.'

'Not just because it's cheaper?'

'I don't believe it is cheaper. There's so much more admin-istration involved in having part-timers. But it's worth it be-cause of the involvement of the public and the independence. If we didn't have such a system, we'd be very well advised to develop one.' This was an encomium indeed and I found myself grinning foolishly, as though being given a pat on the back by the headmaster.

'The other aspect you have to take into account is that if you had to replace all the lay magistrates with professional judges, the calibre of the judge would not be as good as the calibre of the magistracy.' This was a new line of argument to me.

'The lowest tier of the judiciary in many jurisdictions around the world is sadly lacking, for many different reasons. In some jurisdictions you cut your teeth as a professional judge doing work which would be done by magistrates here. You get a whole lot of callow youngsters going out administering justice and gaining experience that way in dealing with the public. One of the problems with such judges is they hide their inexperience by being incredibly pompous. In other jurisdictions, where they have professional judges and have to find large numbers of them, the people who will take an appointment which involves no more than doing magistrate-style work are not always very inspiring.' That, I took it, was British understatement.

'Of course the magistracy now makes more demands, so it's harder to find younger people who'll do it. But I don't know whether we need to have too many young people on the bench. Obviously it's desirable. But judging is an old person's profession.' Lord Woolf, born in 1933, laughed jovially. 'That is one of the things you bring – your experience of life.'

It was time for me to leave. 'I'm giving a judgment at 10.30,' said the Lord Chief Justice unhurriedly. That was in just a few minutes' time. 'I don't think the magistracy needs me as a defender,' he added. 'But if required, it is a role I would readily adopt.'

GUT FEELINGS
If Labour had doubts about JPs, what about the Tories?

I asked to see Ann Widdecombe, then shadowing Jack Straw on home affairs. She was a bit of an enigma: tough on cannabis, tough on fox-hunting, and tough on that toughest of Tory home secretaries, Michael Howard, who she'd said had 'something of the night' about him. Where would she line up on the lay magistracy?

At the mini-branch of Boots beside Westminster tube station there was a queue to buy umbrellas. The rain had caught the tourists unawares. No. 1 Parliament Street is opposite the Treasury, where Chancellor Gordon Brown was biting his nails (one paper had a nauseating front page close-up of them) in anticipation of the next day's Autumn Statement. No. 1 provides offices and the cheapest bar in town for MPs of all parties, but the waiting room gave a decidedly partisan impression. It was presided over by an excellent portrait of Edward Heath in a tweed suit and green tie, his stomach swelling like *Morning Cloud*'s spinnaker in a Force 3 breeze, and a bronze of Michael Heseltine's leonine head sculpted by Anne Curry in 1999. She has given him a protruding right eyebrow you could sharpen pencils on.

Ann Widdecombe was in a plum-coloured suit with a silver cross around her neck. Her office had an anti-abortion poster on one wall and a round table where we drank coffee. She was brisk, as always. She didn't want to see any fundamental changes in the magistracy, she said firmly. 'I will look carefully to see what comes out of the Auld report, and I shall try to approach it with an open mind, but at the moment I don't believe the case for change has been made. There are two issues here. The first is, who is the appropriate person to try the accused, and the second is whether, where you have a magistrate input, that should be lay or stipendiary.'

These issues were of particular importance because of the Government's attempts to get its Mode of Trial Bill through Parliament. 'Our view when it was proposed to restrict the right to trial by jury was that if you were going to remove a fundamental British liberty of that sort, you had to be able to show that the benefits justified doing so. And we believed they didn't. There were savings, but according to the Government's own figures they accrued largely from sending fewer people to prison – because lay magistrates give fewer and shorter custodial sentences. Two-thirds of the savings arose from this. We said that wasn't a valid saving. The other supposed benefit was that it would streamline the system. But because there would be more appeals about mode of trial, this would simply introduce another raft of delays. So we weren't convinced by that either.'

Despite a Tory Home Secretary, the aforementioned Mr Howard, having started that particular ball rolling?

'Oh,' said Ann quickly, 'there was no reason why we shouldn't have looked at it. We were right to consider very seriously doing it and we were right to decide not to. We also thought that the abolition of the automatic right to elect jury trial in "either-way" cases would have meant more stipes. What Jack Straw and Derry Irvine would have said is that magistrates can now try more important cases: therefore we need a bigger professional input. Therefore we need more stipes.' (This was an argument which my fellow magistrates, who were rather keen on Straw's proposals in the hope of getting more big cases coming their way, might not have considered.)

'I think there may be a long-term view in some quarters that we should move towards the European form of justice and have an inquisitorial system and that the professionalisation of the bench would be part of that move. That is our gut feeling about what is going on.'

Whether that would remain the Conservatives' gut feeling after the 2001 general election and the change of party leader it was impossible then to judge. But as she looked forward to whatever Lord Justice Auld might recommend, it was clear that here was one senior Tory who strongly supported the tradition of lay justice and would fight to keep it intact. 'I served on a jury myself in 1983,' she said emphatically. 'The jury is an extremely conscientious body of people. Have you read a book called *The Juryman's Tale*?'

'Well, yes,' I replied modestly. 'I wrote it.'

'Uh? Oh! Of course,' exploded Ann without embarrassment. 'Anyway, the great merit of both the jury and the lay magistracy is that they bring common sense to the judicial system.' As for trying to get a representative balance of JPs from different class and ethnic backgrounds, of course she was in favour. 'I approve of trying to get a good mix on the bench,' she enthused. For a moment Miss Widdecombe, she of zero tolerance for dopeheads and detention camps for asylum seekers, sounded as if she were about to go all soppy and politically correct. Then the no-nonsense bluffness reasserted itself. 'But whatever that mix is, all black or all white, is irrelevant. All that matters is if they are good, sound, sensible people.'

Highgate. A woman applying for a protection order, which will allow her to take over the management of a pub until her full licence is processed, is asked whether she'd like to take the oath on the New Testament, the Old Testament, the Koran, or affirm. 'I don't really mind,' she says coolly. The gravity of what is meant by being 'on oath' no longer seems to weigh very heavily in the public mind, despite the fate of the perjured Jonathan Aitken (and, in due course, Jeffrey Archer).

While we wait for the principals in a trial to gather themselves, we chat about the old days. Jeanette, a librarian, remembers that she was one of the first women on our bench to wear trousers. 'I'd had an operation on my leg and trousers were more convenient. That was in the 1970s. Things were still pretty stuffy then. When we had coffee in the retiring room it was brought to us by a member of court staff. One morning I wanted a refill and there was no one there to help, so I went into the kitchen and poured my own. The chairman of the bench was very disapproving. He made an extraordinary remark. "You forward minx!" he barked.'

Another minor revolution took place around that time, Jeanette recalls. Rastafarian defendants had been routinely asked to remove their woolly hats in the dock in order to show respect. But then someone pointed out that it was surely unfair for Rastafarians to have to bare their heads when Jews were allowed to keep their yarmulkes on and

*Sikhs their turbans. Quite right – though come to think of
it, so far I have seen neither a yarmulke nor a turban in the
dock, only on the bench.*

RIGHTS STUFF
So much for the Act that had caused such concern

The panic over the Human Rights Act was already dying down.
Perhaps we wouldn't be stoking up so much trouble for Lord
Bingham, after all. The one, probably apocryphal, story we had
all heard concerned the case of a motorist caught by a speed
camera who had her case overturned on the grounds that the
police had contravened her right to privacy by asking her who
was driving the car at the time. This example of self-evident
nonsense had not yet surfaced in any of our courts. Other
instances of the Act being cited had been innocuous, while the
requirement for magistrates to give full, public and explicit
reasons for their verdicts and sentences, which had caused so
much advance trepidation, had proved surprisingly popular.
Harry Mawdsley went on record saying: 'I see giving reasons as
an excellent opportunity for magistrates to state clearly how a
decision has been reached in words that the defendant can easily
understand . . . and that can only be good.'

On a winter evening we were summoned to one of our
irregular but fairly frequent training events to practise giving
reasoned sentences. His Honour Judge Shaun Lyons, formerly
of the Royal Navy, now resident judge at Wood Green Crown
Court, was in the chair.

We were divided into groups and sent off to different courtrooms to discuss four knotty hypothetical cases. A spokes-
person for each group would have to stand up and explain
the sentences it had reached once everyone had returned to
Court 1, where Judge Lyons presided. Our group of eight,
overseen by two legal advisers, argued its way through each
case in the approved structured manner. We considered the

seriousness of the offence, the aggravating and mitigating factors, whether or not the offence was racially motivated or committed while on bail, the offender's previous record and any circumstances in his favour. We decided our sentence, reduced it if the offender had pleaded guilty at an early stage, and considered whether to award compensation.

Once we had reassembled in Court 1, His Honour looked down beakishly. One by one each group presented its sentencing decisions and explained them. There was a variety of conclusions and some marginally embarrassing contrasts – one group sentencing to custody in a case of affray, for example, while all the others went for probation. The probationers thought they had 'won' – until Judge Lyons revealed that he, the bench chairman, Ann, and the Justices' Chief Executive, Mr Fillingham, reviewing the case as a troika, had also gone for custody.

'There is no such thing as a *correct* sentence,' the judge beamed when he saw our somewhat abashed countenances. Each bench could only do what it thought was right and just, he said. True but troubling.

It occurred to me that if the Human Rights Act was helping to make the reasoning behind magistrates' decisions more logical and transparent, there could be another area in which its influence might conceivably turn out to be beneficial, contrary to expectations. This was the whole business of case management. Although much has been done to speed up the process, in both adult and youth courts, new magistrates are often dumbfounded by the extraordinary inefficiencies they encounter in the administration of the courts. Time after time cases must be adjourned owing to some simple failure of communication. A defendant has gone to the wrong courthouse or made a mistake about the date of his hearing. A witness has not been given notice of the trial. A police officer is off sick or on holiday in Australia (true). The relevant prosecution paperwork has not been served on the defence in good time. An interpreter has gone to the wrong court.

Obtaining the details of a person's motoring record from the Driver and Vehicle Licensing Agency in Swansea can take half a day. Finding a slot in the court schedule for a trial to take place may bring the court to a standstill for twenty minutes while the clerk makes phone calls to the administration department down the corridor and everyone else sits staring at the ceiling.

Again and again, cases due for committal to the crown court are not ready and the prosecutor asks for an adjournment. The commonest reason for delay is that the hard-pressed and understaffed police have not completed all the paperwork or got it to the Crown Prosecution Service in time. No wonder older JPs look back nostalgically to the pre-CPS days, when the police brought their own prosecutions and were therefore much more reliable about doing their prep. A former Detective Inspector at Scotland Yard told me he used to enjoy prosecuting as a young constable. 'When you had ownership of the case you always wanted to go that extra mile.'

To the novice eye, the present set-up can seem bewilderingly primitive. This is the age of e-mail and the Internet, after all, and it is a very rare defendant or witness who doesn't have a mobile phone – we once had a diddle-ah-da-diddle-ah-da-diddle-ah-da-dee go off in the middle of someone taking the oath. There really ought to be no excuse for everyone concerned in a hearing not to be alerted in time and confirm their intention to appear, or for all the documentation not to be available and in the right hands. Getting a print-out from DVLA or booking a trial date should be the work of a moment. On each of the legal advisers' desks in the Haringey courts sits a gleaming computer screen and keyboard. Yet they are never even switched on. It is baffling.

So I wonder whether this is where the Human Rights Act may be a spur. Article 5, which concerns the right to liberty and security, states that anyone in detention must have its lawfulness 'decided speedily' by the court. Under Article 6, the right to a fair trial, everyone is entitled to a hearing 'within a reasonable time'. This is surely an opportunity defence lawyers will want to exploit, not always for the best of motives. But if it helps to shake up the prevailing adjournment culture, it will be a good thing. Otherwise it will soon occur to someone that if there was a case for privatising the security arrangements in our courts, there is perhaps an even stronger one for doing the same with their administration.

Highgate. A man and a woman are in the dock together. She, in a well-cut wasp waisted grey suit, is charged with being drunk and disorderly and obstructing a police officer; he with threatening behaviour and assaulting two police officers. But there's something odd about all this. We keep going in and out of court while the prose-cutor asks for more time to sort things out. During our repeated visits to the retiring room, the chairwoman finishes off all the pink wafer-creams.

Strangely, the woman prosecutor eventually asks for the defendants to be bound over to keep the peace, which is more or less an admission that she can't get the case together. Either that or there's something else afoot. The altercation arose from a reported domestic incident which never actually took place. A police dog called Charlie was involved. He is outside in the court car park in a police-dog van, waiting to give evidence. The police officers involved also agree that a bind-over would be acceptable. This is all quite mysterious until the defence lawyer produces photographs of what Charlie the dog did to the male defendant during the altercation. Charlie's fangs inflicted a good deal of damage. There were ragged tooth holes in the man's arm, leg and stomach.

Charlie was to have been produced as some sort of canine witness or exhibit for the defence, it seems. We can only wonder why. Perhaps the police were heavy-handed in investigating this false-alarm domestic incident. Maybe Charlie was over-zealous and went into action when his services were, shall we say, surplus to requirements? Aha.

Perhaps the police were worried about an official complaint. That seems the likeliest story. Whatever the truth, we can do no more than speculate, while accepting the all-party proposal for a bind-over. I go outside into the wintry sunshine to catch a glimpse of Charlie, red in tooth and claw. But like an SAS witness or a supergrass, he is kept from view behind the darkened windows of the van, until his handler drives him away. No Bonios for Charlie, I surmise.

I am transferred to Court 2 to fill in for an absent magistrate. A tall white man with the looks of a demented Donald Sutherland is accused of racially aggravated harassment. Racially aggravated anything is pretty serious these days, adding considerably to the gravity of the basic offence. Ironically, given the ethnic sensitivities of the case, the defendant is represented by a young black barrister who appears rather nervous behind her glasses and speaks with soft African vowel sounds, while the prosecutor, Mrs Kwan, speaks with an attractive Chinese accent. Donald Sutherland seems to have difficulty hearing, or at any rate understanding, either of them. He stands in the dock, bending over awkwardly so that he can press his ear against the gap in the security glass. He pleads not guilty with some vehemence.

According to Mrs Kwan, the defendant was harassing the husband and wife in the flat above his for six years by playing music very loudly. There had been official complaints to the council, confrontations. On one of these occasions, the defendant shouted 'Fuck off, you black bastard' at his neighbour and called him a 'black nutter', says Mrs Kwan fastidiously. He told the man's pregnant wife: 'I will destroy your child.'

The defence barrister loses her nervousness. She says her client was himself assaulted by the male victim on two occasions. What was more, on the day of the alleged 'Fuck off, you black bastard' incident, her client was somewhere else and could prove it. 'This was a concoction by the two victims,' she asserts boldly.

The bench must decide whether it should accept jurisdiction or, given the aggravating racial element, send the case up to the crown court for trial, as the prosecution has proposed. To justify this, we would have to consider that, in the event of the man's being found guilty, he might face more than six months' imprisonment – a sentence beyond our powers to impose. In the wake of the Stephen Lawrence report, everyone is acutely aware of the need not to underrate the evil of racism. Nevertheless, we decide pretty quickly that the matter can be dealt with in the magistrates' court. So a date has to be fixed for a half-day hearing. The prosecution will be calling four witnesses, says Mrs Kwan. Donald Sutherland looks defiant. He will want to call fifteen witnesses, he announces through the gap in the security glass. Fifteen? Better make that a whole-day hearing, Mr Legal Adviser, says the chair, concealing his astonishment.

CHAPTER 9

Ancient and Modern

*'The worst offence you can commit round here is hitting a
racehorse crossing the road in Newmarket'*

The St Edmundsbury and Stowmarket Magistrates' Court is in
the old Shire Hall in Bury St Edmunds, an agreeable brick
building erected in 1830. Compared with the great palace of
summary justice in Birmingham, it is little more than a doll's
house, but a rather fine one. There are just two courtrooms,
even though – this being the county town of West Suffolk – the
local crown court also shares the premises.

The Shire Hall overlooks the ruins of the famous eleventh-
century abbey and the sprawling cathedral graveyard, a favourite place for visitors to stroll at warmer times of year. The
juxtaposition of death and the law is appropriate. It was as the
result of local justices or their equivalent sentencing a murderer
that the 25-year-old King Edmund of East Anglia became a
Christian martyr more than a thousand years ago. The killer, a
man called Berne, was punished by being cast adrift in the
North Sea – a sentence which would have some appeal today to
frustrated magistrates, I fancy. Unfortunately, Berne survived
and was washed up on the shores of Denmark, where he
vengefully persuaded the locals that East Anglia was ripe for
invasion.

The marauding Danes duly arrived, raping and pillaging as
was the Danish way, circa AD 870. The saintly young king
offered himself up as a hostage so as to spare his people, but
when he refused to renounce his Christianity he was tied to a
tree and shot to death with arrows, like St Sebastian. Then his
head was chopped off and tossed into a wood. According to
legend, his mourning people found the head thanks to the
baying of an old grey wolf which was standing guard over

the bloody relic. Naturally enough, this horrid but holy sequence of events called for a shrine. The abbey was built in St
Edmund's memory and became a famous place of pilgrimage.

I was standing in the forecourt, gazing at the ancient grave-
stones through the rain and contemplating this cautionary tale
against lenient sentencing, when I heard an anguished shouting
and banging coming from the south side of the Shire Hall. The
walls gave straight onto a quiet little street called Honey Lane. I
went to have a look.

A woman was kneeling on the wet pavement with her head
bent down, plaintively yelling through the heavy iron bars of a
low window. Behind the frosted glass I could make out a
shadowy head. The woman knocked at the glass, the rain fell
coldly on her thinly-clad shoulders and the shadow jerked
about. Down there below street level, I realised with an agreeable shiver, were the old Shire Hall's pre-Victorian cells.

A winter morning in an ancient market town . . . a deranged
woman on her knees in the street, in the rain . . . her indistinct
prisoner of a husband, lover, son, awaiting trial . . . It could
have been a scene straight out of Thomas Hardy. Alas for my
romantic imagination, what she was actually doing was berat-
ing her partner over what he'd done with the keys to the fucking
Fiesta.

Court 1 was a light, handsome, square room with an unusual
box-like arrangement for the lawyers, who sat in a sort of
wooden cockpit around three sides of a large table. The dock
was at the side of the court, not very secure, easy to leap out of.
There was an awkward gap between the stairs to the cells and
the entrance to the dock where a determined prisoner could
make a break, but in fact most of the young men we saw that
morning were led to a pew at the back of the court rather than
into the dock itself.

The first prisoner up was a meek little lad, heeling to star-
board under the weight of a heavy bunch of keys attached to his
belt along with a massive Swiss army knife whose corkscrew
was dangerously open. Was he Mr Hope? asked the clerk.

'Farrell Hope,' replied the lad.

'Is that hyphenated?'

'I dunno,' mumbled the perplexed youth. He faced seven charges of being drunk and disorderly and causing criminal damage. Seven times he said 'Guilty', whereupon we learnt that he was in breach of a conditional discharge for previous drunk and disorderly offences. Despite appearances, young Mr Farrell Hope or Farrell-hyphen-Hope was evidently a one-man bar-room brawl.

Up from the cells came a meagre, rat-faced man. He had been harassing a woman in direct breach of a bail condition while he awaited the outcome of a previous charge of harassing the same woman in defiance of an injunction. The bail condition was that he should not contact her in any way, shape or form. But he had written her a three-page letter, on lined notepaper. It begged her to give him 'another chance' and threatened suicide. Rat-face looked like a man incapable of strong emotions. Yet who could tell? Some hidden passion was driving the woebegone creature back to this woman again and again, even at the risk of imprisonment. Hardy, I thought once more, just as a prolonged wail penetrated the courtroom from Honey Lane.

Gareth Davies, a regular prosecutor in the Shire Hall, told me that before motorways made it so easy for criminals to travel to work, local crime was largely confined to twenty or thirty families whom everybody knew. The next defendant strode up from the cells with a swagger that suggested he might belong to one of them. He winked at his wife in the public gallery. The court was primarily dealing with him for the theft of a closed circuit TV. This was a pretty cheeky offence in itself – the modern equivalent of Bertie Wooster snatching a policeman's helmet, perhaps. But what was even more revealing of his attitude to the law was that he was not only in breach of bail for this matter: he was also in breach of a community service order for another and had, furthermore, failed to surrender to bail in the crown court in regard to a third. So back to jail he must go. He smiled happily as he was taken down, shouting goodbye to his wife, as if a spell behind bars were no more than a routine part of family life – which perhaps it was.

There was a trial going on in Court 2, a large, rectangular upstairs room with lofty windows overlooking the cemetery. The three magistrates, two women and a man, sat at a great table at the end facing the windows. They were on the same level as everyone else, though the bench gained a certain gravity from a heavy, high-backed throne to the right of them. It was an imposing bit of furniture. This was the chairman's chair from the magistrates' court at Stowmarket, Maureen the chief usher explained to me. When Stowmarket was merged with St Edmundsbury, the chair was installed in the Shire Hall as a symbol of the union. A burglar who specialised in antiques and had recently appeared in this courtroom had confided to Maureen that it was worth a bob or two.

The charge was driving while disqualified. The accused sat in front of what had been the focus of the room in the days before central heating, the capacious hearth. Behind him rose a marble fireplace with an oak surround. Peter was a dark, good-looking young man. He wore a sharp grey suit, yellow shirt, striped tie and an aggrieved expression.

A bonny WPC with auburn hair which clashed with her Remembrance Day poppy was giving evidence.

'Tell us in your own words what happened next,' said the prosecutor.

'I got out of my vehicle,' she explained in a calm, clear voice, 'having displayed my blue police light upon my vehicle . . .' She was on the shortish side so she seemed rather swamped by all her kit: handcuffs, CS gas canister, radio and other mysterious bulges. The awkward protection and restraint stick came down to her knees. She had to fight her way through all this clobber to pull her notebook out of a pocket.

As the WPC spoke, the defendant went through a variety of gestures to indicate that she was not telling the truth, the whole truth and nothing but the truth. He threw his eyes to the ceiling. He shook his head violently. He gave sardonic smiles. He frowned in exasperation. It was a performance that might have had some effect with a jury but in this case he merely earned a request from the bench to restrain himself.

The WPC stood up to cross-examination without deviation or hesitation, though with a good deal of stolid repetition. 'I got out of my vehicle, having displayed my blue police light upon my vehicle . . .' The defending solicitor said that according to his client, the WPC knew him well. They'd met on various occasions. She had regularly patrolled near his house. He'd twice offered her cups of tea while she was on duty in her car at the end of his street.

When he gave evidence, Peter made much of this. At which point it dawned on me what the defence line was going to be. Here, it seemed, was a prime example of the particular difficulties associated with local justice among a small population.

Peter was being targeted, claimed his younger brother Mark. 'In Bury St Edmunds, if you give the police any chat, they'll arrest you for it.' The officer had agreed she had met the defendant once or twice in the course of her duties, but said she didn't remember ever being offered cups of tea. On the other hand, she did call him by his first name, Peter, when she arrested him . . . Hmmm. The bench was being invited to think that the police were pursuing a vendetta, by no means an improbable situation in a tight-knit community where, traditionally, as Gareth Davies had said, a small number of families were responsible for a large number of crimes.

A further insight into the nature of local justice was revealed as the prosecutor cross-examined the brother. Mark, too, was wearing a dark suit, with a very long jacket, and thick-soled loafers. He had shoulder-length hair with blond tints and his hands were trembling. 'Do you know what perjury is?' he was asked. 'I certainly do,' Mark replied. But now Mr Davies wanted to ask Mark about his own character. I guessed the prosecutor had come across the witness before and knew what he was talking about. Mark was candid. 'I've had a tainted past,' he whined, sounding like a truculent Uriah Heep. He stumbled reluctantly through his previous misbehaviour: obstruction of police, assault on police officers, theft . . . His voice faded.

'Any other offences?'

'Not to my recollection . . .' Oh, maybe a drink-driving, he added as an afterthought – when he was fifteen.

Peter's girlfriend (fiancée, she corrected), who had brought their six-month-old baby to court in a pushchair, was also aware of what perjury meant, she said. And she insisted that her child's father had driven nowhere that night. It was true he had been in the car when the WPC approached him, but it had been stationary: Peter was merely installing a stereo system in it, she said.

'The bench will retire,' said the chairman, once the defending lawyer had made his closing speech, arguing that there were several doubts in the prosecution case and that the defendant should get the benefit of them. He was at pains to make it clear he was not accusing the officer of lying, merely of having made a mistake. It was not so much a question of whose evidence the bench believed as to which it preferred. He made nothing of Mark's suggestion, and Peter's implication, of police victimisation. Nevertheless, the suspicion remained in the air. And it occurred to me that in the wake of the Macpherson report, had the defendant, his brother and girlfriend all been black or Asian, the suspicion might have been magnified by a decisive factor.

The magistrates took a good fifty minutes to make their decision – quite a long time for a summary case. Peter wandered around restlessly. His fiancée and Mark played with the baby in the waiting room. I chatted to Maureen.

A policeman's wife, she had been doing the job for fourteen years and loved it. Like nearly every court usher I have met, men as well as women, she was an amiable soul, bustling about in her black gown, smiling at magistrates and malefactors alike. Most ushers seem to be well over forty-five. It is a second career for the men (like the jolly ex-butcher who shepherded the jury I was on during a four-month trial at the Old Bailey), and a midlife opportunity for women whose children have grown up and left home. 'You have to be a certain age to do this, you see,' Maureen explained. 'Otherwise you couldn't cope with all these lippy youngsters.' You had to be able to keep the toughs in order, but also be ready to reassure those who were nervous and intimidated.

What did I think about this case, she wanted to know: what would the verdict be? Having not heard all the evidence, I wasn't sure. But it seemed to me the prosecution had not made its case beyond reasonable doubt. I asked prosecutor Davies whether he had indeed come across Mark before. Oh yes, he chortled. He knew all about Mark. So did the defence lawyer. But didn't this raise all sorts of problems, if everyone knew about a defendant's or witness's previous record before a trial even began? It could do, if one of the magistrates recognised him. In that situation, the magistrate might have to step down from the bench. Occasionally, if the accused was too notorious locally, he would have to be sent to a court elsewhere in the county for trial.

The bench were still out, so we carried on chatting. Crime in West Suffolk didn't differ all that much from the rest of the country, Gareth and Maureen thought. The days of witch trials were long gone and it was more than 150 years since Mr Pickwick and Sam Weller tracked that arch-conman Jingle to the Angel Inn, Bury St Edmunds, where I had sheltered from the rain on my way to court that morning. Nor was there much poaching any more. Now it was mostly drugs, burglary, drunk and disorderly, a bit of mugging and occasional ram-raids. 'The worst offence you can commit round here is hitting a racehorse crossing the road in New-market,' said the prosecutor.

But court life in the county was not without its dramas, Maureen wanted me to know. 'You could write a book about the things that go on,' she said, her eyes sparkling. For example, there was the man who'd refused to leave the courtroom and superglued his fingers to the dock. The bench was unmoved.

The man was torn away shrieking, leaving bits of skin and blood behind him.

She remembered an attempted escape over at Haverhill. A boy had been brought up from the cells wearing one of those white paper suits the police sometimes put prisoners in when their own clothes are wet or filthy or have fallen apart. The boy tried to jump out of the dock and was immediately set upon by several burly jailers. In the struggle, the paper suit disintegrated and the boy was left standing stark-naked in the well of the court. The magistrates were amazed. One of them was especially struck by the scene and kept repeating the story. 'There he was, with his little willy flapping,' she'd tell her listeners excitedly.

Gareth had a ruder story. 'It was a Monday morning court. The people who'd been arrested over the weekend were coming up before the bench. As usual, all the defence solicitors were trying to get their cases put back so that they could have time to consult their clients. The court was keen to get things moving, so one of the policemen suggested they proceed with the case of a woman who was certain to plead guilty.

'She was what's known round here as a camp follower. She'd come down from the Midlands for the weekend to drum up a bit of business among the American servicemen at the USAF base at Mildenhall. She came into the dock wearing a halter-top, shorts and flip-flops.'

The PC gravely gave his evidence. He had entered a pub. 'I looked into the bar. I saw a woman standing in the middle of the room touching her toes, with her shorts around her ankles. She was saying: "Go on lads, score a bull's-eye!" Then I noted that she had a target tattooed on her bottom.' It was an open and shut case, so to speak, Gareth concluded. What had the human dartboard been charged with? Neither loitering with intent nor indecent exposure seemed quite to measure up to the incident. Drunk and disorderly, thought Gareth.

Even with ushers scrupulously minding their lists, mistakes sometimes occurred, said Maureen, like the father who had come along to court to support his accused son. The usher called out the surname. The bewildered father was thrust into the dock. When the charges were put to him, all he could do was shake his head and say 'I haven't done nothing'. It was only after a while that the court realised the real accused was the man's son, who was downstairs in custody. On another occasion, sixteen men were charged with affray. Mysteriously, there were seventeen men in the dock and they all pleaded guilty. No one could explain this, until it was discovered that the brother of one of the accused had also been summoned by mistake. Bizarrely, the man had pleaded guilty to an offence he hadn't committed.

Years ago, Gareth reminisced, when the local squirearchy pretty much ruled the bench, there was one particularly purple-faced chairman who became notorious for his *obiter dicta*. He once famously addressed a defendant thus: 'I have been told by the clerk that there is some doubt in this case – but you, sir, are not going to get the benefit of it.' This crusty old party was still in action when community service orders were introduced. He listened sceptically as a defence lawyer pleaded that his client should get a CSO rather than a jail sentence. He asked the probation officer who was in court that day to explain what sort of community service the man in the dock might be made to do.

'Well, Your Worship, since this is an agricultural area, maybe he would be of some use on the land,' suggested the probation officer.

'No doubt,' growled the chairman, then added in a loud aside: 'But how would we spread him?'

Prosecutor and usher were well into their anecdotal stride by now. They were just beginning to tell me about an assault at a fancy-dress party where the chief prosecution witness, a stranger in town, was unable to identify the assailants except as Elvis Presley, the Pink Panther and D'Artagnan, when the clerk asked the court to rise. The bench had reached a verdict. 'We found the evidence of the police officer convincing,' explained the chairman, having carefully run through the evidence that was and the evidence that was not in dispute. The verdict was guilty.

The prosecutor, who had given me not the slightest hint of the outcome he expected while he'd been telling me his stories, looked as though he was about to shoot to his feet, but the legal adviser was there before him. There were other charges against the defendant for the court to consider, he told the bench. There was a further matter of driving while disqualified, at a later date, while the defendant was on bail for this offence. There were two charges of driving without insurance, two of not having an MOT. He had breached a community service order. He had previous convictions for similar offences. He had £1,153 in outstanding fines. None of this had been known to the magistrates any more than to me. Now it was out in the open.

The defendant slumped back in his chair looking sick and white. The young man, despite his respectable appearance, his fluency in the witness box (so strikingly different from the average Haringey defendant) and the testimony of his brother and girlfriend, was now in serious trouble. There would be a pre-sentence report, said the chairman, 'all options to be considered, including an electronic tagging assessment' – and not excluding jail.

It was 2 p.m. The trial had started at 10 a.m. and the three magistrates had a full afternoon ahead of them, but there was just time for a sandwich and a bowl of minestrone across the road at the museum café.

Jane, the chairman, was a health visitor and had been a JP for nine years. Maureen had been on the bench for twelve. She was a counsellor. The other winger was Sandy; he was a health and safety inspector. None of them had recognised either the defendant or the witnesses. 'But there is still a problem of knowing local people and families,' said Jane. 'It happens quite often, and then you have to stand back.' Though there were more criminals from outside the area these days, thanks to easier travel, their court was still chiefly dealing with a small proportion of a relatively small population.

There were forty JPs on the bench, a good deal more representative nowadays than they used to be. 'Nine years ago, when I started, they were mainly county folk,' said Jane, though there was no need to worry about ethnic minorities in this part of the country. But what about all the American servicemen in the area, I asked. Wouldn't it be an idea to have one or two of them on the bench, as well as appearing before it from time to time? My lunch companions were quite tickled by this notion, once I had assured them foreigners were allowed to be JPs.

Alas, in March 2002 the Lord Chancellor suddenly discovered that under the Act of Settlement, 1701, foreign nationals were *not* entitled to be magistrates, after all. My French colleague Gabrielle was furious when I told her the news. 'I will make a stink,' she cried, and I hoped she would. But that small bombshell was yet to come, and in any case would have little impact in West Suffolk.

The magistrates returned to court. Honey Lane was deserted. Outside the low barred window of the cells a fairy ring of cigarette stubs on the pavement oozed coppery droplets, disintegrating slowly in the rain.

EXPERT ADVICE
Where magistrates turn for legal aid

It was in that other fine Suffolk town, Ipswich, that Mr Pickwick had his memorable encounter with the law in the imperious shape of George Nupkins JP, and his long-suffering clerk, Mr Jinks. As a caricature of the relationship between magistrate and legal adviser the scene still hits the mark pretty accurately.

On this particular morning, it will be recalled, Mr Nupkins was in a state of the utmost excitement, 'frowning with majesty, and boiling with rage' because local schoolboys had been breaking windows and hooting at the beadle. Mr Pickwick was brought before him, along with his friend Mr Tutman, accused of being about to fight a duel. Mr Jinks – 'a pale, sharp-nosed, half-fed, shabbily-clad clerk of middle age' – was in attendance. Our hero was not in the least cowed by the magistrate's grand manner. He refused to hold his tongue as ordered and insisted on his right to be heard.

Mr Nupkins looked at Mr Pickwick with a gaze of intense astonishment at his displaying such unwonted temerity and was apparently about to return a very angry reply, when Mr Jinks pulled him by the sleeve and whispered something in his ear. To this the magistrate returned a half-audible answer, then the whispering was renewed. Jinks was evidently remonstrating.

At length the magistrate, gulping down with a very bad grace his disinclination to hear anything more, turned to Mr Pickwick and said sharply, 'What do you want to say?'

'First,' said Mr Pickwick, sending a look through his spectacles under which even Nupkins quailed, 'first I wish to know what I and my friend have been brought here for.'

'Must I tell him?' whispered the magistrate to Jinks.

'I think you'd better, sir,' whispered Jinks to the magistrate.

'An information has been sworn before me,' said the magistrate, 'that it is apprehended you are going to fight a duel and that the other man Tutman is your aider and abettor in it. Therefore . . . Mr Jinks?'

'Certainly, sir.'

'Therefore I call upon you both to . . . erm, I think that's the course, Mr Jinks?'

'Certainly, sir.'

'To er to . . . to what, Mr Jinks?' said the magistrate pettishly.

'To find bail, sir.'

'Yes. Therefore I call upon you both, as I was about to say when I was interrupted by my clerk, to find bail.'

'Good bail,' whispered Mr Jinks.

'I shall require good bail,' said the magistrate.

'Townspeople,' whispered Jinks.

'They must be townspeople,' said the magistrate.

'Fifty pounds each,' whispered Jinks. 'And householders, of course.'

'I shall require two sureties of £50 each,' said the magistrate aloud with great dignity, 'and they must be householders, of course.'

'But bless my heart, sir,' said Mr Pickwick, who together with Mr Tutman was all amazement and indignation, 'we are perfect strangers in this town. I have as little knowledge of any householder here as I have intention of fighting a duel with anybody.'

'I dare say,' replied the magistrate. 'I dare say. Don't you Mr Jinks?'

'Certainly, sir.'

Plus ça change. Court clerks, or better said legal advisers, still 'sir' and 'ma'am' the bench while barely concealing their vastly superior knowledge of the law. Sometimes, as we bumble our way through some minor legal thicket, I think I can detect waves of suppressed irritation radiating from their direction. It is a tribute to their professionalism that they invariably keep their impatience in check. 'It's very frustrating sometimes when you're longing to butt in and say cut the waffle,' said Susie, one of the legal team leaders at Haringey. 'And it's much more difficult to correct the bench these days. Since the Human Rights Act our advice can no longer be surreptitious. It has to be delivered at full volume in open court.'

Susie is married to Derrick, who is also a Haringey legal adviser. We were having lunch at a Greek place in Muswell Hill on one of their joint days off while their small daughter was at school. Susie came to London with an English degree from Lancaster and initially got a job in the Haringey court administration office. She decided to become a court clerk and trained on the job, doing correspondence courses and going to classes. Derrick had been a further education teacher when he became interested in the law and followed a similar route. Both of them enjoyed the work and found the routine suited them. Whereas lawyers in private practice have irregular timetables and un-certain job security, court clerks usually work the same hours every day, nine to five, in the same place, which is better suited to parents with young children. Derrick was now a national official of the 7,000-strong Association of Magisterial Officers, in effect the profession's trade union, though most legal advisers also belong to either the Law Society or the Bar Council. Certainly the profession had come a long way since Mr Jinks's day, and now nursed hopes that, post-Auld, some legal advisers might find themselves reborn as professional chairmen, sitting with two lay JPs in some intermediate types of case.

I think Derrick or Susie would make excellent chairs, as would every one of their Haringey colleagues. The problem for us non-professionals would be that having hung on their every word of advice in the past, it would require an effort of will to contradict or outvote them in the retiring room.

Actually, Susie was quite polite about us. 'Lay justices are far better trained and appraised now,' she said. 'They know about disclosure, human rights, and so on. They know PACE stands for the Police and Criminal Evidence Act. That certainly used not to be the case. The old joke was: why did there have to be three JPs on the bench? The answer: one who could read, one who could write and the other to look after the dangerous intellectuals.' (This last category, I deduced, embraced clerks as well as lawyers, probation officers and lippy defendants.) 'Once upon a time,' Susie went on, 'there was a small coterie of old male magistrates here, typical of a certain generation of JP. They were rude and horrible. One of them used to call me "sweetie" in court,' she remembered with a shudder. The increase in the number of women on the bench had made a great improvement.

Derrick and she both agreed that the lay magistracy was important, in that it brought an element of democracy into the administration of justice. But in the case of our bench, it was regrettable that most magistrates came from the posher parts of the borough, whereas most defendants did not. And perhaps we didn't do enough to liaise with the local communities. JPs did act as a sort of lay filter between the legislature and the ordinary public, though. For instance, when the Poll Tax was in force in the late 1980s and thousands refused to pay, magistrates' courts became the cockpits where the Government's will was put to the test.

'We had special poll tax courts,' Derrick remembered. 'Sometimes they were unbearably tense, with lots of people who couldn't pay but also quite a few who wouldn't, and used the opportunity to stage political protests.' Magistrates were faced with situations where they were supposed to send 75-year-old women to prison. In such cases they often scratched the debt by 'remitting' it – a process which allows fines and debts to be written off, usually owing to a change in financial circumstances. 'There were a lot of remittances,' said Susie wrily.

It was in the magistrates' courts that the inanities of the Tories' Dangerous Dogs Act were exposed. According to Derrick, 'there were days and days of legal argument while vets appearing as expert witnesses for both sides tussled over whether a dog was of a "pit bull type" or not, citing jaw widths and muzzle lengths and so on. There were dogs on death row for months. It was ludicrous.' The magistrates' courts quickly realised it, then the public – and eventually the powers-that-be did too.

Despite the value of the lay input, both Derrick and Susie thought most of their colleagues would probably agree that JPs should concentrate on trials and sentencing, leaving professional district judges to preside over busy charges courts. Stipes were quicker at dealing with non-contested cases, deciding on bail and generally speeding matters on their way without letting defence lawyers pull the legal wool over their eyes with obscure pleas for adjournments.

During their time at Haringey, the kinds of offences people committed had not changed much, Derrick and Susie thought; but offenders had, because of the volatile make-up of the borough's population. 'What you see is the newest people at the bottom of the pile,' Susie observed. 'It's like car-washes. Not long ago the ones around here were all manned by North Africans. Now it's Kosovans. Magistrates' courts know all about what's going on down there in the hidden economy.'

In the case of young offenders, there was a regrettable trend for them to appear in court without an accompanying parent. 'With a lot of the Afro-Caribbean boys, you can just see the desperate lack of a father figure,' said Susie. 'Instead we rely on the girls. So often when a boy is in the dock, his lawyer pleads that he has a steady girlfriend – that's her sitting at the back of the court – who is pregnant and will make sure he sticks to the straight and narrow. We place our hopes on the love of a good woman, even when she's only a teenager, because that's the only more or less solid thing in the lad's life. You *never* hear a girl offender's lawyer putting in as mitigation the fact that she has a good *man*.'

One excellent thing Labour had achieved in government was the speeding up of youth justice. While he was Home Secretary, Jack Straw would call individual Justices' Clerks in for personal wiggings if he considered their courts were backsliding. The wider range of sentences available for young offenders was also an improvement, especially the greater emphasis on reparation, whether it took the form of writing a letter of apology to a victim or cleaning up a damaged bus shelter.

The trouble was that something like 80 per cent of youth trials collapsed because either the defendants had not got themselves represented or the witnesses (usually kids of the same age) were intimidated into not appearing. In Haringey there were only a few dozen repeat offenders, but they were a serious menace. Once upon a time their schools would be involved. Head teachers would come to court. No longer. It was hard not to think of these kids as beyond hope. Did society still believe that morality and the law had some connection between them? These young men neither understood the one nor acknowledged the other.

On this sobering note Susie and Derrick went off to pick their little girl up from school. I returned home to a house rampant with teenagers, doubtful whether any of them would be inclined or maybe even able to engage in a discussion about morality and the law. Instead I read a book I had been sent from Australia, written by a Sydney youth court magistrate called Barbara Holborow. It was called, tellingly, *Those Tracks on My Face*. It did not cheer me up. In one chapter she remembered a thuggish youth called Dmitri. He and a gang of five other boys had beaten and robbed a middle-aged man in a park. They had kicked him on the ground and fractured his skull. There was some doubt as to whether the victim would live.

'These sorts of kids often don't face the bloody consequences of their actions,' Barbara Holborow wrote, 'and when they are confronted with it they are sometimes genuinely amazed at just how much damage they can do when they beat and kick and bash. The real world is not the world of the video store, which is where violence of this nature often starts.'

She recalled closely watching one violent young offender 'to see whether there was a hint of guilt, a hint of emotion, but it was as though he were somewhere else. He had the eyes of a stale fish . . . the mindless aspect of juvenile violence was something that kept on cropping up over and over again in the years I spent on the bench.'

I was already coming to know those stale-fish eyes. Susie and Derrick saw them far more often than I did. Yet the legal advisers as a rule always seemed exceptionally cheerful, as did most of my fellow magistrates and indeed a lot of the lawyers, despite the thanklessness of what most of them did every day. Perhaps it was the case that however grim and dispiriting the world they were all confronting in court – a truer picture than many politicians encounter at first hand – at least they had an opportunity to do something about it. It might be very limited. But it was more than most people had a chance to do and, strangely enough, it was informed by hope rather than despair – the faint hope that one might occasionally right a wrong, or jolt a bad boy into changing his ways, maybe even help to make a good man of him.

SITTING COMFORTABLY
Leeds wins my prize for the best courthouse

The trains were still not running to their usual timetables when I set off for Leeds, though by that time in the winter of 2000–2001 everyone except the railway employees had forgotten what the usual timetables were. 'That'll be £115 return,' said the man in the ticket office. 'That's what I just paid to fly to Malaga and back,' I grumbled. 'Well if you'd caught the train that left five minutes ago it would have been half-price, sir,' he beamed, while agreeing that there was no way I could have known this from a website which was not updated and a telephone enquiries line so clogged it was turning away calls automatically. 'I've got some more bad news, sir, I'm afraid. The journey will take three and a half hours instead of two and a half because of the speed restrictions.' My carriage was half-filled with a party of Chinese businessmen. They chattered excitably for every minute of the three and a half hours, laughing and seat hopping the whole way, joyfully unaware that they were experiencing capitalism on one of its off days.

Leeds Magistrates' Court is a purposeful post-modernist brick building, opened in 1994 by Lord Mackay of Clashfern. It is just a few hundred yards west of the city's grimly magnificent Town Hall, which was opened by no mere Lord Chancellor but by Queen Victoria herself in 1858. In those days it was considered a masterpiece of municipal design, widely emulated throughout the Empire and North America. Besides the council chamber and the city administration, for more than a century the Town Hall also housed the law courts, complete with a set of subterranean holding cells known as the 'bridewell'.

Eventually the demands of contemporary crime overwhelmed these facilities and a new crown court building was opened in 1983 (this time by the Duchess of Kent). Since it is a modern, as opposed to a post-modern, structure it naturally looks brutish compared with the newer magistrates' court, with its pitched roofs and splashes of mauve paint. You could tell the latter was a courthouse because of the knot of hunched youths smoking disconsolately outside the main entrance. Of all the courts I've visited, only the Old Bailey, the Middlesex Guildhall and Birmingham's Victoria Law Courts tolerate the weed within their premises. Bristol did, too, I later discovered, despite the 'No smoking' signs.

The Leeds courthouse was the most thoughtfully-designed I had seen: spacious, well lit and comfortable, formal without being intimidating and with splendid acoustics. In Court 4, the upholstery was in lilac, as were the marble-effect half-pillars behind the bench. In Court 3, the colour scheme was oatmeal. The furniture, including a rather elegant witness box, featured a lot of highly-polished wood and veneer. But for the moderately raised bench, we might have been in one of those private conference rooms you find in the better sort of hotel. There were twenty-one courtrooms in all, the smaller ones being more intimate versions of the remand courts on the lower floor. The waiting areas likewise were airy and reassuring, with plenty of interview rooms for lawyers to meet their clients in privacy and a chic public canteen on the top floor. To judge by the unusually clean, graffiti-free Gents, all this plainly has a calming effect on the passing populace. It was certainly in striking contrast to the gimcrack facilities of the Haringey courts or the haughtiness of Birmingham.

In Court 1 a district judge with a pink and rather crotchety face was at work. Frankly, he would have frightened me had I been in the dock. His manner was decisive to the point of brusqueness. 'Sit down. Stand up.' He wasn't lavish with his pleases and thank-yous. He was dealing with a young man improbably called Beauregard Hancock whose regard, as the judge scowled down at him, was anything but *beau*. In the other courts, lay justices sitting in pairs or threesomes seemed a good deal less alarming. Defendants may find it disquieting when lay magistrates go into a huddle for a whispered discussion about the case, but at least they give the appearance of pondering before reaching a decision. The stipe sitting on his or her own, by contrast, must seem worryingly quick to come to a conclusion.

In another court a young man was charged with assault, having punched his victim, then given him a kicking on the ground. His name was Carlos Sanchez. But what's in a name these days? He looked English, sounded like Geoffrey Boycott and seemed no more Spanish or Latin American than a Yorkshire pudding.

I wandered out into the rain for a break. Opposite the Town Hall was the Quo Vadis, one of those establishments you are prone to find in British provincial cities these days which can't make up its mind whether it is a pub, a coffee lounge or a nightclub. Behind the beer pumps were blackboards recommending American cocktails and Mexican food. The barman was Australian. 'You have to be careful what you say in here,' muttered the landlord knowingly. 'We get everyone from the courts – lawyers and villains alike. Some celebrating. Others drowning their sorrows.'

I lunched with Raymond Curry and Mrs Gill, respectively chairman of the Leeds bench and acting Clerk to the Justices. Over cheese sandwiches and shortbread they told me Leeds was the third biggest court in the country. They had some trouble recruiting magistrates these days. A lot of people were leaving the city, especially the type who might volunteer to be JPs. The press had been rather antagonistic, quick to jump on the courts over controversial decisions and running scare stories about the Auld report. 'Becoming a JP no longer wins the local approval it once did,' they said. 'Sometimes it's not employers but work colleagues who disapprove of the time it takes up.'

Big employers like the clothing factories had gone. Now the city's business was more small-scale – financial services and the like. A lot of magistrates were in public service. 'We advertise every year, hold open days. There's always lots of feedback on the night. But then people realise there are forms to be filled in, and that it's not paid work. The more recent recruits tend to think of it as a stage in their lives – something they'll do for ten or fifteen years and then move on. Which may be no bad thing, though it could lead to a shortage of chairmen, since you have to be five years on the bench before you can be appointed. On the other hand, don't forget the vitality of older people is far greater now than it was twenty or thirty years ago,' said Raymond Curry, who had himself lately retired from the sign advertising business.

Nearly 10 per cent of the Leeds JPs are from the ethnic minorities, which is good going, since the proportion in the local population as a whole is less than 6 per cent. 'We had one of the first black magistrates in the whole country. In fact we're not overburdened with black defendants here, and there are even fewer Asians.'

The university student population of 20,000 or so posed no special headache. The real problem in that regard was the burglary of student premises. I knew about this first hand as my eldest daughter was an undergraduate here. Her unbelievably grotty flat had treble-locked doors and barred windows – not to deter any passing health inspector, but to guard the computers and stereos inside. Despite the club life which accounted for the city's high popularity with UCAS applicants, the courts were not awash with affray cases on Monday mornings – nothing like the football hooligans had been in the bad old days.

Anyway, observed Raymond, one should beware of making local justice too local. 'The prevalence of a certain type of offence in your area is not a reason for arbitrary punishment. It is just something you have to consider.'

It had been a quiet day at Leeds Magistrates' Court. No poisonings or stabbings. But the city's wrongdoers were not idle. According to the local press, Operation Offside had just hauled in three men accused of producing and supplying ecstasy. One of them was described as a 'self-employed horse dealer'. (I wondered whether the newspaper's duty lawyer had hesitated over letting the phrase through, seeing that 'horse' is American gangster slang for heroin.) The crown court was trying a man who had attempted to burn down the family home so as to keep his estranged wife from getting a portion of its value. When that failed, he plotted to murder her by giving her an overdose of heroin, then burning her body. There was also a rapist on the loose, a man with a scratched face whose last victim had been attacked just behind the railway station. And a burglar who had stolen four left-handed guitars.

My last sight of Leeds was of the plaza opposite the Queen's Hotel, where an equestrian statue of the Black Prince cavorted in the rain among an entourage of nearly-naked nymphs holding aloft vandalised torches. Had they all been flesh and blood they'd certainly have been hauled before the beaks the following day for creating a disturbance.

'This is a diesel train,' announced our customer service manager, or whatever guards call themselves these days. 'Therefore passengers with reservations in coach A will find them in coach B and passengers with reservations in coach H will find them in coach G. Those of you who would like to smoke on our journey to King's Cross will find plenty of seats in coach B.' Or did he mean coach A? Four hours later we arrived at our destination. 'Thank you for being so patient and good-tempered,' said the customer comfort provider. Odd that I hadn't so far come across any cases of railway rage, in Leeds or anywhere else.

CHAPTER 10

Deprived and Disconnected

'I would there were no age between ten and three-and-twenty'

Ten-year-old Damilola Taylor was stabbed and left to bleed to death by what was thought to be a gang of children not much older than himself. *The Times* sent my wife to Peckham to report on the council estates in the area. It was a dispiriting experience, except for her meeting with an extraordinary powerhouse of a woman called Camilla Batmanghelidjh, a psychotherapist who in 1996 had set up a centre for young people called Kids' Company. The objects of her bustling energy were children who were outside the system and had no sense of belonging to mainstream society. Many had criminal records before they were even into their teens. As a rule they were woefully neglected, deprived of parental love and guidance, bereft of affection from any quarter at all.

'At the beginning I had no idea of the total breakdown of attachment,' said Camilla. 'The children seemed disconnected from other people. The way they survive is to shut down their feelings in order not to experience their own pain. But the repercussion is that they lose the capacity to empathise. They imagine other people to be equally feelingless, and in that zombie state of mind you can do harm without anxiety or remorse. It's not rebellion they feel, it's sheer lack of care, leading to this suicidal disengagement from the feelings of other people.'

This was the best analysis I had come across of those expressionless youths I had often seen in the dock, with their stale-fish eyes, as Australian youth magistrate Barbara Holborow described them, and their weird air of detachment from their own predicament.

Until now my encounters with such boys had all been in the adult courts, usually because they were jointly charged with someone older. So I asked Cherry, chairman of the Haringey Magistrates' Youth Panel, if I could watch a youth court at work. Only experienced magistrates can join the panel which sits in youth courts, and then only after special training. Normally, outsiders are excluded from these hearings and the press may only report them in a way which avoids identification, but I was allowed to look on as an observer.

The youth magistrates who were to sit that day, with Cherry herself chairing the bench, met half an hour early so as to prepare themselves for the morning's business. They listened attentively as the legal advisers briefed them. I had the impression that everything to do with youth hearings is treated with particular care and sensitivity.

In court, everyone strained to keep the atmosphere as informal and unthreatening as possible. Defendants were placed in the well of the court, not in the dock, and were always called by their first names, even the hulking 16-year-old who looked more like twenty-five. In they came, one after the other, scowling, blank-faced or simply nervous in their puffa jackets and flash shoes. Some had the stale-fish eyes. Others strove to be cool, which had the unfortunate effect of making it appear they had seen it all before – which some almost certainly had. They were each supposed to bring a parent or relative with them. Strikingly, all but one of the Afro-Caribbean youths we saw that morning arrived alone, so that a member of the Haringey Youth Offending Team had to sit beside them *in loco parentis*. The exception brought his sister along. By contrast two Turkish boys each came to court accompanied by an anxious father. One of them had to translate for his dad, who looked dreadfully pained by the whole affair. He made his son take his hands out of his pockets.

By comparison with a typical adult court, with its preponderance of motoring offences, these were mostly pretty serious matters: robbery, assault, affray. One 16-year-old defendant, built like a nightclub bouncer, had apparently been caught on a restaurant CCTV attempting to rob someone and kicking someone else. Nevertheless, he pleaded not guilty and the bench had the tricky task of deciding whether he should be tried in the youth court or whether the charges were so serious the trial would have to take place before a judge and jury. Youth courts have greater sentencing powers than adult courts, but even so the maximum is two years in custody. (This is the kind of decision which the Auld recommendations of 2001 for special youth courts to try even the gravest cases may make easier to handle, if they are implemented.)

Sitting as a youth magistrate on a regular basis must be frustrating as well as depressing. The rate of 'cracked' or aborted trials is high. Many young defendants – and witnesses – simply don't turn up for their hearings. Getting up in the morning is not a teenage skill. A lot of them don't fill in forms or make appointments with solicitors either. They can't turn to adult relatives for help because the family structure barely exists – even though many of these children are parents themselves, thus giving the cycle of deprivation another sickening spin. Most disheartening of all are the repeat offenders, whose regular reappearances are apt to call the whole criminal justice system into question. It might be just about capable of dealing with individual crimes, but it plainly struggles to cope with patterns of criminal behaviour – though by the winter of 2001 there was real hope that some of the new sentences and rehabilitation schemes that had been introduced were beginning to make a difference.

Outside the courthouse the teenage dudes smoked and muttered morosely into their mobiles. Their appearance did not inspire one with hope for their future as good citizens. The gloomiest statistic in the land is the one which shows that half the male population has a criminal record by the age of thirty. As the shepherd says in *The Winter's Tale* just after Antigonus has exited pursued by a bear, 'I would there were no age between ten and three-and-twenty, or that youth would sleep out the rest: for there is nothing in the between but getting wenches with child, wronging the ancientry, stealing, fighting.'

On the day of Damilola's memorial service I called on my friend Sally to find out a bit more about juvenile justice. She must know more about it than most, having sat as a youth court magistrate since 1977. During the 1980s her own children were still young and she worked as a film censor with the British Board of Film Classification, which perhaps gave her a double insight into youthful mores and misbehaviour. Now she sat in South London. A lot had changed, not much of it for the better. 'There's more violent crime about, and a lot of children seem to be totally alienated. Twenty years ago children were more likely to come to court with two parents, and I seem to remember they were readier to own up. The parents would be inclined to say "He's going to plead guilty. Let's get on with it" and not worry about legal representation, whereas now we always advise them to see the duty solicitor. There's more respect for rights now, but that can slow things down, because there are more lawyers involved. At the same time the Home Secretary is urging the youth courts to speed proceedings up.'

The Labour government was certainly showing determination to tackle the problem of young offenders. In my own view, the downside was its tendency to come up with half-baked stunts that hadn't been properly thought through. It was the day after the Queen's Speech, which had announced new and almost certainly unworkable measures to fine drunken yobs and impose curfews on kids up to the age of sixteen. The police were unhappy about these ideas, especially in view of their strained resources. And Jack Straw's previous wheeze of providing them with curfew powers aimed at younger children had not been used even once.

But Sally took a more positive view. Many of the new sentences available to the youth courts were a good thing. She cited parenting orders as an example. The idea is to help parents take charge of their offspring by making them responsible to the courts for their behaviour. As a measure of support,

Youth Offending Teams bring parents to weekly group meetings over several months. There is counselling and discussion and parents meet others in the same plight, which helps them to feel less isolated. YOTs report back to the bench on how the orders are working out. The focus is on the prevention of reoffending.

'If you sit on the family panel you see how it all starts,' said Sally. 'What we see over and over again are these young, drug-addict parents. If we could just rethink the whole of the drugs scene. It's the unerring way in which these sad, damaged young men and women get involved with drugs pretty early on and then team up with someone equally dependent. Then there is domestic violence, and its traumatic effects on children.

'There is a very different pattern of behaviour in other countries towards children. Think of how much more cherishing attitudes are in Italy, for instance. The young here get so much flak these days. There's no positive praise for them. The devaluing of being a mother has not been very helpful to the family either. It's hard for women to find work that allows them to be at home when the children get back from school.

'League tables have increased the number of disruptive pupils being excluded. A high percentage of the young people who come before us in the youth court either are or have been excluded. In the old days we'd ask to see children's school reports, which would give us quite a good idea of what they were like. Now they may not even be at school.'

Sally was on the board of visitors at Feltham Young Offenders' Institution for six years. It seemed plain to her that many of the inmates, those who weren't seriously dangerous or mentally ill, would make perfectly respectable citizens given a decent education and family support. She felt most sorry for the 18 to 21-year-olds. They were the most deprived group in the whole prison system. They got absolutely nothing.

'I sat in on a discussion when a black church worker visited Feltham and asked a group of remand prisoners what they would like their lives to be. In America the boys would say they wanted to be president or a top attorney or a rap singer. But here all of them said "I'd like to live in Essex, have a car, a job, two kids and a wife". Essex and a proper family life loomed very large. It was their target: so many of them had been in care. Nobody wanted to be Mr Big. I remember asking a lad who was a DJ on Radio Feltham, the prison's own station, whether this might help him get a job in a club or the music business. No: that would be a bit too much like hard work, he thought. Maybe he was winding me up, but maybe not: there is so little self-confidence.'

I mentioned Damilola Taylor's memorial service in Peckham. This would have been his eleventh birthday. Sally thought there was something to be grateful for in the huge concern about the little boy's death. In the US it would be just an everyday statistic, though Damilola would probably have died of bullet wounds. 'That would be my one real fear about the future here, if guns became common currency. About ten years ago I went with a group of magistrates to Chicago to observe the penal system, visit the county and federal jails and the night drugs courts. I remember asking a police officer if the accepted wisdom that young offenders would grow out of offending in their twenties applied in America, and he gave a very curt answer. "Lady," he said, "by the time they're twenty, they're dead". '

GESTURES OF SUPPORT
The Lord Chancellor's pep talk

Wherever I went on my magisterial journeyings that winter there were murmurs of woe about the future of lay magistrates. Auld popped up in every conversation. He was the spectre in the retiring room. Older JPs thought New Labour's control-freak tendency spelt doom for amateurs. The more paranoid were convinced the Human Rights Act had been foisted on the country purely to frighten magistrates into mass resignation.

But when the Lord Chancellor had addressed the Magistrates' Association's annual general meeting in Newcastle on 28 October 2000, it was plain he set out to reassure and flatter. This was what he said:

> Let me take the bull by the horns by quoting that great historian Maitland who wrote in the late nineteenth century: *'The JP is cheap, he is pure, he is capable but he is doomed, he is to be sacrificed to a theory on the altar of the spirit of the age.'*
>
> Given that this has not been the easiest of years for you with press prophecies of doom about your future, the same comments, it is interesting to note, were being made by more august sources more than a hundred years ago.
>
> You are, however, still here, all thirty-odd thousand of you . . . The media has run with the scare that there is a hidden agenda and that the Government is plotting the wholesale replacement of the lay magistracy with district judges. But it is not so.
>
> Lay magistrates are the backbone of the criminal justice system. About 96 per cent of all criminal cases begin and end with you.
>
> Let me therefore reassure you. The promotion of volunteering is an objective of government policy. You are volunteers *par excellence*. You represent civic engagement in the justice system. Also, your direct costs represent excellent value for money. Last year, the expenses of more than 30,000 lay magistrates amounted to only two-thirds of the cost of the less than 100 stipendiary magistrates, as they were then known.
>
> You bring a vital knowledge of local conditions to bear on the delivery of local justice – something to which I, and the Government, remain fully committed.
>
> In addition, many of you will know that a review of the criminal courts is currently taking place. Lord Justice Auld is now reviewing how the criminal courts work at every level. It

has been a long time since such a fundamental assessment has taken place. It is the first time that the work of the magistrates' courts and the crown court will be reviewed in tandem and not as two separate jurisdictions.

. . . On magistrates, Lord Justice Auld has stated his belief that there is a sound case for retaining the lay magistracy and district judges.

He has canvassed the possibility of an intermediate court where a district judge would sit with two lay magistrates, which might be an acceptable way of disposing of the less serious 'either-way' cases.

The lay magistracy has a fine tradition of adaptation and reacting positively to change . . .

Aha, I thought, when I read that sentence. We were being praised not for our fine tradition of judiciousness and fair-mindedness but for our adaptability to change. If that wasn't an early warning of upheaval ahead, I was Master of the Rolls.

. . . One major advantage the lay magistracy has over the professional judiciary is that its members do not sit full time. Magistrates are therefore able to bring to the bench a wide range of other experience and knowledge of their community. They are more in touch with life outside the courts, and they should be perceived to be so. The image engendered through television and the media is that magistrates come from a small and generally well-off group of society, out of touch with ordinary people. This is simply not so. Magistrates are drawn from all sections of society and in my now more than three and a half years as Lord Chancellor the social base has significantly broadened.

This brings me to the next area where I offer my thanks for your efforts – increasing the number of ethnic minority magistrates. Britain is a multi-cultural, multi-ethnic and multi-faith society and our ethnic minority communities have enriched this country through their contributions to British culture and economic prosperity. Historically, they have been under-represented in the lay magistracy. I came to the Lord Chancellorship with the belief that more needed to be done to encourage people from these groups to understand the personal contribution that they as citizens could make to their communities by becoming magistrates. So I put in place measures to encourage more members of ethnic minority communities to apply to join the lay magistracy . . . There have been positive results. Last year 8.8 per cent of new recruits to the lay magistracy were from ethnic minorities and the overall representation on the lay bench rose to 4.5 per cent.

So justices were all jolly good fellows and Lord Irvine was pretty jolly good himself, having broadened our social base and ensured that we were more racially representative. Well, fair enough. This was how he concluded:

We are seeing major changes in youth justice; and with the introduction of the Human Rights Act, the platform which has supported our legal system for centuries is itself being strengthened and redefined. For your efforts to adapt to this changing environment, I salute you. I have *confidence* [sic] that *you* have the *confidence*.

It was an uplifting speech if one didn't try too hard to read between the lines. If one did, an element of ambiguity crept in with those curious final emphases. Was the Lord Chancellor placing his *confidence* in that fine old institution the magistracy itself, or in its biddability should it come to be confronted with uncomfortable changes? In other words, were we being softened up? There was not a great deal of *confidence* among my colleagues that they knew the answer.

Two days after the Lord Chancellor's speech an Early Day Motion was tabled in the House of Commons which was cause for unambiguous satisfaction. It proposed:

That this House congratulates the Magistrates' Association on the 80th anniversary of its creation in October 1920; pays tribute to the selfless dedication and commitment of the 30,000 volunteer justices of the peace from all walks of life who generously give their time to the lay magistracy; notes that the lay magistracy, with nearly 50 per cent women and 6 per cent ethnic minority members, is broadly representative of the society it serves and is by far the most representative component of the criminal justice system; applauds the valuable contribution lay magistrates make to delivering local justice in local communities; and looks forward to the continued success of this valuable role.

It was signed by nearly 160 MPs from all three main parties. Julian Brazier, the backbench Conservative MP for Canterbury and Whitstable, was one of the co-sponsors. Afterwards he put out a press release. Not being a very well-known MP – this was before his road accident in 2001 in which an Italian motorcyclist was killed – his remarks attracted little notice, which was a shame. 'Most trials should continue to be conducted by either judges and juries or by lay magistrates,' he stated, and went on:

The Government's Criminal Courts Review was a threat to this, headed by a judge, without a single lay magistrate on his team. Fortunately it looks as though Lord Justice Auld is not going to do the Government's dirty work for them and make recommendations causing lay magistrates to be replaced with stipendiary ones.

This would have caused a fundamental change to the freedom of justice which this country has enjoyed for centuries. The public have justifiable concerns that decisions on guilt and punishment, made by paid government employees, may be affected by personal career aspirations, or some other pressures. The way in which lay magistrates sit in threes, means that they largely reflect the social, gender and racial mix of the community they serve. This is something that an individual could never hope to achieve.

Nevertheless the recent cash cuts by the Lord Chancellor's Department have led to the closure of some court houses and point towards a trend of centralisation. These closures directly affect local communities, especially in rural areas, and undermine the drive to provide local justice. We must resist any further cuts that could choke our justice system.

It is vital that we campaign to maintain the position of lay magistrates within our the courts system.

Well said, Mr Brazier.

Tottenham. The trial of a 34-year-old Turkish Cypriot charged with threatening to kill another Turkish Cypriot, 'intending that he would fear that the said threat would be carried out'. What makes the case unusual is that the victim and his alleged would-be murderer are father and son.

The old man goes into the witness box first. He is wearing a mildewed suit, crumpled white shirt and a loosened tie. He is a big man, but looks ill and grey and stubbly as he recounts how his son came to the house where he lives, threatening to kill him. It was late at night. The son was drunk and had a knife. 'I'm going to slit your throat with this. I will slash you,' he warned his father, and smashed a glass pane in the front door. The father called the police and the younger man ran off. This is the prosecution's case.

The victim had told his story grumpily, barely looking at his son in the dock on the other side of the courtroom. There was a peasant stubbornness in the way he shrugged off the defence's cross-examination, like some disgruntled village elder sulking in the corner of a café. When he is released, he does not go to the public seating to watch the case through to its conclusion but lumbers out of the courtroom without a backwards glance.

The son, by contrast, seems much moved when it is his turn to give evidence. He is almost in tears as he takes the oath, kissing the Koran fervently and pressing the book to his forehead.

'You are the son of Fesih?' his lawyer asks.

'Not after this day,' he gulps, holding back the sobs. He has been a loving son, he says, despite having been thrown out of the family home by his father at the age of twelve. Back in Cyprus, before they came to London, he quarrelled with his father about taking a fourth wife. His new stepmother does not like him. There have been ongoing differences, notably the father's failing to consult his eldest son about his sister's engagement, as tradition requires. The defendant admits that on the night of the alleged incident he had drunk a few pints and when his father wouldn't let him in to collect some things, he had kicked the door in. But that was all. When his sister said 'Brother, leave,' he left.

Neither the prosecution nor the defence evidence has given us a great deal to go on and they are almost flatly contradictory. In due course we all three agree that the son's account is the more believable. We acquit him of the threatening to kill charge and fine him on the lesser matter of damaging the door.

The trial has occupied the whole afternoon, two lawyers, two interpreters, one usher, three magistrates, the police and an unknown amount of legal aid. Who knows how such a family feud might have been resolved back in Cyprus – perhaps with blows, or more likely a couple of glasses of arak. It would surely never have reached a court of law. As it is, the bench has been given an interesting insight into Turkish Cypriot domestic life, learned something of the right of eldest sons to influence their sisters' marriage plans, and done nothing whatsoever to end the feud between father and son.

BRISTOL FASHION
West Country ways with the wayward

It was a sparkling day, but the sight of Bristol Magistrates' Court would lower the blithest of spirits. Summary justice in this ancient, architecturally-abused city was dispensed from a grey, multi-storey bunker, a dingy concrete block opposite a similar monstrosity with its windows and doors boarded up. Fortunately, a new courthouse was being planned. Meanwhile, the graffiti gangs sensed dereliction. Their tags disfigured the walls, all of them inane apart from one prominent piece of work signed with the anarchist symbol which urged, rather wittily: 'Fat cats have cat-flaps: pay them a visit'. A mongrel was whining forlornly outside the court entrance, tethered among the cigarette ends.

Inside the courthouse the spirit of zero tolerance prevailed no more than it did outside. There were graffiti in the corridors, in the lift and in the toilets. As in Birmingham's Victoria Law Courts, some clients seemed to have made a speciality of leaving their mark on ceilings – patterns of small black circles which were hard to explain. Either people were coming to court armed with blowtorches or they were leaping up and down blowing smoke rings at the ceiling from very close quarters. This was the criminal justice system's equivalent to crop circles, I decided.

Lots of people were smoking, despite prominent notices announcing that Bristol was a non-smoking court. No one did anything about it. In the waiting areas, televisions mounted high on the walls were incongruously showing a travel programme about skiing to which no one was paying the slightest attention.

John Budd, chairman of the Bristol bench, was a large, broad-shouldered figure whose powerful presence was enhanced rather than diminished by the fact that he moved around on a pair of crutches. When he was more mobile he played rugby for Devon and cricket for Gloucestershire II. He was an executive at Shell and BP before heading a regional industrial training board.

There were 340 JPs in Bristol, he told me, plus one stipendiary who was only appointed in 1999 after strong resistance to the idea. His presence still caused unease in some quarters ('Where does he fit into the hierarchy?' asked a court official. 'Is he above or below the chairman of the bench?'). Nine per cent of the city's magistrates were from ethnic minorities, which was well ahead of the city's ratio of 5.9 per cent for the population as a whole. Better still, a quarter of the advisory committee, the body which interviews and recommends the appointment of JPs, were from minority communities. That would please the Lord Chancellor.

Bristol had some huge council estates, each with its own special character. The best known, with a high proportion of Afro-Caribbeans, was St Paul's, scene of the notorious riots in the 1980s. Things were much calmer there now thanks to an excellent police district commander, said John Budd, though there was still a problem in encouraging ethnic minorities to take an interest in local policing. This was the very day on which the then Tory leader William Hague made some acid remarks about the Macpherson report, criticising it for lowering police morale and raising political correctness above the requirements of effective crime prevention. Mr Budd didn't want to go on the record on the subject, but I surmised that his own views were not all that far apart from Mr Hague's (and mine). 'I've seen the local graphs,' he said. 'Stops and searches are down; street robberies are up.'

There were eleven courtrooms in the building, which dealt with more than 40 per cent of all criminal cases in Avon and Somerset. This was a statistic which made some of the rural courts a bit jealous. No one was very happy any longer with the old idea of a full day's work for a magistrate being 'a couple of poachers and then dinner'. In Bristol there was plenty of criminal activity and no shortage of recruits for the bench. The intake was twenty to twenty-five new JPs a year. They had welcomed 1,100 visitors on their last open day, which had produced several new recruits. John said he wrote to each new JP personally and met them face to face before they started training.

'At the very beginning they don't know anything. But that's exactly how it's supposed to be. That's what I say in my address to them and their relations when they are sworn in, on their big day. The whole objective of the magistracy is to represent the public. So, theoretically, we could go out into the street and lasso three people and put them on the bench – after careful vetting by the Lord Chancellor's Advisory Committee, naturally.

'There's all the training, of course, but basically you are asking them to use their common sense and local knowledge to dispense justice – in 96 per cent of all criminal cases. The system has worked well for seven hundred years, with three people who don't know much about the law, guided by someone who does, applying common sense principles to what they see going on in their local area. To me this is perfect.'

John had recently gone on a trip to Michigan where local judges were astonished to hear him say he had the same powers to reach a verdict and deliver a sentence as some of them did, though legally unqualified and not paid a cent. He was pretty unenthusiastic about changing the system at all and considered the Auld inquiry with evident suspicion. He was an unapologetic traditionalist. He liked the formality and deplored the lack of it in American courts. When people came into court and bowed to the bench, he stressed, they weren't bowing to the magistrates, they were bowing to the idea of justice as embodied on the bench.

Bristol's Court 1 was very much like our own cheap and uncheerful set-up in Haringey. The handsomest bit of the room was the new £30,000 dock in blond wood and thick, ceiling-high slatted glass, built for security reasons after several attempted escapes. In the last such endeavour the defendant had vaulted over the low security barrier, smashed a water jug and held a shard of jagged glass to the chairman's throat before being overcome. The water jugs, I noticed, were now made of plastic.

In the chair, John Budd was rather forbidding, glowering over his half-moon glasses. If he hadn't looked like the twin brother of the genial Australian who taught me Anglo-Saxon at university I would have found him quite intimidating, as I think he meant to be. He barked at the young men in the dock and issued wiggings with unabashed severity – which seemed to be rather effective. They mumbled apologies, hung their heads in shame and promised to try to mend their ways with affecting sincerity.

During the morning's case load, one man stood out. He had been arrested the previous night. He was a middle-aged man – tall, slim, with silvery hair and an educated manner. The impression he gave was of quiet respectability: a headmaster, perhaps, or a family doctor. Yet he was in custody, accused of raping two girls under the age of sixteen and of three acts of gross indecency against even younger girls, under fourteen years old. His wife sat behind me, sobbing uncontrollably, as the charges were read out. He was to be remanded in custody while the police made further investigations into his past. Looking at him, with his mild appearance and neat grey T-shirt, it was very hard to believe he belonged in the dock. Yet the charges against him were the gravest of the day. His case was much too serious to be heard summarily. In due course he would be committed to the crown court for trial by judge and jury. There was no application for bail.

Now and again the defendant shot his weeping wife a look which I couldn't interpret. Self-pity? Despair? He seemed curiously alienated from both the proceedings and from her. 'Stand down,' murmured Mr Budd, and as the defendant was led away he mouthed something at his wife. It could have been 'Don't believe it'.

Bristol had piloted an imaginative scheme for simplifying pre-trial procedures which is now to be adopted throughout the country. This was the video-link court I had heard about in Wrexham. I was curious to see it. Court 9 had been a staff room, but was now equipped with two large-screen TVs, around which were grouped desks and chairs so that three magistrates, the court clerk and the lawyers could all get a clear view. There was also some seating for members of the public. A small swivelling camera was fastened to the top of the principal television set. It was operated by the clerk by means of a console on his desk so that it could be focused on every corner of the little courtroom.

The TVs were linked by digital telephone line to a special room in each of the main remand prisons in the area, where identical equipment was installed. The prisoner and his guard sat in this room and were directly linked to what was taking place in Court 9. Should the defendant want to have a word with his lawyer, he could do this via a parallel TV and telephone link in total privacy.

The attractions of being able to deal with pre-trial preliminaries in this fashion were obvious to anyone who has wasted whole mornings of court time waiting for a prisoner to be delivered. As far as the prisoner himself was concerned, the advantages were even more striking. Instead of having to pack up his belongings, probably before dawn, and spend hours in a prison van before being returned to a new cell and cellmate long after dark, all for the sake of a brief appearance in court, the whole process could be carried out *in situ*, without disruption and with minimum expense of time and money.

In the case of Category A prisoners, there were benefits to the public, too, as the heavy security measures entailed in transporting them to and from court slowed traffic and caused disquiet. At first defence lawyers were uneasy about not having face-to-face contact with their clients. But their fears had mostly evaporated and prisoners were enthusiastic. Now, so long as the defence agreed, all such hearings in Bristol were dealt with in this fashion. 'It is safer and cheaper,' said deputy Clerk to the

Justices Julie Mills, 'so long as privacy at both ends is adequate and secure.'

After training, the legal advisers had become quite handy cameramen, though it was quickly accepted that the whole court should remain seated when it was realised that tall lawyers were being beheaded by the lens. Prisoners with mental health problems weren't always suitable for this disembodied form of TV justice, however. They had a tendency to think they were seeing visions and hearing voices.

I had not yet visited the cells of a big city courthouse. This was my chance. The entrance was downstairs, through heavy doors and clunking gates. Head jailer Darren met me at the control room. There were twenty-seven cells which at a pinch could hold up to ninety-six prisoners, he said. The cells were forbidding. Just a hard bench fixed to one wall, and otherwise nothing: no furniture, no windows. The walls were bare except for smudged and scratched graffiti. There were several corridors for adult prisoners, another for youths – the youngest prisoner ever held there was only nine years old – and a special cell for potential suicides with a large glass wall in clear view of the control room.

Shouts and murmurs came from behind closed doors. They were the sounds of trapped animals, a human zoo of invisible inmates. Through another locked gate came a more high-pitched cacophony. This was where women prisoners were held. One of them was screaming for a fucking cup of tea. Violent prisoners were brought to this area too, so that if a fight started with the guards it would be out of sight of the rest of the men, who might otherwise be incited to riot. Sitting quietly in one of these isolated cells was the man I had seen upstairs earlier, accused of raping young girls. 'For his own protection,' growled Darren.

He showed me a cell reserved for people with contagious diseases. HIV was a constant risk to the jailers. Darren had been threatened with a syringe more than once. A bleeding prisoner was always dangerous. 'If something like that happens, there's nothing much you can do about it except take a blood test. But then there's a three-month wait before you know if you're in the clear.' Darren grimaced resignedly and unlocked the portcullis that led out of his noisy, neon-lit Hades, back to the world above.

For the prisoner brought up from the cells and suddenly thrust into the eerie calm of a courtroom full of quietly-spoken people wearing suits, the contrast must be shocking. Back in Court 1, a dazed-looking lad was in the dock, charged with committing one offence while on bail for another. His mother was in court, eyeing him sadly. The boy's lawyer made a plea for him to be released from custody on bail so that he could be with his brother and their mother for Christmas. The brother was terminally ill. It would be the last Christmas of his life. Chairman Budd whispered at length with his two wingers, then addressed the defendant sternly. Despite the fact that he was a serial bail breacher, and against all their wiser instincts, they were going to set him free. But first came a good old-fashioned talking-to of the kind that a few decades ago would have made an uplifting paragraph in the local press.

'You've not exactly been a model 20-year-old son, have you?' The defendant looked down at his feet and nodded. 'We're letting you out because of your mother and your family. Do you understand?' said Mr Budd gruffly, peering over his spectacles. Another nod. He would have to report to his nearest police station every morning. 'After all, you won't want to spend all day in bed, will you?' This seemed a very big presumption, but was greeted with another nod. 'Don't let your mother down, or you'll be letting yourself down, too.'

I'd say the treatment worked well with the young bail breacher. He was followed into the dock by a man who claimed to have 'forgotten' that he had £300 in fines outstanding. 'Forgotten?' the chairman harrumphed. 'You wouldn't have forgotten if someone owed *you* £300, would you?' The man looked abashed. 'You know we can send you to jail today for thirteen days.' 'Yes, sir,' responded the defendant smartly. He got a suspended sentence. 'Start paying, or you're a prisoner,' commanded Mr Budd with admirable directness.

We retired for ham sandwiches and buns in the Clerk to the Justices' office. Bristol was now the sixth busiest court in the country, said John, sometimes sitting until 7 or 7.30 in the evening. Thirty years ago there were just eighty-nine magistrates on the Bristol bench. Court started at 11 o'clock. 'It wasn't quite monocles and military moustaches, but it was a bit like that. The ladies all wore hats. In the old courts the stairs down to the cells were very steep. It was quite common for the sergeant to kick a recalcitrant prisoner down them. You could hear them tumbling all the way to the bottom. Those sorts of things had to change.'

Though he obviously enjoyed his crusty image, John Budd was no luddite. 'We spent hours and hours designing the video-link court system.' There were regular court users' meetings. He approved of the mentoring for new magistrates. Regular appraisal, which some benches were said to skimp on, was taken seriously at Bristol, as might be judged by the fact that the head of the panel of appraisers was a former England rugby coach, an appointment which clearly tickled ex-county player John. As a professional in the business, he was all for the various types of training JPs must now undertake, though he warned that there shouldn't be training for training's sake, as in 'Oh, look, here's a subject we could do some training on'.

The pattern of crime had changed dramatically over the past three decades. 'The biggest offending group used to be all about alcohol, now it's to do with drugs. More than half of all our criminal work is drug related. People will skin their own grandmothers to get hold of the stuff. The other thing that's changed is attitudes to prison. In the old days it was shameful to have been inside. One's reputation was tarnished. Now it's a badge of manhood.'

The chairman of the Bristol bench finished eating his Bath bun and hauled himself off to return to the courtroom. The Clerk to the Justices, in whose office we had been lunching, watched him go. 'He's a one-off, as I expect you noticed,' said David Speed admiringly, coming across as a touch old-fashioned himself in dapper pinstriped trousers and a black coat. 'But you always know where you are with him.'

Outside the courthouse the winter sun was blindingly low in the sky, striking cruelly off the strange mixture of fountains and sculptures that now mark Bristol's traffic-girdled city centre. I strolled along the refurbished waterfront. It consisted almost entirely of one enormous bar after another. If these places were ever full, there must be as much drinking going on in Bristol now as there was four hundred years ago in its rollicking heyday as Britain's second busiest port and centre of the slave trade. Drugs might have overtaken alcohol as a major cause of crime, but plainly not because the old seafaring city has lost its taste for booze.

'There's a lot of drinking goes on down here,' said my taxi driver in a thick West Country growl. 'You see they fountains? That used to be graaass. We warned the council what would happen but they wouldn't listen to us and it did. All them drunken students squeezed washing-up liquid into the water. Next morning the pumps were clogged and the fountains were six feet high in foam. It keeps happening. Well, we told them it would.'

I'd have enjoyed hearing chairman Budd dealing with the culprits. As a former rugby man I imagine he wouldn't have been too unsympathetic to such ingenious high jinks.

Highgate. An unusual day for Haringey in that for once Anglo-Saxon and Celtic names on the list outnumber any others, among them Johnstone, Dixon, Scantlebury, Welch, Wallace and the splendidly double-barrelled Skipp-Thacker. Young Mr Dixon has even gone so far as to get himself accused of a pair of almost satirically English misdemeanours. He is charged with being in possession of an offensive weapon, namely a cricket bat and another offensive weapon, namely a tennis racket –

both on the same day. The imagination reels, picturing a white-flannelled youth running amok with his sporting equipment, perhaps under the influence of too much Pimm's. We don't hear details of the case, sadly, since the defendant has elected trial by jury in the crown court and we are merely part of the committal process. Damn.

I imagine the Government's anti-jury tendency would regard this as a prime example of a defendant abusing the right to trial by jury by insisting on taking such a footling matter to the crown court. But who knows? The actual incident may have been graver than it sounded, while Mr Dixon might be right to think that any British jury will give him the benefit of the doubt when the prosecution is silly enough to describe a cricket bat and a tennis racket as offensive weapons.

In any event, the prosecutor wants to drop one of the charges just to simplify matters. He chooses the second. 'I think a cricket bat is more offensive than a tennis racket,' he explains, 'even though tennis rackets are made of tough materials these days.'

'The tennis racket will be discharged,' says our chairman gravely. Beachcomber, thou shouldst be living at this hour.

CHAPTER 11

Banged Up

*'Drugs are an ineradicable problem, as they are in most
British prisons'*

The nearest men's prison to the Haringey courts is Pentonville,
whose beetling exterior used to excite my children whenever we
drove past it on our way to the Holloway swimming baths. On
a dank winter's morning it looked especially grim. The small
party of anoraked and overcoated magistrates gathered at the
foot of its walls was in suitably solemn mood. This, after all,
was the bottom line of what being on the bench was all about,
and why the public image of the JP was both slightly alarming
and a bit creepy: we had the power to deprive our fellow citizens
of their liberty and lock them up for months on end in this very
place and others like it.

So far in my first year and a bit on the bench I had not been
involved in passing a single prison sentence. But there had been
plenty of occasions when I had participated in refusing to grant
bail. This was where most of North London's adult male
remand prisoners were incarcerated. Quite rightly, it was part
of our training to see the place we were consigning them to.

We were met by Gary, who had a moustache, a cheery
manner and the build of a prop forward. He was a senior
training officer at the jail and this morning was doubling as our
tour guide, a task he performed with enthusiasm. Pentonville
was the oldest purpose-built prison in the world, he told us,
completed in 1842. It became internationally famous as a model
of enlightened prison design. The unique feature was that its
wings radiated from a single hub. This was known as the
Centre, and the whole prison was controlled from there.

In 1902 Pentonville achieved another kind of fame when it
became the main hanging prison for the whole of London.

Between then and 1961, when the last execution took place here, a hundred and twenty people were topped. Many of them were despatched by the celebrated hangman Albert Pierrepont. Gary pointed out the windows of the condemned cells, and the very spot where the gallows had stood. Pierrepont, he said, was so efficient he reckoned he could light a cigarette, leave it burning, and put a man to death before even a morsel of ash had dropped. During the Second World War, when Pentonville suffered a good deal of bomb damage, domestic prisoners were sent elsewhere and their places were taken by German POWs. For some reason six of them were hanged, all in a single day, the record for Pentonville. Gary recounted all this with some relish, but he himself was against the death sentence, he said. He had come across too many miscarriages of justice.

Pentonville was an exceptionally busy jail, with 1,100 inmates, 600 staff and 30,000 movements a year. The reason for all this coming and going was that 40 per cent of the population were remand prisoners, which meant that early every weekday morning and again in the evenings the whole place was packed with prison vans collecting men for their court appearances and bringing them back afterwards. Every arrival and departure was logged on a blackboard, including our own as we entered the double set of doors into the prison proper. It reeked of a million roll-ups.

We processed along the length of one of the wings. It was clean enough already, it seemed to me, but there were still inmates mopping and polishing away, as if in an army barracks. The cells, we were told, were 7 foot by 13 foot and 9 foot high. As a result of the drive to end slopping-out, each set of three cells had been turned into two so as to accommodate a loo and washbasin. Prisoners were fed three meals on £1.41 a day, a minor miracle of domestic economy. They ate in their cells and there were showers for each landing. Pentonville operated a system of incentives for good behaviour, sardonically known as the Mad Cow, after its initials – B for basic cell, S for standard cell and E for enhanced. Things got better as you rose up the

BSE ladder, until you reached the peak of prison comfort, with an individual TV set in your cell.

Safety nets to prevent suicides and hurtling missiles were strung between the landings. There was a lot of noise: doors slamming, keys grating in locks, shouts and catcalls, everywhere the sense of big, strong men moving about. The atmosphere was more restless than threatening. 'The staff here are always outnumbered by about ten to one,' said Gary. 'So in effect the prison runs by the prisoners' consent.' There were strategic alarm bells everywhere, plus 'this fine piece of old technology' to fall back on, he chortled, producing a police whistle on a lanyard. 'Whistles don't go off by mistake. If we hear a blast from one of these we know a colleague's in difficulties.'

There were quite a number of female officers, who apparently got very little trouble. On the whole, male prisoners would shy away from attacking a woman. So you see them, not notably tall or beefy, strolling coolly among these powerful men, like antelope among a pride of well-fed lions, showing no sign of discomfiture.

Pentonville was not suitable to hold Category A prisoners. Inmates thought to be particularly dangerous or liable to escape were sent elsewhere. The worst escape risks were prisoners known to have money, who could pay to organise things properly. The most dangerous were the mentally unstable. Attempts at self-harm were a daily occurrence. Gary remembered one schizophrenic character who was well aware of his propensities and used to warn prison officers to knock and ask who was inside before entering his cell. 'If he said he was his brother, you had to be very careful. You just didn't go in. This imaginary brother of his was extremely violent.'

We saw the special reception cells where those going on Rule 45 waited to be processed. This was the protection regime for paedophiles and some other types of sexual offenders, known in jail slang as 'nonces', who were vulnerable to persecution by other prisoners. 'Once a nonce, always a nonce,' said Gary.

Even if they were in for something else, if they'd been on the Rule before, the prisoners' grapevine would know and they'd be marked men. Once upon a time, rapists were given this treatment too, for their own protection. But now, regrettably, the crime had become more acceptable. Most rapists were treated like anyone else. Gary told us that while waiting to be dealt with in these reception cells some inmates started scratching stories on the doors which others would add to, producing mini-sagas written by several hands. Oscar Wilde would have applauded. On one door I made out not a mini-saga, but a laconic verse:

> No *bail*,
> *Just wail*.
> No *dope*,
> *Just hope*.

Actually, the last two lines should have been reversed: *No hope,/Just dope*. Drugs were an ineradicable problem, as they are in most British prisons. C Wing was given over to drug rehabilitation. On a cork board were full descriptions of each main drug and its dangers, from cannabis and speed to heroin and crack cocaine. Prison officers liked working there because they felt they were achieving something positive. But elsewhere, one gathered, drug use flourished pretty well unchecked. 'There's every kind of stuff, mostly brought in by visitors, despite the sniffer dog and the CCTV,' Gary admitted. 'They stick it up their bums and since there are no internal body searches allowed, there's nothing staff can do, even if they've seen the exchange on the TV. You can strip-search them and ask them to squat, but if they've stuck it far enough up, there it stays.'

For a time the exercise yard had been a prime drop-zone for drugs. (Did we know, by the way, that all prisoners everywhere exercise in an anticlockwise circle, even if the ground's rectangular? No, we did not, but it was a pleasing bit of information.) Anyway, the yard was overlooked by that block of council flats over there and people used to toss packets of drugs from the windows down into the yard, where they were quickly scooped up by the circling exercisers. So the yard had been made smaller. Now only the strongest throws could cover the distance.

Inside the jail the drugs market was as thriving as it was outside. The main prison currency was phone cards. A £2.50 card was worth about four times its face value. Phones were good because it meant men could keep in touch with their families, Gary explained. But they were bad because of witness intimidation. At that moment the prison Tannoy system suddenly blared out. 'Mr Smith is now in the stocks on B Wing,' came the mystifying announcement. Was Victorian Pentonville still using the stocks as a mode of punishment?

Gary laughed. It was part of a charity drive. Inmates could throw wet sponges at prison officers for 50p a sponge, and it was Mr Smith's turn to be the victim – a rather heartening state of affairs, I thought.

On the whole, visiting Pentonville had not been as bitter an experience as I had feared. It was a tough place, but not inhuman. I was struck by the number of notices inviting those in distress to contact the Listeners, inmates specially trained by the Samaritans to help their fellow prisoners with counselling and support. It would be horrible to be locked up in Pentonville, for sure. But it would be a great deal worse if you couldn't talk to a Listener, or throw a sponge at Mr Smith.

Highgate. The defendant is accused of kerb-crawling but has failed to show up for his trial. There have been previous failures to attend. The trial goes ahead in his absence. The principal witness is a very pretty WPC in a black trouser suit, who takes the oath briskly, then gives an account of what happened on the night in question in Seven Sisters Road. She was a member of the special clubs and vice squad, she says, and her job was to act as decoy, while two colleagues hung around nearby – 'about ten car lengths away, Your Worships'. She was wired with a concealed tape recorder, and also had an open radio link with the other two, so they could not only eavesdrop on conversations but also come to her rescue if need be.

She describes her decoy outfit: black jeans, black boots, blue jacket. A vehicle cruised by three times, then stopped just ahead of her and winked his brake lights on and off. 'That is one of the ways kerb-crawlers catch a lady's attention,' says the WPC demurely.

She went over to the car and the driver said: 'How much you want?'

She said: 'What for?'

He said: 'Sex.'

She said she didn't do that sort of thing. He asked her what she did do.

She said: 'Not that.'

Then she walked away. The whole thing was recorded. He drove off and the WPC radioed details to her colleagues, who arrested him.

One of the colleagues now goes into the witness box. I was expecting a burly male copper. Instead a slight, bespectacled, rather prim-looking policewoman in uniform takes the oath. She describes how they stopped the man, who was an 'IC2' – police jargon for a dark-skinned European, apparently. They asked him what he'd been discussing with the woman at the kerb-side. He said unhesitatingly: 'I asked her for business – sex.' On being told that was an offence, he said he'd only recently arrived from Poland and didn't know that. Nor did he know the car he'd just bought needed insurance.

We find the matter proved, and impose a modest fine in the defendant's absence for both offences. But the incident leaves me feeling uneasy. The man was very probably some sort of refugee, not yet used to British laws. He learnt that Seven Sisters Road was a famous red-light district. For all he knew this could have been like Hamburg or Amsterdam. He saw a good-looking woman obviously tout-

ing for custom. He responded. And then he was nabbed. It was blatant entrapment and in my view pretty indefensible. Some women colleagues disagree with me about this, pointing out that kerb-crawlers are a major nuisance who often harass innocent women. True enough. But there are far worse nuisances around. I think that in terms of London's policing priorities this was a gross misuse of three officers' time – not just a night on the streets luring sad men when they could have been catching criminals, but also half a day in court.

PASSING SENTENCES
Deciding what's best is seldom easy

As I implied earlier, it is not all that often that magistrates sentence people to prison. Custody is very much a last resort, and rightly so if a more purposeful alternative can be found to meet the case. This is where pre-sentence reports come in. It is usual to call for a PSR when any sentence stiffer than a fine is being considered. This gives the Probation Service a chance to assess the offender's suitability for different kinds of sentence, such as a community punishment or rehabilitation order, or one that involves treatment for drug dependence. The offender's willingness to co-operate is essential for community sentences of this kind. If he has a record of breaching such orders on previous occasions, jail may well be the only alternative.

A typical PSR makes bleak reading. It is generally a three- or four-page document based on an interview and the offender's previous record. It will analyse first the offence, then the offender and his history – all too often a dismal saga of physical and emotional deprivation, delinquency, depression, drugs and drink. It assesses the risk of harm to the public and the likelihood of reoffending should the culprit remain free. It concludes with a recommended sentence, not often a custodial one.

All this takes time to prepare, which means the case must be adjourned and the sentencing bench very seldom includes even one of the magistrates who originally heard it a fortnight or so earlier. This is not ideal, but on balance it is probably for the best. With some 70,000 people in jail we already have the highest prison population in Europe, which is not something to be proud of. A veteran magistrate told me she thought the reason for this was that so many of our lawmakers in the recent past were ex-public schoolboys, who were therefore hardened to the idea of incarceration from their earliest youth. There may be something in that. All the same, it is as well to have a system, however imperfect, which tries to ensure that we only lock up those for whom there is no better option.

My first two sittings of 2001 were sentencing courts. They brought a varied crop of cases. One of the more difficult to decide was that of a 30-year-old man guilty of stealing a video recorder from Sainsbury's. He had begun sniffing glue at the age of five and was now stuck into crack cocaine and heroin. Plainly his whole life had been and still was a complete mess. He had a long history of fines, probation and imprisonment for thieving to finance his drug habits. He was a dreadful sight when he limped into the dock. He looked deathly pale and said he had blood clots in his leg. On a superficial judgment, without the benefit of the PSR, this man was a serial offender of just the type the Government seems eager to put behind bars. On the other hand he was not violent, his thefts were at the minor end of the scale and previous jail sentences had done nothing to stop his offending. From every point of view, it seemed to us, sending this man back to some drug-infested clink would be pointless. So his sentence was a drug treatment and testing order, a new and intensive scheme which everyone hoped would indeed turn out to be tough on one of the prime causes of crime, as Mr Blair had so often promised. Judging by the state of the man in the dock, this DTTO might well be his last chance of survival.

We had another drugs-related case, but of an entirely differ-ent order: two respectable-looking men in their forties, both guilty of possessing and growing cannabis. One had been found with just 22 grams of the stuff, the other a kilo (no metric martyrs in the Met, it seems). The former was growing twenty plants, though of such poor quality, the leaves were really only good for making tea, he said. His co-defendant had a plot of fifty-nine plants and furthermore, unlike the other man, a longish list of previous drug convictions, including time in jail. So how to differentiate between the two, when in legalistic terms both were guilty of the same offences? It was pretty clear the cannabis was only for personal use. Jail, even for the repeat offender, would be pointless – although he didn't help himself with his cheeky plea in mitigation. He argued that he was performing a public service by growing his own weed, thereby doing the drug dealers out of business. Anyway, he was remorseful: this had been a regrettable lapse, he said, not altogether believably.

We put him on probation, which meant he would be supervised and would have to keep out of trouble for a good long time. We fined the other man, with his poor quality crop and previously clean record, but not very severely. While the debate about decriminalising cannabis continued outside the courtrooms, within them magistrates were daily faced with applying the law as it stood – except in anomalous Brixton where, at the time, police were cautioning rather than charging those found in possession of small amounts of soft drugs. As previously mentioned, since then David Blunkett has announced his intention to reclassify cannabis as a Class C drug. But how that might affect the small-time cultivator, growing the stuff only for his own consumption, nobody seems to know.

Light relief came with a man convicted of shooting someone with an air rifle. The victim was a builder who was shot in the backside while he was up a ladder. That would make a fairly damning headline, on the face of it. But as usual, the headline wouldn't have told the whole story. The guilty party was a young man of previously unblemished character who had bought himself a new air gun. Foolishly, he had let off a few shots out of his bedroom window to try it out. One of them had ricocheted and hit the builder, fortunately not causing him any serious injury. The shooter was deeply embarrassed, as well he might have been: he worked as a security guard. We gave him a conditional discharge, confiscated his gun and charged him £50 towards costs. He looked immensely relieved. '*Magistrates free security-guard gunman*' might well have been the local paper splash, had it sent a reporter to court. Fortunately it did not.

The matter of professional embarrassment is something magistrates quite often find themselves having to consider. A conviction can derail a person's whole career. There was a very agreeable, shamefaced young woman who pleaded guilty to drink-driving. It was a complete one-off, she said; something she would never normally do. What was really upsetting her was that she had just applied to join the police force. She was worried this might stop her being accepted. But there was nothing we could do. The courts have virtually no discretion when it comes to motoring and excess alcohol. Her licence had to be endorsed and she had to be disqualified for at least a year. On balance, we thought – we hoped – the police were probably so desperate for recruits they would take her anyway. But it was irritating that there was no way our sentence could reflect our confidence in her.

One more PSR sticks in the memory: a white-haired, kindly-faced, 65-year-old Somali in a dark suit and silver tie. He was a vet, formerly the deputy dean of veterinary science at a leading Somalian university. His father was an ex-Somali ambassador. He had been done for drink-driving – three times over the limit. This was seriously bad news, because it was the second time within ten years. Not only did this mean an automatic three-year disqualification, but the sentencing guidelines indicated a community sentence or even custody. He was doing valuable work for the exiled government of Somalia, helping with refugees in Britain. Well, so what? The fellow was a menace on the roads. Well, so then we learnt that this apparently able and decent man's wife and five children had all been massacred in Somalia. No wonder he took the odd drink. We disqualified him for three years, as prescribed, and sentenced him to two years' probation, or community rehabilitation as it would now be called. But nothing could rehabilitate the family he had lost and mourned.

CHAPTER 12

Nothing to Brag About

'As for the public . . . they just think we're a bunch of middle-class busybodies'

I had now been a magistrate for eighteen months. I was beginning to feel a bit less of a fraud sitting in judgment on fellow citizens charged with there-but-for-the-grace-of-God type misdemeanours. With the help of Barbara, my mentor, I was working my way through the Magistrates' New Training Initiative and filling in my Personal Development Log. This last was a somewhat laboured business, requiring one to conduct a progressive self-assessment exercise by ticking boxes and scoring oneself on various 'competencies' [*sic*], while keeping up a self-critical running commentary on how things were going.

Sometimes this could be awkward for both mentor and mentee. For example, Competence 3, which concerned how to 'Think and Act Judicially', required one to demonstrate one's knowledge of: 'Participating in using a systematic, structured approach to the decision-making with regard to evidence and information as presented in court with awareness of the impact of 1) One's own conditioning and personal prejudices; 2) Labelling and stereotyping; 3) Language and cultural differences; 4) Body language.'

Through the gobbledygook one could of course discern what was required. But to demonstrate 'competence' in such matters, to the extent of being able to tick a box with assurance, as though one had passed some refined sort of test of racial, cultural and social non-discrimination, was just plain silly. Nevertheless, in general the scheme ensured a purposeful approach to the training, which was undoubtedly helpful. Barbara and I ploughed on. The end was in sight, when all my 'competencies' would have been confirmed and Barbara could sign me off, no doubt to her great relief.

On the whole, I said to my friend Rhoda, I had found my first year and a half rewarding. It was as interesting as she had said it would be when she first urged me to apply. She seemed relieved. Her own early experiences when she started eight years earlier had been a bit discouraging. Soon after she was sworn in, when she boasted to a lawyer friend about her new status, he replied shortly: 'That cuts no ice with me, Your Worship.' That was a bit of a blow, but it helped give her a realistic attitude towards the magistracy which had not changed.

'I've never been particularly proud of being a JP, as some people obviously are,' Rhoda said. 'It's not something I talk about socially. The fact is the lay magistracy is not well respected by lawyers. It is condescended to by the clerks. And as for the public, if they know anything at all about us, which most of them don't, they just think we're a bunch of middle-class busybodies. The general image of the bench is of a lot of interfering bossy-boots, committee people, school governors and so on. Of course people like that are necessary. But one reason I do it is that I think there should be more JPs who aren't busybody types.'

I scanned the café where we were talking to see if there were any busybody colleagues in earshot. But the rest of the clientele were reassuringly laid-back. 'I hate it when the host at a party grabs you by the arm and says you must meet each other: you're both magistrates,' Rhoda went on. 'I distrust people who want to talk about it all the time. I approve of JPs giving talks to schools and that sort of thing, explaining the magistracy, but that's another matter. There's a clubbiness about the bench which I don't like, a sort of smugness.'

I thought I knew what she meant. I had detected it myself now and then – maybe I was guilty, too. A cynical observer would say there is an unspoken refrain wherever two or more magistrates are gathered together which goes something like: 'Here we are doing this difficult and demanding work for which no one pays or thanks us. Aren't we public-spirited?'

But the quality of our own bench had improved since she joined, Rhoda said. She remembered being shocked at how some male magistrates in those days were quite open about having become JPs to help them with their business and social lives. They actually bragged about it. More training and regular appraisals had made things better. In one of her first sittings she was mortified when the chairman kept announcing 'We are minded to do so and so' without even glancing at herself and the other winger, never mind consulting them. That sort of thing didn't happen any more.

After five years as a winger she had done her training to become a chairwoman. Being a chair was hard but rewarding, she said. You had to be on your toes the whole time. At one of the first sittings over which she presided they were hearing a bail application. The prosecutor finished his argument against granting bail and sat down. Rhoda promptly said the bench would retire, got up, and led her wingers off to go and discuss their decision. Lawyers, clerks and lay magistrates are always to some extent in competition with each other: this was a bad moment for the amateurs. Humiliatingly, the clerk had to call them back in, explaining to madam chairman that they had left the courtroom without having heard the defence. Poor Rhoda. Covered in confusion, she apologised to the court for being 'a little hasty'.

Still, the amateur status of magistrates was important, she believed. 'I think we are more like jurors than judges. A lot of JPs object to that view. They want to be seen as professionals, though the same people brag about being volunteers and grumble about the training.' Anyway, judging the credibility of a witness was no easier for a professional than it was for a layman.

'The hardest thing is when you've got a victim in court as a witness. It alters things quite a lot. Once we found a man not guilty of common assault simply because the prosecution evidence wasn't strong enough. The look the woman victim shot me as we pronounced the verdict went right through me – and I knew we'd done the wrong thing.'

Rhoda thought there was still a depressing lack of sentencing options in adult courts. 'Lord Chief Justice Woolf talks enthusiastically about community sentences, reparation and so forth, but the scope for them is often so limited. There was a film on TV the other day with Kenneth Branagh playing someone who'd been given a community sentence which consisted of helping to care for a motor neurone disease sufferer – Helena Bonham Carter. It was all very touching. But I've never come across anyone being given a punishment as imaginative as that!

'The strangest sentence I've ever been involved in was soon after I became a JP. We were doing a means court, dealing with people who hadn't paid their fines. Most of them had not turned up. We issued warrants for arrest like there was no tomorrow. One woman did show up, however. She flatly refused to pay her fine. We warned her we'd have no alternative but to send her to prison. That's OK, she said: she *wanted* to go to prison. Her woman lover was in Holloway and she missed her terribly, so please would we send her there to join her friend? Well, we had no choice really. So off she went.'

Highgate. A long, long day of charges, one after another, as if a crime wave has deposited all its flotsam at the courthouse door in a single morning. We have assaults, bladed weapons, muggings, shoplifting, criminal damage, fraud, crack-dealing, and a racially aggravated harassment. There is a man accused of robbing a 70-year-old woman newsagent with a crowbar – on being arrested and charged he apparently said to the police 'Robbery? I don't do robberies.'

A Russian Lithuanian charged with drink-driving does not open his mouth much as he can't speak English. But when he does it is so astonishingly full of gold teeth he could surely pay off his fines with a single molar.

The saddest case of the day is that of a large, handsome, Latvian woman accused of stealing a cheap handbag. She was drunk at the time and befuddled with Prozac, says the defence lawyer. The reason for this was that she had been under extreme stress, he explains, then hands up a recent edition of a local newspaper. Puzzled, we look at the front page, and immediately see what the lawyer is driving at. The whole page is taken up with a horrifying story about an 18-year-old Latvian girl who was kidnapped and forced to work in an Italian brothel. This was the defendant's daughter. She is with her mother in court today. For five weeks the girl was repeatedly violated and gang-raped, until she managed to escape and find her way back to London. Not surprisingly her mother, as well as herself, was deeply traumatised by what had happened – hence the Prozac and the booze. The girl looks at the bench, sadly but without self-pity. It is difficult to return her gaze.

FELL SWOOP
Local justice in a plagued land

I felt like an intruder on private grief. From the train window the Cumbrian fells looked beautiful but strangely desolate. In March 2001 these were not pastures sheep might safely graze. Foot and Mouth Disease was raging. There were clusters of white dots to be seen here and there, but for all I knew they were already under sentence of death. The Ministry of Agriculture, Fisheries and Food and the National Farmers' Union had closed their minds against vaccination. The result was a rolling catastrophe and this was one of its epicentres. I wondered how the effects of the plague would manifest themselves in the magistrates' courts I had come to visit. Assaults on visiting politicians and London journalists? Murdered MAFF inspectors? Mere townies like me were angry enough at what was taking place. How enraged must the locals feel?

I wandered the late afternoon streets of Carlisle on the alert for signs of crisis. But to my surprise there were none: no frantic newspaper bills, no ruined farmers selling the *Big Issue*. I never got to spot a car sporting one of those Cumbrian car stickers denouncing the 'Ministry of Arseholes F***ing Farming'. I sensed no atmosphere of communal despair. To be truthful, there was no atmosphere of any kind. Had this been France, the old market place in front of the town hall might have been filled with protesting farmworkers burning tractor tyres. What is more, it would have *looked* like a market place, the buildings around it proclaiming centuries of decent rural prosperity. Instead they have been dehumanised and disfigured by the same blandly inappropriate high street façades one finds in almost every town in England. The once-rollicking Roman garrison town, the 'merrie Carlisle' of Border ballads, seemed a touch soulless. By 6.30 p.m. it felt lifeless too. The only interesting crimes in the Cumbrian capital that night, I decided, were less likely to be committed by desperate farmers than by the guests at my dismal hotel, driven mad by the piped music endlessly repeating *Send in the Clowns* and *The Power of Love*.

I found the magistrates' court, though architecturally undistinguished, oddly cheering when I arrived at its entrance the following morning. Courthouses ought to be sombre places, but they also stand for a lot of things that are good about this country, such as the tradition of local justice, the independence of the judiciary, civic pride, public duty and so on. Markets may have stopped being markets, churches may no longer bind communities together and town halls have lost much of their clout, but the courts continue to occupy an important and interesting place in the life of any town still so fortunate as to have one.

Cumbria had lately had the number of its courts reduced from ten to six, despite protests, said Chris Armstrong, Clerk to the Justices, as we drank coffee in his office. Wigton appealed against amalgamation on the grounds that summary justice was constitutionally meant to be local, but was overruled. However, it was true to say, Chris admitted, that in the old days when there was less crime around, rural Cumbria had rather an oversupply of local justice. For example, the court in Keswick used to sit for just half a day a week, and even then there was so little to do they sometimes had the magistrates sitting in fours instead of threes so as to give them some action. 'It really was too many,' said Chris. 'Not only did we get split decisions but every time they retired it was like a flock of starlings leaving the courtroom and then bustling back in. There was another danger with small benches of only a dozen or so JPs – they could become a bit of a club.'

Carlisle (pop.125,000) had the biggest bench in the county with about eighty members, though that was still twenty below strength. They were having recruitment difficulties, especially with men. Just a few days earlier Chris had vainly tried to argue with a magistrate not to leave. The young man had only recently been sworn in but was already having to resign because of pressure from his employer. By contrast Kendal had a surplus of JPs, thanks to the number of retired people settled there, though that meant quite a few of the bench were not native Cumbrians. The county was considering putting in for a full-time district judge to help with the case load. At first, the lay magistrates had resisted the idea of letting a professional stipe into their midst, but their suspicions diminished after Graham Parkinson, the then Chief Metropolitan Magistrate from Bow Street (the same who presided in the Pinochet extradition case), came up to deal with a backlog of trials. The local JPs were impressed by his approachability and effectiveness and felt reassured, having seen how a pro went about his business.

Chris Armstrong was a contented-looking man. Even without the tie one might have taken him for the type of chap who is happiest with a rod or gun in his hands and a dog at his heels. But the burgundy neckwear was a give-away: it depicted stags' heads, leaping salmon and tumbling pheasants. This was the tie of the Countryside Alliance, of which Chris was an enthusiastic supporter. He would of course have been on the Liberty and Livelihood march in London the previous week, where half a million pro-hunting, pro-countryside demonstrators had been expected, had it not been cancelled because of Foot and Mouth.

He said the courts had so far had only one case arising directly from the epidemic – a man pleading not guilty to moving his livestock without a licence. But there had been several occasions when the police had called on magistrates at home seeking warrants to remove shotguns from farmers thought likely to be a danger to themselves – or possibly to the man from MAFF. 'The isolation and fear are making some of these people very volatile,' said Chris. Later that day I was present when a magistrate called Melvyn had to go off to issue a shotgun warrant. A farmhand had tipped off the police that he feared for his boss's state of mind. (Back in London, out of curiosity, I asked that well-known Cumbrian Lord Bragg whether Melvyn was a local name. No, he said. Middle-aged Melvyns like himself had been christened after Melvyn Douglas, the Hollywood heart-throb who starred with Garbo in *Ninotchka* – usually at the insistence of their star-struck mothers.)

It was ten o'clock and time for the day's hearings to begin. I spent some of the morning observing a drink-driving case. This would have been a singularly unoriginal thing to do, given the number of such cases we routinely dealt with in London, but for the fact that the defendant was a minor local celebrity. He was a pleasant-looking young man wearing a tie and a smart overcoat, and he was the Carlisle United goalkeeper. The press were outside. There was a bit of a buzz in the small courtroom. He had been caught in a Ford Escort in the Tesco carpark at 3 a.m. the previous Saturday. He registered 76 on the intoxaliser (a new word to me), two times the limit.

'I know I did wrong,' said the footballer. 'I went out with a few of the boys for a couple of drinks after the match.' He earned £21,000 a year. He said he would be prepared to take a rehabilitation course which would reduce his automatic disqualification period by a quarter. When the magistrates retired to consider their sentence, the atmosphere in the courtroom changed abruptly. Suddenly the prosecutor, the defence solicitor, the clerk, the usher and the defendant were all chatting about that evening's game against Halifax as animatedly as if they were in the pub rather than a court of law. The goalie said he thought they'd do OK.

When the bench returned he was fined £500 and disqualified for two years, the mandatory period according to the amount he was over the limit. Fortunately for everyone else in court, including the magistrates no doubt, he seemed untraumatised, since *le tout* Carlisle was anxious for the home team to do well that night. They were near the bottom of the Third Division and acutely nervous of relegation. It turned out they drew 0–0 with Halifax. Perhaps it said something for the sensitive behaviour of the bench that our man didn't let a goal in as a consequence of his brush with the law.

In a different courtroom a 26-year-old woman was to be sentenced for hurling a bottle at another woman, the cause of the altercation being her ex-husband. Her demeanour was a model of crafty courtmanship. She had brought her smartly-dressed family along with her. The epitome of respectability, they filled most of the public seating. The defendant herself looked very fetching in a sleeveless cream jumper which showed off her tanned arms. Her blonde hair was neatly coiffed, but with a stray lock falling artfully over her forehead. Throughout the proceedings, she held her specs at an attentive angle beside her face, giving the strong impression of a pretty, intelligent, reliable young working mum, obviously embarrassed to find herself in a criminal court. This was a young lady who could have given masterclasses in eyelash-fluttering. 'She would be something like a fish out of water in Low Newton,' said her lawyer, referring to the nearest women's prison, in the course of an interminable plea of mitigation which was naive in even mentioning the possibility of a custodial sentence and would have been much, much abbreviated before a stipe. The defendant got a suspended sentence. It was what she had schemed for, I guessed. It was also what she would probably have got even without the scheming.

During the breaks I talked to a knowledgeable usher called George. He was a former British Telecom employee and very up on his local history. Carlisle's last public hanging was in 1879, he told me. That was when the city had had its own jail. It was knocked down in the 1930s along with the neighbouring Jail Tap, the pub so called because the prisoners could send out to it for ale. They were replaced by Woolworths – a poor exchange, I found myself thinking, which must mark me out as the definitive conservative: someone who prefers an old prison to a new shop. Now the closest prison was Durham, two hours' drive away on the other side of the Pennines, across roads that could be exceedingly treacherous in winter. Another consequence of 'rationalisation' was the curious security setup in the Carlisle courthouse. Although there was a police station right next door, the courtroom panic buttons were connected to the police HQ at Penrith. In the case of trouble, the alarm had to be relayed first to Penrith and then back to the Carlisle police just a few feet away from where the emergency was taking place.

A number of magistrates gathered around a large table in the retiring room for lunch. We ate delicious Marks & Spencer sandwiches. I asked them about the prison problem. They said not only did it mean regrettably long journeys for prisoners and visitors; in Durham jail there was also a good deal of North-East versus North-West hostility between the inmates – a sort of Wars of the Roses behind bars. Local loyalties were strong in this part of the world. The border with Scotland was still an issue, as it had been over centuries, though the signs saying 'Haste ye back' were not so prevalent as they used to be. Otherwise Cumbria had no racial problems to speak of. There was one Indian and one Sri Lankan JP in the whole county, which didn't sound much but was actually a higher ethnic minority ratio than in the population as a whole. A number of displaced people – Poles and Latvians, mainly – were settled here after the Second World War, but they were all immensely law-abiding.

'I still remember people staring in the street at the first

Chinese restaurateurs who came to Carlisle,' said one magistrate. 'There are almost no coloured faces around even now. It's too cold for them.' Another JP said: 'I was looking at the visitor's book in one of the Lakeland churches the other day and there was an entry from a Korean family. They said they loved living in Cumbria, but were sorry they felt so lonely.'

Like everywhere else in the country, Carlisle had suffered a steady rise in drug-related offences. But a lot of the more serious crime remained the responsibility of only a small number of families. Jane, a legal adviser in an eye-catching check jacket, had been telling me about this before lunch. Cumbrian born and bred, she had been a court clerk for thirty-three years. 'When I first started, people were frightened of appearing in court. Today it's just routine. I recognise lots of people who come through the court – and now their sons and daughters. JPs know some of them, too, so for a trial we try to get magistrates who don't know the defendants, sometimes from a neighbouring bench. But,' she added, 'I can't recall a single appeal arising from this problem.'

One of these criminal clans pioneered ram-raiding in the area, a magistrate was saying. They were out on a job one night when a steel security shutter crashed down suddenly and caught one of the villains on the hop, so to speak. It broke both his legs. His companions dumped him out on a country road, so that the police would think he had been run over – which they did not, of course, even for a second.

Generally, though, ram-raiding was a less typical Cumbrian crime than sheep-rustling – not that there was much of it going on at present, with every farm under 24-hour scrutiny. There used to be a lot of salmon poaching, too, particularly on the Derwent, one of the lunchers reminisced. The poachers were notably unsporting in their methods. They used dynamite, devices called double-armoured trammel nets and sometimes a heavily-weighted hook which gaffed the fish and was ironically referred to as a Longtown fly. The Salmon Act of 1986 put a stop to much of this business by penalising hotels caught 'handling salmon in suspicious circumstances' – that is, serving their customers what used to be known with a wink as 'twice-poached salmon'. Almost as nefarious was the offence of passing off crossbred Aberdeen Angus as purebred beef. There was meat here, I thought, what with the ram-raiding and the wicked Longtown fly, for a Lakelands version of the Sopranos.

But these were light matters compared with what was happening right now, as the vets went about their lethal business among the flocks. A dozen or so Carlisle JPs were farmers, but every member of the bench shared their interest and concern. Apparently there were three or four more cases of moving sheep illegally in the pipeline. 'You must understand the heartbreak of what is going on,' said one magistrate. 'You people in the south simply don't appreciate the scale of what's happening. We will deal with these cases sensitively, which is where local knowledge comes in.'

It was as well the justices took this understanding attitude, I thought, as I left Carlisle for Kendal. Without the rule of law, there would be danger of the farming populace treating anyone flouting the regulations in much the same manner as an eighteenth-century cattle thief from north of the border, which is to say pretty heavy-handedly.

There was a prominent notice at Kendal station: 'It is currently an offence to use all footpaths and bridleways across farmland, including the fells, in Cumbria. This is to help combat Foot and Mouth Disease which is now threatening the way of life of everyone in rural communities.' This was a sobering sort of welcome to the home of the famous mint cake. Besides having tried this sugary delicacy and not much cared for it, I had no previous acquaintance with Kendal. It was a pretty town, garrotted by a one-way traffic system which for much of the day turned the main street into something resembling a car factory assembly line. By one minute past six that evening every shop was shut and the pavements were almost empty. I resorted to the bar of the Union Tavern, where I was staying. It was not terribly welcoming, but there was little alternative except for ubiquitous B & Bs, with their promise of horrid intimacy around the sauce bottle and TV set.

I would not recommend the Union Tavern to Lakeland visitors hoping for a rural inn with a cosy fire and a Cumberland sausage. Instead of *Send in the Clowns* and *The Power of Love* we had non-stop TV competing with disco thump and a whimpering fruit machine. I don't think there was a single local dish on the menu, which led off with lamb rogan josh and deep-fried Camembert. I settled amid the din and the smell from the deep fryer to read the paper. The *News & Star* ('At the heart *of what's happening all over Cumbria'*) had a crop of crime stories. There was life-threatening arson in Carlisle and pornography in Penrith. The most intriguing report of the day concerned a naked Cockermouth man who had dragged his pregnant wife around the garden by her hair, threatened to break her arms and legs, trashed their home, smashed a neighbour's window, spat at police officers and rubbed CS spray in their faces. Magistrates heard that the bizarre behaviour was the result of consuming hallucinogenic mushrooms. The couple, plus their newborn child, were now living peacefully together. The sentence was probation for two years. One could only salute the bench's unexcitability.

There were five pages on the progress of Foot and Mouth Disease, including interviews with schoolgirls who had been exiled to live with relatives to do their A Level revision, because their own farms were out of bounds. I tried getting the views of some of the men at the bar. They looked at me stony-faced. In his *Good Guide to the Lakes*, my friend Hunter Davies says that because of the violent history of these borderlands, Cumbrians can be suspicious folk, 'preferring to winter you, then summer you, and winter you again. Then if you're lucky, they might say hello.' The men answered my questions curtly, making no effort to disguise their dislike of Blair and New Labour but certainly not after my sympathy. 'We've got to go now,' they said at around 11 o'clock. 'It's not because of you, you understand,' they added kindly.

I breakfasted among heeltaps and unemptied ashtrays to the roar of the vacuum cleaner. The sight of Kendal courthouse lifted the spirits. Opened in 1992 by Princess Anne, it was an airy, pitch-roofed building in pale grey, blue and white with the smartest court loos I had yet encountered. Picture windows overlooked the River Kent and views of the fells beyond, where scattered sheep waded nonchalantly through mist up to their bellies. Next door was a garden centre. I was greeted by friendly Ron, who doubled as court receptionist and manager of the little kiosk selling orangeade and Kit Kats. It was about as rural a courthouse as you could find.

I joined the three magistrates for their pre-court briefing over coffee and chocolate digestives. The very efficient court clerk, a young Michael Palin with a Cumbrian accent, took them through the list. The worst cases were an assault committed with a broken snooker cue and the theft of a bottle of Jack Daniels by a notorious local drunk. To describe someone as a drunk in these parts, I realised, was quite serious. I had already been told that heavy drinking was pretty common, especially on Friday nights. For example, one heavy toper recently had his lawyer admit that he had drunk seven pints on the occasion in question. This was his plea in *mitigation* – it was *only* seven pints. His normal intake was twenty pints a night.

Court 1 was a lovely, spacious, predominantly white room with a high ceiling reminiscent of a Dutch barn. Lamps like upturned kidney bowls illuminated the walls, with spotlights shining down from the beams above. The acoustics were perfect. What was weird was that, in keeping with this trim, well-designed courtroom, defendant after defendant was also smartly turned out. They wore suits and ties. They spoke politely. The reason for this, I soon realised, was an accident of geography. They were all young business execs and salesmen caught breaking the speed limit in their Ford Focuses on the nearby M6 motorway.

They were invariably racing to meet an appointment in Scotland or catch the ferry at Stranraer. They were fined a few hundred pounds each and given penalty points on their licences. This was the court's daily clientele. What the girls from the Seven Sisters Road were to Haringey these chaps from the motorway were to Kendal. A typical offender drove 30,000 miles a year, apparently. For these people disqualification was a serious matter, as they would almost certainly lose their jobs if they couldn't drive. Several of that day's defendants were totters, which meant they already had a number of penalty points on their licences. If, with that day's additional points, the total totted up to twelve or more, then they were automatically disqualified for at least six months. Oh dear, one thought, as one watched their faces crumple in despair. The only hope was to persuade the court, on oath, that they would suffer exceptional hardship as a consequence. But this was not an easy task with a bench so accustomed to such pleas.

The stream of speeding drivers was interrupted by a farm worker with blond-streaked hair who had come to court to explain why he couldn't go on paying his fines at £20 a week for a previous offence. The reason was that he had just lost his job thanks to Foot and Mouth Disease. It was as though a spectre had entered the courtroom and jogged the chairman's elbow. They gave the lad time to sort out his affairs, and let him go.

The bench retired to the neighbouring garden centre café for lunch. Over mushroom soup and rolls the talk was all of the great disaster plaguing the countryside. The chief worry was that flocks of Herdwicks, Swaledales, Cheviots and other hefted sheep would be wiped out. For centuries it had been possible to graze these animals on the hundreds of square miles of unfenced fells because they were genetically attuned to know their own patches and not to stray, which was what the term 'hefted' meant. If they were slaughtered, it would mean either replacing them with non-hefted sheep, which would have to be walled or fenced in for several generations, to the great detriment of the ancient landscape – or the end of this kind of farming altogether.

One could sense the depression at the café tables. This was

not Carlisle, which had seemed to me so strangely unstirred by what was going on. People exchanged news and rumours in low voices. Someone said he'd heard farmers were hiding their prize sheep away in lofts and cellars, like escaping airmen in France during the war. Someone else said there was a worry about the geese in the Solway, which were about to migrate to Norway. Could they carry the disease on their feathers and spread it across Europe?

Elsewhere in Cumbria that day the government chief vet was addressing farmers and the press in an attempt to justify the cull. Those opposed to the policy, it was said angrily, were excluded from the meeting. I wondered whether such opponents might eventually end up in court for some act of resistance, and if so how local JPs would view the matter. My lunch companions said they believed the bench had a democratic, representative role as well as that of simply applying the law: they must dispense justice, but tempered with local understanding. That was well put. Mischievously, I then asked a question from which I had found that other magistrates, and the Magistrates' Association itself, tended to shy away. How might rural JPs act if Labour eventually passed a ban on fox-hunting? This was Cumbria, after all, home of that most famous of huntsmen, John Peel.

One of my lunch companions, who was a farmer, did not hesitate. If there were a hunting ban, he said, at least a dozen people would resign from his own bench, including himself. 'I wouldn't sit there and sentence old friends,' he said determinedly. I suspect this attitude would be echoed all over the country, though I don't suppose the Government has bothered to take it into account.

On the train back to London I glanced at the correspondence page in the *News & Star* (*At the* heart *of, etc.*). Among the readers' letters, mostly indignant at the Government's ineptitude, was one taking a different line. The writer denied that the Lakelands landscape was under threat from livestock depopulation. 'The current number of sheep is higher than ever before,' he wrote, 'and acts to the detriment of the scenic beauty of the Lake District. The fell slopes are grazed back hard by the sheer numbers of sheep, harming heather and bilberry. In the autumn these plants would provide a blaze of gold and purple interspersed with rowan and silver birch if grazing levels were lower.' In short, he said, less intense grazing would be better for the landscape and reduce the potential for future transmission of disease.

It was a point of view, one that would presumably delight the hearts of those alleged plotters in MAFF – soon to be culled itself and be replaced by (or perhaps reborn as) DEFRA, the Department of Environment, Food and Rural Affairs – who yearned for the end of uneconomical hill farming and saw Foot and Mouth as the means of attaining it.

This set me to musing, as one is prone to do on a long train journey. The region I had just visited, one of the best loved in the entire country thanks to its sublime fell and lakeland landscape, thanks to Wordsworth and Beatrix Potter, already seemed in some danger of losing its sense of self. The only places to eat well, apart from top-of-the-range spots such as the Miller Howe and Sharrow Bay hotels, were French, Thai or Chinese. Eating badly in a pub was also a foreign experience. The brochure for the museum in Carlisle somehow managed to emphasise its shop, café and educational events over and above telling you the history of the city. If the place and its history were not remarkable, why should anyone be interested?

In Carlisle's splendid Market Hall the old Butter Market had gone, where every week people would flock into town to sell local produce. The reason was partly the supermarket culture, but also the plethora of food hygiene inspectors and regulations. Now the stalls sold cheap bed linen and nasty tableware. The disassociation between the town dwellers and the surrounding countryside was already well advanced, thanks to bureaucrats and shopping chains. MAFF's Foot and Mouth death squads might well complete the process, aiding New Labour's unsubtle campaign against the country-dwelling classes, aka the 'forces of conservatism'.

What was at stake here was a sense of rootedness and belonging. It was only a little far-fetched to think that the idea of modernising the magistracy likewise posed a threat to the old idea of community and place. Get rid of the farmers, the butchers, the blacksmiths and the huntsmen, amalgamate the parishes, close the police stations, do away with the local courts and justices, and where would you be? Answer: but for the scenery, almost anywhere in turn-of-the-millennium Britain, alas.

Highgate. Court interpreters are a study on their own. They are obviously among the most successful of the immigrant and refugee communities, always well dressed, fluent and polite. They look like school teachers or university professors, which maybe some of them are as well, or were before they came here. Sometimes the contrast between the bewildered, recently-arrived defendant and the poised, long-settled translator is rather poignant. There is one interpreter whom I especially enjoy: a small, bustling lady of middle age who always gives the appearance of being totally at home in the courtroom. She whizzes through the oath they all have to take, promising to 'well and faithfully interpret and true explanation make', then huddles up beside some monstrous lout in the dock, several feet taller than herself, as confidently as if she were his mother. Sometimes the briskness of her translation makes it sound almost as though she were giving the boy a dressing-down herself, and one is not surprised when he responds in a crestfallen way by pleading guilty. But then occasionally she will spread her arms, cast her eyes ceilingwards in a resigned sort of way and inform us that, well, 'he says he is not guilty'. I'm sure it is only my imagination that detects a very faint emphasis on the word 'says'.

RATIO AWARENESS
More ethnic minority magistrates, please

A Cumbrian JP visiting one of our courts in Haringey would be struck by a very obvious difference: the large number of non-white defendants. As against this inescapable fact of inner city life in the twenty-first century, most metropolitan benches still fail by some way to reflect the ethnic make-up of the local population. This is despite the strenuous efforts by the Lord Chancellor to recruit more blacks and Asians, which have in fact had a good deal of success. The problem seems to be, at least as far as the eight North London boroughs of the Middlesex area are concerned, that the ethnic minority populations have been growing faster than was realised. In 1999, for example, Middlesex thought it was doing quite well, with around 20 per cent of black and Asian JPs on the bench compared with 25 per cent in the area as a whole. The snag was that this last percentage was based on the 1991 census. One research body calculated that by the end of the decade the true figure was nearer 33 per cent, which was not so good at all. We would have to await the full analysis of the 2001 census to get a more accurate idea of what was going on, but in Haringey the previous year it was estimated that while the percentage of non-white magistrates on the bench was a meagre 12.6, the ethnic minority proportion of the borough's populace had risen to 45 per cent.

This was pretty dismaying. The explanation put to me was that despite all sorts of efforts there were simply not enough suitable ethnic minority volunteers putting themselves forward, though of course that left the prickly question of what exactly was meant by 'suitable' rather hanging in the air. In 2001 Lord Irvine launched a scheme for black, Asian and Chinese people to shadow local magistrates for six months so they could learn how the lay justice system works. It was hoped the shadows would then carry the good news – that you don't have to be white and middle class to be a JP – back to their own communities. The idea seemed laudable enough as a gesture of inclusivity. But it struck me that anyone keen enough to become one of these shadows in the first place probably didn't need much persuading that the lay magistracy was a worthwhile institution and that ethnic minority citizens ought to be a part of it. I would have thought it more sensible, less time-consuming (and perhaps less condescending) to get them onto the bench themselves as soon as possible, and *then* urge them to go out and spread the word.

Leslie is a black JP who joined the Haringey bench in 1996. An imposing man of over six foot with a trim bread and a purposeful manner, he works as a public health specialist and management consultant for the voluntary sector. I suspect he would have been rather scathing about the shadow magistrate wheeze. He himself was only twenty-six when he was sworn in and did not need much cajoling. He grew up in Tottenham, where he still lives. He studied public health at Sunderland Polytechnic, became a National Union of Students officer and enjoyed his public duties enough to think of becoming a politician or a lawyer. In fact, after doing an MA at King's College, London, he returned to Tottenham to work in the local authority health department, and quickly found himself involved in community activities. It was a local Tory who urged Leslie to apply for the bench. Remembering how interesting he had found a stint at the Old Bailey as a 19-year-old juryman, he did so.

He joined when training had already improved a good deal. 'We were among the first to get a proper training manual,' he remembered. 'This was very important. As you broaden the base of the magistracy you can't rely on everyone sharing the same sorts of values. You have to establish a common ground, and the training helps to do that. The only problem was that everything was focused on the heavy end of crime. My first sitting was a traffic court. Dealing with people for parking offences didn't feel like what we were supposed to be doing.' Fortunately, the feeling didn't last.

There were a dozen people in Leslie's intake. One was a Greek Cypriot and there was another Afro-Caribbean besides himself. More than half the Haringey bench were Jewish then, he said. What had he thought of the other magistrates?

'They were lovely. I met all sorts of people I would never normally have come into contact with. There was a Lady Someone and a retired Major Someone-Else. I'd never even met a major on a personal level before. One woman I sat with in a fines court listening to people's accounts of their financial troubles amazed me. "I can't believe people don't pay their bills on time," she said in genuine wonderment. She was from another world. So I supposed it was a part of my job to put another view, from a world I am familiar with. It was about making sure we didn't tar everyone with the same brush.

'No, I don't think magistrates like that woman should be banished from the bench. Why wipe those characters out of the picture? It's important to have their voices. They have a contribution to make, too, and they need to be exposed to other views of life. Being a JP keeps them grounded. Otherwise you're just encouraging the upper strata of society to wash their hands of it all and say "Let the riffraff run themselves".'

Being a black magistrate, Leslie said, made him especially conscious of the oath to 'do right to all manner of people without fear or favour, affection or ill-will'. 'When a young black defendant sees me on the bench you can see him do a double take. That's good in one way, but in another it gives him false hope. You can almost hear him saying "Root for me". He doesn't understand that justice isn't about the way you look or the colour of your skin. Justice is blind. The magistrates aren't there for the good of the defendant. They're there for the greater good, because they are concerned members of the community.'

In any case, a black or Asian presence on the bench didn't affect a lot of the defendants we had to deal with in Haringey one way or another. For example, as far as East European refugees and the like were concerned, none of us was a friendly face. 'Through the Haringey courts you can almost map the

countries from which the latest batch of immigrants is coming,'
Leslie observed. 'You can't always tell whether it's poverty that
pushes them towards crime or whether they are being picked
on.'

A comparable sense of alienation prevailed in the youth
court. Leslie had been on the youth panel for two years,
watching the law scrambling to keep pace with the phenomenal
rate of change in children's lives and attitudes. 'As a Tottenham
local I have some idea of the context of their lives. I can follow
the story. Youth magistrates are rehabilitative in their outlook,
almost nurturing. But still, often you feel there's no dialogue.
We should do more to access young people. It's not about court
open days; it's about reaching out in schools and shopping
centres.'

Race remained a barrier in this country, however politically
correct people were trying to be. Leslie was on a prison visit to
Pentonville with some other magistrates a while ago. The prison
officer who showed them round didn't at first believe he was
one of the group. 'Are you sure you're a magistrate?' he asked
Leslie, eyeing the young black man suspiciously. 'As we toured
the wings I was worried I'd run into an inmate I knew. Well, I
didn't, which was a relief. Then, just as we were about to leave, I
looked up and saw this guy leaning over one of the balconies.
"Hey," he shouted, "Leslie! What are *you* doing in here?" Then
he raced down. It was someone I'd grown up with from Ferry
Lane Estate. Everyone looked on in astonishment as we shook
hands. The prison officer stared hardest of all.'

Leslie laughed as he told the story, though he was making a
serious point. Well-meaning white people can pooh-pooh Macpherson's notion of 'institutional racism' all they like, but they
shouldn't be too surprised if well-meaning black people respond with cynicism. 'Why is there now this drive to get more
ethnic minorities on the bench?' asked Leslie pointedly. 'We've
always had inner cities. Have we suddenly become nicer people? I don't think so. The drive is occurring because our
democracy is in crisis: there is a crisis of legitimacy. The system

needs shoring up from a broader base. So they turn to us to provide it.'

There was a lot in what he said. But there might be another motive, too. Some of the sharpest criticism of the Mode of Trial Bills, which sought to restrict the right to elect trial by jury, had come from ethnic minority communities. They argued that black or Asian defendants had more chance of a fair hearing from a randomly picked jury than from predominantly white magistrates. If the Government, perhaps with the support of Auld, was determined to pursue its plans in this quarter, which would mean thousands of previously 'either-way' cases being heard in the magistrates' courts, then obviously recruiting more black and Asian JPs could help to soften some of the hostility.

GROUP ACTIVITY
How persistence changed the colour of justice

Not every Middlesex borough was doing as poorly as Haringey in recruiting ethnic minority magistrates. Soon after my meeting with Leslie, I learnt that in 1999, the same year that I became a magistrate, all but one of Brent's new JPs were from an ethnic minority, whereas in my own intake the ratio was exactly the reverse, with only one non-white magistrate out of the ten of us. In 2001 our North London neighbours again outperformed us in this respect, with two-thirds of Brent's new magistrates being black or Asian. This seemed so remarkable I decided to pay a visit.

Brent's 1980s courthouse in Willesden is a persuasive advertisement for modern local justice. Its design is smart and approachable, its brickwork bright. On the other side of the road is a former cinema whose discoloured paintwork and graffitied walls suggest terminal neglect. One would be tempted to see the juxtaposition of these two buildings as pleasingly symbolic of law and disorder, were it not for the large sign running right across the front of the old Willesden Empire.

'Miracles Signs & Wonders Ministries,' it proclaims. 'Restoration of Lives & Needs. Jesus is Lord, Jesus is Lord.'

Jesus is certainly Lord for many of Brent's inhabitants, but there is also a large Jewish and Muslim population and an ethnic mix at least as diverse as Haringey's. How was it that Brent had successfully co-opted so many members of these minorities onto the bench in recent years? They made up nearly a quarter of the 150 total, compared with our own puny 12.6 per cent. Admittedly, the proportion of ethnic minorities in the borough as a whole was also larger than Haringey's, an estimated 53 per cent, so in a perfectly balanced world, the bench should have reflected this. But still, Brent's was a considerable achievement.

One of the reasons for it, I gathered, was the existence of a vigorous Equal Opportunities Group of JPs which had helped to transform the way the Brent bench was viewed by the local communities. It was three of the most active members of the group whom I had come to see: Phil from Barbados, its chairman, Winston from Guyana and Vipool, a Tanzanian Asian. They were clearly able and agreeable men but also, I felt, a touch impatient with my rather mealy-mouthed approach to the subject we were there to discuss. I had the impression they had experienced too many encounters with well-intentioned middle-class white folk inclined to avoid the real issues.

Phil, a very direct character, launched into me straight away to demand what I meant by 'ethnic minorities'. I said it was a definition which troubled me, too, since it was both loaded and imprecise. Phil nodded. His concern, he said bluntly, was with Caribbean, African and Asian people. 'The term "ethnic minorities" is a deliberate attempt to flatten the distrust caused by racial disadvantage,' he asserted. 'Lumping people of different cultures and backgrounds together broadens the whole issue too much. The prime issue is race equality.'

'There are about 161 different nationalities in Greater London,' said Vipool. 'So we're all minorities. But we don't all have the same problems.' For the moment, Kosovan refugees and asylum seekers were a disadvantaged minority at the bottom of the pile. But how long would it take them to belong to the community, those who stayed here long enough to become a part of society? Not all that long, we thought. 'For the likes of me and my children and my children's children,' said Winston firmly, 'it will take many generations to become assimilated. But the Kosovans have got white faces. The primary problem we're dealing with here is one of colour. It is about black and white.'

Phil joined the Brent bench back in 1973, knowing there had been strong opposition to his appointment because of his race. What got him through was the fact that he had been nominated by the (white) chairman of a neighbouring bench, who happened to be a fellow hospital governor, and that he won the strong support of the chairwoman of the interview panel, Lady Macleod, a JP herself and widow of the senior Conservative politician Iain Macleod. 'But I was under no illusion why I was appointed. I was a black face – for some years the only one on the whole bench.'

'You mean it was tokenism,' said Winston.

'Yes.'

Phil's work as a community relations officer with the local authority did not help. If anything it increased the suspicion of some of his white colleagues on the bench, who seemed to think his job compromised his impartiality. But he toughed it out, not just from cussedness but because he felt the rest of the bench needed to hear what he had to say. 'I had a responsibility to make them understand what the problems were really all about.' Once he was joined by other black and Asian magistrates, such as Winston and Vipool, the drive to make the Brent bench more racially alert grew increasingly effective.

They did not regard it as a part of their role to be recruiting sergeants for black JPs. 'What I saw as my chief duty was to help make changes among my colleagues so that newcomers should find this an open-minded bench, free of racist undertones,' said Winston. Vipool remembered a Tory Home Secretary visiting the borough as part of a clumsy initiative to persuade more Asians to become magistrates. He had no success whatsoever. Instead of the direct approach to potential candidates, Vipool felt it was more effective to rely on Brent's lively community grapevines to convey the message that Asians were not merely tolerated but welcome on the bench. Plainly, the strategy works.

'A black face on the bench does make a difference,' said Winston. Like his colleagues, he was on the youth panel as well as sitting in adult courts. 'Chairing demands all your attention, but as a winger you have a chance to watch what's going on and pick up the vibes. I think you can see sometimes the black kids gain confidence from the fact that one or more of the magistrates is black or Asian. That doesn't mean we're a soft touch. We don't treat them any differently from white kids.' On the other hand the black and Asian presence on the bench has certainly helped teach white magistrates to treat black defendants with more understanding than they used to, said Phil. 'These days everyone makes a real effort to pronounce people's names correctly. They're not so quick to jump to cultural conclusions as they were. We used to have to correct their perceptions, like the idea that there was something fishy about a young black guy owning a car.'

Winston said: 'A few years ago, some white magistrates were much too prone to believe police witnesses unquestioningly, especially when there was a black defendant in the dock.' Structured decision-making and better training had contributed tremendously to counteracting that kind of thoughtlessness, these three agreed, as had the growing presence of blacks and Asians on the bench. They also had three court clerks from the ethnic minorities. (Haringey, come to think of it, has none.)

'Back in the seventies the local people thought of this as a police court,' Phil recalled. 'Now there is confidence among the black, Asian and other ethnic minority populations here that the Brent bench will treat them fairly.' A sign of that was the respect people had for the new courthouse. This seemed to be true. Unlike many I had seen, it was strikingly free of graffiti and cigarette butts both inside and out, whereas its predecessor had actually been firebombed.

The next step, said Phil, was to set up some sort of country-wide association for black and Asian JPs, a network which could exchange experiences and act as a lobby, just as already existed among lawyers and in the police, probation and prison services. As I left, the three of them got down to work drafting the letter they planned to send to the Magistrates' Association putting forward the idea. With the Brent Equal Opportunities Group behind it, I'd say it had a high chance of success.

Highgate. A trial that's more EastEnders than North Londoners. Cherisse, the defendant, is accused of assaulting two neighbours on her council estate. She has failed to come to court. We decide to proceed in her absence, as all the witnesses are present and she has had plenty of warning. She can always ask for the verdict to be set aside under Section 142 of the Magistrates' Court Act, the clerk advises us.

The first witness for the prosecution is one of the alleged victims. Lisa is a tiny woman with a pinched face who is probably in her late thirties but looks like a waif, a starveling Cockney sparrow. She is unable to read the oath and is so cripplingly inarticulate she can barely even say it, as the usher leads her through it word by word. She keeps looking at her friends at the back of the court, like a child seeking approval. Unbelievably, she has six children under twelve. 'On the day it 'appened,' she says, 'I was doin' me arsework.' The dispute was about the key to the shed where her son kept his bike. She thought Cherisse's son had run off with it.

'I asked her politely if she'd got my shed key. She effed and blinded at me,' says Lisa with an embarrassed giggle. 'I don't like to say the words.' Then Lisa went off to talk to her friend Teresa. 'We was joking and laughing 'cos it was a nice sunny day.' Next thing, Cherisse came running up to

them. 'She banged me 'ead against the door and punched me on the nose. She got her fist and punched it.' Lisa demonstrated this by scrunching her own small hand into the shape of a walnut and flourishing it above her head. After that she had run upstairs to her flat and her husband called the ambulance.

Lisa becomes confused under cross-examination by Cherisse's lawyer, unable to remember whether the head-banging had come before the nose-punching or the other way round. 'I got mixed up,' she says, looking shyly at the bench. 'I'm sorry, Your Honour.' Her friend Teresa's reaction to Cherisse's assault was also to run upstairs. 'She's got bad nerves, Teresa has,' Lisa explains.

It is Teresa's turn to give evidence. She cannot read the oath either. She is a big, slow woman in a denim dress. She tells the story of the attack, saying Cherisse knocked her into a ditch. 'How long did the assault on Lisa go on for?' asks the defence lawyer. 'A couple of hours,' says Teresa after some thought. Everyone looks astonished.

'A couple of hours?'

'Well, maybe it was a couple of minutes. I can't tell the time.'

'How many EastEnders programmes would you have seen in that time?' asks the prosecutor unhelpfully. Teresa is quite baffled by the complexity of this concept. She remains completely silent, then starts shaking and finally bursts into tears. Our chairwoman kindly asks if she'd like a break to recover, but when she returns the same thing happens again and she is led away weeping.

The police constable who went to the scene gives evidence. When he got to the flats he met Cherisse. She said: 'It's me you're looking for. I lumped her one. Them fucking cunts are getting away with it. I'm fucking nicked.' In the police interview tape she gives her account of how Lisa and Teresa had accused her boy of having the shed key. 'He was scared. He was literally crying his eyes out. I *said leave my kids alone. She deserved everything she got. Round that area if you don't stand up for yourself you'd be battered.'*

We find Cherisse guilty and issue a warrant for her arrest.

CHAPTER 13

Catching Them Young

'They don't value themselves and so they're not valued by anyone else'

I would soon have been a magistrate for two years, which meant I would be eligible to volunteer for specialised work in the family and youth courts. Both panels were always eager for fresh blood, and they were critically short of men. I knew a little about the youth courts by now, but had had nothing to do with family, so I asked David to fill me in. Our daughters had been at the same primary school – he was the chairman of the governors – so we were old acquaintances. He had been on the Haringey family panel for a couple of years. I often saw him in the retiring room, scratching his head, bent in thought over heaps of daunting-looking files.

'There's always a lot of documentation in these cases,' David said. 'Most of what we do concerns the protection and care of children. Typically we are assessing applications from local authorities to carry out some kind of intervention where a child is thought to be at risk – a supervision order, maybe, or an emergency protection order.

'It's not like an ordinary criminal court. It's a non-adversarial setup. We sit in one of the smaller courtrooms and try to keep the atmosphere informal. The lawyers representing the council, the child and its family are arranged in a horseshoe facing the bench. Usually at least one parent is present and, if he or she is old enough and the facts of the case are thought not too horrific, the child too. Everyone is introduced to everyone else.

'Mostly our task is to scrutinise and approve what the council wants to do in order to safeguard a child, under the provisions of the Children Act 1989. Given that this very sweeping legislation was brought in under Mrs Thatcher, who thought there was no such thing as society, it's a very good piece of lawmaking. It gives absolute primacy to the best interests of the child. But at the same time it establishes as a point of principle that families should not be interfered with unless it is plainly necessary for the child's welfare.'

David enjoyed his family court work. Although he had encountered some sickening cases of children being physically and sexually abused, what the court was interested in was not punishment for the perpetrators but simply a positive outcome for the victim. This often required very delicate negotiation with the parties concerned. For example, David's own wife was a social worker, and he was aware that some of her colleagues were sometimes inclined to attach too much importance to the sanctity of the parent–child relationship, even when there was evidence of serious neglect or abuse by the parents. On the other hand, the cautious approach could pay dividends. He recounted the case of a vegan mother whose small child was 'failing to thrive' because of protein deficiency. In other words, the child was alarmingly undernourished. Guided by the court, the mother had been counselled as to how to feed her offspring properly without contravening her vegan principles, and having done so successfully, the authorities were able to back off.

The family court also dealt with disputed applications for adoption, hearings which generally took two or three days. David, who gave up his interior design business to work for a charity, had the time to spare and liked the sense of engagement such relatively long cases gave the magistrates. He also liked our bench's tradition of marking the successful solution to one of these adoptions by presenting the child with a teddy bear, paid for by donations from the Haringey JPs. It was a small gesture, but one which aptly summed up the spirit in which the family panel went about its work.

David made the family court sound thoroughly interesting and worthwhile. But I still felt myself more drawn towards the youth courts. If magistrates ever entertain a hope of reforming offenders rather than merely punishing them, it is surely here that they have the best opportunity. The ITN newscaster Carol Barnes had recently written about becoming a JP herself and homed in on the problem of juvenile offenders. 'When and why do they take the first step on the crime ladder?' she wanted to know. 'Can they be guided off it, or must they end up as habitual criminals?' They were questions I asked myself. So, even though I knew younger magistrates were preferred for the task, I thought I would put my name forward for the youth panel. But first I would try to learn a bit more about the whole business by visiting the Haringey Youth Offending Team. Its headquarters were in an office block in Crouch End.

One thing New Labour really did put its mind to in its first term was youth offending – young offenders being defined as those aged from ten up to but not including their eighteenth birthday. Under the aegis of the Youth Justice Board a number of admirable objectives were laid down. They included speeding up the progress of youth cases through the courts, the introduction of more imaginative sentencing, encouraging reparation to victims by young offenders and the greater involvement of parents. To achieve these aims on the ground every local authority in the land was required under the 1998 Crime and Disorder Act to establish a Youth Offending Team. This was to be a multi-agency body, including representatives of the police, the Probation Service, the social and education services and the health authorities. If it worked, it would be a rare example of Labour's much-vaunted 'joined-up' government in action. By the spring of 2001 there were some promising signs. The pace of getting youths through the courts had not quite halved, as intended; but it had greatly improved, from an average 142 days per case to ninety.

Fundamental reforms of this kind could not simply be imposed from the top by political diktat. They had to be built from the bottom upwards. Much of 1999 was spent simply setting up the Haringey YOT, said Paul Dugmore, showing me a daunting flowchart-cum-network of interconnecting tasks and responsibilities whose purpose was at once to succour, guide and contain young offenders, and when necessary supervise their punishment. It was a major organisational undertaking. Paul, though only thirty, seemed calmly on top of matters. He was operational manager of one of the two main arms of our YOT, the Community Supervision Team, which dealt with established offenders. The other arm, the Early Intervention Team, was chiefly concerned with nipping offending behaviour in the bud, as its name implied.

The old days of serial police cautioning had gone, Paul told me. Now there was a pretty severe routine that amounted to three strikes and you're out. A garishly coloured pamphlet issued by the Metropolitan Police explains things in no-nonsense terms. 'If you don't break the law,' it says, 'the information in this leaflet probably won't affect you. But if you DO, you will find that the police deal with young offenders in a different way now because the law has changed.'

For a first minor offence there will be a Reprimand (printed in day-glo cerise). For a second, a Warning (toxic orange). 'If you break the law for a third time, whatever the offence, even a minor one, you will automatically be sent to court and be Prosecuted (blood red) . . . Why does being taken to court matter? If you are taken to court and found guilty of an offence, you will be sentenced and convicted as a criminal. This criminal conviction can then ruin opportunities for you in the future. Remember (acid green) if you are a convicted criminal your police record may last all your life.' Good stuff, I thought. This was giving it to the kids in clear, plain language – always assuming they could be got to read it in the first place.

The idea is that the Early Intervention Team is notified by the police every time a reprimand is issued. This triggers a visit to the offender's home and an extremely thorough twelve-page assessment of the boy's or girl's character and circumstances. Ideally, this will cover every kind of problem that might lead to offending, from drug abuse to truancy, from bullying at school to violence or neglect at home. The team tries to redirect the reprimanded youth before he or she settles into a pattern of misbehaviour, offering volunteer programmes, counselling and so forth. It also does preventive work through the schools.

From the reprimand stage onwards, young people can be given, or sometimes compelled to have, a mentor or 'personal trainer' to help them with their difficulties and act as a role model. These mentors, Paul explained, were all volunteers, of whom there seemed to be an encouraging supply. They had to be over eighteen but usually not a lot older, since the idea was to match mentor and young offender as closely as possible in terms of age, sex and race. Mentoring was apparently proving very effective. Amazingly and hearteningly, Paul told me that in Haringey 80 per cent of those reprimanded were not reoffending.

All this sounded highly desirable, though extremely labour-intensive. There would be about forty people on the Haringey YOT when all the vacancies were filled, dealing with 150–180 clients at any one time. The funding from the Youth Justice Board was quite generous, but recruitment was not always easy. For example, they had not yet got a health officer, said Paul, because it was hard to find someone who was not only qualified to deal with mental health problems and substance abuse but also had youth experience. Being able to engage with young people was probably the most important skill of all.

Those who failed to respond to early intervention and continued to offend would become the responsibility of Paul's own Community Supervision Team. Its job was to keep an eye on kids on bail to make sure they turned up to court, and to work closely with those who had been sentenced, whether in or out of custody.

The range of sentences now available in the youth courts is impressive. For example, as from April 2002, children from ten to seventeen with no previous convictions who plead guilty at their first court appearance automatically get a referral order of between three and twelve months. This is an imaginative idea whereby the offender is in effect 'sentenced' by a panel of volunteers from the commuity, whose chief purpose is to prevent the youth getting into the habit of offending by devising an individual programme of reparation and rehabilitation. I like this initiative, particularly because it is an extension of the principle of involving local lay people in the administration of justice.

Another bespoke penalty, further down the sentencing road, is the action plan. This might include an element of reparation to the victim together with weekly visits to an attendance centre. The prime aim is to get the offender to address his antisocial behaviour. For instance, violent offenders might be made to attend the special first-aid course which Haringey runs with the Red Cross. A young thug would not only be confronted with the flesh-and-blood consequences of violence but also learn worthwhile skills. Likewise a young arsonist might do work with the local fire brigade.

This sounded like a promising approach, though it seemed to me that, like some other aspects of the Government's youth justice reforms, there was a strong element of wishful thinking here. This also applied to the concept of reparation. It was now routine, according to Paul, that the victim should be consulted when a youth was convicted, and invited to take part in victim–offender mediation, if both parties agreed. The court could propose suitable reparation, either to the victim personally or, if the latter could not bear the idea of seeing the youth again, to the community – say by scrubbing graffiti off a wall or collecting litter. The trouble was that so far victims had not been as willing to become involved as the Government intended. Reparation was always considered, but the take-up had been disappointing.

Another new penalty which was proving only patchily effective was the parenting order, requiring parents to see their children to school, be responsible for their good behaviour, and if need be, accept counselling on their own behalf. Again, this was a well-meant initiative, but in fact, said Paul, only some courts in the country were using it. The difficulty was knowing what to do if parents – especially a hard-pressed single parent – breached the order. In Haringey the legal advisers took the view that if a father or mother were punished, there could be trouble under the Human Rights Act, since he or she would not actually have committed a crime. One had to agree. Regretfully, even in the best-run households these days parental authority was something of a spent force. No mere law could conjure it back into existence.

Recognising the problem, the Haringey YOT has a parenting co-ordinator, who is often contacted by parents themselves when they become desperate for advice and support – like the group of Somali mothers who had recently approached the team, anxious about their children's misbehaviour. But not all parents are that concerned. So one of the YOT's tasks is to provide 'appropriate adults' to attend the court and police station with young offenders when they have no parent or relative of their own to accompany them. Haringey has more than thirty of these saintly volunteers, recruited through advertisements in local newspapers and libraries. They save masses of time for the YOT workers and are a godsend to the police, who used to have endless difficulties with parents unwilling to come and stand by their offspring when they were hauled into the station at 2 a.m. on a Saturday night.

For the hard nuts who resist the improving efforts of the Early Intervention Team and end up being convicted as persistent offenders, the usual custodial sentence is a detention and training order. This can run from four months to two years. Like adult prison sentences, the DTO means you only serve half the time. But in the case of youths the other half is supposed to continue the 'training' you started in custody. What is wrong with this worthy concept is that prison education, so shamefully run down by the Tories, is still something of a disaster area. And the idea that a youth can move 'seamlessly' from custody back into the ordinary school from which he probably used to truant anyway seems wildly optimistic.

A perennial problem is the breaching of non-custodial orders. After two failures to attend offenders are supposed to be brought back to court, and usually are, but soft-hearted magistrates don't always punish them for the breach. Paul thought they should, even if it was only a £5 fine, just to make them realise they had committed a wrong. Non-punishment was liable to lead to a further breach, in which case the YOT might feel there was no alternative but to refuse to have them back. That was as good as a custodial sentence, a course which was only ever pursued with the greatest reluctance. 'Our ethos is let's keep them out of custody if we can,' said Paul. 'Most of these young people are damaged. Sending them to a prison full of other damaged young people is not going to help either them or society.'

In Paul's office there was a blackboard with the names of thirty youths currently serving DTOs. 'If you were on the youth panel,' he said to me, 'you'd recognise most of them. There is a core of persistent offenders in the borough. Our most relentless offender once committed thirty-three crimes in twelve months, and those were just the ones the police knew about. He did a DTO at Huntercombe, where he was a model trainee for three months. That's a long time for a chaotic young offender. When he was released he went straight on to a course. We thought maybe he was in the clear. And then, just two hours after his detention and training order expired, he was found driving a stolen car.

'With young people like him the offending is entrenched, and the people they hang about with are the same. They either bunk off school or they're excluded. They live in crap housing. They're disenfranchised. They don't value themselves and so they're not valued by anyone else. Their investment in society is so small, what have they got to lose? For them offending is a way of being recognised. It makes society notice they're there. For us it's about limiting the damage they cause.'

It was a pretty bleak assessment. But it showed that, for all the pie charts and glossy pamphlets, the Haringey YOT had a grip on reality. One could raise an eyebrow at the idea of a fire-raiser working with the fire brigade, or a barely literate mugger writing a letter of apology to a traumatised pensioner. Some of these bright new community punishments might indeed turn out to be pie in the sky. But they were unquestionably worth trying, as was anything that might make a young offender think a bit better of himself and, as a consequence, a bit less contemptuously of others.

The frightening rise in crime among the desocialised young was the gravest social ill facing this country at the start of the new millennium. In seeking to halt or at any rate slow the trend without adding to the already bulging figure of young people in detention, the Youth Justice Board was aiming high. But its funding was generous, its cause admirable and the potential rewards were enormous. Youth magistrates had a crucial role in helping it succeed. If Lord Justice Auld's recommendation for a new kind of youth court for very serious cases were approved, so that child defendants would no longer appear in the adult courts before a judge and jury but before a tribunal of a professional judge and two JPs, the role of youth magistrates would become more important still.

Highgate. A young black man is hauled up from the cells and accused of stealing an A Class Mercedes. At first he slumps back in the dock in an epic sulk. But then he begins to shout. 'These are not the proper procedures,' he yells. 'I am not guilty.' And he won't shut up, despite the patient attempts of the clerk and our chairwoman to pacify him. The problem is that this guy is not just tough: he looks as if he is made of solid muscle, every fibre of it combat-tuned. Someone says he's a boxer. I believe it. His neck is as thick as my thigh. And boy, is he getting stroppy. The anxious-looking security man in the courtroom vanishes. I look around and gauge the distance to the door. The defendant has now left the dock and is looking very dangerous. Interestingly, however, he does not march out of the courtroom but sits at the back, muttering and cursing. When the security guard returns he has three colleagues with him, plus two policemen. They do their best to loom threateningly, but the young man is not remotely intimidated. Fortunately, he has decided he wants to see the duty solicitor and play it by the rules. Had he not done so, says our unflustered chairwoman, she would have ordered him to be jailed for contempt of court. But as she knew and we knew, even six strong men would have had an almighty struggle getting him down the stairs into the cells. In that bout, my money would have been on him. His disdain for the nervous-looking forces of law and order mustered to deal with him had given a whole new meaning to the word 'contempt'.

CHAPTER 14

Them and Us

'There is no love or reverence for the magistracy as there is for the jury'

The second anniversary of my becoming a magistrate arrived. I had finished my basic training, ticked all the tedious boxes in my Personal Development Log and had my last mentored session with Barbara. I was now ready to be appraised. This would be a novelty both for me and for the senior magistrate who was to carry out the appraisal, since this was the first year in which wingers, as opposed to chairmen, were to be formally scrutinised in this manner.

First I had to complete a paper which was a cross between an exam and a self-assessment exercise. Its snappy title was 'Appraisal Questions for the Knowledge-Based Competences' (not 'competencies', thank goodness). Although I did this at home, with reference manuals to hand, it still took a couple of hours and revealed deserts of ignorance and forgetfulness. I sent the paper off to my appraiser, Barry.

Barry watched me from the well of the court for all of one July afternoon, which must have been deeply boring for him. More usefully, he sat in on our discussions in the retiring room to judge what sort of contribution I was making and how I made it. Then we drank tea, went through in depth each question in the paper I had sent him, and chatted in a general way about the magistracy and its future. Thus passed my Adult Court Winger Appraisal, patiently and penetratingly conducted by Barry. I say 'penetratingly' because he indicated that he was going to recommend to the Bench Training and Development Committee that I be given the green light. In due course I received a letter saying that the members of the committee were satisfied I had reached the standards expected of a 'competent winger in the Adult Court'. I could put away my L-plate.

By now I had around eighty court sittings on the clock. I was no longer a novice, though I often felt like one. There were times I had the sensation of being one of a small team of useful idiots trying to stop the advance of a giant glacier of crime and fecklessness by hacking away at it with penknives. There were a few when I thought we might have made some progress. There were others when I couldn't make out whether I belonged to 'Them' or 'Us', or which was which (King Lear: 'change places and, handy-dandy, which is the justice, which the thief?'). Like the day I received a letter bearing the seal of the Lord Chancellor marked 'RESTRICTED – PERSONAL' and signed by the Assistant Secretary of Commissions.

For the first time in my life I had got a speeding ticket. It was on the North Circular, a road notorious for its varying speed limits, which jink abruptly between 30, 40 and 50 mph. I was caught by one of those cameras whose exact location was known to every minicab driver in London but not to me. Guiltily, I reported the matter to my bench, as one was required to do. The admonitory letter from the Lord Chancellor's Department arrived soon after. 'Lord Irvine views the commission of an offence by a magistrate with concern,' wrote the Assistant Secretary, 'but does not propose to take any action on this occasion. He has, however, asked me to draw to your attention the need for magistrates to comply with the law at all times.' Well, there was a radical notion.

I didn't know whether to be surprised or impressed at being dealt such a personal reprimand – the letter was topped and tailed in the Assistant Secretary's own hand. In *The Changing Image of the Magistracy* (Macmillan, 1983), the late Sir Thomas Skyrme says that letters of this kind 'sometimes arouse indignant reaction from magistrates, who take exception to the Lord Chancellor's rebuke for what is regarded as a trivial matter. On one or two occasions a justice convicted of a speeding offence has resigned in protest.' Well, even if I was a mite indignant, I had no thought of resigning. Instead I became super careful about how fast I drove and of course a trifle more sympathetic to speedsters on the North Circular than I might otherwise have been.

Perhaps that's as it should be. The great virtue of lay magistrates, as I see it, is that they are both 'Them' *and* 'Us'. We sit in judgment – but we also get speeding tickets. Far more than professional judges, who are inevitably somewhat cosseted in their existence, magistrates are part of the real world outside the courtroom. We work – at something other than the law. We are made redundant. We use public transport. We shop at Sainsbury's, watch TV, use the Internet. We are not likely to say, as the judge did in my Old Bailey trial, 'I must be the only person in England who doesn't have a mobile phone'. We get burgled and have our cars broken into.

John Humphrys, the sage of Radio 4's *Today* programme, penned a stirring piece in the *Sunday Times* about magistrates. 'Justice,' he wrote, 'is about more than simply creating a machine that churns out judgments efficiently, speedily and at the lowest possible cost. Professional lawyers may be frightfully clever people, but they are different from you and me. A judge in the higher courts wears a wig to reinforce that difference; we talk of the majesty of the law. He or she is there to interpret the law and pass sentence – a high calling, it's true, but there is more to justice than that.

'A bench of lay magistrates – guided on points of law by a professional clerk – brings something else: not just judgment based on the law, but a bit of common sense and often, dare one say it, a touch of humanity and human sympathy. If the people sitting up there on the bench are people like us, from our own community, with our backgrounds and some of our foibles, then we may be more likely to feel that we have been fairly judged.'

My fellow magistrate Clive, he of the beard and ponytail, put it like this. 'I'm very uneasy about stipes,' he said (though I am sure he did not have in mind our own admirable district judge,

Mr Wiles). 'Sitting up there on their own they give the impression of routinely dispensing sentences with no evident reflection. I'm surprised the system isn't criticised more. It makes summary justice look a lot too summary. I don't just mean defendants will feel they are not being given a fair hearing. I mean that when they are found guilty they should be made to believe and understand that their behaviour is wrong, not just in the eyes of some case-hardened professional judge but in the view of three ordinary people who have argued through the matter carefully before reaching their decision.'

It is quite hard, I have discovered, to make the case for these three ordinary people. There is no love or reverence for the magistracy as there is for the jury. No one has written a play or made a film called *Three Angry Men*, or ever will. Though Justices of the Peace are as ancient an institution as juries, they have never been a popular part of our civic tradition.

An article about the modern magistracy in *Prospect* magazine a few years ago, by a writer who had often been on the wrong side of the bench himself, expressed a view which was both benign and uncomfortably telling. 'The overriding impression,' wrote Jeremy Clarke, was of 'well-dressed, well-fed, well-meaning people conducting complicated legal business around the shortcomings of the weak, the meek, the slow, the addicted and the destitute; of an erect, confident people presiding over a race of cowed, tattooed, smoking folk.'

Juries, by contrast, are garlanded with praise, even though they deal with only a minute proportion of all the criminal cases that come before the courts. The eighteenth-century judge and jurist Sir William Blackstone called the jury 'the sacred bulwark of the nation'. De Tocqueville deemed it a 'peerless teacher of citizenship'. Most famously, Lord Devlin said the jury 'is the lamp that shows that freedom lives'.

As the author of a book strongly supporting the jury, I see it as the jewel in the crown of our criminal justice system. For centuries, it has been our defence against the we-know-best instincts of the police, the judiciary and the overmighty state.

But almost more important than this idealised role, it is the daily means by which the public plays a key part in the administration of the laws that rule our society. It epitomises and protects the notion of government by consent.

In *The Juryman's Tale* I wrote: 'I want to believe in the jury system because it seems to me not only a tolerably effective method of judging serious crimes but an inspired means of helping a society to believe in itself . . . To let justice rest in the hands of its own citizens is the highest expression of a mature, civilised, self-confident democracy. Whether one agrees or not, to undermine it or abandon it would be catastrophically dispiriting. It would be to admit that as a people we no longer trusted ourselves.'

For much the same reasons, I have come to believe that the lay magistracy, with its strong local roots and detachment from the legal establishment, its voluntary and independent spirit, performs a similar democratic function. I don't think that is pitching it too high.

The defence lawyers to whom I talked in writing that earlier book were apt to look a bit askance at magistrates, for being too case-hardened compared with jurymen and women, too reluctant to give the defendant the benefit of the doubt, too much a part of the establishment. At the time, since I was rooting for the jury system, I went along with that wholeheartedly. Since then, however, I have come to a different view. I have seen that the social spectrum of the magistracy is much broader than people think. I have witnessed how scrupulously fair-minded most magistrates strive to be.

Of course, in a grave matter, the judgment of twelve citizens must have greater democratic authority than that of just three. And of course there is truth in the allegation that magistrates are more sceptical than jurors, most of whom have never been in a courtroom in their lives until summoned to do jury service. Magistrates do become familiar with certain types of defendant, certain lines of defence. But in my experience as both a juror and a JP, this does not make as much difference as I had imagined.

First, it is important to realise that the number of sittings a magistrate may do per year is strictly limited. Much more than half a day a week is frowned upon, precisely to avoid case-hardening. In fact the average is just over forty half-day sittings a year.

Second, magistrates conduct trials very rarely. Thanks to the preponderance of guilty pleas and the number of JPs on a bench, I reckon I have sat on no more than seven or eight trials in a year, the rest of the sittings being taken up with first hearings, bail applications, sentencing, community penalty breaches, non-payment of fines and so on – matters where the comparison between innocent juror and supposedly cynical JP does not apply.

Third, when it does come to a trial, one very quickly learns that no two cases are *ever* exactly the same. Often you think the prosecution evidence is not only remorselessly familiar but also watertight: yet almost invariably the defence case makes you revise that opinion. After all, if the prosecution's account of the matter were so open and shut, it is unlikely it would have come to trial in the first place, unless the defendant were extraordinarily stupid or very ill-advised by his solicitor.

Fourth and finally, magistrates do seem to me to take their oath to 'do right to all manner of people . . . without fear or favour, affection or ill-will' very seriously. They have the volunteer's conscientiousness. Some critics think they are conscientious to a fault. It is a fact that district judges sitting on their own are more likely to refuse bail or issue a custodial sentence than a bench of three lay magistrates – which is one reason, no doubt, why the authoritarian-minded would prefer to see the bench professionalised.

I was an admirer of the idea of lay magistrates long before I became one. I had grown up in South America, in a place where dictatorship was more or less the norm, and it seemed to me a marvellous thing that in this country, the vast bulk of all criminal cases were dealt with not by professional judges employed by the state but by ordinary, unqualified, unpaid members of the public. After two years on the bench, I still think this a marvellous thing. Together with the jury system it represents a unique tradition of lay justice that is admired and envied the whole world over. As such, I believe the magistracy deserves to be cherished and defended quite as vigorously as the jury system.

Bruce Hyman, the producer of Radio 4's excellent *Unreliable Evidence* law programme presented by Clive Anderson, told me, after I had taken part in one of his broadcasts, that he did not agree. Making democratic claims for the magistracy, he argued, could only encourage the Government's schemes to restrict the right to trial by jury.

There was something in that. But I persist in supporting both juries *and* justices. I think it is misleading and, from a democratic point of view, self-defeating to defend the one by attacking the other, as distinguished QCs like Michael Mansfield and Geoffrey Robertson have done. I know them both and we see eye to eye on the value of juries. But I was annoyed to see Geoffrey denouncing magistrates as 'ladies and gentlemen bountiful'. I hope JPs are bountiful, as in generous, but certainly not in the *noblesse oblige* sense he implied.

Likewise Helena Kennedy QC, a Labour member of the House of Lords. She wrote a brave attack in the *Guardian* on her party's plans to restrict the right to trial by jury, suggesting that JPs were a much less satisfactory alternative. 'Magistrates do a great job,' she said. 'However, anyone who sits on cases too regularly tends to become case-hardened, and cynical about the people who appear in the dock.' That is doubtless true if you do sit *too* regularly. But forty half-days a year does not seem to me an excessive number of sittings, especially when only a handful of them are trials.

Case-hardened? I am perfectly sure a defence barrister as persuasive as Baroness Kennedy could still soften our hearts any day of the week.

AULD ACQUAINTANCE
The Criminal Courts Review – at last

In October 2001, after two years of research, cogitation, rumours and delays which had almost exactly coincided with my novitiate as a JP, Lord Justice Auld's report saw the light of day. But for events in Afghanistan, it would have been every broadsheet's lead story. It was impressive in both size and scope: 700 pages, 328 recommendations and engagingly well written for such a document. There it was on Auld's own much-visited website, www.criminal-courts-review.org.uk. It was so huge my computer gave a bleat and announced it could only download the summary – but that was enough to make it clear that JPs could stop holding their breaths. At least so far as Sir Robin was concerned, the lay magistracy was to soldier on as before. Indeed, it was to have its role enhanced.

Magistrates and district judges should continue to preside in summary hearings, the review recommended. But in addition, Sir Robin proposed a new layer of intermediate courts – to be known as the District Division – which would deal with matters of middling gravity carrying sentences of up to two years in prison. They would include the more serious 'either-way' cases where the defendant currently had the automatic right to elect trial by jury – a right which would be abolished under his recommendations. In these courts, the bench would consist of a professional judge flanked by two lay magistrates, he suggested.

Well, on the face of it this was excellent news for lay justices. 'The report is an enormous vote of confidence in the magistracy,' said the chairman of the Magistrates' Association. He welcomed not only the retention of magistrates' present jurisdiction but also the opportunity for his members to play a key part in the District Division courts, should they materialise.

In the months following the publication of Auld, however, it became increasingly apparent that the District Division proposal was getting the thumbs-down from most of the interested parties. As well as opposition from defence lawyers and the pro-jury lobby, there was concern about the complexity and expense of setting up a whole new layer of judicial administration. Word began to circulate that the Government's determination to restrict the right to trial by jury might be slackening somewhat. One suggestion was for magistrates' courts' sentencing powers to be increased from the maximum six months' custody to a year or even two (as is already the case in youth courts). This would allow magistrates to accept jurisdiction in a whole range of more serious cases, which could help reduce pressure on the crown courts.

By the spring of 2002, the Government's position as regards Auld was still unclear, pending a white paper expected in the summer. But the probability was that, one way or another, lay magistrates would end up dealing with more cases than before. This being the likely outcome, there is all the more reason to protect and strengthen the magistracy's lay identity and to resist any temptation to manage higher caseloads by simply appointing more stipes. The graver the matters that might be tried summarily, the stronger the argument for the bench to be composed not of a single professional judge but of three ordinary mortals.

Ideally, those ordinary mortals will be people from every walk of life, distinguished only by their interest in public service and a belief in the rule of law. Just as I think jury service ought to be all-inclusive and not so easily evaded by the professional middle classes (a view with which Lord Justice Auld and David Blunkett agree, I am glad to say), so I believe the magistracy should be as inclusive as possible, and not be dominated by those same professional middle classes – a view with which Sir Robin also agrees, urging that 'steps should be taken to provide benches of magistrates that more broadly reflect the communities they serve'.

Magistrates cannot help being 'Them' in the eyes of those who come to court as defendants or witnesses. But if they are to have the trust of the public they must recognisably be 'Us', too.

For the lay magistracy to survive and flourish it must do what it can to deserve that recognition. I think that to a large extent, it already does. Judging from what I have seen and experienced of the lay bench, I agree with Lord Bingham: it is a democratic jewel beyond price. What it needs is polishing up, so that society can see itself reflected there with greater confidence and clarity.

A Mock Trial

In England and Wales nearly all run-of-the-mill criminal cases in which the defendant pleads not guilty are heard not by judges and juries in the crown court but in the magistrates' courts, before three lay Justices of the Peace or, less often, a district judge. Trials in the magistrates' courts are seldom sensational, but rarely uninteresting. There is something quite fascinating about the way the formality of the law strives to encompass and bring order to the minor anarchies of real life.

This simulation of a morning's hearings in a magistrates' court gives an excellent idea of what goes on. It was devised by Peter Milford, a teacher at St Vincent College in Gosport, who was prompted by the proposed closure of the local courthouse in 1992. 'There was quite an uproar at the time,' Peter told me. 'So we felt it was a suitable topic for discussion with the students – and built a whole week's personal and social education activities around the role-play experience. We had support from the Hampshire constabulary, local JPs, the Crown Prosecution Service and local solicitors.

'We had a real magistrate as chairman; the CPS sent a lawyer to prosecute; a member of the college staff (a fully qualified solicitor) defended; a student took the role of defendant, with witnesses being called from staff. The police acted as custody officers. Oh, and the local press attended. They behaved as normal – took their seats, made notes, and yawned.'

A role-play simulation for schools

THE PLAYERS
Court Usher, Chairman and two other Magistrates,
the Clerk to the Court.
The accused – David Martin. The witness – Karen Johnson.

The Police Officer – Sergeant Thomas.
Prosecution solicitor (CPS). Defence solicitor. Reporters.
The public.

It is morning. 10 a.m. The beginning of another day at a magistrates' court. A reporter arrives and takes out a notebook. Solicitors for the defence take up their places with their bundles of documents. The prosecuting solicitor leafs through his papers. The public seats are filling up. The clerk to the court enters from behind the bench, carrying a large bundle of documents and sits at his desk below the bench. The clerk checks the time and nods to the usher.

Usher All stand.

The three magistrates enter, exchange bows with the court and take their seats on the bench, the chairman in the centre.

Clerk The first case this morning, Your Worships, is that of Terry Dicks of Furnace Road, Brierley Hill. Mr Dicks has been summonsed under the Road Traffic Act for driving without due care and attention and has pleaded guilty by letter (*hands copies to the bench*). Mr Dicks was involved in an accident on the 5th January at the junction of Grange Road and North Hill. Two other cars were involved and two people received hospital treatment.

Chairman Do we have Mr Dicks's licence?

Clerk Yes (*opens file and passes licence to the chairman*). There are no previous convictions.

Chairman (*Confers with other magistrates*). We have taken into account Mr Dicks's means, as stated by him in his accompanying letter to the court, and we therefore fine him £500 and his licence will be endorsed with six penalty points.

Clerk The next case this morning, Your Worships, is that of Darren Rowe, number three on your list. Mr Rowe was convicted, in his absence, of offences under the Road Traffic Act on February 18th and has been summonsed to appear here today for disqualification under the totting-up procedure as he has more than twelve penalty points on his licence.

Chairman Is Mr Rowe here?

Clerk (*Shakes his head*) No, sir, he has not appeared.

Chairman How was the summons issued?

Clerk (*Leafs through papers*) The summons was issued on February 20th and was sent by first-class post. The summons was sent to Mr Rowe at the address we have on all of the documents, including the print-out from DVLA in Swansea.

Chairman Are we sure he has received the summons?

Clerk As I am sure Your Worships are aware, ordinary letter post is now deemed to be acceptable for the issue of documents. We have no indication that the letter was not delivered, nor have we received any communication from Mr Rowe. You can reissue the summons or you can issue a warrant for Mr Rowe's arrest with or without bail so that he can be brought before the court.

Chairman (*Confers with other magistrates*) A warrant will be issued, not backed for bail.

Clerk (*Makes notes on document, places documents on desk and picks up a large bundle*) The next case, sir, is that of David Martin, number five on your list. Mr Martin appears for trial today on three matters, having pleaded not guilty on the last occasion.

Clerk David Martin to Court 1 (*David Martin enters court. Usher shows him to a seat.*)

Clerk (*Motions to defendant*) Please stand up. You are David Anthony Martin?

Martin Yes.

Clerk (*Refers to file*) Your address is 16 Aston Street, Dudley?

Martin Yes.

Clerk Your date of birth is 5th May 1977.

Martin Yes.

Clerk You are here to answer to three charges. (*Looks across to defence solicitor.*)

Defence (*Stands*) Good morning, sir. I represent Mr Martin.

Clerk Sir, Mr Martin pleaded not guilty at the last hearing to taking a vehicle without the owner's consent, driving without insurance and driving otherwise than in accordance with a licence. Sit down please, Mr Martin.

CPS (*Stands, opens file*) This is a relatively simple case, Your Worships. The defendant, David Anthony Martin, was seen to enter a motor vehicle at about 2.15 p.m. on the afternoon of the 20th March 1995, a Ford Escort XR3i, registration K100 ABC, the property of Miss Karen Johnson of Naish Road, Dudley, and to drive the vehicle away without permission. Some time later, the defendant was seen driving the vehicle in Mill Lane, Brierley, by a police officer. He parked the vehicle and made off on foot. A few minutes later he was apprehended by the officer.

I would like to call my witness, Miss Karen Johnson.

Chairman Yes please.

Clerk Karen Johnson to Court 1. (*Miss Johnson appears from the back of the court and is conducted to the witness box. The usher hands her a book and a card.*)

Usher Please take the book in your right hand and read the words on the card.

Karen (*Holds the book up and reads from card*) I swear that the evidence I shall give shall be the truth, the whole truth and nothing but the truth.

CPS Miss Johnson, I would like to take you through the events of the afternoon of 20th March. Now, can you tell us where you live?

Karen At 15 Naish Road, Dudley.

CPS Where were you at the time this incident took place?

Karen At home. I was cleaning the front room when I heard someone opening the door of my car. I went and looked out of the window and saw someone sitting in the car and fiddling around by the steering.

CPS This was your car, was it?

Karen Yes, an XR3i. I haven't had it long.

CPS What did you do when you saw someone in the car?

Karen I banged on the window and then rushed out of the door. But, as I got the door open I saw the car drive off. I went back inside and phoned the police.

CPS Did you recognise the person in your car?

Karen No. Well, not then anyway. I now know who it was.

CPS Could you explain that further?

Karen I went to the police station to take part in an identity parade and picked out the man that I thought it was.

CPS What was the man wearing?

Karen A black leather bomber jacket and jeans.

CPS Can you see the person in this court?

Karen Yes. It was him (*points to Martin*).

CPS Thank you Miss Johnson. Stay there, please.

Defence (*Rises*) Miss Johnson. There are just a few questions I would like to put to you. Where were you when you saw this person in your car?

Karen In my front room. I was using the vacuum.

Defence Are there curtains by the windows?

Karen Yes, of course. They were pulled back as usual.

Defence Do you have any other curtains, nets etc?

Karen Yes, there are net curtains across the windows.

Defence So, you were behind net curtains and you were using the vacuum. You weren't looking out of the window?

Karen Yes I was. No, I wasn't.

Defence Now, you say you went to the door and saw the car being driven off.

Karen Yes. When I opened the door he had got the car started and was driving off.

Defence So you could not have seen the driver clearly. You were at your front door and the car was being driven away.

Karen I saw him drive my car away (*points to Martin*).

Defence But you could not have had a clear view of the driver so you cannot be sure that it was Mr Martin who was driving the car. Thank you Miss Johnson (*turns and sits down*).

CPS What could you actually see out of your window?

Karen I could see him.

CPS Did you have a clear view.

Karen Yes, very clear.

CPS Did you have your room light on?

Karen No. It was early afternoon and quite bright.

CPS Have the Bench any questions for this witness?

Chairman No, thank you.

CPS Thank you, Miss Johnson.

Usher This way please, Miss (*leads witness to the back of the court and then returns*).

CPS My next witness is the police officer, Sergeant Thomas.

Clerk Sergeant Thomas to Court 1.

Thomas (*Enters and goes to the witness box. Usher hands him a book and a card.*) I swear that the evidence I shall given shall be the truth, the whole truth and nothing but the truth . . . I am David Thomas. I am a Sergeant of the West Midlands Constabulary and I am stationed at Dudley police station, Your Worships.

CPS You are here today in connection with an incident on the 20th March 1995.

Thomas Yes.

CPS Are there any notes that you wish to refer to, Officer?

Thomas Yes, Your Worships. I wish to refer to my pocket book.

CPS When were the notes made, Officer?

Thomas Directly after the incident, Your Worships – within thirty minutes.

Defence No objections.

Chairman Carry on, Officer.

CPS Please give your evidence.

Thomas It was about twenty past two and I was driving a marked police car in the Mill district of Dudley when I received a radio message. I went to the Naish Road address and spoke to Miss Karen Johnson, the owner of the vehicle, a blue Ford Escort, registration K100 ABC, who reported it stolen. As a result of what she told me I then passed the vehicle details and a description of the male over the radio.

I then left Miss Johnson with another officer.

As I turned into Grove Road, I saw the Ford Escort, registration K100 ABC, being driven towards Mill Lane. I gave chase and saw the Ford pull into a parking bay opposite the entrance to the leisure centre. A young man got out and ran away from the car. He was dressed in a black leather bomber jacket and jeans. I gave chase and caught the same man, Mr Martin, behind the flats off Mill Lane. I asked him if he was insured to drive the vehicle or had a driving licence. He replied: 'I have got a provisional licence. I don't have a car so I don't need insurance'.

I cautioned Mr Martin and took him to Dudley police station.

CPS When you arrived at the police station, did you search Mr Martin?

Thomas Yes, sir. I found that he had a number of bent paper clips that could have been used to open the lock of the Escort. He had some loose change and a small screwdriver – the electrical type.

CPS Are you absolutely sure it was Mr Martin (*indicates Martin*) that you saw driving the car?

Thomas Yes, sir.

CPS Is it within your knowledge that an identity parade was held?

Thomas Yes.

CPS Is it right that Mr Martin was interviewed at the police station by yourself and PC Green and gave a no-comment interview?

Thomas Yes.

CPS Thank you, Sergeant Thomas. No further questions.

Defence (*Stands*) There are one or two points that I would like to clear up now. Sergeant, you have told the court that you attended at Miss Johnson's house in response to a call over the radio.

Thomas Yes, that's right.

Defence You saw the car after you had left Miss Johnson's house.

Thomas Yes

Defence And you have told the court that you saw Miss Johnson's car as you approached along Grove Road.

Thomas Yes.

Defence You followed the car into Mill Lane. How far behind the car were you when it pulled over and stopped?

Thomas (*Pauses to consider*) I should think that I must have been about 100 yards away. I had turned out of Grove Road and had accelerated to catch the Escort. It was going around the bend into Mill Lane as I pulled out of Grove Road.

Defence When the driver got out of the car, what happened then?

Thomas He ran off, behind the Glass Close flats. I left my car and ran after him. I caught the accused in the alley behind the flats.

Defence What was the defendant doing when you caught him?

Thomas He was walking – in fact he came towards me as I ran around the corner of the block.

Defence He came towards *you*?

Thomas Yes.

Defence Didn't that strike you as being rather odd? Hardly the action that you might expect? Would you not have expected him to run away when he saw you?

Thomas He was very close when I came round the corner. He didn't have time to turn and run.

Defence So you only saw the back of the man running away?

Thomas Yes.

Defence How far away were you when he left the car?

Thomas About 75 yards.

Defence Is it not true that there are many young men of my client's age who are dressed in similar clothing – black leather bomber jackets and jeans?

Thomas Yes.

Defence I put it to you that this was not the same man that was driving the car. The defendant that you see in the court had nothing to do with the taking away of that vehicle but just happened to have the misfortune to be in the wrong place when you arrived.

Thomas No, sir. I am quite convinced that he was the man who was driving that car and that he was the man that I followed.

Defence Now, the matter of the defendant's possessions. You say that you found a number of items that you thought were tools for opening locks.

Thomas Yes, that's right. The defendant had a set of what I thought might be lock picks.

Defence What were these items?

Thomas He had a number of paperclips that looked as if they had been opened out and then folded back again. Some of them had had the ends cut back.

Defence Paperclips?

Thomas Yes.

Defence So, on the basis of a pocketful of paperclips you assumed that the defendant had been guilty of stealing a car?

Thomas I know that you can use paperclips to enter a car. Only last month we had to help the deputy head from the school – her son had picked the lock of her car with a paperclip.

Defence Thank you, Sergeant. It would seem that there is some considerable doubt as to whether the defendant was indeed the person who took this car. No further questions.

CPS Sergeant Thomas, you have already told the court that you are sure that Mr Martin is the man who had been driving the car. Have you any reason, following what my learned colleague has said, to doubt that opinion?

Thomas No.

CPS (*Turns to bench*) Have the bench any questions for this witness?

Chairman Are Ford Escorts easy cars to get into?

Thomas Yes, sir, they are one of our most commonly stolen cars.

CPS I submit the statement of Inspector Saunders, served on the defence and accepted by them under Section 9 concerning the identification parade (*hands document to clerk*).

Clerk (*Offers document to defence*).

Defence (*Nods*).

Clerk (*Hands documents to bench. Bench read the statement*).

Chairman On the subsequent identification parade, the witness Miss Karen Johnson did pick out Mr Martin.

CPS Those are my witnesses (*sits*).

Defence I would like to ask the court for a short adjournment whilst I discuss these matters with my client. (*Defence confers with Martin. Martin shakes his head.*)

Defence (*Stands*) My client is not guilty of the offences with which he has been charged and to answer which he appears here today. The evidence of the witnesses has not shown the conclusive proof of his involvement. All we have heard is that a person of a similar appearance and description was seen getting into the car and then driving it and subsequently running away. Sergeant Thomas only saw the running driver from some distance away and has told the court that he apprehended the defendant when he was walking towards him.

Not the attitude, I would suggest, of a man who has committed a crime and is running away from the police. There was nothing in the defendant's pocket that could be held to be solely for the purpose of committing a crime. The objects that he had were perfectly ordinary objects that anyone might have in their pockets. The evidence against my client is totally circumstantial and certainly does carry enough weight to warrant conviction.

I do not propose to call my client to give evidence.

I submit this case has not been proved beyond reasonable doubt and I ask you to find that my client is not guilty in these matters (*sits down*).

Chairman Thank you (*turns and confers with colleagues on the bench*). The bench will retire to consider its verdict and we invite our legal adviser to retire with us to assist in any points of law that might arise.

Usher All stand! (*The bench leave the court*).

(*After some time, the magistrates return.*)

Usher All stand!

(*The bench take their seats.*)

Clerk David Anthony Martin: stand up, please. (*Martin stands and faces the bench.*)

Chairman Mr Martin, we find you guilty of the three charges tried today. The bench is satisfied beyond reasonable doubt that you took the vehicle without the owner's consent and drove it without insurance and without a licence.

We have drawn inferences from the fact that you have not given evidence today and from the fact that you failed to give an explanation to the officers of your behaviour when detained. That is your right. It is for the prosecution to prove the case. We find that the prosecution witnesses, Miss Johnson and Sgt Thomas, are credible. We also took into account the ID evidence and the fact that you were found to have lock picks on your person.

The court will adjourn for sentence in three weeks from today to give time for the preparation of reports. All sentencing options are open. Until then, Mr Martin, you remain on unconditional bail, but you must co-operate with the Probation Service in the preparation of the pre-sentence report and you must be back at this court without fail at 9.30 a.m. on the day in question

Three weeks later

Chairman Stand up, please, Mr Martin. You have been found guilty of a serious crime, that of taking away a motor vehicle without the owner's consent. This is a crime that is far too common and one that places the public in considerable danger. You are fortunate indeed that you were seen by a police officer and stopped before you could do any damage to the car, to yourself or to others.

We have considered the pre-sentence report carefully. We have read that you have had a difficult life and have not offended since the commission of this offence. We have noted that you are in receipt of income support and have no savings. The aggravating features of the offence are that you were found with paperclips in your possession which we believe were used or to be used to break into vehicles. You did not co-operate with the police. There are no mitigating features.

We feel that the most appropriate way of dealing with this increasingly prevalent offence is by way of a community punishment order for 200 hours. You will do unpaid work in the community in your own time as directed by the relevant officer. If you do not present yourself when required to do so, you may be brought back before this court for sentence to be reviewed. Do you understand?

Martin Yes, I do.

Chairman For the no-insurance offence you will pay a fine of £150. Your licence will also be endorsed with six penalty points. For the licence offence your licence will be endorsed and you will pay a fine of £50. These fines have been reduced to reflect your low income. You will be aware, Mr Martin, that if you accumulate twelve points or more on your licence you may be disqualified under the totting-up procedure.

Can you pay any of these fines today?

Martin No, sir.

Chairman Very well. We have heard from your lawyer that you would be prepared to pay at the rate of £10 per week. Is that correct?

Martin Yes, sir.

Chairman Don't forget, paying these fines comes before everything else, before any other kind of debt you may have. Do you understand?

Martin Yes.

Chairman Good. You may stand down.

Usher That completes your list for this morning, sir. (*The bench rise and make to leave the court.*) All stand.

Applying to Be a Magistrate

I hope some of those who read this book will be sufficiently intrigued to think of volunteering for their local bench themselves. The wider the pool of applicants, the more representative the lay magistracy will be.

Before sending off for the forms, however, my advice would be to find a friendly JP to talk to, and to spend at least a couple of mornings or afternoons watching the goings-on from the public seating in your local courthouse. It is important to have some idea of what you might be letting yourself in for – i.e. at least one such morning or afternoon most weeks of the year, plus quite a few hours of training.

The application process is simple, but prolonged – and can lead to disappointment. Aside from the nosy forms you have to fill in, would-be magistrates must undergo two pretty inquisitive interviews. In the year 2000, some 5,320 people applied but only 1,366 were appointed.

The rejects should not be downhearted. They will probably have been turned down for all sorts of reasons which have nothing to do with their own eligibility but everything to do with the need for the local Advisory Committee, the body which recommends the appointment of JPs, to ensure a 'balanced' bench as regards age, occupation, ethnicity, etc.

You must brace yourself, all the same: an eminently suitable friend of mine who went through the whole year-long selection process is still smarting from having received a curt note telling him he was not, after all, wanted on his South London bench. There was neither an explanation nor even a signature. If this sort of thing is general practice, I hope it will be amended.

Anyway, bearing all these obstacles in mind, here is what you need to know about applying, as set out in the admirable Magistrates' Association website:

WHO CAN BECOME A MAGISTRATE?

Magistrates
- must be of good character
- have personal integrity
- have sound common sense
- have the ability to weigh evidence and reach reasoned decisions
- live or work in the area
- have good local knowledge and understanding of the local community
- be able to work as a member of a team
- be firm yet compassionate

WHO CANNOT BECOME A MAGISTRATE?

Almost Anyone Can Apply But The Following Will Not Be Appointed:
- anyone who is not of good character and personal standing
- an undischarged bankrupt
- a serving member of Her Majesty's Forces
- a member of a police force
- a traffic warden or any other occupation which might be seen to conflict with the role of a magistrate
- a close relative of a person who is already a magistrate on the same bench
- anyone who, because of a disability, cannot carry out all the duties of a magistrate

BENCH REQUIREMENTS

A Balanced Bench
The Lord Chancellor requires that each bench should broadly reflect the community it serves in terms of gender, ethnic origin,

geographical spread, occupation and political affiliation. Achieving a balance is, however, a secondary consideration to the essential and pre-eminent requirement that a candidate must be personally suitable for appointment, possessing the qualities required in a magistrate.

Age
The retirement age for magistrates is seventy. The Lord Chancellor will not generally appoint a candidate under the age of twenty-seven or over the age of sixty-five.

The Lord Chancellor has temporarily suspended the requirement that benches should be balanced in terms of age. He is of the view that his policy on age will make it easier for advisory committees to find more candidates with the appropriate social and political backgrounds and so achieve a more balanced bench.

Gender
Each bench should have a roughly equal number of men and women. There should be sufficient magistrates of each sex who are eligible to sit in the family proceedings and youth courts, which must be made up of three magistrates and include a man and a woman, unless this is impractical.

Ethnic Origin
Advisory committees are making strenuous efforts to recruit suitable candidates from the ethnic minorities. Advisory committees should be aware of the ethnic composition of the area for which they are responsible and seek to recruit sufficient numbers from the ethnic minorities to reflect that composition.

Geographical Spread
Advisory committees should aim to recommend candidates proportionally from the areas for which they are responsible but ensure that there are not too many magistrates on any one bench from the same village, neighbourhood or street.

Occupation
Advisory committees should seek to recommend for appointment, candidates from a broad spectrum of occupations. No more than 15 per cent of the magistrates on a bench should be from the same occupational group.

Political Affiliation
The political views of a candidate are neither a qualification nor a disqualification for appointment. However, the Lord Chancellor requires, in the interests of balance, that the voting pattern for the area, as evidenced by the last two general elections, should be broadly reflected in the composition of the bench.

Membership Of Clubs/Organisations Including Freemasonry
It is important that there are not too many magistrates on the bench from the same clubs or organisations. Candidates for the magistracy are specifically asked on the new application form if they are freemasons. If a candidate has completed the old form, they should be asked at interview if they are freemasons. Those recommended for appointment will be required to inform the chairman of the bench or the clerk to the justices if they subsequently become a freemason.

WHERE TO APPLY

The local advisory committees who advise the Lord Chancellor (or in the case of areas of Lancashire, Greater Manchester and Merseyside, the Chancellor of the Duchy of Lancaster) on the appointment of magistrates in England and Wales welcome applications from people in all walks of life who have the qualities and the time to serve as magistrates. Individuals may put themselves forward for consideration or any person or organisation may recommend a candidate for appointment.

Application forms and information on the selection process

are available from the secretary of the local advisory committee, whose name and address can be obtained from the office of the clerk to the justices in your local magistrates' court, or from the office of the Secretary of Commissions:

> Secretary of Commissions Office
> Third Floor, Selborne House
> 54/60 Victoria Street
> London SW1E 6QW
> Tel 020 7210 8990

or from the office of the Chancellor of the Duchy of Lancaster (for Lancashire, Greater Manchester and Merseyside):

> Duchy of Lancaster Office
> Lancaster Place
> Strand
> London WC2E 7ED
> Tel 020 7836 8277

Before making an application you are strongly advised to visit your local magistrates' court to observe a court in action.

Useful Contacts
Helpline for Potential Magistrates: 0845 606 1666
The Lord Chancellor's Department website: www.lcd.gov.uk
The Magistrates' Association: www.magistrates-association. org.uk

Index

A NOTE ON THE AUTHOR

Trevor Grove grew up in Argentina but was educated mainly in England. After Oxford University he became a journalist, working for the *Spectator*, the London *Evening Standard*, the *Observer* and the *Daily Telegraph*. A former editor of the *Sunday Telegraph*, his first book, *A Juryman's Tale*, was published by Bloomsbury in 1998.